# Cornwall Cree

# Cornwall
# Cree
# Nation

## Alan Davis

To Steph

Best wishes.

*Alan Davis*

## Johnston Hope

Copyright © Alan Davis 2007
First published in 2007 by Johnston Hope
13 Carnsmerry Crescent, St Austell
Cornwall PL 25 4NA

Distributed by Gardners Books, 1 Whittle Drive, Eastbourne,
East Sussex, BN23 6QH
Tel: +44(0)1323 521555 | Fax: +44(0)1323 521666

British Library Cataloguing in Publication Data
A catalogue record for this book is available from the British Library.

ISBN 978-0-9553904-0-1

Typeset by Amolibros, Milverton, Somerset
This book production has been managed by Amolibros
Printed and bound by T J International Ltd, Padstow, Cornwall, UK

This book is dedicated to – Catherine, Alice, Celia and Faye,

is written with gratitude to – Suzannah Dunn, Jane Tatam

and in appreciation of – The Northern Medical Unit, Manitoba,
and all the communities which they serve.

From the air no two squares look the same.

Each one is the precise same size as its neighbours but is variegated with its own unique watermark of soil porosity and unseen geology. Landscape hieroglyphics, significance unknown. It is May the first and the newly molten snow is only now revealing the huge brown prairie mesh which stretches away to the Rockies, hundreds of miles to my left. The only interruption to the skyline is the stolid geometry of Winnipeg, now behind us, and the occasional farm. But soon everything changes and agricultural order gives way to a wilderness, a scrub of vague vegetation still listless from winter. Streams meander along its surface, lethargic from the absence of gravity's drop.

Now, suddenly and gloriously, there is a dazzle of white. Lake Winnipeg appears ahead, stretching flat and massive to the horizon. But nor is its surface uniform. The thaw is fissuring the ice into random cracks, and deeper collections of turquoise try to glow through. Further north, the snow appears, as clean and unbroken as the day, half a year ago, when it first fell. Occasional trees break through it, and although they are spindly they bestow drama and contrast to the land. We think of continents agog with cities and highways and mountains, but much of North America reduces to nothing but this.

The tiny plane, in which we twelve or so passengers are tightly sat, is noisy. We have been issued with pink polystyrene earplugs, but mine keep falling out. I am sitting at the back and immediately behind me the haphazard luggage, which includes a howling kennelled dog, is restrained by a loose blue nylon net. The in-flight refreshments comprise a carton of orange juice and a clingfilmed bun. The reading matter clamped to the seat in front of me is a magazine called *The Elite Traveller*. Plump and glossy like collagen lips, it advertises timeshares in Mauritius, Lexus cars and Rolex watches. There are features on African safaris, Adriatic cruises and Alpine spas. This seems to me to be distastefully, even insultingly, incongruous. I do not wish to be seen showing an interest in this so I return my attention to the view.

The truth is—and my naivety approaches stupidity here—I had not expected to be the only white person on this flight or, by implication, the settlement where I am heading. My previous experience of Canada, twenty-seven years ago, was of small town Saskatchewan, yee-ha rodeo country, rural and conservative. There were no natives there.

Even Winnipeg, where I have spent the last few days, seemed homely and European. Everyone spoke English, they were polite, there were buses and shops and bars. A few indigenous people were usually to be seen outside the mall on Portage, scruffily drunk, but infringing on nobody but themselves. Which city in the world has no such gathering on its streets? I stayed for two nights in the oddly grandiose Prince Albert Hotel, exploring the mild delights of the city, but mainly in order to attend my interview at the College of Physicians and Surgeons, whose missives and demands have dominated my recent months. Their office topped an anonymous edge of town block shared with, among others, DKD Holdings, Express Moto-Refrigeration and the Northern Mineworkers Pension Fund. The view was of the perimeter highway, foursquare suburbia, the occasional light plane droning by. But my meeting with the dean and his assistant was amicable. They asked briefly about my practice in Cornwall and my student experience in Saskatchewan and then they gave me information, a briefcaseful, on: child abuse; alcohol abuse;

2

bronchiolitis; the West Nile virus; diabetes; aboriginal ethics and the role of the elders; sexually transmitted diseases; iron deficiency anaemia in children; tuberculosis; end-stage renal failure; notification of sudden death. They politely demanded a further cheque and wished me well in my stay.

But only at the airport this morning did I appreciate the otherness of the place where I have agreed to spend the next six months. Travellers to the outposts of the north do not avail themselves of the coffee bars, bookshops and Canadiana outlets which civilise the main terminal. Instead they report to a cabin on the far periphery of the runway, between engineers' offices and fuel stores. There is a rudimentary check-in, a toilet, a dozen plastic chairs. One machine vends chocolate bars and crisps (or chips as they are over here), the other fizzy drinks. Around them a sticky brown circumference of Pepsi has caramelised to the floor. On arrival I was excited to see an Inuit woman in traditional dress—an elaborately adorned white hide cape complete with slumbering baby in the voluminous hood—but once she departed to Rankin Inlet I found the remainder of my fellow fliers, natives all, to be sullen and dowdily dressed. Their only excitement occurred minutes before boarding when a young man burst through the doors from a taxi to be greeted loudly with cries of, "Hope you got some beer in that bag, Marshall!" and, "Hey, they finally let you out!" He greeted everyone with smiles and handshakes before catching my eye and nudging his neighbour with a whispered sniggered aside aimed at me.

Now I inspect my fellow passengers as they seem to lapse into collective torpor. Nobody reads or talks, they just stare through the windows or ahead. The men wear sham-leather jackets such as might be flogged from white Transit vans at Midlands Sunday markets, and some have what I take to be their family name emblazoned on their back—FRASER and MacPHERSON sit ahead. Everyone appears overweight, they seem jaded, and one or two of the women look distinctly ill. How conspicuous I am in my Barbour jacket and new nubuck boots. These are people I may well encounter during my stay, but now they show no interest and do not acknowledge me. Instead I am treated as they are in Whiteworld—I am ignored.

Lake Winnipeg has disappeared, the sky is perfect blue, and below us is an infinity of snow and trees. For an hour there is not one sign of human impact on the land, it is immense and unmarketable, and all the more impressive for that. Now, though, we are starting to descend, and I assume we are nearing London House, the only habitation en route. From here it looks magical— a few scattered cabins are in view, sharp and dark against the backdrop of snow and frozen river. As we bump to a halt I check my map to see that this plane is their only connection to the outside world. There is no road in or out.

The pilots are also porters and stewards. Two people get off, stooping past and clunking down the little metal ladder to the adjacent shed. Nobody takes their place, so within a few minutes we are clattering back down the runway. Just when it seems that so much energy has been expended on vibration and noise that none can be left for flight, we take off again. Our speed does not seem too great, yet we are chugging blithely through air. The view is resumed of trees and snow and lakes, snow and lakes and trees, lakes and trees and snow. The horizon in all directions remains remorselessly flat.

After forty minutes we start to descend again, the view now peppered by the outline of skinny spruce. They are miniature from malnourishment, we are deceptively close to the ground. Below us Churchill River dilates to form what arbitrarily becomes Jackfish Lake. Houses and the occasional attached car are scattered on the western side of it, along the linear black slash of road. We bank and drop, engine noise slows, then runway scree suddenly scrunches under the tyres. I have arrived.

The airport facilities comprise a hut, even huttier than the one at London House. A few friends and relatives have gathered to greet our arrival, and they slip between English and a language I don't understand. There is only one white face, and I presume it belongs to Sharon, the clinic manager who has helped me organise this trip. Through many hours of phone calls, usually involving her suave voice soothing me through another bureaucratic obstacle, I have developed an intimate and grateful bond with her. Now it seems like meeting a pen pal or a blind date. Sure enough she steps forward to shake my hand. She has a streaky bottle-blonde mullet and she wears all black. She is also enormously fat.

"Hi, Philip, I'm Sharon. It's really nice to meet you. How was your journey?"

"Hi. It was fine, thanks."

We make our way outside, where seven or eight cars have collected. The sky is cloudless but the wind spins off the not so distant Arctic and through my clothes. Everywhere but the gritted road and car park is still concealed under a foot or more of snow.

"You'll see the baggage reclaim facilities aren't too sophisticated here," Sharon says, as the pilots unload the luggage onto a platform under a ramshackle wooden canopy no more than six foot square. My brand new suitcases are easily recognisable among the scruffy holdalls, plastic bags and dog. Ah, the Englishman abroad!

We make towards Sharon's pick-up, punchy and gluttonous on its big wheels, coated to the hilt with mud. And within seconds my new boots and clean trousers are also spattered slushy brown. After loading my bags alongside her fishing rods and zipping the canvas cover over them, we get in the front of the car. I am taken aback by the overwhelming smell of dog, and then the actual presence of one, bounding and yapping from the seat as I open the door. It is an ugly animal, of indeterminate breed, scruffy coat, bulldog proportions and bulk. As I try to sit down it clambers all over me, slobbering wetly at my face.

"Philip, I want you to meet Roth."

"Wrath?"

She heaves him off me. "As in David Lee."

"Oh, right, the author. Didn't he write *Portnoy's Complaint*?"

Sharon stares at me, confused. "He's a singer, Philip. Aren't you into metal?"

We pull out of the car park and immediately past a sign which reads

**Welco   to Jackfish Lake Cree Nation**
C Population (1994) 2035
Altitude 637 fe t

For a moment I am distracted by the surprise of being so far above sea level, but then an uneasy reality sets in. I hate rock music, I hate fat women, and I hate dogs. How Mary would laugh to see my grand arrival here.

Mary? Mary is my ex-wife-to-be, and I have been trying not to think too much about her now I am embarking on this new instalment of my life. I certainly don't like to recall the night, twenty-three years into our marriage, when she came home and said, "Philip, there's something I have to tell you."

"What's that, then?" I asked, anticipating another of her Amnesty International meetings or some Family Planning conference. She had been spending a lot of weekends away at that time.

"Philip—" this said standing before me in the kitchen, staring somewhere beyond my right knee, "I've been having an affair."

The tense she used made me think this thing was past. "I've been having..." not, "I am having..." she said. I was shocked, stunned silent, and momentarily relieved. "But it's all over now," I waited for her to say.

"Oh, Mary—" I stepped towards her, arms outstretched to welcome her back—as if I'd known she'd ever been away.

But she froze into herself, contracted, small fists braced to beat me back.

"Mary?"

The rejection in her stance hurt me badly, and there was dismay in my voice as realisation set in. The worst of the many bad things which engulfed me in that instant and in the trillion instants since was the utter sheepishness I felt. I knew at once that it must have been avoidable. It was like telling a smoker he has lung cancer, that he has the all too finite interval between now and his death to rue those warnings he ignored.

"Mary, since when?"

"About eighteen months."

"Eighteen months!" Christ, how could I not have known?

"But—but who with?"

"Nobody you know."

"Mary! Who?" I shouted. "You can at least tell me that!"

"It's nobody you know," she insisted, turning away. "I met him at the AI meetings."

"Oh, great! So thanks very much, Amnesty Fucking International. Instead of addressing human rights in Burma, it just ends up as some sort of dating agency for bored housewives, is that how it works?"

"No, it's nothing to do with AI," she protested.

I made some inarticulate noise of disgust, and cringed at the memory of my jovial comments at her attendance over the years. Off to your Artificial Insemination meetings again, then? What? You know, AI? That's just not funny any more, Philip.

Too sickeningly right it wasn't funny. Anyway, that was how Nobody You Know, this NYK, exploded like a bomb in my life.

Desperate as I was to retrieve time and all those opportunities to be a true husband, I knew deep within me—even from that first minute—that there could be no recovery from the blast. We had a trial period, we told ourselves we were trying to resurrect our marriage, but I think it was simply something she felt she owed me after my years of overwork and partial fatherhood. I tried to force some happiness back into it, for yes, we were once content. But our (well, my) efforts only lasted a few weeks because Mary's heart clearly wasn't in it. All she wanted was to get away from me and move in with NYK.


Of course it was all down to work. It sounds idyllic to spend twenty years as a GP in the Cornish village of Tregaskis, but I can look back now and see its price. It was fine to have a comfortable salary and Dene House, our nice detached home in Rose Lane, but it cost a ten-hour working day, with nights and weekends on top. The popularity among patients was always welcome, though given our population of reverent Cornish families and well-heeled London émigrés it would have taken a deliberate effort to offend. Admittedly this ever growing wealthy brigade always demanded their full quota of time and attention for their daily concerns ("Ah, Philip, could you refer me back to my dermatologist again? That annoying little patch of eczema behind my ear seems to have recurred. I'll go private, of course."), but that was the way they were. A number of them were actually seen privately by us, a lucrative arrangement whereby we made ourselves available at nights and weekends to save them the uncertainty of seeing some locum or foreigner on the regular out-of-hours service, or maybe we did a relaxed Saturday morning session for those who worked away or travelled a lot. It all boosted the income, though Mary became increasingly annoyed by my commitment to these select patients over the years.

At least they always assured a bountiful Christmas in the Cormack household, and when they irritated me I asked myself if I would prefer to deal with the opposite end of the social spectrum instead. Drug addicts, homelessness, domestic violence? Answer—a resolute no.

There were other family pressures too. Our daughter Beth had left home, almost unnoticed by me, to go to university. Her sister Stella remained and we would pass civil words in passing, me off to work and she to college, me back from work and she off with friends, rarely with time to discuss anything but the mundane. I assumed that this was normal, me in the emotional back seat, for it was Mary who had always invested time and energy and common interests as they grew. In later years she would complain ever more bitterly of my perceived lack of interest in the girls, but how could it have been any different? The demands of work exhausted me, and I had to have *some* time for myself.

Meanwhile my parents were steadily failing some two hundred

miles away. My sister Eve would reinforce my guilt at not seeing them, phoning me with sporadic bulletins about their state of demise. But how could I forestall this with an occasional weekend visit? Mother wittered on about her endless anxieties and was long immune to any reassurances on my part, while Dad's cantankerous independence rebuffed any offers of physical help.

Stressed and overworked as I was, it would be wrong to suggest I had no outlet from the pressures of the practice and family demands. I would not have survived at all without cricket, I feel sure. I would have had a coronary or a complete nervous collapse, would have been one more addition to the list of Doctors Who Thought They Could Cope. And who can ever be too old for cricket? What could surpass a Sunday afternoon with the sun high over Tregaskis church, walking out to the crease with lazy pavilion applause crackling in your ears? Or ambling round the boundary to retrieve a cross-bat slog and arc it precisely back into the scuffed cupped gloves of Wally at the wicket? And how about the grace and timing of a sweep, as the grunting effort of some swaggering young lad is dispatched to the boundary by the twist of a wrist, the perfect co-ordination of eye and brain, strategy and style?

Batting yoga, skill in action. Such moments were perfect, they could only have been created by a cricketing God.

But oddly enough it was one such September Sunday—my fiftieth birthday, as it happened—when I decided I must escape. My marriage was irretrievable, work was more demanding than ever, and, worst of all, it was the last game of the season. We were playing St Petrocs, I recall, chasing a modest total of 121. We started off briskly, then a couple of wickets fell. I was going in at my usual number six and was alone in the changing room, buckling up my pads when the thought occurred to me—utterly uninvited—that from now on my innings was in decline. Any day now God could declare and summon me back to His pavilion. This startled and saddened me, for there were still many shots I wanted to play.

This unaccustomed introspection must have affected my concentration, for I was out third ball for a duck. It was a poor delivery, too, short and wide, the sort I normally thrive on as the bowling tires. Maybe I visualised it whipping across the boundary before I even made contact, but I spoon-fed mid-off with a catch.

"Shit!" I shouted. Yes, it was only one Cornish village team against another, but I was annoyed with myself. I have always been accused of having a competitive streak—my sister Eve would certainly claim that, though now I think it's more an innate orderliness. At work I have always been more methodical than my partners, it always bugged me (and bemused them) to leave paperwork and dictation undone at the end of the day. This often made me late home, but it couldn't be helped, it's the way I am. And if I am batting, I want to bat properly and tidily, otherwise what's the point? That's why I am still selected, because I'm reliable, there are plenty of other people to supply the flair. Anyway our collapse that day continued and we lost by forty runs. With a bit more application on my part we could have worn down their attack and won.

Afterwards we congregated in the pub, engulfed in bonhomie at the season's end. Some of the team pressed me into birthday pints: Jon Tullo, local author of some renown; Mike Donnelly, captain and solicitor; ENT surgeon Jeremy Walsh. Then, as was our custom, Gareth and Lyn had invited me for a birthday meal with my neighbours Steve and Kim. I suppose I would describe Gareth as my best friend, and a real cricketing man too. He was actually on Worcestershire's books in his youth, rubbing shoulders with the likes of Headley, d'Oliveira, and the great Tom Graveney. (His tales of these days always made me envious, for I had dreamed of being a cricketer myself. But Jack Jarvis, our PE teacher, took me aside one afternoon and told me I would never have been quite good enough. He was very kind, sat with an arm around me for an age, said he understood I only wanted to do things if I could be the best. I was devastated, of course, and without really knowing why I ended up doing medicine instead.) When Gareth realised he wouldn't cut the top grade he dropped out altogether and made a successful career for himself in the property market. Indeed he still has a good few holiday lets scattered around the county that generate a tidy income even after his various minions have been paid for the necessary maintenance work. However. Perhaps I was still brooding on my inadequacy with the bat, for I do, long after team mates have submerged thoughts of their failure under the first pint. Maybe the thought of my birthday was subduing me. Or, most discomfiting, I was reflecting on the fact that our regular harmony had been wrecked by Mary's defection.

For I felt this asymmetry dominate the evening. Two couples and me. In future years I saw myself sliding off the guest list and—the anguish!—being replaced by Mary and NYK. For Lyn and Mary were very close, and I knew they still met. I found myself wondering, again, how long she had known of Mary's infidelity, and whether she had told Gareth. Presumably she had, and this background of collusion tainted the whole evening. Despite more drinks I could not rid myself of the anger at Mary spoiling my special night. On the surface our chatter was that of any comfortably-off people of our day—witty, gossipy, opinionated and inconsequential in turn—but it was guarded all the time. The subject of Mary and me was studiously avoided, a steaming dog turd in the middle of the conversational park.

Suddenly I had a vision of my future. There might be token match-making attempts at dinner parties ("Philip, this is Lucinda, she's a potter...") but I would reject them or, more likely, be rejected on first impression. My well-meaning friends would soon give up and leave me to look forward to cricketless winter evenings as another sad old git in the pub, eating chicken in the basket, drinking ever more Guinness, getting sucked into the ambience of *Daily Mail* opinions and rancid jokes.

It was suddenly clear to me that I had to get away. The realisation of this left me quite calm, which made it all the more absolute, something I simply had to do. I knew that I could take a sabbatical from the practice if I provided a locum, my partners George and Julia would be pleased and relieved that I was taking positive steps to deal with my stress. So, yes, I could do it, for I was fifty and unattached. I could now do exactly what I liked.

I knew at once that Canada was where I should go. It would have to be somewhere English-speaking and well paid, as employing a locum would not be cheap. But as a medical student I had been to Wynsdale, a small town on the Saskatchewan prairies. Dad's brother Geoffrey was then a physician there, and although the relationship between him and the rest of the family had been strained by some bygone rift, he took a long-distance interest in me when he learned of my choice of career. So I spent two contented summer months in his practice and in his comfortable home.

As soon as I made the decision to return, reminiscences of my time there kept flooding back. I went to bed feeling happier than in months because the flat prairie skyline lay not too far ahead. Most people found the prairies monotonous, but to me they were utterly exhilarating. Perhaps I liked them because they were so organised and neat. I recalled the phenomenal range of the sky, the drama of August storms, great hail-laden clouds trundling by as farmers in Estevan or Fairlight willed their course of destruction away. They watched this natural display of shock and awe and all they could do was pray—please not my crops, God. Not mine.

Wynsdale was supremely amiable. Residents would know me as the doctor's nephew and would stop me in town to chat and enquire about my family tree. They watered their lawns and drove their chromed post-war Buicks to the library or the store or the John Deere dealers lining the highway out of town. They went to evening history lectures in the town hall, joined the Air Club, played golf and bridge. Old men chatted beside the fountain, waving at their fellow townspeople outside Kittie's Flower Shop or the offices of the *Wynsdale Messenger*. Everyone knew, and cared for, everyone else. Hospitality prevailed. Here in the heart of bucolic Canada everything was in gentle abundance, and people took pride in that.

One evening I strolled through the churchyard to consider some gravestone names. Many of them seemed spiky and cumbersome,

Nordic or Eastern European I guessed. Kovalczyk and Kutarski, Thordarsson and Weiss. No one had been interred there for more than sixty years, and as I was sitting on a bench to reflect on this I was joined by a small bespectacled man, almost as old as the town.

"Nice evening," he observed.

"It sure is."

"My name's Ralph, by the way."

I shook his offered hand. "Good to meet you, Ralph. I'm Philip. How long have you lived here?"

"Let's see now," he pondered. "Must be sixty-three years."

But the lilt of his voice certainly wasn't Canadian, in fact it sounded Geordie to me. "But you're from Newcastle, aren't you?"

He looked at me, deeply offended. "Nay, lad, nay—South Shields!"

Twenty-seven years later, fifty today, I smiled at the memory of this. And next day, a solitary Sunday, I dug out my old maps of Canada and spread them all over the floor. Nostalgia, trapped in them for years, burst out and overcame me. And it was not possible to study the geography of the country, even of staid and rectangular Saskatchewan, without considering its history. The two were intertwined. I imagined the pioneers setting out their foursquare fields, nothing but the ocean of land around them, the constancy of the horizon ever behind and ahead. The railways and roads and farms were methodically laid out, securing the future of grain. The westward halts to Saskatoon were staked, one by one, to Yarbo and Zeneta, then started again with Atwater, Bangor and Cana until they reached Young and Zelma. Then they resumed with Allan, Bradwell and Clavet...I searched in vain for their destination Z.

The names said much about the founders. Strasbourg and Lillestrom spread before me, as did Bodmin and Penzance. Over in Manitoba I found Gretna and McTavish, St Malo and La Rochelle. Some, like Mafeking and Kipling, clung unashamedly to their past. Eyebrow and Elbow awaited me, as did Resource, Revenue and Reward. I marvelled at the double act of Wabowden and Rawebb. Friendly old Roland and Myrtle were there, and also Arabella, Beulah, and Corinne. I envisaged those wives and lovers left at home, some maybe lost to childbirth along the unchartered way. I wanted to see the goose-laden splendour of Clear Lake and Gods Lake, even of Wrong Lake. Most of all, though, I pined for places like Eden, Vista and Justice, I wanted to experience the sheer everydayness of them all, and find out if that optimism was still in the air. I felt sure in my heart that it was, and that was the reason I had to go. I felt sure in my heart that it was.

Exhausted after the next day's work, I refreshed myself with a large G and T, followed by a larger one, and maybe a larger one still. Now was the time for Philip Andrew Cormack to act! I knew that certain provinces were unglamorous and unattractive to Canadian doctors, so these were where I would most likely find work without the tiresome requirements of an exam. So I asked my computer to search for medical locums in Manitoba and Saskatchewan, and, what do you know, it did! It was so easy! Pages of opportunities scrolled before my eyes, and mellowed by gin, I vowed to secure my venture forthwith. I decided that I would go wherever the fate of the keyboard took me. It would be an adventure, a new beginning. The only thing I decided in advance was that, having experienced life on the prairies, this time I would head for the north...

**Arborg.** Immediately available long-term locum...no good, they needed Obstetrics.

**Lloydminster**. Lucrative 6 man practice requires additional help...but the date had already passed.

**Moosomin**. Urgently required...no, that's too far south.

**La Ronge**. Friendly practice urgently seeks locum...too much Obstetrics again.

**Jackfish Lake**. The great outdoors! 300km N of Thompson. Short or long term locum available. $210,000 pa basic plus on call. Accommodation supplied. Occasional intra-partum care only. For further details contact...

I checked the conversion rates and rubbed my hands with greed. I found Jackfish Lake on the map. There was no mention of it in my guide book, nor, oddly, of Thompson. But this did not deter me, for I wanted to experience the authentic backwaters of Canada, not a tourist trap.

It seemed ideal. If I procrastinated now, I feared I always would, so I sent an email to express my interest and attached my cv. I wondered what life must be like in these outposts of the north as I sipped on another drink.

Next afternoon at work I received a phone call.

"Can you speak to Sharon Ballantyne?" Janice the receptionist asked.

"Who?" I demanded. "What's it about?" They all knew of my dislike of taking unscreened calls. After all, this could have been a disgruntled patient, an interfering relative, a market researcher, even a social worker, heaven forbid.

"Hi, Dr Cormack, this is Sharon, the clinic manager from Jackfish Lake. Do you have a moment to speak right now?"

Jackfish Lake? It took a moment to register. "Oh—yes, go ahead." I would give as much time as necessary to fix up this escapade abroad, especially as Sharon's voice was rich and alluring, a provocative yet wholesome drawl. A woman emitting such lovely purring tones could only be young, sexy and slim.

"Now I don't expect you had much experience of working with the aboriginal population in Wynsdale?"

"No, I didn't."

"Well, it sure makes for challenging work, Dr Cormack—"

"Philip, call me Philip," I insisted.

"Thank you, Philip..." She told me a little about the local population, that there were normally two doctors sharing on call, that I would be paid a bonus for weekends and weekday nights, that there were usually no more than a dozen labour cases a year. "And it's really not a problem, Philip, the Cree just cough them out..."

She promised she would steer me through the bureaucracy

ahead. These days the process had gotten really slow, she told me, and it usually took six months to fix it all up. But nothing she said would have deterred me. My mental application form was already on its way.

All of the necessary and inexplicable processes took time— application for hospital "privileges", membership of the College of Physicians and Surgeons of Manitoba, clearance by the Human Resources Department, authorisation of a work permit by the Canadian High Commission, subscription to the Canadian Medical Protective Association, personal insurance cover with Manitoba Health—but over the winter Sharon's voice soothed me through every obstacle. Without her I would have been paralysed by the paperwork. Without Sharon I would have given up.

"Don't worry about those forms, Philip, this is what you have to do…"

"It's really not a problem, just fax everything to me…"

If a week went by with no palpable progress, I would phone her to be reassured. Sometimes—lonely evenings here, bright afternoons there—I would simply want to chat.

"It's really cold, here, Philip, minus thirty-three…"

Minus thirty-three? Wow! It all added to the adventure of the place. I just wanted to be there to experience the extremeness of it, and, of course, to meet the fount of that voice.

A minute later, without passing any noticeable habitation and just before a sign to the hospital, we turn off to the right. After fifty yards the road forks either way into a cluster of seven or eight houses, wooden built and detached, all overlooking the lake. Mine, it appears, is the last but one on the left. A path leads through to the hospital from the back of them, and Sharon lives conveniently next door.

We unload my belongings and Sharon says, "Okay, Philip, it's now three o'clock. How about I give you a couple of hours to unpack and clean up, then I'll come back at five to give you a tour of the reserve. After that you can come eat at my place. I've invited some of the guys from work so we can all get to meet. Showing you round the hospital can wait until tomorrow."

"Sounds fine. Thanks, Sharon."

"You're welcome. I'll come back about five."

Space, in this house as in this country, is not at a premium. The rooms are large, and warm air sweeps in through floor level vents at the touch of a switch. The house is double-glazed and double-doored, with fine metal meshes on every window warning of insects to come. The back door opens into a small porch containing a broken fishing rod, a bottle of meths, barbecue equipment, and a mildewed volume of the Northern Lights telephone directory for 1994. There are three sizeable bedrooms upstairs, and it seems obvious to choose the front one with its view over the whiteness of Jackfish Lake. There are masses of storage space, especially in the kitchen. I open door after door and although most cupboards are empty I find I have been provided with tea, coffee, milk, bread, butter, eggs, sausages, cereal and cheese. In the lounge is a comfortable settee, television, phone and a modest CD player and radio. I make myself tea and toast, unpack my clothes, sit down to await Sharon's return, then realise that if we are going straight on to this social function after our tour I ought to make myself presentable. So I change into my new linen jacket and black moleskin trousers, which, like most of my replenished wardrobe in these post-marital-split days comes from Johnny Boden's catalogue (in which in moments of whimsy I appear in my new modelling career. **Philip**: Sporting hero— Sir Garfield Sobers. Shaken or stirred?—Stirred. Ideal date—Juliette Binoche.), as I reckon this would be the least that people expect from the new doctor in town.

"Hey, you're looking pretty smart," Sharon greets.

"Thank you."

"You're welcome. Ready to roll?"

"Sure." I climb onto the big bench seat of her truck and instantly an electro-static reaction of previously undescribed force hoovers every dog hair in the cabin onto my trousers. Roth greets me like a long-lost friend and deposits half a litre of canine saliva onto my groin.

"Hey, he likes you," Sharon observes.

Back on the road we pass a few houses with tumbledown sheds alongside, then immediately we turn left and cut into the vast arboreal expanse. "I'll take you to the mine first," Sharon says. There are a few sporadic houses among the trees, but they seem somewhat decrepit. There is not much sign of life. Suddenly the tarmac gives way to gravel, and we bounce harshly from bump to bump. "You can tell we're off reserve now," she shouts above the noise.

"How do you mean?"

"The band gets a considerable sum of money to maintain roads—"

"Hang on—the band?"

"Sorry. That's the name for the tribal councils here. Each reserve has its own band, and they're in charge of social services, civic amenities, stuff like that. They'll spend money on keeping roads in good shape, but as soon as you go off reserve it's not their problem. So if you want to drive to Thompson, you've got four hours of this." As she says this a truck passes in the opposite direction, spraying the car with a clatter of gravel and mud. Only now do I notice that the whole of the windscreen is traversed by an east-west crack.

"Sounds great."

"Actually it's better in the winter, the snow kind of evens it out. Anyways, take a look at that."

She slows the car to show me a log cabin—no, more like a log mansion—a stout but elegant building made from tree trunks. And not northern Manitoba tree trunks, for sure, but substantial masses of wood, red and robust, laid horizontal atop each other with their corners neatly chamfered square, interlocking precisely to keep the weather out. A few yards on is another house, similar though smaller, then another one, then a fourth. Each one a dream home, thoughtfully integrated into the wild, but each one deserted, each one bleak and dark.

"So who lives here?"

"No one."

"No one? Why not?"

"Well, five or six years ago, the mine was doing just great. It employed about five hundred people and was looking to take on more. Most of the locals thought they would get work here, there was money coming into the town. The engineers and surveyors built these houses for their families, the school was full of kids from every part of the country, and everything looked bright."

"So what happened?"

"So politics happened. First of all the mine got taken over. It used to be owned by Munro Minerals, which was originally a Manitoba company, but they got swallowed up by EMH, some multi-national with no loyalty whatsoever to Jackfish Lake. Then

20

the copper market collapsed. There's still no end of the stuff down there, but it no longer makes economic sense to get it out. Suddenly it's cheaper for people to import it from Poland or Thailand or wherever, even the States. The company started laying people off, and of course the locals were first to go. A lot of the labourers were Newfies, so they—"

"Newfies?"

"Sorry. Newfoundlanders. I think they're equivalent to Irish people in the UK, they've always had the reputation for travelling the country to find manual work. But there was a lot of ill-feeling because the Cree, as you can imagine, thought they should have been kept on instead. So when they started getting argumentative, it just reinforced the prejudices about the Indian being drunk, aggressive, and unwilling to work. It was pretty unpleasant a year or two ago, there were lots of fights, but now most of the jobs have gone anyway and the Newfies have left, apart from one or two who built homes here and decided to stay."

"So who did these belong to?"

"The big house belonged to Dave Bartram, the chief engineer. Cost him about 200k to build, now he can't give it away."

"Can't any of the locals buy it?" I know as soon as I ask what a dim question this is.

"No way. There's no one here can afford two thousand bucks, let alone a hundred times that."

"What about the band? Can't they do anything?"

"Ah, now that was the other problem. That was the politics on a local scale fucking everything up. When the mine was expanding, Munro's realised that they would have to smarten up the town if they wanted to attract people to live here. So they were prepared to fork out a substantial sum of money to build a new community centre, a hotel, apartments and houses—there was even talk of a new hospital. But they wanted to build off reserve, and the band wanted everything on reserve, partly for the tax reasons, but mainly because they wanted to be in control, they wanted to own it all. They always knew they would outlive the mine. One argument led to another, things got delayed, and

21

the result, of course, was that nothing ever got done. In the end EMH took over, got fed up with all the wrangling and withdrew the offer. They blamed the band, the band blamed them, and there were rumours of people in high places on the lookout for bribes."

"I presume the local people were pretty fed up with that."

"You bet. Now they've seen the mine come and go they're feeling pretty cheated. Nobody in Jackfish Lake has a cent to show for it."

We rumble up the lane to the mine entrance. Its gates are firmly closed, but unoccupied offices and sheds can be seen beyond. "There's not much to see as the copper is about half a mile below ground," Sharon explains.

"Isn't there anyone left working here?"

"They've kept some maintenance staff on until the end of this month. They were kind of hoping someone would come up with a rescue package, but it doesn't look like that will happen. Once they quit, the pumps will be shut down, and the mine will flood. And that's when the security people's contract runs out. When they move out, then the fun will really start."

"How do you mean, fun?"

"Everybody will be fighting to get these empty houses. The band are trying to allocate them fairly—even though they're not theirs to allocate, they want to be seen to be doing something useful—but unfortunately it's pretty much a case of every man for himself. We've already had a couple of nasty stabbings."

My concern at this potential for social unrest is rapidly converted to a far more personal and immediate alarm. If there are more knife fights in the offing, where will these severely lacerated victims be brought? To Jackfish Lake Indian Hospital, that's where. And who is likely to be on call for the emergency room? An outdated and dissipated GP from Tregaskis, Cornwall, that's who.

The road circles back into the town, and as soon as it acquires a decent surface, the houses indeed become ramshackle and surrounded by the debris of collapsing sheds, old cars or what I take to be snowmobiles skewed into ditches or across paths. Most homes are detached, shouldered with snow and surrounded by a rough unfenced outcrop of rocky land. One small shack boasts a satellite dish almost the size of itself. I am surprised how scattered the small population is, though the housing becomes a little more concentrated as we near what might loosely be called the centre of the town—for there is simply a junction with a cluster of shops. Most prominent is a metal windowless hulk of a place, its double doors camouflaged by a dull frontage of rust. It looks like some sort of penal institution but turns out to be the main store. Across the road is a handful of equally bleak buildings which prove to be post office, bank and a hardware dealer. ("Knives a specialty," Sharon says.) A shop proclaiming **Gifts & Local Crafts** appears to have been boarded up for many a day. Next to it is a rudimentary car park which backs away to the shore.

Sharon turns left to drive along the lake again, to show me a further scatter of houses. These are similar, though a little closer together, to the ones I have seen before. They are of basic construction, their innate shabbiness offset by the remnants of snow. Their only concession to decor seems to be the dangling wires which skirt every roof to form artificial icicles, now dripping weakly in the sun. Further on a large square of land has been cleared of trees, apparently earmarked as a site for the new hotel when it was envisaged engineers and businessmen would be attracted by the booming enterprise of the mine. The only building of quality or elegance is an octagonal structure of glass and pine which turns out to be the band's main office. Then we pass a sprawling complex which accommodates schools, police, fire and ambulance, a petrol station, and then, bizarrely, The River Café. This too appears to be long closed.

"I'll take you down to Fraser's Point, it's really lovely down there." So, I suppose, it is. A disused wooden jetty is crumbling into the lake, its shapes of slats and gaps and suspended tyres sharp against the white. And yes, the houses here are perceptibly bigger, surrounded by less disorder than the ones I have seen so far.

We turn round in silence and it does not even hearten me to

see that the final building before we return to the hospital is a slightly newer but nonetheless scruffy two-storey edifice, simply labelled **Athabasca Bar**. In its car park a handful of people loll, their fleetingly caught expressions, postures and ragged clothes and teeth the hallmark of drunks everywhere. As we pass them Sharon says, "Well, I guess that's it."

It is difficult to find any positive comment, in fact I can't say anything at all. Instead I stare out at the desolation, the nothingness, the drab desperation of the reserve. I feel sick with the realisation that in coming here I have made a colossal mistake.


Sharon's house is a mirror image of mine. Roth welcomes me to his territory by boring his snout into my crotch. I try to push him away, though Sharon doesn't seem too concerned by his olfactory explorations. Maybe it's normal behaviour around here. The decor is hardly feminine, and the starkness of the walls is exaggerated by her choice of posters, most of which are predominantly black.

"Who's this?" I point to a tattooed, big-bicepped collection of 1970s' throwbacks.

"That's Nickelback," she says, appalled by my ignorance. "Canada's finest. Anyways, would you like a drink?"

Too right I would. "Ooh, yes please. What have you got?"

She inspects the contents of a kitchen cupboard. "Hm, supplies are getting a little low, guess I'll have to make a trip to Thompson soon. I have beer, whiskey, rum or red wine."

"A red wine would be nice."

"Good idea, I think I'll have the same." She unscrews a half full litre bottle and pours out two glasses. "So, Philip, here's to your stay in Jackfish Lake."

"Cheers." I down a mouthful of the cheapest, most acidic, tannin-laced plonk I have tasted since my student party days.

"Mm, that's good," Sharon approves. "Cheers."

She has provided a tableful of pizza, bread, chips, jacket potatoes, chicken drumsticks, sausage rolls and potato salad. Soon after six the doorbell rings, and the people with whom I am to be incarcerated here for the next half year begin to arrive. First there is Ellie the radiographer, slim and blonde, with her big policeman husband Brad. They seem pleasant enough, and within a few minutes are inviting me round for an unspecified meal. Then comes the pathologist, my neighbour from the other side whose name is Doug. He is tall and angular, his straggles of hair, flutters of beard and dense specs helping confirm all known stereotypes of the socially incapable scientist consigned to a solitary life in his lab.

"Hi, Phil," he greets.

"Hi. Actually, I prefer to be called Philip."

"Gee, I'm sorry for the presumption. You know what, my left brain processes seem a little disturbed today. I think my magnesium levels may be low. Or possibly boron. I guess I should eat more nuts."

This is not a line of conversation I feel I can confidently pursue, so I am glad to be distracted by the arrival of Donald, the pharmacist. He is older, seems gentle and affable, and is keen to fill me in with a brief history of his life. When his wife died three years ago he decided to sell up his drug store in the cosy security of Brandon, MB, and see a little of his country by taking on locum work wherever he could. "Let me tell you, Philip, since I sold up I've been all over the place—Whitehorse, Dawson Creek, Baker Lake—I really love the north. You really must get to see as much as you can."

"I intend to."

"It's a hard life, of course, especially in winter, but I don't miss the city at all. I've got a contract here till the end of the summer, then I guess I'll move on. It's real liberating not to have any ties, you know. Are you a family man?"

Before I can give him a run-down of my marital collapse, Sharon nudges my arm. "Sorry to interrupt, but Arie's here. Come and say hello."

Arie, the other doctor, greets me with a bounding shake of the hand. He cannot realise how much I am relying on him to be my mentor and tutor in the weeks ahead. He is South African, about thirty, with a thin intelligent face and spiky young blonde hair. His wife Florence is, by comparison, short, dark and round. She speaks quietly and smiles wanly. They have two young boys who are already chasing each other loudly around the house.

"Hi, Phil, how was your journey?"

"Fine, thanks. And it's Philip, not Phil."

"Oh, sorry. Anyway, it's really good to see you. I've been working single-handed for the last six weeks."

"Is it that long since Reinhard left? I guess it is," Sharon muses.

"You've been busy then?" I ask. After all, two thousand people is hardly more than the average list size back home. In an environment of sensible activity, reasonable health, and a modicum of self-reliance, two doctors here shouldn't have *that* much to do.

"Yeah, pretty steady. I could do with a good night's sleep."

"Me, too," adds Florence. "What with the phone going every night, and those two."

I follow her gaze to the boys who are now throwing lumps of food onto carpet and dog. She calls, "Thomas! Thian! Stop that!" but weakly, and her words have no effect.

"So where in England are you from?" Arie asks.

"Cornwall, down in the south west."

"I've heard of that. You know, I really want to work in England. So green! All those country pubs!"

Oh, that's it, rub it in. Make me yearn for the back bar of The Dog and Pheasant. Bring my attention to my empty glass. Even a top-up of this *Chateau Pisse du Chat* would be preferable to the torture of abstinence. "What about you, Arie?" I distract myself. "What did you do before coming here?"

"I worked four years in Cape Town. A bit of Orthopaedics, but mainly Anaesthetics and Intensive Care. I tell you, it was major trauma every night on call—gunshot wounds, thoracotomies, neurosurgery, the works."

"A far cry from here, then?" I suggest.

He smiles. "Well, actually it seems like useful experience when you're on for bash and slash weekends."

"Bash and slash weekends?" I try to conceal my panic—what the fuck are they?

"You know, when they get their welfare cheque and head for the pub. You get some—"

Florence gives him a sharp nudge. "Arie, don't put Philip off yet, he's only just arrived."

As if to make his point he is interrupted by his bleep, which is the size of a half brick and resembles a prototype walkie-talkie. "*KrrrcanyoucomeseeheadinjryinemergAriekrrr.*"

He phones to get more details, leaving me with Florence. We chat stiffly, me with an eye on the prospect of a steadying drink (Would it confound Canadian etiquette to go help myself? Would it confirm me, straight off the plane, as a hopeless alcoholic?), while Florence listlessly watches her offspring pull at Roth's fur and try to cadge a ride on his back. He, to his credit, does not object, but I find myself willing him to proffer a playful nip.

Arie goes to assess the head injury and does not return. Meanwhile some of the nurses have arrived, so they say, "Hi, Phil," and I say, "Hi, by the way I prefer to be called Philip," and they say, "So how was your journey?" or, "All the way from England, ay?" Their accent, I notice, differs from Sharon's, it is flatter, lazier, more slurred. These women, it seems, are Cree, they are in their thirties and forties, and they live with their families on reserve. They are all products of The Northern School of Nursing, which encourages indigenous people to train—in Winnipeg, Thompson, and isolated hospitals such as this—before going back to serve their own communities. They are jovial, intelligent and hospitable, and, boy, do they know how to eat.

But at nine o'clock people start to diffuse away. My glass has been in receipt of one meagre top-up, and Diet Pepsi appears to be the staple drink. It seems I am in danger of being left here with Sharon and, much as I feel I should stay to help clear up, weariness intervenes.

"I need to turn in now, Sharon, if you don't mind. Thank you very much."

"You're welcome. I'll call for you about nine in the morning and show you round the hospital."

"That's fine. Good night, then. Good night, Roth." Shit, I curse myself as I step outside into the cold clear night. Did I really say good night to that stupid dog?


But of course I cannot sleep. It is not belated jet lag so much as outright anxiety which keeps me awake. Panic prevents me absorbing any useful eleventh-hour medical facts from my masses of leaflets or *The Oxford Textbook of Emergency Medicine* which the pretty Glaxo rep gave me before I came away, its bookmark still lodged at page nine. Anyway it doesn't seem to have a chapter on Bash and Slash Weekends. But at least I can thumb through a little red booklet from the College. *Working With Aboriginals*, it is called.

And yes, I learn from the foreword, "aboriginals" is the correct term. "Native" is not acceptable, unless you are in the USA, while "Indian" (a major misnomer, of course—could you imagine white Americans tolerating two centuries of being called Australians?) is positively derogatory, even though I am working in Jackfish Lake Indian Hospital. "First Nations People" is also approved, though not all aboriginal tribes are strictly First Nation. I get the impression that hundreds of man-years' worth of committees has been spent deliberating the politically correct terminology here. After generations of oppression and abuse, at least they are trying to make amends by decreeing that no man shall take offence by being called an Injun.

I read about the appalling treatment meted out by the white man (more specifically the Anglo-Franco-Scottish imperialist Christian missionary white man) right up to the twentieth century, when the confinement of children in residential schools was still being imposed. Despite this, it says, the aboriginal has always responded with a quiet Zen-like dignity, always reluctant to offer criticism or praise. He has an "intuitive and flexible" approach to time. I read that he has a passive view of his place in nature, he has a profound intrinsic respect for the land. Even the nomadic Arctic tribes have always understood that they must tend planet Earth. They were dispossessed because they never had the concept of possession to start with, so now here they are despatched to their isolated ditchwater reserves.

The following pages tell me about powwows and sweat lodges and potlatch ceremonies, about sweetgrass and various sacred herbs. They describe the four stages of life, and in particular how the elder is revered. Each community appoints respected senior citizens whose wisdom and experience can be sought by others. This seems to me like a good idea, one we should adopt back home.

My concentration fails, but when my eyes close they let in floods of apprehension of my months ahead. This is an alien place, I feel, but what really scares me is the work. I can't help thinking of the myriad things which could barge through midnight emergency room doors and find me utterly unable to cope—myocardial infarction, subarachnoid haemorrhage, ectopic pregnancy, pneumothorax, burns, acute renal failure, pericarditis, psychoses, cardiac arrhythmias, meningitis, alcohol poisoning, alcohol withdrawal, overdoses, diabetic ketoacidosis, all the gory possibilities of trauma, and, dread of dread, all those complications of labour—haemorrhage, shoulder dystocia, undiagnosed breech, fetal distress, newborn babies refusing to breathe. Then I try to comfort myself by listing all those conditions which I, an experienced and trusted British GP, could confidently treat. Let me see—tonsillitis, eczema, gout...

It was all very well doing those weekend courses in obstetrics and resuscitation in preparation for coming here, but they were several months ago. Manoeuvring a ragdoll baby through a mannequin pelvis was fine, but this is now for real, and it is only a matter of time before my utter incompetence will be revealed. I fear I will be phoning Arie on his every night and weekend off to come and bale me out.

———

On the dot of nine o'clock Sharon rings the door bell. I feel I have barely slept, and the knot of nerves in my stomach is tighter, I think, than the one before finals or the interview for any job. And this is supposed to be my sabbatical, my rejuvenating escape!

We take the path which cuts through a handful of thin trees to the back of the hospital. It seems to have been built on the model of hospitals everywhere, its ageing nucleus accumulating over the years a haphazard and badly built satellite of annexes, sheds, storage areas, and cheapskate offices for secretaries, social workers and physiotherapists. The corridors linking them are gloomy, lined by bulky pipes of uncertain function, and they retain the stale reek of hospital food. The basic plan is U-shaped, the ward and emergency room on one arm, the clinic running parallel along the other, offices and the staff canteen in the connecting limb. Between these is what Sharon calls the garden, but it is no more a garden than any other scrawny clump of land I have seen in Jackfish Lake. Anyone entering the hospital from the set of double doors here is greeted by a faded monochrome photo, circa 1957, of Elizabeth II, Her Majesty the Queen.

At least I am to have today, Thursday, for orientation. After that I am hoping to attach myself to Arie as a helpful underling until I feel confident enough to cope. Will, I wonder, six months be enough? I try to picture myself after that time as an assured and competent physician, but the image does not appear.

"First and foremost, here's the coffee machine." She inserts two dollar coins, and it clatters out a cup for each of us. It is thick and chemical, bitter and lukewarm. "Mmm, that's good," she says. "Now I can start the day."

She sits me down in her office and presents me with a substantial red folder. "These are the hospital bye-laws, you can take them away and read them at home. Maybe you could sign the last page and give it back to me tomorrow." Then she opens the file she has already constructed, containing my contract, my references, and copies of correspondence from the College, already several pages thick. "Here's a list of privileges you signed up for. Could you check that it's still okay?"

This notion of hospital privileges baffles and unnerves me, though she has already explained it on the phone. It seems I have to state which clinical services I am willing to provide, and I was presented with a four-page list of procedures and operations which left me quaking at my desk. "Don't worry about it, Philip," she had said. "It's just a technicality in isolated places like this. In an emergency situation you would do whatever you feel you can. But for billing purposes the College need to know what elective procedures you might be able to offer here, and what would have to be sent out." So I stare uncomfortably at the list of things I have accredited myself to do (my confidence must have been boosted by a goodly intake of gin)—aspirate pleural effusions, insert supra-pubic catheters—interventions I last carried out under supervision twenty-five years ago. Despite my terror the choice of terminology still amuses me, "Excuse me, madam, but it would be a privilege to insert this proctoscope into your bottom…"

"Hey, Philip, something funny?"

"No, sorry, it's nothing."

Then there are forms for rent agreement, telephone rental, banking details, and tax, before we confirm my salary. Basic payment is $210,000 a year, with a bonus of $175 for each night on call and $500 a day for weekends. As an immigrant worker I will be taxed 15% at source, so even with that and an exchange rate of $2.40 to the pound, that makes… but instead of comforting me, the thought of all this money is deeply worrying. They must be expecting a hell of a good doctor for that.

We drink more synthetic coffee, then Sharon takes me to the ward. "Rose is the sister in charge. She can go through all the clinical stuff with you, then you can grab some lunch and I'll see you back here at two."

Rose greets me gruffly. Greets is in fact the wrong word, for she acknowledges my presence with a fleeting handshake and stony face. She is short and squat, middle-aged. I follow her around the ward, managing to catch key words on the way, "Four bed women's ward here…four bed men's ward…two paediatric cots...two single rooms...labour room here...dialysis room through there—"

"Dialysis! You have your own kidney dialysis unit?" I exclaim. Why didn't anyone warn me about this? What other horrors lie in wait?

"Sure, two beds, but you don't have to get involved, the renal nurses do it all." Instantly we move on: "This is emerg...plaster of Paris in those cupboards...guess you're familiar with the resus trolley—"

"Actually, hang on—not this particular model—if you could just go through it—"

Her stare unnerves me, and I feel she has already rumbled this long-awaited English doctor as being useless. "Paddles here and here...button here to charge...here to discharge...drugs in here...IV stuff underneath...guess that's it."

I thank her and make an urgent mental note to learn up how many Joules to zap into unresponsive chests, the doses of adrenaline and atropine, rules for giving bicarbonate and calcium, all of which I have forgotten. Then, oh shit, there are the scary new drugs like adenosine and amiodarone which lie casually on the trolley. When do I give them? What do they do?

Rose dispenses with me in barely ten minutes, so, as Sharon directed, I make my way to the clinic. It seems eerily empty with just one elderly man sitting immersed in sad isolation, and it occurs to me that anyone here for a psychiatry appointment could be triggered into suicidal despair by the country and western wailing which is constantly piped into the waiting room. Arie is in the office with a mound of letters, notes and lab reports, and he waves a sheaf of forms on which he has been dashing his signature. "As far as the patients are concerned, your most important function here is to sign these."

"What are they?"

"Travel warrants."

"What are they for?"

"You'll find out."

He introduces me to the staff. We say hello, I forget their

names, and the typist stares and asks, "You the one from England?"

"That's right."

"So that's overseas, ay?"

I assure her that it is, then Arie explains how the system is supposed to work. When there are two doctors, one runs the nine-to-five clinic, which deals with the usual non-urgent sore throats, asthma, blood pressure, diabetic, pre-natal clinics and all the rest of the routine stuff. This leaves the duty doctor to cover real emergencies and any acute problems when the clinic gets overbooked, and to take care of in-patients. We try to meet up once a day to hand over problems on the ward, and we alternate duties from day to day and weekend to weekend.

"The problem is, when you're the only doctor you have to deal with everything. You can't be in two places at once. We try to educate them to bring their snotty kids into clinic at a sensible time, but when they do that and you've been called over to a chest pain, they get a little pissed off, and the system breaks down. So they just turn up at emerg all hours of day and night with all sorts of trivial crap."

I feel that, given our backgrounds, it would be sensible for me to do the clinic every day, and Arie to do the emergency work, then sharing nights and weekends. Maybe I will suggest this when I am fully bedded in. At least I might be able to organise some health education, and get people to use the services in the way they should. By eleven o'clock, when the morning rush of troublesome throats and coughs and backs back home would be starting to subside, just three people have turned up.

"Is this normal?" I ask Arie.

"Sure. It's early yet."

"Do you want me to do anything to help out just now?"

"No, it's all under control, you can just spend the day finding your way around, and start properly tomorrow." He hesitates, then asks, "Philip, I know it's a bit soon, but I've been on call every day for the last six weeks, and Florence is desperate for a break—could you do this weekend?"

"Um—" What can I say? How can I deny the man such a request? "Sure, Arie. That's fine."

He thanks me and his bleep crackles from sleep, "*Krrrxraysonthatshoulderareherekrrr.*"

For a moment I think I should accompany him, but how can I correct a career long ignorance of x-rays in just five minutes? He hurries off, thanking me again, so I head for the library next to Sharon's room. It seems that in 1956 someone decided it would be a good idea to subscribe to the quarterly *Pediatric Clinics of North America*, and half a wallful of them have now accumulated, almost certainly unread. There are sporadic copies of the *Canadian Medical Journal*, a few outdated tomes on Obstetrics and Orthopaedics, and not much else. I am rather hoping to find *ECGs for Dummies*, and something ultra-concise on resuscitation and fractures, but I search in vain.

After a leisurely lunch in the house, glazing over more hand-outs, I return to Sharon's office. She introduces me to a large taciturn man named Larry, who is one of the social workers here. (One of? How many social workers does a place of this size need?) He takes me to his office and proudly displays the computer on his desk. It seems he is very keen to give me a tour of the reserve, so I can see how the people here live. I don't have the heart to tell him Sharon has already shown me round, so I follow him into his Chrysler SUV. It is awash with empty sweet packets, Pepsi cans, paper and mud, but at least it has no dog. We bump along the same tracks to see the same houses, the same dismal town, though this time we stop at the band headquarters, and he points to one of the cars outside.

"Looks like the Chief's in. Want to say hello?"

I suppose I do, not from any socially aspirational point of view, but simply to see what the head of this community might be like. We leave our shoes in the porch, and are greeted by an attractive young receptionist. While she dials a couple of numbers to locate the Chief, Larry proudly shows off the memorabilia encased on display around the foyer—models of traditional boats, a Bible translated into Cree, a stuffed eagle, floridly feathered headdresses, a gigantic moose head, and various grainy photographs of the reserve's past. One in particular, maybe a hundred years old, catches my eye. It shows two aboriginal women, young but darkly suspicious of the camera, flanked by two men who are clearly European. They are both formally dressed, their jackets, waistcoats and stiff collars at odds with the scrubby land they have invaded. One stands stern and powerful, his prominent hands dwarfing those of the small girl beside. The other man is tiny, hunchbacked and heavily moustached, his expression smug with acquisition. The caption tells me, **"Wee Jock" MacPherson lands at Jackfish Lake, 1927**. I feel queasy at the layers of abuse hinted at in one small photo. I wonder why they feel they should display it here.

"Ah, doctor, pleased to meet you!"

"How do you do."

Larry exchanges names on our behalf and we shake hands. Bernard Bell is in his fifties, he has a substantial paunch, dense glasses, and grey hair tied back long and straight into a pony tail. His smile is easy, his voice firm, his welcome seems genuinely warm.

"So where are you from?"

"England."

"Ah, very good. Makes a change from all the South Africans we usually get, ay, Larry?"

"If we have anyone at all."

"For sure. We're very glad to have you with us, Philip. I apologise if you come across any resentment during your stay here, but there are always a few people who find it difficult to get away from their history."

"I think I can understand that."

"Good. For myself, I think we should just look ahead. We're trying hard to train up our own doctors and other professional people, but of course it will all take time. I think there are four or five Cree in the medical school in Winnipeg at the moment, so at least it's a start." I wonder if the pick of local youth from this or any similar reserve who are granted access to five years of university life will really want to return to what they left behind,

35

but that is not my problem. "However—" Bernard continues, "that's all for the future. For now I'm late for a meeting. Do excuse me if I rush off. Enjoy your stay!"

We conclude our tour, Larry pointing out features I missed first time round. It surprises me to see so many churches here, five at least, given the history of the last two hundred years.


When I report back to Sharon she is speaking on the phone, "He's just walked into my room...sure, I understand that...well, I can't really say no...I'll speak to you about five, you can let me know if you have anything definite by then..."

I loiter outside the door, not wishing to intrude. "Everything all right?" I enquire casually when she has finished.

"Sure, no problems. How was your tour?"

"Interesting. I got to meet the chief."

"Lucky you. First day, too." There is a hint of sarcasm in her voice.

"Is he not what he seems?"

"I think he's a good guy at heart, Philip, but being Chief in a place like this is an impossible job. Anyway, consider yourself orientated. Why don't you take my car and go for a ride? I expect you'll need to go to the store at some point." She tosses me her keys.

"What—I can just take your car?"

"Sure, any time. I'm not going anywhere. I don't expect you to buy a car for six months here, but sometimes you just need to get away. Any time you want to go to Thompson, just take it. That's a spare set of keys, you can hang on to them."

"Thanks, Sharon, that's very kind of you."

"You're welcome. And if you want to take Roth with you he'd be only too pleased. But it's entirely up to you."

"Hm, is it okay if I pass this time?"

"Sure," she laughs. "He's not everyone's idea of a best friend."

So, for the third time in twenty-four hours, I find myself heading out of the hospital complex. This time I turn left, away from town and past the airstrip. **Thompson 312km, Winnipeg 958km**, the sign informs me. **Tregaskis, 200 light years**, it might as well add. But there is half a continent before me, and isn't this why I am here? However each kilometre is the same as the last, and, I presume, the next three hundred and ten. I catch glimpses of the lake to my left, between the (what else?) snow and trees, and I look out for somewhere to stop so I can walk down to the frozen water's edge. However the concept of the cosy lay-by with picnic tables is not one they have adopted here. After five or six miles the road veers away from the lake, and eventually there is a hint of a clearing. A thin path heads into trees, so I follow it, glad to stretch my legs and breathe unadulterated air. My new boots leave crisp prints, though in some places the snow has now thawed to expose the soggy brown undergrowth, below which feeble roots compete with each other and grapple with the permafrost below. Some trees even sprout directly from the rocks. The lanky trunks struggle twenty or thirty feet upwards, where their sparse bursts of green also seem inadequate to sustain them. I had assumed the track would lead to a clearing or the lake, but it simply disperses to nothing, leaving only me and the trees. My eye is caught by a splash of lurid colour and I wonder why two dozen or so spent cigarette lighters have been discarded into the pure seclusion of Manitoba air.

The temperature is falling, below zero I feel sure, so I decide to return. My route, though, is not as clear as I thought, and I lose trace of my foot marks. The road is but a hundred yards away, but I cannot see it. The skyline is uniform in all directions, there are no landmarks, no reassuring buildings, no buses or pylons or hills. Suddenly I feel anxious. If I keep the failing sun to my left I know, rationally, that I will soon reach the road, but the freedom engulfs me, and I glimpse the panic of immersion in the immensity of the natural world. So how awesome does that make the skills of the aboriginal? He will spend weeks in the wilds, submerged by trees or adrift on the lake, armed only with homing mechanisms I and my neighbour have lost. Within five minutes I get back to the car—of course I do, I was but a pitiful distance away—turn it round, and, a little chastened, head towards the store.

Inside UP (United Provisions) I am immediately confronted by a truck-sized display of Pepsi, brashly advertised at ninety-nine cents for six. I estimate this at seven pence a can. Then there is a pile of polystyrene bread, with two token granary loaves languishing near the floor. I pick one of them up and head for the fruit and veg, but the entire display is no more than six feet wide. There are plenty of potatoes and carrots, a few bashed bananas, a cauliflower turning brown. A shrivelled pepper costs $2.95, the tomatoes are pale and hard. A carton of mushrooms looks about a month old, its occupants all crinkled and limp. Maybe I have arrived too late in the day.

There is no fresh fish or meat, everything is frozen or tinned. About a quarter of the store is devoted to megabags of crisps/chips, their array of E-flavours ranging from BBQ Mesquite to Lemon & Dill. There are tins of baked beans with maple syrup, and tins of baked beans with sausages and molasses. There is a prodigious supply of candies, chewing gum, fizzy drinks, bleached bloated cakes, frozen burgers, and packet upon packet of Choco-Pops, SugaWeet, and Honey Nutz. There is no muesli or exotic fruit, there are no stuffed olives, no aubergines, no organic food, and—my second panic of the afternoon sets in—there appears to be no drink.

At the till a grumpy woman unloads my basket of third-rate fare. "Treaty number?" she asks.

"Here are your keys, Sharon. Thanks very much."

"You're welcome, but please hang on to them. Did you have a good trip?"

"Um, yeah. I drove a few miles out past the airport."

"Oh, great. It's really beautiful up there, isn't it? And did you get to the store?"

"Mm. It wasn't the most exciting shopping expedition I've ever done."

38

"No, but it'll be better tomorrow, deliveries come in on Friday. I forgot to tell you that."

"That's okay. Isn't there anywhere to buy drink here?" I ask with enforced casualness.

"Sure. You could go into the Athabasca, but it's not the kind of place I'd wish to be seen in, even for ten seconds. They also do takeaway pizzas and burgers if you're *really* desperate. But most of us stock up when we go to Thompson. If there's anything you want I'll get it for you next time I go—or maybe we'll ask Arie to bring back some supplies this weekend."

This brightens me briefly. It's not that I have a problem with alcohol, not at all, but right now I yearn for the Waitrose wine section with its array of Bordeaux, Corbières, Muscat sec, Mouton Cadet, oh and Rioja of course, seducing my visual field.

"Anyways, stay and have some dinner," she offers.

"But I've just got some food from the store."

"That doesn't matter. I don't like to think of you eating alone when you've only just arrived."

It would be churlish to refuse. So I perch on the sofa with a cheap sweet sherry she has found, while Roth bores his snout into my crotch like a pig in search of truffles. Sharon puts Nickelback's latest CD on the stereo. "Sit down and relax," she says.

So I try to relax, I really do, but the sherry tastes like sugared paraffin, the music sounds like someone cutting a car in half with a chain saw, and her infernal dog continues to explore my bite-sized testicles. Sharon busies herself in the kitchen and prepares *chilli con carne*, which is to say she opens a tin, heats the contents, and pours them onto a bed of sticky instant rice. We sit down to eat and she asks me, "So I guess you're missing your daughters?"

"Well—" I falter. I have been giving her regular updates on the dissolution of my marriage, in fact she became my trans-Atlantic confidante as I had no one nearer home on whom I could unload all those feelings which had gathered over the months. Now I feel a need to retract that intimacy. (Why? Because the protective space between us has been closed? Because she is fat?)

So I say that, yes, I miss the girls. But I don't disclose that I still resent Mary's accusation that it was somehow all my fault. I slaved long and hard for a comfortable salary to support them, then Mary had the nerve to say I gave her no time or emotional support. God, did she think I was out on the golf course all those years? I worked flat out while my girls grew up and away, and for much of that time my wife was in bed with NYK.

But then I remind myself that this is a new chapter of my life. Unpromising as page one may be, there is no point in getting bogged down in the episodes of what might have been. "Anyway, Sharon," I say, "so much for my misfortunes. Tell me about you."

"I guess I'm just a simple prairie girl," she says. "From a little place called Morris, just south of Winnipeg. My dad was a mechanic, he had a business fixing tractors and farm machinery in the town. He set it up himself, and he worked long hours, six or seven days a week, so I never saw him awful much."

"So were you unhappy?"

"I don't know. I mean, I never thought about it at the time, so that must mean I was happy enough. That was just the way it was. My mom was lazy, and I think she drank too much, though I wasn't really aware of it at the time. I had lots of friends in town, so as I got older I spent less and less time at home. Dad was always working, she started messing around with other men, but I think she was just lonely, you know. But basically I was okay until I was eighteen."

"What happened then?"

"First I had an accident. Some idiot guy I was dating drove his car off the road, with me in it. The only bend between Winnipeg and the US border, and he fucks up. I got a real bad fracture of my right femur, and it took nearly a year to mend—I had operations, traction, pins and plates, bone grafts, and nothing worked. Then, while I was on the ward, my dad went and died. Dropped dead in his workshop with a stroke."

"I'm sorry to hear that."

"So was I. I couldn't get to the funeral because of my leg, then when I finally got home, everything had changed. I'd already been accepted for the nursing school at Grace Hospital in Winnipeg, only to end up in traction there for months instead. They said I could postpone my training a year, but Mom just told me I had to go find a job. Apparently Dad left loads of debts—nothing dishonest, he just took on too many loans to get his business started and try to keep it going. He wasn't very efficient at handling the money side of it, and she was certainly no help. Anyhow she said she couldn't afford for me to train as a nurse, I had to get out and take care of myself.

"And that's when I began to put on weight. About thirty pounds while I was in hospital, miserable and unable to move, but when I got home I just kept on eating. I was unhappy, I couldn't exercise, I got work in offices, I argued with my mom, I moved into Winnipeg. But I found a job as secretary in a clinic, found that I liked it, got myself promoted to deputy manager, then—how long have I been here?—two years ago I came to Jackfish Lake."

"Why?"

"Got a bit restless, I guess. I just wanted to see if there was more to Manitoba than grain elevators and Osborne Village bars."

"And have you ever been anywhere else? Have you ever been abroad?"

"Went to Minneapolis once, just for a weekend. It was no big deal."

"What about the rest of Canada?"

She stops to think, chomping on a mouthful of garlic bread. "Tronno n R2R."

"Where?"

"Sorry. Toronto and Ottawa. That's about it."

"Don't you have the urge to go anywhere else?"

"Not really. I think it's something to do with coming from the prairies, Philip. After all those wide open spaces anywhere else seems so noisy and crowded in. Anything larger than Winnipeg just freaks me out."

"So how long do you think you'll stay here?"

41

"Another six months, then that will be long enough."

"And then what?"

She looks at me, as if weighing some important question in her mind. Nickelback finally screech to a halt, and Sharon hauls herself up from her chair. She pulls a thick brown envelope from a drawer of her desk, comes to sit close beside me and hands it over.

"Back to Winnipeg, I guess. But first—you can look inside on condition you don't tell anyone. I don't want word to get round about it, but—well, I know I can trust you."

"Sure. I won't say anything." The envelope contains a glossy brochure with a photograph of a ranch like establishment nestling under blue skies and snow-topped mountains. **Phoenix Farm, Lethbridge, Alberta**, it is called. "What it is it, a hotel?"

"No, it's a kind of health club. Oh, what the hell—it's a fat farm, Philip, a fat farm."

"Oh, I see." Roth powers his nuzzle into my scrotum once more, and I wonder if there are such things as canine farms, where people can get rid of their surplus dogs.

"I've booked in for October, for two months. It's real expensive, but by the time I finish here I'll have saved nearly twenty thousand bucks. That's why I came here really, to save money, and the most important thing I can buy myself is the opportunity to get back to 150 pounds."

I skim through the pages showing the gymnasium, the jacuzzi, the bracing Rockies walks. There are fitness instructors, nutritionists, masseurs and motivation coaches, all sleekly healthy, tanned and eager to ease you back to your ideal mental and physical shape. There are testimonies from ex-tubbies, saying how they have been transformed.

"I have everything I want in life thanks to Phoenix."

"Words can't describe my gratitude to the wonderful staff."

"Thanks to Phoenix I have discovered the potential I always felt I had."

It looks impressive. "It looks great, Sharon. I hope it works out."

"Thank you. I know people can say it's my own fault, but it's no joke being trapped in a body like this. So I've decided to do something about it. After that all I want is to buy a little house in Winnipeg, get myself a job, and find a husband. I wouldn't worry what he looks like, or how old he is, I'd just like to settle down with a decent honest man, someone like my dad."

For a moment she looks as if she might burst into tears, but she composes herself and looks at me. "And you know what, it sure would be good to have some sex."

# 1.4

If there is one guaranteed way of acquiring insight into the true nature of a community, then spending some time in its hospital emergency room must be it.

My first day, Friday, begins quietly. Arie urges me to call him if I have any worries, but by three o'clock I have seen a couple of snotty kids and a man with a nose bleed. I would like to think that this is not going to be too bad after all, but I check my watch every few minutes, obsessively counting off each fifteen-minute aliquot as, near enough, another one per cent of the day elapses. By mid afternoon, thirty-five per cent of the way through the first of my predicted ninety-one days on call (let's see, $35/100 \times 1/91 = \ldots$), he phones to ensure that I am not struggling with some cardiac crisis, wishes me well and heads for his weekend off.

Tonight's nurse is Edna, a feisty lady who views my apprehension with amusement. A wailing boy is brought in with his head bloodied by a chucked stone. Edna asks my requirements for suture materials and when I ask for good old-fashioned silk her "Doctor knows best" voice is scarcely disguised by her indulgent "Nurse knows best" smile. She restrains the boy in a blanket while I slowly mend his gashed scalp. It is satisfying to complete the task, but by the time I do there is a queue of people to be seen, and it is clear from their expressions that they do not like the idea of a wait.

There is a child with a cough, and when I ask why he was

not brought to clinic at a more convenient time, his mother shrugs and says, "Aahhdno."

This is the tribal mantra, the answer to everything, words slurred together and clipped off at the end, as if to conceal that "Don't know" is what they mean at all.

"So how long has he been unwell?"

"Aahhdno."

I sigh and examine him, not expecting the need for veterinary qualifications here as well. There is clearly nothing too much wrong, so I advise the mother that this viral illness will run its course, he will get better by himself.

"You're not gonna give him anything?" she asks, amazed.

"No, he doesn't need any medicine, he just has a cold."

"So you're not gonna give him anything?" she accuses once more.

I launch into my Antibiotics Aren't Always The Answer spiel, words polished perfect from years of practice, while Edna looks on. But before I can finish, the woman grabs up her baby and huffs away through the door.

"They usually get Amoxil," Edna says.

The next child presents a similar story, though she has had ear infections in the past. This time her ears look okay, and when I begin my advice to carry on with the Tylenol, mother and Edna fix me with a disapproving look.

"I think you'll find she already has a pretty bad hearing loss," Edna hints.

"Well, there's no sign of any ear infection at the moment," I say. "Mum can always bring her back at a reasonable time of day if things don't improve with the Tylenol."

The mother looks at Edna for support. Edna raises her eyebrows to disclaim responsibility for my foolishness. Mother and child follow their predecessors by storming from the room.

"Look, Edna, most ear infections are viral and get better with symptomatic treatment. We have to encourage these people to take responsibility and apply some self care, don't you think?"

"She'll be back," is her reply.

Before I can turn my attention to the next in line, the doors burst open and two ambulance men wheel in a trolley on which lies a flabby, groaning mass.

"Hey, what's going on?" Edna snaps. "Why don't you guys phone us up?"

"Sorry, Edgar must have forgot. He's just sent the reserve crew to an MVA up at Jewel Falls."

"It would be nice to get some warning," Edna complains, heading off for the necessary triplicate forms without even looking at the occupant of the trolley.

Meanwhile the men transfer their considerable load onto the emergency table. "Hi, doc," they greet. "Do you know Ken? He fell downstairs in the bar."

Ken is middle-aged, deeply dishevelled, and unconscious. His chest heaves in great irregular spasms and his cheeks vibrate noisily against his tongue, which has fallen back to throttle his throat. He wears an ancient tweed jacket covered in mud, and his trousers have solidified with the slow seepage of urine over many a year. He stinks.

"Um—any obvious injuries?" I ask.

"Minor lacerations on his hand and the back of his head."

"His respiration's obstructed like that," I observe. "Maybe we should turn him onto his side."

"Sure, but what about his neck brace? You want to check out his cervical spine first?"

Do I? I suppose I do. How exactly? Aahhdno. I avoided doing an Accident and Emergency job in my junior hospital years. I was never really cut out for all that blood and guts stuff, or that lumbering orthopaedic business of sawing bones and wrestling grotesque dislocations back into place. I have always been more refined, more suited to the role of a dermatologist or a traditional country GP, but now, in the reality of this drunken Friday night hinterland, these paramedics are looking to me to take charge. There is not much chance of building a meaningful therapeutic alliance with Ken, as he grunts and slavers away. I gingerly prod his neck and inspect the back of his head as best I can.

"His obs okay?" I ask the attendants, trying to distract attention from my tentative examination. As I undo his shirt to examine his chest, a shower of grit, dirt, tobacco and general muck cascades onto the trolley. I imagine whole populations of scabies, bed bugs, ticks and mites burrowing sociably into the underworld of his skin.

Edna returns and exclaims, "Oh, not Ken again! Put him in the corner for now, let's get the rest of them seen."

"I take it he's a regular?" I ask her.

"You could say that. If you only learn one word of Cree while you're here, remember *ki'skwe'pe'w*."

"What?"

She writes it out on his chart then translates, "He is drunk."

Thankful to be relieved of my ER role (for now) I am grateful that the next few patients are not too taxing—a sprained ankle, a vomiting child, an asthmatic who has run out of her inhalers. It comforts me a little to know that I can deal with these things, here as at home. Then I remember the words of the ambulance crew.

"By the way, Edna, what's an MVA?"

"Motor Vehicle Accident."

Oh, God. How is it possible in this sparsely populated semi-continent, with one vehicle per four billion square miles, for collisions to occur? The answer, as it inevitably turns out, is drink. A car has skidded into a ditch, and the youth wheeled in with a minor head injury and a very stiff neck swears he was the passenger. The "driver" is nowhere to be seen. Police barge in to question him and he maintains he was not in charge of the car. If this is true, a search party will have to be sent to locate the driver. He is not believed, of course. This is not really my problem, but he may have been knocked out.

"Can we admit him for head injury observations?" I ask Edna.

"You want to admit him?" Edna asks with more polite incredulity.

"Um. Well, he's had a possible loss of consciousness and he's had alcohol—"

"That's pretty unusual around here on a Friday night." I feel

I am being seriously undermined here, and if this guy collapses during the night with an intra-cranial bleed it will be my responsibility, not hers. But she smiles and puts an arm round my shoulder. "We don't have to formally admit him to the ward, Phil. We can keep him on the trolley in a corner for six hours if you're happy with that."

"And after six hours?"

"After six hours we either send him on his way or we have to formally admit him. And the paperwork for that is phenomenal."

"Okay, I'm with you, a trolley in the corner will be fine. And it's Philip, not Phil."

So he ends up with Ken behind the curtain which partitions the room. This enables me, for the next few hours, to deal with the succession of minor illnesses and injuries which have turned up to be seen. It is as if the life of the reserve is nocturnal. When my book mentioned them having an intuitive and flexible approach to time, I had assumed that related to a sensitivity to the wiles and tides of nature, not the opening hours of the pub.

It also seems to me that the Cree are a graceless and ungrateful people. Yes, I know about their history, but how does that excuse their sheer ignorance towards someone who is here to help? There don't appear to be any words for please or thank you. Everyone enters and leaves the room with an expressionless grunt, stony-faced and hard done by before they are even seen.

Edna's attitude to them is one of amused disgruntlement, and I think I will like her a lot. She gets particularly irritated when the patients, newly stitched or clutching their supply of antibiotic, immediately demand that she phones them a taxi home. "You'll have to wait!" she snaps back every time.

"What's with this taxi business?" I ask her when finally, at four in the morning, we sit down for a rest.

"They get a free taxi service—provided they have a treaty number, of course—to and from the hospital twenty-four hours a day." A treaty number, she explains, is the priceless certificate

48

of First Nation pedigree, a guarantee of racial purity as might be handed out at Cruft's. It entitles the holder to all manner of concessions, health entitlements and tax cuts. Those who are pure in lineage get free prescriptions, those whose Granny was once contaminated by some Icelandic fisherman don't. Sometimes whole tribes, like the Métis, are refused treaty numbers because they were a bit too willing to mingle with the French.

"It all seems very arbitrary," I observe. "Don't people abuse the system?"

She laughs. "Abuse it? My God, no. It's complete coincidence that everyone turns up at emerg on the way back from the pub."

"But—that's a terrible waste of resources. Who pays for that?"

"The band. Why do you think they have a two-million-dollar debt? That's a thousand looneys for every person on reserve."

And of course this is all part of the hand-out culture which deadens the motivation of aboriginals and infuriates everyone else. How did it start? How can it change? Discuss.

Just as I think it might be safe to head towards bed, the phone goes. The ambulance is bringing in a stab wound with severe lacerations to his hand.

"Oh, shit," I exclaim.

"Don't worry, it's probably nothing. Edgar makes everything sound like a really big deal."

But it doesn't sound like nothing to me. I sit sandwiched between exhaustion and apprehension at what the night may still hold, then start thinking of my cosy little practice in Cornwall. Why did it all seem so bad? I have not yet completed my first night on call, and I am seriously wondering if I will make it through a week, let alone six whole months. It is tempting to go and see Sharon in the morning and admit that I am really not up to it, but the only thing which stops me booking an immediate flight home is the ridicule my premature return would provoke. "Did you hear about old Cormack? All the way to Canada and only stayed a weekend!"

Ten minutes later the doors burst open and the paramedics accompany an unsteady young man to the desk.

"Hey! Mister Marshall Snape!" Edna greets him. "Long time, no see—you been away somewhere?"

He is in his early thirties, I guess, with classic Cree good looks, his lean face and long black hair set off by a drunken swagger. I recognise him as the man at the airport who drew his fellows' attention to me with his darting sneer. Now awash with alcohol, he shows no sign of recalling this. Edna takes him through to remove the boxing glove of a bandage which has oozed through with blood. After a few minutes she summons me to have a look. There is a clean straight slash through the web between the base of his thumb and index finger of his right hand, the injury sustained when someone unwittingly tries to grab a knife which is being wielded at them.

"How did you do this?" I ask.

"Aahhdno."

Edna nudges him sharply. "Don't be stupid, Marshall. You can tell him, he's a doctor, not the police."

"They're all the same to me."

"In that case you want me to call a cop to stitch you up?" she asks, and he shrugs a wordless reply.

"So what happened?" I ask again.

"Somebody stabbed me."

"What with?"

"A fucking banana, what you think?"

"It could have been a bottle," I point out. "There could be glass in there." He grunts but allows me to examine him. It is clear, even to my inexperienced eye, that he cannot appose the tips of his thumb and index finger together. He must have severed a tendon deep in the gore of his palm, and I explain this to him. "I'll need to speak to one of the orthopaedic surgeons about this. I guess you'll have to go to Winnipeg to get it fixed."

"Fly me out? No way!" he shouts. "It's just a cut, give me a couple of stitches, man."

So I spend an age on the phone trying to find an orthopod willing to see him. I feel like a telephone salesman trying to tout a transparently dodgy product. Eventually I complete a full circle

50

of the city's hospitals and end up with the same cocky intern I started with an hour ago. I am advised to clean and cobble up his wound for now, then send him down on Monday morning when he will grudgingly be seen for a formal tendon repair. In the background I hear Marshall arguing with Edna, complaining of the time I have taken, and she replying he should have thought about that before getting into a fight. I fear she will provoke him into storming off into the night, which is all very well but I am not sure that this "serves 'em right" attitude is entirely defensible, and anyway he would only return to pester us when the drink wears off with his hand in an even worse state than it is now.

I sit down to perform my surgery, keen to offer something presentable to the experts in the city after the weekend. Marshall dozes off, then wakes to start a slurred conversation with Ken and the recovering motorist (or passenger) behind the curtains. Then he flaps his hand around while I am trying to fix it, before slumping into senselessness again. He oscillates between stupor, aggression and drunken bonhomie with bemusing speed. He curses me for being so slow (he evidently has numerous previous operators for comparison) and then launches into some rambling anecdote, confident in the knowledge that he is the wittiest and most entertaining person alive.

Edna, meanwhile, has arranged his transport. She writes the details down for him on my referral letter and sends him on his way. "Don't forget, Marshall, be at the airport Monday morning eight o'clock."

"Sure thing, Edna."

"Do you think he'll make it?" I ask her as we watch him leave.

"Aahhdno," she grins.

"If he doesn't get that tendon repaired properly," I point out, "he may never be able to write again."

It is unkind, I know, but I have the excuse of tiredness and a good deed done. We slump into our chairs and laugh.


Despite my fatigue I cannot sleep. My nervous system is on red alert for the first ting of the telephone, and the disaster it may herald. I am used to packing every mini-emergency into an ambulance, sometimes without even bothering to see it myself, knowing it will be in hospital—even from the most remote corner of our practice—in little more than half an hour. But here in the middle of nowhere the medical buck stops at me. Apparently the bronchiolitis season is still going strong. How do I assess it? What do I treat it with? Or a dehydrated child? What if it needs intravenous fluids—how much of what sort, and where? Or meningitis—shit, what if I have to do a lumbar puncture on a baby? Sure enough, at five-thirty, when sleep has barely intervened, I am clattered awake by the phone.

"Heurrh?"

"That you, Irvine?" a gruff voice asks.

"No, it fucking isn't!" I yell.

Thus the weekend proceeds. Saturday's nurse is Karla, who is conspicuous here by being young and slim! She has coffee-coloured eyes and, for this race, pale and faintly freckled skin. She smiles readily, which again distinguishes her from her peers.

"Hi, Dr Cormack, can I ask—?"

"Call me Philip. Please."

"Okay, Philip. This guy with an ACS who Arie admitted on Monday night—"

"Um—ACS?"

"Sorry—acute coronary syndrome, maybe you call it different—does he still need heparin?"

My God, how should I know? Arie just said he was okay, and never mentioned anything about major therapeutic interventions. "Um, yes. I guess so."

"I'd better let Doug know, then. He may not be too pleased."

My expression must reflect the blankness of my brain.

"He'll need his IPTT checked every twelve hours, won't he?"

Will he? I haven't used heparin for twenty years, and I didn't think they used it these days for cardiac stuff. "I suppose so. Didn't Arie write anything in the notes?"

"No, but he's been on it five days and this morning's enzymes are normal."

"Oh. Well, we'd better carry on till Monday anyway."

"Whatever you say," she says, in a tone she has clearly copied from Edna. "And does Joe still need his sliding scale insulin?"

She shows me his glucose results, which seem not too bad, but caution again seems the best course. This decision, too, can be deferred until Monday and Arie's return. My hope that she does not ask any more awkward questions and expose my ignorance further is interrupted by the phone.

"Okay, see you soon," she answers. "That was the ambulance. Chest pain coming in."

I can't decide which is more agonising—to be warned of such horrors in advance or have them dumped on me in a precipitate panic. At least this gives time for his notes to be retrieved from the office, and they are the size of a telephone directory. Volume 4, it says on the front. Within five minutes an elderly man arrives, sweaty but chatty, well known to Karla and her assistant. "Hi there, Edwin," she says.

He talks to them in Cree, and I realise that nearly every patient must be related in some way to a member of staff. At first I am relieved that he looks quite well, but when I feel his pulse it is almost too fast for me to count. "Can we have an ECG?" I ask.

"A what?"

"An ECG. A cardiogram?"

"Oh, you mean an EKG. Sure."

She slickly attaches electrodes to his chest and within a minute I am staring at the most bizarre tracing I think I have ever seen. The only thing I feel sure of is a relief that it isn't mine. "Um…" I opine.

"Shall I get Doug in to do his enzymes?"

"Yes. Good idea."

At home, of course, our state-of-the-art ECG machine, kindly donated by our Friends of the Surgery to protect our oh-so-paltry income, gives out an instant computer interpretation of the result.

Not so here. I stare nervously at it and my perspiration soon exceeds Edwin's. "What do you reckon?" Karla says.

"Hmm, not too sure. It's certainly not normal."

"You could always fax it through to the cardiologist in Winnipeg," she suggests.

Bless her. I do as she says and he phones back, sounding dismissive of my skills. Do I not know SVT with escape beats when I see it? Evidently, no. Have I never heard of beta-blockers? I give Edwin intravenous propranolol and stop when I feel that my need for it is greater than his. His pulse slows, he admits to feeling better. Karla is impressed.

But later in the day when I phone an orthopaedic surgeon he is pompous too, as is the endocrinologist whom I phone about another diabetic. How it contrasts with home. ("Hello, Monty, how was the skiing?…You remember that delightful old dear with the Crohn's?…) Are all Canadian doctors as arrogant as this?

When I mention it to Karla, she shrugs and says, "Welcome to the north."

"What do you mean?"

"Let's say they won't be expecting you to send them many private patients from up here."

All in all it's a depressing day, and I fear that she is wondering, like everyone else, if I have ever qualified at all. But, at seven in the evening when she goes off shift, she flatters me by saying, "Bye, Philip, it's been real nice working with you." Unfortunately she adds, "By the way, the cops just phoned. They're bringing in two MHAs."

MHA? Motor—? No that's an MVA. "Oh, right. Good night."

It turns out that MHA stands for Mental Health Act. My experience of its equivalent in England is of prolonged and heart-searching discussions with psychiatrists, social workers and relatives about the pros and cons of signing the forms which authorise compulsory detention of a mentally ill patient in hospital for the protection of himself and/or others. There is usually intense debate because the patient, by definition, refuses admission, so we are left to assess his mental state, the wishes of his family, legal and ethical considerations, and other worthy social workery stuff like that. Once more—not so here.

Extreme drinking and extreme weather conditions do not mix, and inadequately clad drunks stumbling home in minus thirty degree conditions fare badly. One can imagine the spring snow melting from roadside ditches to reveal a cache of winter revellers, "Gee, I thought I hadn't seen Lorne for quite some time…" The RCMP (long since dismounted, by the way—the RCDP, perhaps? The Dismounties?) have long had the power to apprehend the poor dears for their own good. So, as I discover, they can be banged up in the cells for twenty-four hours, whereafter a medical opinion must be sought as to whether they are of sound mind. I never encountered such interventions in southern Saskatchewan, mind, but there weren't any aboriginals there. But in practice this means that anyone under the influence of drink who is overcome by the general demoralisation which abounds here and expresses some maudlin wish to end it all is rounded up by the cops and left to contemplate his gloom in solitary confinement until the alcohol wears off. Next day he, or she, is brought along for his mental state to be expertly assessed.

First I see Gina, a wild-looking girl in her twenties. She is almost gypsyish and sports hacked-off hot pants, goose-pimpled legs, and a glut of amateur tattoos. (JERRY and SEX feature prominently, the second such adornments I have seen this weekend. Jerry must have made quite an impression in his day.) It seems she is a regular Mental Health Actor. Most weekends when she is about to go off drinking, which she does to excess, her mother phones the police and claims that she is brandishing a knife and all hell is breaking loose. So they unquestioningly pick her up and she spends the night in the cell instead of the pub. Now, twenty-four hours up, it is my turn to confirm she has no severe mental illness, whereupon she is free to go home and beat the crap out of her mother, who will retaliate next week by phoning the cops once more.

Next, though, is Raymond, who is not a frequent attender. He is young and embarrassed, polite and shy. It seems that last night, drunk and argumentative, he pointed a loaded shotgun at his own head. Now, in the cold and sober light of day, I ask him about being an impulse away from blowing out his brains. He scratches his wispy chin and reflects.

"Nope," he tells me. "Ah don't remember that."

By the end of this, my first weekend, my exhaustion and feelings of inadequacy are being expressed as extreme irritation.

"What the fuck is wrong with these people?" I demand of Bertha, Sunday night's nurse, who is indeed big. "Why can't they just turn up at a reasonable time of day instead of dribbling in at all hours of the night?"

"Aahhdno," she says. It does not help that the nurses are not permitted to dispose of patients by themselves, except in the most trivial of cases. The problem is that this is a supremely unhealthy community, and although most children whipped in at the first hint of a cough, sniff or irregular shit will indeed not have much wrong with them, there will always be the odd one who is seriously ill. Kids get septicaemia and meningitis here. Kids die.

So the doctor on call has to cast an eye on every child brought in. At half past three on Sunday morning they finally seem to have stopped. I desperately need to sleep, and I leave a message with Bertha that I will turn up in the morning when I am ready, rather than a precise nine o'clock. (Yes, damn it, I am adopting Cree habits already.) After all, Arie will be back, refreshed from his weekend away, to sort out problems on the ward.

At five-thirty Bertha rings back to say, "Remember the kid with earache you sent away yesterday?" I groan but flatly refuse to see him. They can bring him back at ten.

At seven I am wakened again. "Heurrh?"

"That you, Irvine?"

"No, it isn't! You've got the wrong number again!"

"So what number is that now?"

"Oh, God—6223."

"Well, that's what I have here. 6223."

56

"Well, it must be wrong."

"So Irvine isn't there?"

"No, he isn't fucking here!" I slam the phone into its cradle as hard as I can. I expect shards of Bakelite to shower the room and wonder how much impact its delicate microphonic innards can withstand.

Then I get a call from Rose on the ward. "Sorry to disturb you, but could you come and see Joe? He's having a hypo."

Joe? Oh, shit, the diabetic on the ward whose insulin I declined to stop. Well done, Cormack. "Oh, okay," I groan. Then I look at the clock and see that it is nine-thirty. "Hang on—where's Arie? Isn't he around?"

"No, apparently he's been delayed."

"Delayed?!" My panic thoroughly wakes me up. "How delayed?"

"Aahhdno. You know what the planes are like here."

I don't but I can guess. By the time I pull on some clothes and dash over to the ward Rose has resolved the Joe situation, and he is now smiling groggily in bed. "He was all pale and sweaty and his Accucheck was 2.8, so I've given him 50ml of 50 per cent glucose and 1mg of glucagon."

"Oh, well done, Rose. Maybe we should stop his insulin," I suggest.

"Good idea," she says.

I tell her I will go for a shower and some breakfast, then come back in half an hour to see the other patients on the ward. On leaving, though, I bump into Sharon, flustered and stern-faced.

"Oh, Philip, there you are. Do you have a minute?"

"Sure, what is it?"

"Arie's just been on the phone."

"Oh, good. I gather he's been delayed?"

"That's what I wanted to talk to you about. He's really worried about Florence. She's got so depressed, he feels they have to get away from here."

Gloom envelops me. "I suppose that's understandable. But when does he think he'll be back?"

Sharon's face expresses unease, and this immediately transmits a flood of nauseous apprehension over me. She says, "That's the problem. He says he's not coming back."

So—I have been deserted again. But despite my despair and panic at having to manage alone in this forsaken place, I can understand why Arie has left. He must, first of all, take care of his wife. If only I had declared to my partners fifteen years ago that I had not been devoting enough time to my family, and that I would just work part-time or resign from seeing our private patients. We could have managed financially, of course we could, and it would have been for the best. I would have seen something of my daughters growing up, Mary could have got a foothold in a career and avoided the idle resentment which plagued her quietly for so long. We could still have been together.

"Can we get a locum?"

Sharon pities my naivety. "Philip, our advert is on all the locum agencies' websites as a permanent feature. They send us Christmas cards. We just can't attract people up here."

This only emphasises my own gullibility. No wonder Sharon knew so much about the bureaucracy of registration and work permits. Why didn't I notice that? Why didn't I ask? So, unless another misguided fool comes along (Two in a week? It seems unlikely.), it will be left to me to man this medico-social disaster area alone. It seems too brutal to wonder what might happen if I decide to leave as well.

Florence's plight also reminds me that in the chaos of my first few days here I have hardly given a second of thought to Mary, to my ageing, ailing parents, or, shame on me, to Beth and Stella.

I have vaguely thought of myself as a good and caring father, but absence has been such a feature of my relationship with them that a physical separation of three thousand miles has not materially affected us. I have every right to be angry with Arie but I wouldn't want to see him becoming a stranger to his sons. They need his love and attention, not to mention a periodic clip round the ear, and I know he has done the right thing.

One week passes, then another. By the end of the third week I have not been outside the hospital once, so I borrow Sharon's car to go to Unspeakable Provisions. The fact that I cannot placate my grumpy self-righteousness with a simple gratification of my senses makes me feel ten times worse. Oh, for one of Mrs Gantry's home-made pork pies, washed down by a pint of Skinner's, or a Stilton Ploughman's or some decent pâté or a delicately cooked sea bass fresh off the Newlyn boats…

"God, the food in here is unadulterated shit!" I accuse a teenage shelf-stacker as I settle for frozen yellow peas and a tin of tuna, which at least is bathed in brine and not molasses. I am trapped in a labyrinth whose walls fluoresce with additives, all their carbohydrate refined to death to cater for the need for another cookie fix. Despite my depleted food cupboards I feel sick with disgust and have to get out of the place at once. The crabby cashier unloads my meagre purchases. "Treaty number?" she asks.

"**Good Lord, woman!**" I shout in my best public school accent. "**Do I look as if I've got a bally treaty number? Well, do I?**"

Every night's sleep has been broken and I can tell that everyone is worried that I might leave too. The nurses put themselves at risk by turning people away to come back at more convenient times, nine o'clock at night being the favoured hour for the day's injuries and illnesses to amass. My fear that serious problems might be missed is balanced by the knowledge that I must protect myself. I simply cannot be available as a round-the-clock, round-the-calendar convenience, and in three short weeks my attitude is sharpened and my martyred irritability is heightened, though I do not feel less scared. I have no one to ask for help.

Worst of all is the trauma. The aboriginals project their anger onto themselves and each other, leaving the more legitimate target (me, the white man) to patch them up. As the last weekend in May approaches I am filled with trepidation. Not only do the welfare cheques arrive but Victoria Day makes it a long weekend, and if the local populace is aware of any irony in celebrating that queen's birthday, it blots this out with beer. Long weekend from what, incidentally, is not too clear, for employment here is limited now the mine has closed. Nobody can survive on hunting and trapping alone, and the few remaining fishermen are restrained by quotas too. A handful of men work as guides out at Muswagen Lodge, where rich Americans pay megabucks to shoot moose. Other than that, it's down to the service industries like the Hydro plant up river and the band's little collection of officials, labourers and mechanics. The only flourishing business is social services, who employ mainly women as carers, nurses in the old people's home, and workers in the various agencies which abound—Carers' Support Group, Diabetic Support Group, Alcohol Support Group, Victims' Support Group, Health Education, Youth Counselling, and so on. This all leaves a sizeable body of young and middle-aged males to ponder their idle future and unjust past at home or in the pub.

Not that the violence is confined to men. Friday begins with the arrival of Maria, who is in her thirties with four or five kids. Late last night she answered a knock at her door to be dragged outside by a gang of women for a damn good kicking. She didn't want to report it but has been brought in by her sister for a check-up because both eyes are occluded by bloated purple bruises. As far as I can tell there is no damage underneath, but how can I be sure? The x-ray of her skull looks okay to my untrained eye, but I advise her to stay on the ward for twenty-four hours so we can observe her. She refuses, saying she needs to get back home. As she waits for the inevitable taxi I wonder what gangland grudges might have caused this unwomanly spat. An affair,

61

perhaps, or money owing? Her lift arrives and she heads wordlessly back to her kids.

From then on it seems to be an endless succession of drunks, and God, how I hate them. Ken is brought in again, not injured, just pissed. He was found unrousable on the road so an ambulance was summoned to bring him here and make the problem mine. I really want to disown him, but fear that if he was dumped back home he might indeed choke on his own vomit and then my name would be even muddier than I suspect it is now. Thus he is confined on a trolley in his usual corner for the statutory six hours.

It also turns out to be a weekend of fractures. In the big outdoors I have vaguely noticed that the snow has finally cleared, the days are lengthening, the temperature rising. Apart from anything else this means the return of trampoline season. It seems that every garden has one, and now children who have been cooped indoors all winter boing madly in the sun. Inevitably this involves small kids getting squashed by bigger ones or bouncing off onto rocks. At two-thirty on Saturday morning a small blubbing boy is brought in, clutching his swollen and obviously deformed wrist.

"Excellent!" Edna approves. "The year's first trampoline accident—summer must be here!"

His mother smells of alcohol and, unsurprisingly, is not amused.

"What time did this happen?" I ask.

"Aahhdno."

"You must have some idea. Surely he wasn't out trampolining just now?"

"Aahhdno, I been out. What time you do this?" she asks him.

"Aahhdno," he confirms, as I knew he would.

His arm is clearly broken but there is no point in dragging Ellie from bed right now. I decide to immobilise it and bring him back in the morning to be x-rayed. I am a complete neophyte where plaster of Paris is concerned, and it does not help that he begins wriggling and screaming as soon as I start to apply the hot (possibly too hot) white wet bandage to his arm. Edna moves in to restrain him, but of course the struggle hurts him more. I try to contour the rapidly setting mould but he flails frantically at the air, and it sets grotesquely, lumps and gaps and protruding angles everywhere.

"Neat back-slab," Edna observes.

"Actually, I thought I might enter it for the Turner Prize," I tell her.

"What, you mean you actually have a competition for crap casts?" she asks.

For two solid days this stream of illness, injury and drink-driven excess is relentless. I am seriously thinking about a belated change of career, I am so heartily sick of being treated as an unskilled jobsworth by these bloody Cree. Don't they know I am Medical Officer to St Lanyon's Country Club, luxury rural retreat for executives, declining boxers and daytime TV chat show hosts?

By now I have realised that I am in the wrong Canada. There should be someone I can phone to rectify my mistake. Maybe Uncle Geoffrey's old practice in Wynsdale or any of their neighbours could provide me with work. But this would mean having to register in a different province, which would take forever, so maybe the College in Winnipeg would have a list of other vacancies? If no replacement for Arie is found in the next week I resolve to give them a ring. For this—this medical and societal mess—is not what I came for. I am fifty years old now, I deserve a little comfort and respect, I can leave the world-changing crusades to those much younger than myself. Yes, I am prepared to work, but in an atmosphere of small-town prairie courtesy, just as my uncle did. I recall how he was worshipped by the elderly ladies who attended monthly so he could fine tune their blood pressures. I picture him whistle-stopping round the nursing home to convey his concern for everyone with a hearty shake of the hand. Okay, so he claimed each handshake as a technical home visit when the item for service claims were sent off at the end of the month, but what the hell. "There's nothing wrong with a spot of gratitude," he would reflect.

At times like this my mind wanders back to Tregaskis, which is ironic given that in my last months there my attention was so frequently occupied by thoughts of here. I imagine everyone congregating on the beach for the informal Friday at Six gatherings at St Anselm's Bay. Even if the weather is poor the assorted kids will be exhilarated by the free run across the sand, the wind and spray and drizzle giving them some elemental lift. Toddlers will watch with fruity chuckles as dogs bound daftly after chucked sticks. How Beth and Stella used to enjoy our trips there, and now I look back it seems like those evenings were the pinnacle of my family life. But things change. The children have all grown away into their own lives, and everyone there will be basking in a successful middle age. This week Kim might comment about how dishy my locum is, and Steve will be able to tease her because their marriage is so secure. After all these years they still speak and look and touch like young lovers, their public devotion and durability a source of entirely unselfish admiration to us all. Then she and Lyn will joke about Gareth's new sheepskin coat, which makes him look like a used car dealer, they'll say. Barnaby and Caroline will turn up late, she affected and apologetic, though everyone forgives her for that. Jon Tullo will be raising money for some charity triathlon, because that is what he does. He is also our star batsman, though the women will be pressing him for details about his new book. He writes historic romantic novels, all set in Cornwall—predictable Poldark stuff, but it makes him plenty of money and attracts hordes of permed admirers to his annual reading at the du Maurier festival, so he's not going to change his formula now. When the temperature drops, the Friday at Sixers will adjourn to the pub and be served with robust steaks on wooden platters or sizzling hot dishes of fisherman's pie. The conversation will turn to new arrivals in the village or offsprings' gap years, and my presence will not be missed.

But at least I am making new friends here, for our isolation unites us outsiders with a grimly humorous bond. Sharon frequently calls round for coffee, offers to get my shopping, or invites me for weekend meals. I do not expect classic cuisine and am simply grateful that she conjures a microwave feast to eat with me whenever the demands of work allow. She makes a receptive audience, easily amused by my rantings against the hapless Cree. Thankfully she makes no further comment about being deprived of sex, though her attentive eyes and flattering comments confirm that she likes me a lot.

Doug drops by at unpredictable hours for unpredictable conversations (yesterday—the homing mechanism of ducks; the day before—a debate about determinism versus free will, with specific reference to the question of whether the decision to hang a toilet roll with the free end dangling nearer to or further from the wall has a genetic basis), though he does not reciprocate by inviting anyone into his home. This has become a joke amongst the rest of us, the favourite theory that he is constructing a latter-day Frankenstein, a nerdy boffin humanoid in the image of himself. Sharon worries that he harbours darker secrets, stashes of gay pornography perhaps, but I see him as one of those rare beings who operates on a plane which does not include the energies and frustrations and mangled hang-ups of sex.

As for Donald—I have felt a pleasing affinity to him since the first time we met. At first I presumed it was some subconscious message of body language which engaged me, maybe the clear blue fixity of his gaze. Then I thought he must remind me of someone and puzzled who this could be. Why, yes! This occurred to me at three o'clock one night, in the limbo between awareness and sleep, when uncontaminated thoughts and ideas and recollections break through. It was dear Uncle Geoffrey all over again, a charming and dapper embodiment of that happy instalment in my life. And, like him, Donald is a quiet and kind man, forever asking after my welfare, enquiring about England, inviting me to travel with him when our circumstances permit. At other times he invites me into his house and rarely speaks, and we sit in a surprisingly easy silence over coffee and a newspaper or one of his classic music CDs. "Thank you for coming round, Philip," he said one evening last week. "After all those years of marriage sometimes I just miss having someone else in the house."

At two o'clock on Sunday morning Marshall Snape reappears, clearly the worse for drink. I recognise him from the dishevelled cast somehow still attached to his arm to protect the tendons which were repaired.

"I need to see a doctor," he insists.

"What's the problem?"

"I come out in this rash."

Edna sighs. "Well, we're real busy, but you can wait if you want."

He slumps in the waiting room while I attend to the range of bugs, sprains and lacerations in the queue. It really irks me that people abuse the system like this, especially when he rouses himself to ask how long he must wait. I resolve to keep him until last.

After three frantic hours I see him slumped asleep and wake him with, "Okay, what is it?"

He lifts his shirt to reveal a widespread scratchy rash, almost certainly scabies. I guess he has had it half his life, and that he fancies a free taxi ride home from the Athabasca.

"How long have you had this?"

"Aahhdno."

"Have you been in contact with anyone with scabies?"

"Aahhdno."

"Does it itch?"

"Aahhdno."

**"For God's sake, man, you must know!"** I explode. **"Not knowing is not an option here. It is not ontologically possible not to know whether or not you itch!"**

He stares at me calmly, then gets up. "Hey, fuck you and your attitude, mister, fuck you! I'll get you back for this some day."

"Oh, help!" I plead with sarcastic bravado.

He glowers at me then turns to stride unsteadily out, denying Edna the pleasure of refusing him a taxi.

"You're welcome!" she shouts after him.

"I'm going to bed," I say.

"Good night. Hey, Philip, what does that long word mean?"

"What, ontologically?"

"Yeah."

I shrug, for I am not entirely sure. Nor, I am willing to bet, is anyone in the whole of Jackfish Lake.

But on Sunday the work suddenly slackens off. My phone does not go until eleven-thirty—seven hours of undisturbed sleep! From my bedroom window I inspect the clarity of the lake and vow that today, somehow or other, I simply must get out. Meanwhile I treat myself to a full Cree-style English breakfast, featuring the most pallid yolk in egg history, and search the radio waves for some soothing relief.

Ah, the radio! What a fabulous and unparalleled device for opening up the world and making it a more tolerant and educated place. At home I oscillate between Terry Wogan, Classic FM, the political deliberations and panel games of Radio Four, and the global cricket situation wherever its waves might be borne. I still mourn the loss of Brian Johnston's mellow meanderings on *Test Match Special*, and swear the moral fibre of our nation has gone significantly downhill since it was axed. I yearn for a connection to my previous world, in which *Sport on Five* will be following the cricket season as it endures chill showers and sparse crowds in Chelmsford and Chester-le-Street, Nigel Parsons will be introducing *Just A Minute* from somewhere like Devizes town hall, *Poetry Please* will be taking an affectionate look at John Betjeman, and *The Archers* will be wondering whither farming if we join up for the Euro. And here? As I frantically sweep the dial across its extremes of range, it is confirmed once more that in this wilderness only two stations can be received, Radio Manitoba and Radio Jackfish Lake. The former isn't actually called that, it's CFMD or RTFN or BNCM, or something equally unrememberable, but it repeatedly hails itself as "The Spirit of Manitoba" with such unwarranted smugness it makes me want to puke.

It spews out Johnny Cash, Willy Nelson, Dolly Parton, and Garth fucking Brooks—nothing but Country and Western the whole day long. Some evenings they broadcast "talent" competitions, and aspiring performers wail plaintively about God, fishing, or the woes of domestic life. One inspired composer has managed to combine all three of these essential threads into one stupendously maudlin song, slide guitars cranked up to every last vibrato of pathos:

> Mah woman gorn left me but mah heart won't break
> Long as Gard puts pickerel out in that lake.

Another number alerts me to a profound and incontrovertible philosophical truth which, I must admit, I have never really appreciated before:

> There wouldn't be no truckers
> if it wasn't for the trucks.

"Yup, that was 'The Truckers' Song'," announces the presenter. "You don't say," I reply. "I'd never have guessed."

Between songs he makes the average Radio One DJ sound like Bertrand Russell, with banal chat, requests, and interminable weather bulletins ("Flin Flon and The Pas, maximum eight degrees, minimum two degrees, five per cent chance of precipitation. Swan River, Dauphin, Gypsumville, Grand Rapids, maximum nine degrees, minimum two degrees, five per cent chance of precipitation..."). And he, like all his colleagues, talks up every miniscule meeting and two-bit concert into such a massive event that it makes Winnipeg sound like the most happening city between Alaska and Tierra del Fuego. Seven-thirty tomorrow night, the Prairie Poets perform at The Forks. This, the first

Tuesday of the month, the Architectural Heritage Group meet at the Fire Brigade Museum. Next Sunday, don't miss the Teddy Bears' Picinic in Assiniboine Park.

"So make sure you get yourselves down to The 'Peg for that one," he exhorts.

**"The 'Peg?!"** I shout in appalled amazement. **"The 'Peg?!** Jesus Christ!"

But this does indeed sound gloriously expansive and cosmopolitan when compared to Radio JFL. I suppose it is easy for we wealthy people to take our everyday communications for granted, for the reality is that many people out here still don't have a household phone. (And they certainly aren't likely to get mobiles for another millennium or two, as network coverage peters out about four hundred miles to the south. I wonder if those well-to-do mummies who protest with such indignation about what Orange transmitters might do to their offsprings' precious brains would prefer to live up here.) So the radio has become a message board. The minutiae of life on the reserve is infiltrated into every home. I was shocked when I first switched it on to hear a reminder for Elsie Ingmarsson to come to clinic that afternoon for her Pap smear. I waited in intrigued horror to see if the public health nurse give an update of the week's positive pregnancy tests along the same lines.

This morning's announcements are typical. Lucille Monias is holding a garage sale tomorrow at noon...Ed Rivers phone 4338...Wilson MacRae meet Marshall at the jetty, usual time...Robert MacDonald go home to your mom...Charity Muskego is having a birthday party this afternoon at four. The following children are invited—Paula Foubister, Dallas Carter, Eugene Carter, Stacey Parks...

I picture the children of Jackfish Lake sitting around their radios with ears agog, then bursting into tears as their rejection is made public all over the reserve.

But Sunday radio is devoted mainly to church. It seems inexplicably ironic that a tribe of people so abused and oppressed in the name of Christianity should flock to their weekly services in such numbers and with such gusto. Pentecostals, Methodists, Catholics and Baptists are all represented, though they seem to drop into each others' services with admirable tolerance. Today's transmission is from the Revival Centre, and if the length of a sermon is directly related to the piety of the speaker, then this morning's preacher is right at the top of the celestial stairs. He finally gives way to the congregation, and their rousing Lordy-Lordy chorus escalates into something akin to speaking in tongues. When this abates, worse is to follow, some rescued alcoholic who pays homage to Gard in his dreary nasal monotone and two chords of guitar.

"Thank you, Lester," the cleric MC concludes, "for inspiring us all with your music for the last twenty years."

Twenty years? Two notes? Fucking hell, Gard, can't you bestow greater gifts than that?


I snap the radio off and phone emerg to confirm that all is quiet. "If it's desperate you can bleep me, but I'd quite like some time to myself."

"Sure thing, Cormack," Bertha says. "Sure thing." Like some of the student nurses and assistants she baulks at the informality of calling me Philip, but as a concession drops the Doctor prefix. So "Hi, Cormack!" is a common greeting on the ward, despite my invitation to first-name terms. It still grates faintly because it reminds me of the horrors of school. Philip Andrew Cormack was P A Cormack, which became Pacamac, every single day for thirteen years. On arrival at university I thought I had finally freed myself of this childish nickname, only to be greeted by fellow boarder Simon Bingham in the Union Bar one night, "Hello, Pacamac! I managed to scrape in here to do Maths! Good to see you again!" "Pacamac?" my new-found friends tittered, and I was never able to rid their brains of this.

Anyway I have arrived here with some aspirations for personal development. I was passably good at art at school and now I have resolved to resume painting in some form. I have decided on pastels as a good and portable medium, and now I finally unpack them. After pausing a moment to admire the lush chunky hues in their pristine box, I head off towards the shore with my pad of paper and folding aluminium easel.

The predictability of the view does not deter me, for I have to capture basic techniques first of all. So I gently pencil out the slim horizon of trees, the nearby rocks, the corrugated interface of lake and sporadic islands between. Ideally I should have some interesting foreground feature, but I do not want to stray too far from the house in case work calls. Indeed, I would be perfectly happy to come down to this spot every day and try to perfect its colours and record them as they progress through summer and fall. Pastels, of course, are harder to master than one might think, but I am happy to stand here exploring their basic properties. The subtleties will follow in due course. First I fix the pine skyline, then I turn my attention to the rocks and coarse grass at my feet. I smudge brown into yellow, trying to record this unique and delicate distillation of shape and substance and light. An hour passes happily by, unimpinged by worries of work, occupied exclusively by the problem of mastering this simple creative task. How, I wonder, should I depict shade? How will I make this artistic impression recognisably mine? How can those subtle gradations of—?

I swear silently at an interruption to my field of view. A young boy, aged eleven or so, is ambling across the rocks. As I try to glare him away, a woman's voice behind me calls, "Hi, Philip, is that you?"

"Oh—hi, Karla."

She walks towards me and, "Hey, you've got a talent there," she admires.

"Come on, you can't mean that."

"No, you have. You've gotten the colours real good."

"Well, it's nice of you to say so."

The boy strolls towards us. "This is my son Alex."

"Hi, Alex."

He is a slim and attractive-looking boy with his jet straight hair and sharp eyes. However, his stare at me and my embryo work is unforthcoming. He is clearly a true Cree.

"Don't you think that's good?" Karla prompts.

He shrugs and, amazingly, speaks. "That a potato?"

"No, it's a rock."

Karla rebukes him but she smiles too. "Hey, don't you have anything to sit on?"

"No, I didn't have room to pack an armchair."

I like the sound of her laugh. It is clear and spontaneous, feminine without being girly or shrill. "Well, we have a folding stool at home. My dad used it for fishing, but it's stuck in a shed somewhere now. I'll bring it over for you if you like."

"That would be ideal. If you're sure you don't need it, that is."

"No, it's all yours, if you don't find it smelling of fish."

"Thanks, Karla. Hey—I was just about to stop for a coffee—do you want to come on in?"

She checks her watch and agrees. "Alex, why don't you carry on over to Howard's? I'll pick you up from there in about half an hour."

Without expression, he nods and wanders off. So I find, oh my God, I am entertaining someone—a young, attractive female someone—in my bachelor home. (All right, I am not strictly a bachelor, nor yet a divorcé. A separaté, I suppose, or a dumpé.) I attend to the coffee while Karla quite openly inspects the house.

"Do you have any children, Philip?"

"Yes, two daughters."

"So why don't I see any photos of them?"

"I don't know—" Why indeed? I suppose I've always slightly objected to the public display of cosy two-point-four-childrenness which a certain breed of GPs and other men feel obliged to air. And domesticity has been a sore point throughout the last year.

"Have they disappointed you?"

"No, of course not! What makes you think that?"

She smiles. "I don't mean to be rude. It's just that the Cree really love their children, they like to show them off whenever they can. If you don't, they think you're hiding something. So that's sad you didn't bring any pictures of them—do they look like you?"

"Not really. More like their mother, I guess."

"So what does she look like?"

She can see I am taken aback by her directness, but instead of veering the subject away I find myself describing Mary. Small, slim, always smartly dressed. Dark, enquiring eyes. Hair dense and short, prematurely grey but no less attractive for that. Charitably, I omit the detail of the eyebrows furrowed into dissatisfaction, though maybe that feature has now been erased by the attentiveness of NYK. Before I know it, I am telling Karla how we drifted apart. And this time it's not a factual précis of a routine marital split which happened in a third-person distant past, this is an outpouring, a bereavement, an unexpectedly unleashed deliverance of grief and, yes, resentment. Forgotten fondnesses then sneak back into my brain. The joy of our first flat together. Me locking us out of the car in a thunderstorm. Walking home through deserted midnight Bristol streets after Beth was born. I don't know whether Karla teased these intimacies out of me or they were due to be off-loaded anyway to whoever happened along. (Doug? Larry? I prefer to think not.) My recollections could continue, but I wind down to a stop.

"You must feel very lonely out here," Karla observes.

"No, no," I protest too eagerly, "I'm doing okay. Anyway, what about your family? Tell me about them."

"Some other time," she smiles. "I really have to go."

I am amazed that more than an hour has gone. She accompanies me back to my easel then heads off to collect her son.

"I'll bring you that stool," she says.

"Thanks. You know where to find me."

As we wave goodbye I turn and catch Sharon at her window, a momentary glimpse before she backs away into shade. I can't really concentrate on my art work now and anyway, two minutes later the silence is shredded by my bleep. Bertha is apologetic, *"KrrrsorryCormackbutthey'restartintopileupkrrr."*

Yes, the Cree love their children. And here they are now, hundreds of the little buggers, it seems, running irritably wild while they wait for the Big White Doctor to arrive. It is difficult not to feel sorry for them, knowing what fate holds in store. The life-cycle of the female seems particularly harsh. Most young girls display that undifferentiated beauty which genetic purity so often brings, but by their early teens they will have gravitated into one of two types. The first become plump, mirroring their mothers, gobbling up fatty calories to comfort their sullen souls. They will become old and undesirable before their time, offer sex for passing affection and thus get lumbered with dumpy babies. After that, years of drudgery and diabetes lie in wait.

The others preserve their beauty, but this may turn out to be an even greater curse. They are pestered by marauding boys, and given the intensive boredom which abounds, sex soon prevails. Pregnancy of course ensues, some years earlier than their fatter sisters, and these babies are entrusted to grandmothers who are barely thirty themselves. More hybrid children follow, education ends, resentment intervenes. The only solace is drink and escape in the form of some squalid flat in a cold block of Winnipeg, where street corner dollars are exchanged for further sex. They lie back and endure it, thinking of their children who trampoline the short summer away, five hundred miles to the north.

Every child I see on this bright spring afternoon has rotten teeth. At least half look anaemic, no surprise given the horror which is their diet. I tell their mothers to bring them back in the morning for a blood test, though I am prepared to bet that they won't. Many have eczema, many have impetigo, and many have scabies.

"Full house!" I declare to Bertha after seeing a boy with all three, but she looks offended and perplexed. Only Edna seems to appreciate my disrespectful quips.

Four solid hours of sick kids later, I finally get to the end. The last one is a baby with gastroenteritis whom I discharged from the ward only yesterday. His mother sits him on her fat lap and feeds him peckings of her Athabasca Special, a Monster Offalburger with Double Glop.

"He won't keep nothin' down," she says, staring accusingly at me.

After a short rest the night unveils another relentless cavalcade of disease. I see more pathology in an average day here than in a month at home. Everyone, but everyone, smokes. There are more drunks, of course, and the other lethal activity which goes on here is eating. Everyone does it, and in public, too! They never stop! Even in the clinic the nurses and secretaries can be seen any time of day munching on cookies or chips. Their hunger is never satisfied, they munch, munch, munch, their hamster cheeks bulging all day long. The incidence of diabetes here is a staggering seventeen per cent, and it is predicted to treble in the next twenty years. It reminds me of the lectures of my medical student days, when the Pima Indians were demonstrated to us by excited academics as a genetic curiosity because of their tendency to maturity onset diabetes. I pictured a proud tribe of people, complete with headdresses and tomahawks, battling against their unkind hereditary hand with quiet dignity as they fished and hunted their days away. Well, future students, I guess it ain't like that. The Pima just happened to be first in the queue to acquire those fashionable Western illnesses, and now the Iroquois and Ojibway and Cree are not so far behind. Once we gifted them TB and measles and gonorrhoea, and now—life out here is just full of ironies—they have overtaken us in their affinity for the world's most civilised disease.

Yes, they are lumbered with a genetic tendency to this, as are Chinese and (Indian) Indians who also become westernised. But otherwise, it seems to me, the problem is medical only in that stop-gaps like me try to patch up the damage when it is irreparable, twenty or thirty years too late. It is ultimately political that United Provisions stores have a stranglehold on the north, and condemn the people to a diet of lifeless fatty crap which will ultimately cause their death. If I can go to Truro to buy coriander from Israel, beans from Gambia, or potatoes from Egypt, then why can't simple fresh food be transported to Jackfish Lake? I am told that the previous manager of the UP store here actually tried to encourage healthy produce at the expense of bottom-of-the-range burgers, and the move was popular. However after three months he was moved on elsewhere with no explanation, and the quality of the store fell back to its normal abject state. He might have been promoted for his enterprise, of course, but the word is that he got the sack.

And yet I read in the newspaper today that farmers on the great Canadian prairies are in crisis. Their profits are falling, many are going bust, some are squeezed literally to death as WalMart demands eat their profit margins away. Ever more topsoil is eroded, and the Monsanto stranglehold on GM crops and heavy duty pesticides tightens by the day. Meanwhile nobody, but nobody, on this reserve grows their own fruit or veg. It is not a native tradition, for sure, the growing season is short, for sure, but the thin layer of soil is surprisingly rich and summer days are long. It can be done and it would be cheap, so why doesn't anyone bother? Is this genetic too?

There are drives to educate people, of course. Every wall of the hospital features posters displaying diagrams of clogged coronary arteries and terminally infected and semi-amputated feet. Smiling Cree families are shown in their incongruous Ikeoid kitchens eating wholesome meals and plentiful portions of fruit. There are health fairs, workshops, diabetic groups, screening programmes, school visits, fitness clubs and cookery classes, but none of this makes any impact on the colossus of collective denial. Because every family is blighted by diabetes, has someone who is blind or on dialysis or vegetates in the aftermath of a premature stroke, the problem is simply too great.

It is huge and unopposable, it is like the white man, it is like the USA.

---

My own diet is, by necessity, dire. Even the store's top-of-the-range fare cannot be disguised as anything but junk. The cheese I buy is a chunk of bland rubbery fat. The bread tastes sweet, for someone behind a desk at UP headquarters has decreed that nothing will sell to these dumb Indians unless it is saturated with sugar. Sharon continues to feed me once or twice a week, and on Saturdays there is usually a barbecue in our communal "garden" where we can at least savour pickerel or black market moose and admire the sunsets or the barely dark midnight sky.

These get-togethers usually comprise Sharon, Donald and Doug, sometimes Ellie and Brad, and me. Edna and Bertha occasionally come, and although their husbands are polite in a monosyllabic sort of way, I sense they see us as odd-bods whose company is not what they would willingly choose. I don't think it's necessarily a racial thing, just that they have their families, and we are a disparate gaggle of incomers, Cornish or Canadian or what. Tonight for once the Saturday evening is quiet and there is no intrusion while I eat. I still can't claim ever to be relaxed, as I am conditioned to any thoughts of leisure being interrupted by random and increasingly irritant bleeps. Sometimes I think of performing Pavlovian observations on rats, implanting them with mini-pagers which crackle into activity every time they settle into food or sleep, and I wonder how their progressive breakdown would compare to mine. At least the continuous on-calls mean I am drinking less, admittedly not from choice. Doug and Ellie are in the same position anyway, and Sharon is too worried about the calorie content to take much alcohol. Tonight I have allowed myself one glass of mediocre white wine before moving on to some fizzy placebo.

Donald does not appear to drink much either, but he seems particularly mellow tonight. The outside temperature has dropped so we have moved in to Sharon's house, with Roth and Nickelback for further company. "So, Philip, how much longer do you have with us?"

"Oh, let's see—four months, two weeks, five days, nineteen hours…"

We laugh and he says, "Well, if you find yourself at a loose end after that, and want a tour of Canadian outposts, I'd be glad of your company."

"Thanks, Donald, I'll bear that in mind."

"I know you'll probably want to fly off to Vancouver, or Montreal and Quebec, but I was thinking of taking a few weeks out about that time and driving up to the Yukon."

"Wow, sounds great."

"Keeping to the minor roads as much as possible, of course. It's the best way to see the country, and it doesn't really matter where you end up."

"Watch out, everyone," warns Ellie. "Thelma and Louise are planning a big trip."

Donald chuckles. "You know something, Ellie, when I was a boy the one thing my mom and dad used to instil in me was the need to settle down. 'You need to find yourself a profession, a nice wife and a family,' they'd tell me. 'You need to Settle Down.' And every time I phoned them or came back from college they'd quiz me about my plans, what jobs I should apply for, where I would live. 'It's time you Settled Down,' they invariably said."

His eyes switch off from us, relocating in the past. "It was understandable, I suppose, because they came from the Ukraine. They had a terrible, terrible life there, labouring on some farm. Then they were evicted, and it was only because my uncle was already in Canada that they were able to escape. They would probably have starved if they'd stayed, but they managed to get into Lithuania, then on a boat to England, then get from Liverpool to Toronto. From there they had to get to Saskatoon, where they moved in with my aunt and uncle and their several kids. The whole journey took three months, and I think my mother nearly died.

"So when people complain that Canadians are bland and boring, Philip, I think that's probably why. Many of them are only second or third generation immigrants whose families have escaped from something like that, so the last thing they're looking for is adventure. All they want is stability and security, and a nice cosy home."

"Yes, sir, that's me!" Sharon volunteers with a raised hand.

"Well, my parents would have loved you," Donald tells her. "They loved me, of course, and I always felt I owed it to them, given all their hardships, to do what they wanted. So I did it, I Settled Down. I lived in the same house in Brandon for thirty-two years. I had a wife and a son—just one child, it seemed we couldn't have any more. I had my own little pharmacy, and I worked in it six days a week, fifty weeks a year. I gave myself two weeks summer vacation, but only when I was sure I had someone reliable to take care of the store. Even then I'd phone up every day to make sure everything was okay. When my son Peter qualified as a pharmacist too, I always had this idea that he would take over the family business, that I could wind down and hand it over to him."

"So what happened?" I ask.

"He didn't stay. He wanted to see his country, he wanted to see the world. He was a bright and popular young man, he could always get work. He went to Calgary, which he loved, and although I was sad he wasn't going to take over my business, I was proud of him and happy he was doing so well. If Medev's Pharmacy faded away when I died or retired, it wouldn't be the end of the world. But, one day—three years ago this week, as it happens—he phoned us up. I answered, and I knew straight away from his voice that something was wrong. He just said, 'Dad, I've got leukaemia. It doesn't look too good.' We immediately went to see him, and he wasted away before our eyes. In three weeks he was dead."

We mumble our condolences. Sharon looks away and I wonder if she has heard this story before.

"Anyway—" Donald pauses and sighs, bracing himself to say more. "Anyway, the only thing I knew was to get back to work. I couldn't talk about it, I just tried to blot it all out by carrying on exactly as before. Oh, you wouldn't believe what a busy guy I was. And it didn't even occur to me that Wendy, my wife, was affected as badly as me. So off I set, eight o'clock every morning to work, leaving her alone for ten or twelve hours every day. Except that..."

His eyes glisten, and I know this is going to be bad. "Except that I came home one evening, about three months after Peter died, and she wasn't there. No note, no message, none of her friends had seen her, she'd just disappeared. Then I was in a real panic, of course, because it was only then I realised how devastated she must have been too, and I'd been ignoring her. Me, her husband for over thirty years, ignoring her. I phoned the police, and I vowed that as soon as she came back I'd take time off work just to be with her, you know, I'd even sell up if I had to. I could see in that instant what was important, that my nice secure business meant nothing.

"Then I got the call at midnight, two cops knocking on the door..." his voice tails off, he swallows hard. "'Mr Medev?' they asked, 'Mr Donald Medev?' And of course it was every bit as terrible as I'd feared. They told me that she'd gone down to the rail track, waited for the night train to Thunder Bay, and then stepped right in front of it."

If he starts crying now, then I know I will too, we all will. Nobody can speak for fear of triggering a mass outpouring of tears for Donald.

"I'm sorry to burden you with all that," he finally says. "But I've known you all for quite some time now and I didn't feel it was right to keep it concealed. And what I really wanted to say was—well, the lesson I wanted to share with you is that I spent thirty years of my life Settled Down. I did what my parents expected—and I don't blame them for anything, not one bit—but look where Settling Down got me. It isn't everything, you see."

I don't see how it's possible to break this silence which ensues. What can anyone say? I am almost hoping for my bleep to go off, but it is unexpectedly Doug who acts. He gets up from his sprawl on the floor to sit beside Donald on the settee. He puts his arm around the older man and lets him drop his head onto his shoulder.

"It's all right, Donald," he says. "You're with your friends now."

Sharon is silently crying in her chair, and I simply have to leave the room. I step outside to marvel at the vast silvery darkness of the sky and the suffering our universe imposes in its same inexplicable breath.

# 1.6

After that I am busy, not with anything too drastic, but from midnight until three I suture the customary scalps and lips. Chucking stones at heads seems to be a common children's pastime around here. This constant throughput of injury makes me no less cross than before, even though I am now tackling the tiredness by taking short afternoon naps, especially at weekends. I am frustrated because I would prefer to have some waking time to myself—to explore the country or pursue my painting, but I will simply have to give over some time to address my sleep deficit if I am to survive. When I get into bed I am still thinking of Donald's story, more awake than asleep when the phone goes once more.

"Hello?"

"That you, Irvine?"

"Yup."

The caller hesitates. "You okay? You sound a bit strange."

I muffle my voice into a semi-Canadian drone. "Ah'm okay."

"Okay. Anyways, you thought any more 'bout what I said to you last night?"

"Yup."

"And?"

"And Ah've decided you're the biggest ass-hole Ah've ever met. Don't you ever dare phone me again, understand?"

"Hey, Irvine, get serious! What's wrong with you?"

"Ah'm serious. Ah don't want to speak to you again long as I live."

I put the phone down, laughing with exaggerated satisfaction at my own wit. This time I fall into a definite sleep, only to be woken again just after four.

"Heurrh?"

"Hi, Philip?"

"Heurrh."

"It's Karla." I am aware of loud music thumping in the background and I wonder what the hell is happening in emerg. Then I remember that Karla wasn't even on duty tonight. What is going on? "Philip, I'm at a party. Could you give me a ride home?"

I am jolted into serious wakefulness. "What?"

"I'm at a party, but my friend who was supposed to be driving me home has gone without me." Her words slur drunkenly into each other, and she adds, "It's okay if you can't make it, I'll get a taxi, only I thought—"

"No, it's no problem. Where are you?"

"I'm at my friend Lorraine's."

"Where's that?"

"Fraser's Point. But I can walk to the fire station, I could meet you there."

"Okay, give me ten minutes."

"Thank you, Philip, you sure you don't mind?"

"No, no. I'll see you soon."

I lie there for a minute, nervous with anticipation as the implications of her request sink in. Only then does the fact that I have no car occur to me—but I have the keys to Sharon's dogmobile, so I fumble into my clothes and sneak out to the rough patch of car park where our little road divides. The vehicle throbs into action and I hope that Sharon's ears are not tuned in to its nocturnal mission. (Well, I remind myself, she said I could use it whenever I liked.) As I approach the town I note that even now a straggle of youths seem to be staggering back from the bar. Other than that it is deserted, and the moon blesses the reserve with its ironic brilliant light. Within five minutes I pull onto the fire station forecourt but see no one there. I ask myself why I am feeling so horribly guilty; after all, I am only, am I not, doing a favour for a friend?

When I see her walking towards the junction I pull away to meet her. She is unsteady and giggly as she hauls herself into the truck. "This is real kind of you, Philip," she says, seemingly untroubled by the canine whiff.

"It's no problem."

"Could you turn the heating up? I'm cold." She is wearing a denim jacket over, as far as I can see, a thin blouse and jeans.

"Sure. So where do you live?"

"Just by the school. But I can't go home," she adds.

"Why not?"

"I must have left my key in Jackie's car, and I daren't wake my mother at this hour. She'd be *so* mad."

I know what's coming when I ask her, "So where do you want to go?"

"Aahhdno. Guess I'm kinda stuck."

"Okay, you can stay at my place. There's a bed in the spare room."

"Philip, are you sure that's okay? That's real kind of you."

"It's no problem."

"Or a settee would be fine," she says. "You don't have to go to any trouble."

Before we can settle the niceties of this we are speeding past the youths from the pub, and I hope they are too drunk to register our identity. Karla seems unperturbed, she is telling me about her best friend Lorraine, a teacher, a real nice woman. She says I'd like her a lot. I park the pick-up precisely where I found it and as we walk past the four houses I hope that their occupants, particularly Sharon, are asleep. As I let Karla into the front door the first streaks of daylight are already hoisting themselves above the lake.

"Would you like a drink?"

"God, I've already had too much of that."

"You could have tea or coffee."

"Sure, I'll have tea. Thank you."

She slumps into the settee, so I make the drinks and sit next to her. "You said you'd tell me about your family," I say.

So she does. At first I think she is too drunk to keep to the point, but over the next hour I learn of another history, one more cameo of Canadian life randomly exposed to me in my stay in this strange place. There is loss here, too, another father dying too soon. He was taken by diabetes, of course, reinforced by its henchmen coronary and stroke. That was two years ago, but Karla is no longer distressed by this. Indeed, she recalls him fondly, with a soft smile. Now she is left with her mother and older sister Evelyn, whom I recall seeing in the clinic. She has what we politely call a learning disability, she is heavy and dark and slow. Something—maybe a sly genetic twist, maybe a struggle for oxygen in a difficult birth—deprived her of that spark, that last magic ingredient which makes most of us rounded and intelligent and alive. She is forever a child, a solemn and limited child, but accepted for who she is, not who she might have been.

"Then there's my brother Wilson," says Karla. "But I prefer not to talk about him."

"Why not?"

"Because he's a bit of a crook. I love him dearly, but he's a crook. He's always been in trouble, since he was a boy, but he could get away with anything because of his nice big smile. Maybe Dad favoured him, being the only boy. Now it's nothing violent, but minor stuff, thieving, scheming all the time, he just gets into these things for the devil of it. It really scares me to think where he might end up."

Such diversity! A dull handicapped girl, a petty thief, and here, sitting beside me, this bright and popular young woman. I turn to find her rich brown eyes are staring straight into me and I cannot help but smile. I don't know who instigates this, it seems involuntary, but it is the most natural reaction in the world for our faces to merge into a kiss.

After a few minutes she breaks away to stand, stretching her arms towards me to haul me up. "Come on, let's go to bed."

The ease with which she sheds her clothes is marred by the

unsteadiness of her balance. As she helps remove my shirt I am entranced by the raw beauty of her. She is slim and lithe, but she is real. Her belly is furrowed by stretch marks, her breasts are unobtrusive (frankly, they sag) but I swear she is the most beautiful sight I have ever seen. Her fine film of bodily hair concentrates at a black triangle, earthy and sexual and raw. We fall into bed, holding and kissing, legs intertwined, but despite my great physical desire a part of me feels this is not the right thing to do. Perhaps I have inherited the middle-class English prudery gene. I have always been slightly appalled by the casual abandon of the one-night stand.

"Karla?"

"Mm?"

"I'm not sure that—well, I think you should just go to sleep."

"Don't you want to make love to me?"

"Of course I do—but you're terribly drunk, I just don't want to take advantage of you."

She stares at me and smiles. "Philip, you know what?"

"What?"

"You must be the first man in the history of Jackfish Lake ever to say that."

We laugh, and within two minutes it seems my gallantry is justified for she has slumped into oblivion beside me. However I have never been more awake. As she sleeps I cup her breast, and my long-neglected erection presses against her hip. Maybe it is because I have not slept with anyone but Mary for nigh on twenty-five years, but I just want to freeze this moment, untainted, in time. I cradle the heave of her chest and study her silhouette against the slowly breaking light, hoping to preserve these imprints for the rest of my days.

She wakes at half past nine. "Philip, my head hurts."

"You know what you need, don't you?"

Her eyes dilate. "I'm sorry, but I'm too hung over. You missed your chance last night."

"I was thinking in terms of a nice cup of tea."

"You and your tea! Did you sleep?"

"No, not really."

"Why not, did you get a call out? I didn't hear you get up."

"No, it wasn't that. I was just so excited to be in bed with you."

"Philip, you're very sweet." She kisses me and, stale drink taste or not, it is intensely thrilling. That, I recall, is one of the things Mary and I stopped doing. Perhaps that was the biggest index of the decline of our marriage. It belatedly occurs to me that it is not sex which sustains and enlivens a relationship, but touching and serious kissing, this delicious tactile exploration of—

"Philip, I have to go. Sorry."

"Oh—okay."

"I have to be back before Mom goes to church, she'll be wondering where I am. Someone needs to be with Evelyn."

"Do you want to phone?"

"No, thanks, I'll just get on back."

"Hang on, I'll give you a lift."

"Are you sure? I can walk, I can go out the back and through the hospital."

I hesitate. "No, it'll take ages. I'll drive you."

She shows no embarrassment as we dress, gives no intimation that this is something we should not have done. I wonder if this assuredness, this ease at being naked and imperfect with a man, is somehow an aboriginal trait, or whether it is simply *her*. Then I realise it is not possible to separate the two, any more than one can differentiate between the untrammelled me of here and now and the me which is a product of English middle-class parents and public school.

As we walk back past my neighbours' houses again, yearning for invisibility, I realise that this is one more drawback of living on a reserve such as this. Privacy is not even a luxury here, it is an impossibility. I drive quickly and ask, "Karla, when can I see you again?"

"Tonight, I guess," she laughs. "I'm at work."

This is not what I meant, of course, but now we are at the band hall and she instructs me to stop. As she is leaving she asks simply,

"Philip, you won't tell anyone about this, will you?" and before I can reply she is gone.

Back home elation and exhaustion compete. Now, of course, I am wishing I had made love to her, but all I can do is close my eyes and fulfil the fantasy of her as I lie in the solitude of my bed.

Nobody needs to tell me that embarking on a relationship with Karla would open up a very large can of social worms. Last night may have been a one-off drunken folly, but I suspect (and admit it, Cormack, hope) not. Karla's invasion of my personal and sexual space has made me realise how isolated I am now. My only function in life is being a doctor and it is simply not enough.

So I phone Beth, I phone Stella, and I phone Mary to remind me of the role I still have as a father and, technically at least, as a husband. I even think of ringing my parents and my sister Eve, but am happy to procrastinate on that. Beth is walking to work through rainy Camden streets. She has a weekend waitressing job to supplement her student loan. She has just managed to acquire a last-minute ticket for Glastonbury so she is happy. I comment on the contrast between life in London and Jackfish Lake, and she asks what I miss most about home. Apart from her and her sister, I tell her, I am taken by the sudden yearning to spend an afternoon in a city bookshop, relaxing with a *café latte* and pondering a welter of CDs and books. She asks what I would buy; Fairport Convention, Eva Cassidy, anything by Justin Cartwright, and the new *Wisden* of course.

Stella is depressed by being in the throes of 'A' levels, and I reassure her that actual results almost invariably exceed those expected on the day. I am sure she will do just fine. Mary surprises me by taking the phone keenly from her daughter. It is unsettling that I can speak to her so readily when our history has driven us so far apart, but she seems happy to talk to me and relay Tregaskis gossip. My locum Ben Whitehead seems to be charming and efficient, from which I conclude my presence in the practice is not missed. Indeed she seems to be suggesting that the current arrangement is actually an improvement. Gareth has bought himself a new BMW, Steve next door has done his back playing squash. She confirms that the girls are fine, but does not divulge much about her and NYK. All I can tell her about Jackfish Lake relates to work and the plight of the Cree, for I decline to mention that I shared last night's bed with some drunken totty but gallantly declined her offer of sex.

"*KrrrMHAwaitingforyouPhilipkrrr.*"

"What on earth was that?"

"Our state-of-the-art communication system."

"How quaint."

"Apparently it was very popular in Eastern Europe in the 1950s." I could use this interruption as an excuse to sign off, but we carry on with our chat. Mary falls into a reminiscence about the girls, their early school reports, one of Beth's birthday parties, and for some reason she seems more relaxed and forthcoming than she has for an age. I am not quite sure why that should be, but hope it has nothing to do with any new-found access to contentment, fulfilment and frequent phenomenal sex.

Finally she says, "Well, you'd better go and deal with that call."

I suppose I do. "Mary?" I add, after an uncertain pause.

"What?"

"Well, you know—about us—?"

"I know what you're going to say, Philip, but my mind's made up. I'm very happy now, and I'm not going to give that up."

"Oh. Okay."

"I'm not angry with you any more, it's just the way things have turned out."

"Oh. Okay," I repeat. "I just wanted to be absolutely clear."

We say goodbye and then I think, hang on, why should *she* be angry with *me*?

For once the MHA is genuine. Jodie is sixteen. She has a six-month old baby and she has been depressed. Her mother called the cops because she was threatening an overdose, and they sensibly brought her straight here rather than confining her in the cells. The police, I have come to realise, have a thankless job. They are all outsiders too, so are despised by the locals on account of their role and their race. Most reserves have now introduced their own community policing scheme, whereby locals are trained up to the equivalent of our special constables in the hope that they can have a greater rapport with regular reprobates. The theory is fine but in practice such volunteers are regarded as traitors, and the few I have come across so far are more officious than the RCMP. Most of these seem to me to be reasonable people, trying to see out their unwanted posting to the north with a grudging tolerance. Brad, for instance, seems calm and affable, though there is still a detectable undertow when he speaks of them. He regards them all—with the best will in the world, of course—as drunks and criminals at heart. Nor it does not help that, even when escorting a distraught young girl to hospital, they make no effort to conceal their bulky holstered guns.

On this occasion Larry the social worker has also been asked to attend. His big presence seems to calm the girl, though today's two policemen look on suspiciously when he talks to her in Cree. Before I see her, Larry takes me into the corridor to give me some background. The family are well known to him, and Jodie has alleged that her stepfather has been sexually abusive, the baby may even be his. The implications of this, in terms of legal action, family loyalties, Jodie's mental health, and the welfare of the child, are clearly enormous, and her mother is worried that she plans to harm herself, and maybe her baby too. They are right to be concerned, for the Children's Hospital in Winnipeg receives a steady trickle of teenagers, ninety per cent of them girls, who have taken an overdose of Tylenol—sorry, that's paracetamol back home. This rite of passage is manageable if it is immediately declared, there is treatment which works (I have even become competent at administering it myself—a new skill to add to my list of privileges), but after twenty-four hours it is too late and the sullen overdosee will find her liver remorselessly beginning to rot. Out in the desolate reserves of Shamattawa, Tadoule and Lac Brochet, teenage angst is potentially lethal. London House has the highest suicide rate for young people in the country. Jackfish Lake is in the top ten.

The average sulky self-engrossed youth back home has nothing on her counterpart here. Refusal to communicate is taken to unparalleled realms. Jodie sits by the window, staring through it at some fixed middle point of space.

"Hi, Jodie, I'm Dr Cormack. How are you feeling now?"

She does not respond.

"Okay if I sit down?"

No response.

"Do you want to tell me about what's been happening?"

Apparently not.

"Would you like your mom or anyone else to come in?"

Nothing.

So have you been feeling depressed? Do you still feel like harming yourself? Are you having problems with the baby?

No response. No response. No response.

"Okay, I can come back later. Can we get you anything to eat or drink?"

I know this will take time, I know all about the density of the unseen barriers in the few feet between us, but I am also aware of the queue of impatients outside. Not that I feel I should put myself out for them when there are more urgent things to do, in fact I am starting to take a cynical pleasure in sauntering past them, taking my time, watching their irritation rise with the wait. It is tempting to go back to the house for a leisurely lunch, but I do my duty and dole out to the natives their rations of Amoxil instead.

When I go back to Jodie she refuses to speak to me some more. I am beginning to wonder if she has lapsed into some obscure catatonic state, but when I edge Larry outside the room for his opinion he says she has opened up to him a little while I was away, and he feels she will be all right with some support at home.

"Look, Jodie," I tell her, exasperation seeping through, "it's my job to decide whether you're safe to go back home. I can't know if you're going to be a risk to yourself and your baby unless you speak to me. If you don't, I'll have to assume you're seriously depressed and therefore need to be in hospital for a full assessment. Do you understand that?"

She still doesn't say anything, but everyone here knows what invoking the MHA means. It involves an escorted journey involving two planes, with ambulances at either end and endless waiting between, to the province's single psychiatric hospital, four hundred miles and one culture away. There, white men in metaphorical white coats will opine on her mental state and countersign the papers committing her to detention inside. It's residential schools all over again, except that the western model of psychiatry has taken over from the church.

I ask her, as gently as I can, "Do you want to go into hospital, Jodie?"

There is a barely perceptible shake of the head.

"What do you want then?"

Tears sidle into her eyes. "Go home to my baby," she says.

The thought later occurs that the Cree, and their counterparts throughout this country, are like one big sulky teenager taking collective umbrage against her white officious parent. Let's hope she doesn't do too much damage to herself in the process of growing up.

Everything else is crap. I am hungry and irritable, and every time I finish dealing with one self-limiting illness or self-inflicted injury, another one takes its place.

A small boy breaks his wrist falling from a trampoline, just as he did last summer.

Ken the drunk discovers a jagged dirty laceration on his leg. He has no idea how long it's been there or how it was caused.

93

An old recluse is brought in, his house said to be uninhabitable, rat-infested and empty of food. To Rose's displeasure I say he can lodge on the ward.

A very fat woman has had back pain for three weeks. When I ask why she waits until now, Sunday afternoon, to come in, she replies—astonishingly, not "Aahhdno," but—"When the weather's hot it puts my blood pressure up and I just have to stay in bed."

Seven o'clock takes me by surprise and I am brightened by Karla's arrival. For a moment I wonder whether to refer to last night's liaison, but she simply smiles at me and says, "Looks like you've been busy, Philip, why don't you go away for a couple of hours? I expect you could use some rest."

It is difficult to think of anything but Karla. I feel as if I have been transported back thirty years, when any new relationship caused turmoil in my brain, and I wonder why maturity has not settled my emotions down. But first I have the fundamentals of food and sleep to address. My easiest and safest meal option is frozen fish, which I put in the microwave with chips. I would desperately like a gin and tonic, but I simply don't have any, though I have placed my orders for Sharon's trip to Thompson next weekend. While I wait I click on the radio and shout in approval when they broadcast my favourite song (sad, I know, to have a favourite, but I have been in solitary confinement here for seven weeks). A yowling male, discordant even by Radio JFL standards, wails:

> Pukatawa-gan, that's where ah come from
> Pukatawa-gan, that's where ah come from
> Pukatawa-gan, that's where ah come from
> Pukatawa-gan, that's where ah come from
> Pukatawa-gan, that's where ah come fro-om
> Pukatawa-gan, that's where ah'm from.

However, this is followed by a live broadcast from the Revival Centre, which I know I will be unable to stand. As an alternative the "Spirit of Manitoba" has its weekly talent competition, and some screeching juvenile makes a point of dedicating the next song to her paw. The poor unfortunate has a paw? Or does she mean her pore? Oh, God, I switch the radio off while my sanity is still intact.

But, deep joy, at least I have the weekend *Winnipeg Free Press* to occupy me. I seem to be one of the three people on the reserve to buy a newspaper whenever I visit the store. National papers do not get this far, and the choice of magazines seems to be limited to *Wrestlers Monthly*, *Celebrity Chat*, and, oddly enough, *Rolling Stone*. Anyone with an eye for what's happening in the wider world (anywhere like Overseas, ay?) will be disappointed. **Man charged in fruiting incident** catches my eye. The defendant, upset at discovering his girlfriend was cheating on him, responded by hurling oranges and bananas to the street three storeys below. "I so loved that woman," he informs the court. "You seem like a kind and decent man," the judge concludes.

There are pages of other such trivia, then readers' letters as petty and parochial as any in the *West Briton*. A woman writes to complain that she had to wait fifteen minutes in her car for a freight train to pass through a level crossing. "You stupid, stupid bitch!" I shout. Doesn't she know that the very fabric of her province, her country, is dependent on transporting this grain to the wider world? Then there are dozens of obituaries, most of them with photographs, and many of them surprisingly young. The politics section is dull to the point of coma-inducing—to my understanding the two main parties here are the Middle of the Road and the Even More Middle of the Road. There are whole pages of humourless cartoon strips and the reviewers swoon over upcoming local events. Once again I am crestfallen to find the sport is incomprehensible, columns solid with baseball and American football stats but without a single mention of cricket.

However, I am saving the best to last—the puzzle page usually occupies a good couple of hours each weekend. There are anagrams and word-plays, and the crossword splays out over half a page. Many clues refer to Canadian sport or television; others are silly, oblique, or obscure, and their solutions come to me by guesswork or default as the massive grid slowly fills. For example, **67 across**: What? (3) Answer: HUH.

At nine o'clock Karla calls me to deal with the little collection of pukers and coughers she has gathered, all of them routine. Then it is pleasant to sit with her drinking coffee, not that I have much else to do. Considering I don't have anything in common with her apart from our engagement in this little medical outpost, she chats easily, telling me of her friend Lorraine, Alex's progress at school, and asking me about life in my Cornish home. But soon I am aware that another wave of fatigue is threatening to engulf me, and feel I will have to tear myself away to bed, this time—regrettably—alone. However we are interrupted by the crackling of the intercom, the Marconian hot-line which connects us to ambulance control.

"*KrrrEdgarherelookslikewegotadislocatedanklecomininkrrr.*"

"Oh, shit," I declare.

"It's probably just a sprain," Karla anticipates, but panic is established yet again, and I wish that Arie were here.

And this time my fears are confirmed. Screams herald the arrival of the paramedics, and the ankle of the young man their trolley bears is horribly twisted, ninety degrees or more out of shape. Seemingly there was a skirmish in one of the deserted houses and he was thought to have been kicked downstairs.

"Hmm, Johnny Moose," Karla observes.

His foot skews out to the side. It is swollen, deformed, and—far more alarmingly—white and pale. Karla phones for Ellie while I confirm my worst suspicions, that the pulse in his foot cannot be felt, its circulation is severely impaired.

Even I, with my encyclopaedic ignorance of orthopaedics, know that this is an emergency. While I wait for Ellie I put up a drip, and know that the next thing is to give him pain relief. But he has been drinking, and the mixture of alcohol and opiates can stop respiration in its tracks. I ask Karla to get some diamorphine, and I dribble a milligram or two into him, petrified that his breathing will cease. It seems to have little effect.

"Give me something for the pain, man!" he shouts.

"Hang on, we need to get you x-rayed first."

We lump him onto the radiography table, his screams ringing in our ears. Karla and the paramedics look to me, and I repeat the baby dose of morphine, still to no avail.

The x-ray is no less horrific than the reality, and I know that I am simply going to have to correct this because the circulation to his foot is at stake. Back in emerg, I trickle in more analgesia to try to curb his noise.

"We need to reduce this," I announce. "Someone hold on to his knee."

Sweat pours from me, and the merest tweak of his foot provokes more agony. "Give me something for the fucking pain!"

I offer a few more molecules, convinced they will cause a respiratory arrest. I pull again against the paramedic's counter-traction, and Johnny Moose yells.

"How about some Entonox?" Karla suggests.

"Good thinking." He gasps frantically on his gas. I try again, he shouts some more, the ankle does not budge. By now most of the ampoule has been given, and after four more yanks to his foot there is no progress. I must be doing something wrong.

"I'll just have a word with one of the orthopods," I say, as calmly as my panic and incompetence permit. To my surprise I am connected almost immediately to the consultant (or whatever they are called here. I am still muddled by their grades, and get some bumptious junior when I want an expert opinion, and some bumptious expert when I want the day-to-day approval of an admission.). I explain the situation and ask if I can Medevac him down.

"You'll have to reduce his dislocation first," Dr Orthopod growls.

"I've tried, I can't reduce it."

"You have to. Otherwise he loses his Goddam foot."

"I know that, but I've had four attempts. I was wondering if you had any suggestions how to—"

"Put some effort into it, man. Don't send him down until you've done it."

With that, the phone goes dead, and I am left to test my strength against this misshapen foot. I inject more diamorphine and pray that he continues to breathe. It slows, for sure, and as his eyes finally register a welcome oblivion, I haul on his foot for all my worth. Johnny cries, the bones of his ankle grate loudly, a fifty per cent improvent is achieved. "Hold on," I urge, and with sweat dripping from every pore I heave one more time. He yells yet again, but this time his foot starts to suffuse with the belated arrival of blood. I feel like I am going to faint.

It takes an hour or more to apply a back slab, phone Dr Grumpy Bastard's hospital with details, organise transport and write up the paperwork. By then, of course, Johnny is happily serene as the morphine and beer run wild in his brain. Finally he is whisked off to the airstrip and I only hope I can make it to my bed before I collapse.

"Sleep well," Karla smiles. "And hey—you did that really well."

I give a wry smile and stumble off to my house and bed. In the minutes before sleep sets in I reflect on my panic and feel a sudden surge of satisfaction that, bumbling or not, I achieved what I had to achieve. This is a feeling I have not experienced for many a year, and suddenly my presence here is justified, I feel it will all be worthwhile. Then I remember that today is summer solstice, and I drift away with the image of Johnny's plane flying through its dawn, the vast expanse below it suffused in the soft pink slant of light from the north.

Over the next few days there are more fights, and a parallel rise in the number of parties. At four, five or even six o'clock in the morning. an insistent *thump-thump-thump* pulsates across the reserve, backed by laughter and raucous female squeals. There is nothing traditional or aboriginal about the music, it is the crass electrified grating of Nickelhead or Motorback or whatever they are called. Emerg is unduly busy and nearly every day I have to transfer some victim or other to the city, and I imagine their doctors' mess gossip carping about the English guy up here who can't seem to cope with anything at all. It seems that half the population of London House has arrived, as they periodically do. There are a couple of big weddings in the offing, and, as they are all here to celebrate, they might as well drop by the hospital for a supply of T3s and Valium while they have the chance.

There seems to be a cop car outside emerg most of the time while Brad and his colleagues take statements or photos of offending wounds, then invite the victim to accompany them back to the cells. We have our impromptu barbecues and discuss what we have heard about the rival machinations on the reserve. Brad hints that there are scores of suspects regarding the assault of Johnny Moose.

"Some of these feuds go back for generations," he says, "but Johnny's determined to get those houses for his folks. He's got a lot of enemies on this reserve."

Sharon asks, "But what's the big deal? There are dozens of empty houses around."

"For a start, Bartram's—the chief engineer's—is the best house, so it's regarded as first prize. Johnny fancies himself as the number one gangster here, so he's out to get it. And Bartram always refused to give Johnny a job because of his reputation, so now it's a matter of Moose pride to get revenge, even if Bartram's left."

"Where did he go?" I ask.

"Nobody knows for sure. But he upset a lot of people by taking up with that Muskego girl."

"Which one, Lydia?" Sharon asks.

"Yeah, that's right. And the locals sure don't like it when a white guy takes up with one of their women." I freeze with suspense that they will all shoot accusing glances towards me, but nobody does.

"I guess she took a fancy to his bank account," says Sharon. "It couldn't have been his looks."

Brad muses, "Well, she was as pretty as you can get. Could have been a model if she weren't a native."

"Brad!" Ellie protests.

"It's true. When did you ever see a Cree on a catwalk?"

"I heard they went to Niagara and got married," Sharon says.

"No, I think that was just a rumour."

We turn to the interruption of a loud thwack, caused by Doug slapping the back of his own neck. "Rumours! They're just like these damn mosquitoes—you can't get away from them in this place."

"Hey, you've just reminded me!" says Donald. "How'd you like to try out Medev's wonder insect repellent?"

"You bet!"

Donald scurries into his house and returns with a large plastic tub which he opens to reveal a thick black paste whose smell makes our eyes water at twenty yards.

"Jeez! What the hell is that?"

"I've been checking the pharmacy stock, and found a pile of time expired stuff. I thought I might put some of the creams and lotions and cough mixtures to good use, so I experimented a little and came up with this. It's based on good old-fashioned glycerine and ichthyol, with white soft paraffin to ease application and *mist ammonia et chlor* for the killer ingredient. Doug?"

"All yours, baby!" Doug rips off all his clothes except, thankfully, his underpants, to expose his thin and pallid six-foot frame to the world. He scoops handfuls of Donald's patent pungent concoction and daubs them all over himself while Sharon does his back. He stands, black and glistening in the fading light like some deranged lanky minstrel, and shouts, "Come on then, you bloodthirsty little bastards! Come on if you dare!"

We are helpless with laughter and I observe, "I don't know about the mosquitoes, Doug, but you're sure repelling us."

At times like this, relaxing in the pleasure of new friends, I wish Karla were here. But I hear nothing from her for over a week, and I start to think that our encounter was just a one-off drunken mistake. Rationally, of course, this would be just as well, but I look out for her at every change of shift, and rush to answer every ring of the phone. I have realised that this is the first time I have ever done anything remotely unconventional in my life, but am

I now getting carried away by that? Is Pacamac trying to make up for lost time? For, yes, there are probably a good few past acquaintances who would be rather surprised to hear of me taking on an adventure such as this. Mary once told me about a conversation she overheard between two nurses in our hospital days, "I think that Philip Cormack's quite sweet." "Well, if you like that kind of thing, I suppose. Straight as Jesus if you ask me." I remember being quite upset by that description, though Mary was very amused.

Sharon still visits or invites me over for food. Sometimes I walk with her and Roth to the shore. She asks how I am, and it is not just the fear that I may leave which fuels her concern, more the fact that she is so intrinsically nice. But she, too, is tired of being here. She is looking forward to her fat farm, and after that she aims to launch herself, transformed, back into city life. Already she is eyeing situations vacant in the *Free Press* to get an idea of what she might do, and unashamedly checking out the lonely-heart columns to see which dependable type of man she might meet.

More days lapse, shortening already, and each one adds to my urge to escape. I have been thinking I might tell Sharon that I will leave at the end of August, for by then I will be desperate for a break. Even though this will leave me with two unpaid months when I must still pay my locum back home, I do not care. Then there is the complication of my impending divorce. How much will it cost me? Will Mary be able to leech half my earnings, claim rights on my pension and half the house, even though she is the one who has left? I have no idea, and in a way it suits me to be here protected from all of that. Yes, there are indeed times when playing the denial card seems like the best move.

But these technicalities are troubling me when my doorbell rings. It makes me jump because there is a woman in labour, and the list of things that can go wrong with her are prominent at the front of my brain. I am especially peeved because she should be in Winnipeg, her delivery was booked there because her last birth ended with an alarming haemorrhage. But this would mean elective transfer three weeks before term to the city, where she would languish in the stark hostel provided, kicking her heels with women from other outposts while her children miss her as she misses them. So she simply ignores our advice, runs the risks (denial again!) and decides to stay home. Understandable as this is, it is no help to me if obstetric horrors set in, for I as ever will be expected to bale her out of her irresponsibility. When things go wrong I will be the one on the end of the fucking phone.

"Oh, hi, Sharon, come in. Coffee?"

"Yeah, that would be great. Thank you."

I pour the coffee, we chat, and she tells me, "Anyway, the reason I'm here—I've got some good news."

"Oh, yes?"

"Yes. I've got a locum."

"You've what?!"

"That's right, starting Friday."

"This Friday? Sharon, you're a marvel! How long for?"

"Three months. It's a woman called Lena Khonje, she's been here before."

"She's been before? And she wants to come back?!"

We laugh at the masochistic absurdity of this. "She was here briefly when I first arrived. She's a bit of a free spirit—splits her time between South Africa and here, doing locums where she fancies. She's already got registration with the college and the medical protection people, that's why she can start at short notice. And she's really good, I'm sure you'll like her."

"Oh, my God, I can have a day off!"

"A day off? Philip, you can take a holiday!"

"I think I'm going to faint. I'd open some champagne if I had any."

"Well, you could come to Thompson with me at the weekend to buy some."

"Oh, brilliant idea! Is that what you're doing?"

"Driving down Friday after work, coming back Sunday night, you're welcome to come. Don't expect too much from Thompson, though."

"Sharon, I don't care. After eight weeks here, even a Siberian salt mine would be great."

"It's a deal. There's a real good hotel on the river with swimming pool, jacuzzi, good restaurants, bars—"

"Restaurants! Bars! Decent food! I can't wait, it sounds wonderful—"

The doorbell rings once more and I interrupt myself to answer it.

"Hi, Philip, I finally brought you that stool."

"Oh, thanks, Karla. Come in."

The women eye each other and say, "Hi, Karla," and, "Hi, Sharon."

"Coffee?"

"If you have some."

"Top-up, Sharon?"

"No thanks, I can't stay."

This wasn't meant to be offered as a hint to leave, but she is already downing her drink and rising from the chair. "No, don't rush off," I urge.

"It's okay, I have things to do, emails and stuff. You'll let me know about the weekend?"

"Yeah, sure, it sounds good."

She leaves me to pour Karla's coffee, and I unfold the little seat to try it out. "That's perfect, thank you."

"You're welcome. So what's happening at the weekend?"

As I rise from the stool she is standing close. Our eyes meet and she smiles. "Oh, God!" I exclaim as the possibilities hit me. "Karla, what are you doing? Are you free?"

"Sure. I'm working the next three nights, then I'm off."

"Karla, we could go away together!"

"Are you kidding? A threesome with you and Sharon?"

"No! Just the two of us!"

"But you were just fixing up something with Sharon."

"No, no, that was just a shopping trip to Thompson, that was nothing. There's a locum coming on Friday for three months, I can actually get away—we could go away for a weekend together, we could go on holiday."

"Holiday!? Hey, slow down!"

"Sorry, I didn't mean to be presumptuous, I'm just so excited at having the freedom to get away from here at last." I find myself squeezing her hand. "But seriously—this weekend—would you like to go away somewhere? What do you say?"

"*KrrrbettercomequickPhilipshe'sapushinkrrr.*"

"Oh, shit!" I shout.

"See you later," Karla grins.


I have seen smaller crowds at county cricket games. The corridor outside the labour ward seems to be heaving with relatives, friends, neighbours and anyone else who might have lurched by from the pub. All eyes turn to me, and I squeeze past them and through the delivery room doors. Beyond them I have the vague expectation of the woman, her husband and a nurse huddled in the throes of this most intimate act, maybe with subdued lights and atmospheric native music to match. But there are at least half a dozen women in there too, clustered round the incipient mother who writhes and squeals, her bulging vulva exposed to them all.

"Who are all these people?" I whisper to Edna.

"Oh, family and stuff."

"Well, can we ask them to leave?"

"Leave? Why?"

"Well, it's all a bit intrusive, isn't it?"

She shrugs. "Aahhdno. But you can't ask them to leave."

"Why not?"

"Because this is what happens here. This is what they do."

I should have known, for suturing is the same. Attendances at emerg are family events, part of entertainment on the reserve, with kids clustering round and shoving in under my elbows for the best view as Dad's split lip is repaired. I greet the labouring mum with the nearest I can get to calm authority, omitting to tell her that it is at least twenty years since I last did this kind of thing. Examination of her state of progress is unnecessary as the baby is clearly imminent, thankfully head first. After three meaningful contractions I do no more than escort its head into the world and fumble the wriggle of slippery limbs as they slalom out behind.

"A girl!" declares Edna, and the women all shout their delight. The news is relayed to the corridor and elicits further cheers. Thankfully the placenta follows with no great gush of blood and I briefly confirm that the baby is fine. I congratulate the parents and both of them shake my hand.

"Thank you for delivering my baby," the mother says.

"It's a pleasure," I reply, for—retrospectively—it is. No matter what deprivation and endurance may lie in store for the child, this is still a time for optimism and delight. "And a privilege," I add.

# 1.8

As we immerse ourselves in the luxury which is Jackfish Lake International Airport waiting room (Terminal One), my excitement is darkened by worry about the reaction our presence might provoke in fellow travellers. Karla seems unconcerned, she sits next to me and drums her fingers on the bag on her knee to imagined music. She smiles, waves or chats to these friends or neighbours she has probably known all her life. Do they think her relationship with this visiting doctor is benign? Maybe they have seen it before, maybe she chases after them all. I would like to squeeze her hand for some sort of reassurance but that might not be such a good idea.

We are herded onto the miniature plane and have to sit in single seats. At least I have two hours to study the back of her neck and count down the minutes until I can kiss it. At Winnipeg Airport there is a complimentary bus to take us downtown and its driver asks for our destinations.

"Polo Park."

"Osborne an' Ellice."

"Bus station."

"Prince Albert Hotel," I mumble.

"Huh?" the driver demands. I have learned from my crossword that this means "What?"

"Prince Albert Hotel, please."

He looks to Karla. "Yeah, that would suit me," she smiles.

The bed is swathed in pristine linen. It looks big enough to sleep about eight people and inviting enough to sustain a major all-night orgy. Karla inspects the bathroom with its opulence of chrome, its explicit mirror and its gaping tub. I hope she is impressed.

"So how much did this cost?" she asks.

"Karla, I'm not telling you! Is there a problem? Is it too extravagant?"

She shrugs. "No, it's fine, it's very generous of you. Anyway, what shall we do now?"

What else? I complete my raid on the back of her neck. "Oh, my God, I'm *so* sensitive there!" she giggles as we slide each other's clothes onto the floor and roll onto the bed. Her laughter assures me this is a natural and joyful activity, and the question crosses my mind (it does not linger, but nonetheless it occurs) of whether Mary has discovered this degree of uninhibited passion now she has taken up with NYK. Is this display of overtly frenzied enjoyment normal in a woman? In my own twenty-five year study of the subject I only have a control population of one, in which case I should conclude that it is not. I cannot recall the last time I felt such unashamed exuberance, such physical bliss. Because this is being reciprocated, it adds to my joy. We caress each other for a long time afterwards, beguiled by each other's bodies on the extravagance of the bed and then in the slippery scented bath.

"Hey, you're in pretty good shape for an old guy," she observes.

"Thanks."

This is flattering, for this is not what I have come to perceive. I am all but six feet tall, and my excess weight is reasonably disguised but for the chubby bolstering of my chin. Above it, the rounded face of my mother looks anxiously out, while my hair has always remained immune to order or style. You could look at a photo of me aged seven or eight and my hair would be unchanged. I know full well that people wondered what attracted Mary to me, but I was once, in an overgrown schoolboy sort of way, considered a handsome man. With Karla the disparity is even greater, but it seems not to worry her. But one thing is certain—

my appearance would be a further generation older if I lived and ate on a reserve.

We rub each other dry in our warm shawl of towel and my penis impresses us by re-erecting and nuzzling into her groin.

"So when did you last have sex?" she asks.

"About an hour ago. Didn't you notice?"

"I mean before that."

"Getting on for a year ago, I should think. What about you?"

"Yeah, the same sort of time, I guess."

The thought unsettles me, I'd rather not know who she was with. "Looks like we're in for a busy weekend."

"Busy, busy, busy," she agrees, resurrecting my organ further with the lustful look in her eyes.

After dressing, I suggest a drink in the bar. It is in the mode of hotel bars worldwide with its leather chairs and oak panels, its white-shirt waiters and miniature dishes of nibbles, its expensive cocktails and the contented murmur of people who have money to spare on a meeting or a meal or a getaway weekend. The scent and secret of our recent intimacy makes me confident and replete, but as I stroke Karla's hand I see she absorbs the surroundings with suspicious eyes.

"What's the matter?"

"I always wondered what this place was like inside, ever since I was a little girl."

"So what's it like?"

"Okay, I guess."

"But?"

"Well, it's the history of the place."

"What about it?"

"Did you notice that big building across the road?"

"The station?"

"Yeah, that's why this hotel is here. People stayed on the site here to supervise and work on the railway when it was being built, and then it was somewhere for early travellers to stay." She looks in vain for my response. "Don't you see, Philip, the railroad has very bad connotations for us. It symbolises the invasion of the white man, the destruction of our culture, taking all our land."

"I'm sorry, Karla, I'd never thought of it in those terms—"

"Of course you hadn't, you just thought the station was somewhere to get on a train. You thought the hotel was somewhere to seduce an impressionable native girl. But you're English, you're a white man, not a Cree."

"Look, I'm sorry if I've been insensitive—"

"You're not insensitive, I don't expect you to know any different. I'm not blaming you, that's just the way it is."

"If it's a problem, we'll book in somewhere else. I won't mind."

"No, it's okay," she says. "We can't run away from every bit of history we're reminded of, it's something we have to face every day. I was just pointing it out."

"Anyway, let's go and eat. Last time I stayed here I noticed there's a really good, um, curry house a couple of blocks up the road."

"You're allowed to say 'Indian restaurant'."

"Thanks. So is that all right? Have you ever had curry before?"

She bursts into a shout, and I am aware of people looking reflexly her way. "For fuck's sake, Philip, of course I have! I have been to cities before, you know, I spent two years here as a student nurse. I might be from a different culture, but I'm not from another planet."

"Sorry," I mumble. Again.


As we eat she seeks out more details of my middle-class middling life:

*My childhood home?* A rambling, detached, five-bedroomed, shrub-gardened house in Penscott Abbas, a comfortable Dorset village.

*Dorset?* A southern English county, rural and twee, its people jolly well bred.

*My parents?* Father—an architect. Never had time for much else.

*A good father?* In his restricted way. Cold and distant, never in his life offered physical contact to his children or his wife. (Shit, that sounds like a description of me. Make that a no.)

*What about her?* A housewife all her life, utterly dedicated to her husband, and one of the few women in the world capable of tolerating him.

*So why did she?* I'll probably never know. That was what she did.

*And school?* In Shahbn. Not the famous school there, but Mountstephen, a lesser, cheaper one.

*Shahbn?* Our nearest town. It's like two places in one—Shahbn, which is where the wealthy folk live and send their offspring to school, and Sherrborrne (yes, spoken with exaggerated stereotypical country idiot burr), home of farmers and bakers and other common people. I never knew it much. But my school was public, meaning private. Boarding. One had to pay.

*Oh my God, you went to a residential school too? Your parents actually paid money to send you away? Didn't they like you?* Difficult to say. Liking and loving wasn't a concept that troubled them much. But my younger sister Eve stayed home, she was a day girl, girls' education didn't matter so much then. During the holidays we constantly fought.

*I guess you were jealous. Did you hurt her?* No, no. Well, not really. Well, yes, I suppose I did.

*That's awful. Do you like her now?* I suppose so, but I hardly ever see her.

*What weird sort of family do you come from? Is this normal in England?* It's certainly not unusual.

*Then what?* Medical school, average student, made friends, met Mary, hospital jobs, married Mary, general practice, two lovely daughters, nice house, too much work but plenty of money, marital neglect, separation, mid-life crisis, here I am.

"Hm," Karla concludes. "That's kind of sad."

"Is it? How?"

"Well, your marriage splitting up, of course. Your cold parents. Fighting with your sister. No warmth, no affection in your life.

110

Anyway, what about now? What do you do when you're not working? How do you enjoy yourself?"

"Enjoy myself? Music, I suppose—folk music. And—aha! I haven't told you about cricket! You know, it's always surprised me that Canada has never taken to cricket, with all that flat land everywhere you look. And it's part of the Commonwealth."

"The what?"

"The British Commonwealth."

"What's that?"

"You've never heard of the British Commonwealth?" No, I can see she hasn't. "It's a loose union of English-speaking countries like Australia, New Zealand, India, various African nations—"

"You mean all the countries you've ever invaded?"

"We've never invaded Canada!"

"**The hell you haven't**!" she shouts, attracting more stares.

"Okay, sorry, I take your point. Anyway the Commonwealth is just an affiliation of countries who were once bonded by British rule. Yes, I suppose it is a colonial thing in a way, but I'm surprised you've never heard of it. Why do you think there's a picture of the queen in the hospital?"

"Is there? Where?"

"In the main entrance, that very old black and white photo. Who did you think it was?"

"Aahhdno."

"That's Queen Elizabeth the second."

She looks at me, overwhelmingly unimpressed. "So why's her picture there? Do you think she gives a shit about the Cree?"

Probably not. Anyway, to get back to cricket. I explain the rules, the tradition, the history, the etiquette, The Ashes, *Wisden*, and the layers of statistics and averages which underpin every over of every day of every feebly spectated county game in the land. Over coffee I set out the field placings on the table with cubes of sugar, and our little waiter comes along and instantly recognises them, "Ah, you are a cricket fan, too!"

He introduces himself as Deepak from Chennai and within a couple of minutes, oh, we are flying! Karla looks on, amused and

111

bemused, while Deepak and I discuss great Indian cricketers of our years—Gavaskar, of course, Bedi and Chandrasekhar—

"And Venkat," he recalls. "They were a joy to watch."

"I think I saw them at Lords in, what was it, 1986? When you won the series."

"No, before that, I think," he says. "'86 was Kapil Dev. Wait, I'll get my brother Kumar—I think he may have been there too." So the three of us recall some classic encounters and favourite players, delighting in our brief retreat back to those civilised lands where willow and leather meet.

Afterwards Karla links my arm and we stroll through the warm evening, past the city hall and along the river. Back at the hotel we make love again, and I plunge into my deepest and most serene sleep for months. The only disturbance is the vague joyful awareness of Karla beside me, her body hot and sleek.

When she wakes she looks at me and laughs.

"What's so funny?"

"You?"

"Why?" I demand. "Look, if you just think I'm some sort of curiosity, then I'm—"

"Whoa, calm down!" She restrains me but gently, smiling. "Don't be so touchy, Philip, I just found it amusing that you spent all that time last night telling me about your family and the breakdown of your marriage in a real cool matter-of-fact way, but as soon as we got on to cricket, you were so excited."

I want to explain that what she perceives as coldness is in fact normality, at least for me, and I don't *really* value cricket more than my family. Before I can say this she starts kissing me and her hands and mouth begin an exploration of my body of which any Shahbn boy could only dream.

But afterwards the day finds me oddly nervous—partly, I think, because I am not entirely sure what we are going to do. Although I only have two day's experience of this city, I have the vaguely old-fashioned feeling that I should be showing her round. At breakfast I pick up the *What's On* magazine, which assures me, of course, that in the streets outside palpitating excitement abounds.

"Where do you want to go then?" I ask.

"Philip, put that away. We don't have to *go* anywhere, we don't have to *do* anything. I've seen Winnipeg, I just want to relax."

I watch the middle-aged men in short-sleeve shirts and well pressed golfy slacks as they queue for the egg chef and return to scoff their mountainous fry-up and scan the business supplement. Their tubby wives eat more daintily and between each mouthful smile across the room with inanely good-natured intent. While I might blend in with the menfolk here, I realise that Karla is, in her faded T shirt and short cotton skirt, a little underdressed. Under the tablecloth I run my hand lightly up her brown thigh.

"How about the art gallery?"

"Sure. If you like."

So the art gallery it is. But its focus is a collection of turn-of-the-century paintings of pioneers staking out their farms and defending themselves against vicious warmongers like the Cree. As soon as I see it I flinch with embarrassment and apologise to Karla.

"Don't worry about it. It wasn't your fault."

Upstairs, though, there is an exhibition of aboriginal sculpture and jewellery, most of it Inuit, from Nunavut and the far north. The carvings are intricate and light, made from natural artefacts like whale tusks and vertebrae, symbolising ancient legends and depicting the seasons, the elements and the gods. I comment on how skilful and moving they are, but Karla inspects them all impassively and, catching her diffidence, I ask her what she thinks of the work.

"Oh, fairly insulting, on the whole."

"But why? I know the paintings come back to a touchy subject, but some of this Inuit work is beautiful."

"I'm not saying it isn't. But the Inuit have had their entire lifestyle destroyed, so it's a bit of a sop to turn round and say,

'Okay, we've oppressed you for generations and now we're fucking up your environment, but at least we'll sell some of your cute craftwork to well-off white folk in our nice shops in the cities. That'll make amends for two hundred years of shit, won't it?'"

"Come on, Karla, aren't you being a bit cynical?"

"**Me**?" she shouts, and now it is the turn of the gallery's well-heeled white ears to twitch. "**Me**? You're calling **me** cynical? You should be a little more aware of the history of this country before you start—"

"Okay, you're right, I apologise."

There is a difficult pause, then, "Apology accepted," she smiles. "Don't take it personally, Philip, at least you're here and at least you acknowledge our existence. That's more than most Canadians do."

She may not regard it as personal, but I am beginning to worry that every innocent comment I make will trigger a major cultural clash. Perhaps I need to find some safe, uncontroversial and emotionally neutral ground. What price Lancashire for the championship this year? Is Murali's bowling action a no-ball? I peer through the doors of the gallery's sedate coffee shop but fear that the province of art might be best avoided for now.

"Anywhere I can buy a couple of shirts?" I ask.

"Sure," she says. "Let's go."


I am not the world's keenest shopper but on a good day I can tolerate an hour or so in one of southern England's green and pleasant cathedral cities. Truro, Exeter or Bath, for instance, Salisbury at a push. Downtown Winnipeg, however, seems like a scruffy grey mish-mash of hidden malls, car parks, junk shops and drug stores. But at least it is a city centre of sorts, and I assume this is where we should go.

"There's a taxi rank right here," Karla points out.

"Why, where are we going?"

"You wanted to buy clothes. The best place is Polo Park."

"Okay, whatever you say."

According to my dictionary, a park is a large area of land preserved in a natural state for recreational use by the public. Polo is a game similar to hockey played on horseback using long-handled mallets. Polo Park, however, is a colossal mega-mall, one tier of multi-national consumer addiction outlets above another, the choice of ten thousand Korean sweat-shop trainers or mobile phone covers beckoning through every plate-glass door. It is a heaving, gleaming, skyless, anonymous shopper warren—Merry Hill, Cribb's Causeway and the Metro Centre rolled into one.

"Is it okay if I scream?" I ask.

"Why, what's the problem?"

"I just feel a little claustrophobic."

"Philip, this is nothing. You should see the one in Edmonton, it's the biggest in the world."

"Amazing. I really must get to visit it while I'm over here."

Her voice rises again. "Look, it's all very well for you to be sarcastic, but when it's minus thirty degrees for three months of the year we appreciate having somewhere dry and climate-controlled to shop. If that's okay with you."

"Okay, point made."

"And anyway, if you want to buy clothes, all the best places are here."

Maybe they are. We find a menswear shop and I pick out a couple of lightweight shirts before panic intervenes. "So that's it?" Karla asks. "You're gonna buy the first two that you find? There are plenty other places, you know."

"I like these, they're fine." But now I have accomplished the shopping thing in two minutes, what are we to do here for the rest of the afternoon? "Karla, look, let me buy something for you. Are there any clothes you'd like?"

This time she really shouts, causing—for the fourth (or is it the fifth?) time today—heads to turn. "**Hey, for fuck's sake, what are you trying to do**? Am I too dowdy for you? You want to turn me into a nice little whitey lady with pretty summer dresses—?"

"Hey, no, calm down!"

"I hope you're not patronising me, Philip, I hope you're not doing the missionary thing and trying to buy me."

"Karla, I'm not, I just asked if there was anything I could get you as a gift."

"I am what I am, you can't convert me into your ideal of something—"

"Karla!" I grab her wrist to staunch her flow of anger. "I just want to thank you for coming with me, I just want to show my affection, I didn't mean to offend you. I'm sorry."

She considers this, looks at me with a wry shake of her head. "Anyways, if you buy me an evening gown, where the fuck am I gonna wear it? You gonna take me to karaoke night at the Athabasca?"

"Why not? My Johnny Cash impressions are coming on a treat."

We laugh, I put my arm round her shoulder, and we stroll on through this palatial, air-conditioned homage to commerce, with its country 'n' western muzak a-twangin' in our ears.


So what can we do on a stifling Winnipeg Sunday? We can lie in, loll in the bath together, and make our way down from our room with the expectation of breakfast. But to our surprise the entire hotel foyer is taken over by a colossal buffet. Table after table boasts a culinary extravaganza—salads, salmon, fruit, cheese, seafood, meat, a riot of colour and immaculately presented food.

"Can we just get normal breakfast?" I ask a waiter.

"No, sir, today is Sunday brunch. Would you like to reserve a table?"

It is clearly the place for well-off 'Peggers to gorge. At eleven o'clock it is packed with smartly dressed families stuffing into their rightful sabbath treat. My mind is filled with the horror of my last two months of pisspoor UP fare, and my long-neglected salivary glands limber up for action. It is promising to be a bumper weekend for glands.

"Come on, Karla, what do you say?"

What does she say? "I'm not hungry," is what she says.

"But look at all this—it's wonderful food!"

"It's not the food that's the problem, Philip."

Sorry, stomach, but I am starting to understand what she means. "Come on, then, we'll get our things from the room and find somewhere else."

"You sure you don't mind?"

"No, I don't mind. It's your weekend too."

I turn towards the lift but she blocks my way. Oblivious to the throngs of Sunday-best noshers, she reaches up to fling her arms round my neck and kiss me full on the lips.

"We can go to the Folkfest!" I suggest. I show Karla the feature on the freebie paper's front page. I am surprised that I have not spotted this before, and surprised she has never been. It seems to be a big tradition round here.

"Well, if you really want to, I guess. Do you go to stuff like that back home?"

"Oh, yeah, I've been to all the big festivals—Trowbridge, Cropredy, Sidmouth…"

"What's that really big one everybody goes on about, it was in the news the other week?"

"Glastonbury? No way! My idea of hell, all those crowds, all those drunks, all that screeching music."

There is an hourly bus service to the venue, twenty miles out of the city. Most people will have camped out there for the weekend, but an assortment of young and less young people, pretty damn hippy-looking for this country, are scattered about the seats. The journey takes nearly an hour, and I am intrigued as we cleave through the phases of this grain-belt city, as thirty-storey banks give way to shabby hotels, then to pizzerias, to travel agents, to mini-malls, to grey-slab apartments, then to avenues of geometric settlements with glimpses of SUVs, house-tall aerials, obedient pedestrians at traffic-light junctions, and all-day sprinklers feeding the blindingly green lawns. I get a glimpse of understanding that people with less than conventional lifestyles don't have much of a place in this town.

"You wanna buy tarp tickets?" a man at the entrance asks.

"Der what?" In vain, I look to Karla for a clue.

"Did you bring your own tarp?" he persists.

"Well, no. Do I need one?"

He shrugs. "I guess it's up to you."

I decline his offer, but feel slightly disorientated by it. I like to do things properly, and now I fear I might be missing out on something. When we enter Tarpsville all is made clear. The area in front of the main stage is staked out with hundreds of identical square groundsheets, the prairies in miniature, territory claimed. But until six o'clock precisely, singers perform on the smaller stages in, it pleases me to see, the old folk tradition. Five or six acts take turns and then combine to do some impromptu songs, with fiddles and voices and accordions in spontaneous unison, the effect of it remarkably uplifting. Most of the bands are North American, which would explain why I've not actually heard of any of them. We watch Bob Benbow's Banjo Boys, Darlene Duchenne, The SasKats, and The Les Broadbent Folk Fusion Project, and they sure hit the groove together. They sure do. We stand watching them in the afternoon sun, my foot tapping recklessly away, and before I know it Karla is dancing—I mean *really* dancing at my side. Some people (am I allowed to say some races?) have innate rhythm, and Karla is one of them. I patently am not, so while she gives her whole consciousness and her whole body over to the swing and movement of the music, I jig stiffly beside her like a cross between Prince Charles and Mr Bean.

We move on to different stages and different acts. Some, it has to be said, seem a little corny, though these are the ones which are most rapturously received.

"Fancy a beer?" I suggest later in the afternoon.

"You bet."

We head to the big marquee outside which people lounge good-naturedly with their drinks. It seems that people *en masse* conduct themselves well in this country, there are no lager louts here. I get two bottles of Miller Lite from the bar, and we stroll off to see what further entertainment we might find. But suddenly there is an outburst of shouting, the happy order is disturbed.

"Hey, you! Whoa!" We turn to see two security guards, po-faced and sweaty under their fluorescent tabards, bearing in our direction. We look around us to see who might have ruffled the decorum of the day but there is no incident to be seen. Suddenly they are confronting *me*, glowering with authority, "Whaddya think you're doing, Bud?"

"Heurrh?" There must be some monumental mistake.

"You can't take drinks away from the beer tent."

"You what?" I laugh, for I think they must be practical jokers, or drama students doing a festival stunt. But no, they are serious, drinking is allowed only at the bar. "But I thought this was a festival," I protest.

"You tryin a be funny?" they demand. "You tryin a get thrown out?"

But I am amused more than angered, I am not going to let the incident mar the happy Folkfest ambience. In the evening everyone congregates round the main stage and only then do I appreciate the true significance of the tarp. We tarpless ones are consigned to the very back, it is forbidden to sidle through and forage for a bit of space in the midst of the crowd because every square inch is designated to families who sit neatly with their alcohol-free hampers of food. But we don't care, for when the music warms up Karla is free to dance again—

"Hey, siddown!" come cries from behind. We turn to find she is in receipt of much indignant pointing. "You wanna jig about, go over there!"

It appears that dancing is confined to a single area in the far corner of the arena, where a couple of dozen reckless gadabouts can be seen flaunting themselves out of sight of the neatly betarped. There are one or two mutterings, which I take to be uncomplimentary, from folk behind. Karla grabs my hand, I pick up our rucksack and we decide to move away.

"Would you say that Canadians as a nation are anally retentive?" I ask her.

"I'm not exactly sure what that means, but it sounds about right."

119

But despite this, again, we enjoy the evening. We find something to eat, go back for more drinks, then return to our position at the periphery of the tarps. Karla is no longer alone in dancing freely, and I find that the beer has loosened my limbs. Even my arms, which usually dangle passively as I jerk dysrhythmically from foot to foot, discover a spontaneous life. This is a momentous new development on my personal bodily expression front. In the past any attempts at arm movement have unerringly, if subconsciously, resulted in a total inability to move my legs and feet at the same time, to the extent where I look like, in Mary's astute words, "a complete prat".

"Hey, you're really in the groove now!" she teases, and I hug her to me, unable to remember the last time I had such—here's an unusual word in the Pacamac thesaurus—fun.

The night winds down and we head off to find our bus. But it seems we have just missed one and, incredibly, we are now faced with a wait of over an hour before the stragglers are collected at one. Most people, of course, have come by car, and as they head back to the city some of our fellow bussers successfully thumb a lift. I decide to try my luck, and a baseball-capped driver soon stops.

"Downtown?" he offers.

"Please," I accept.

But his passenger nudges and mutters, and the driver spots Karla standing behind. I catch, "Sorry, no natives," and the car revs away.

"You racist bastard!" I yell after it.

"Philip, don't worry," Karla soothes. "We'll just wait."

I put my arm around her and we stand at the mercy of the night's mosquitoes. Only now do I realise that for the whole day, at this celebration of the people's music, she has been in a racial minority of one.

# 1.9

Ways of being violently wrenched from sleep at four in the morning, variation 24: this time it is not a phone call for Irvine, for work, or a lift, nor is it a bleep or the throb of a distant drunken rave. Instead the hospital siren wails and its red light flashes. I have never really noticed it before, one wouldn't, but now we gather outside in our rudimentary clothing—Sharon, Donald, Doug and I—and stare up at its wilful skeletal frame. It emits a noise as baleful and unsettling as anything I have ever heard. It excludes all thought except the certain foreboding that there is disaster somewhere—a war, a fire, or a boat lost in the black depths of the lake.

Brad emerges from his house and runs towards his car.

Sharon yells, "Hey, Brad, what's going on?"

"Bartram's house is up in flames."

"Shit!" she exclaims. "Johnny Moose will be some mad."

"You can smell it," says Doug.

I'm not sure about that, but there seems to be a red glow beyond the trees to the north, more than one would expect from the imprint of the emerging sun. Fire engine sirens can now be heard, the whole reserve must be awake to the knowledge that something bad has occurred. Brad speeds off to contribute to the flashing and wailing of the night.

"I'd better go over to emerg and see if Lena needs a hand," I volunteer. Typical that this should occur on my night off.

"I'll come with you," Sharon says.

We turn towards the path but are arrested by the sight of Doug, hands on hips and head thrown back so the tip of his nose is the highest point of his anatomy, sniffing loudly at the night air. "Did you know," he asks, his voice garbled by the unnatural pressure on his larynx, "that the human nose is ten thousand times more sensitive than any artificial smelling machine? It's a very neglected area of science. My own theory is that there's a whole variety of olfo-receptors up here (he jabs a finger up his nostril) which haven't yet been researched. I think there's great potential in it, not only for medicine, but also the cosmetic industry. I think I may make that my next project."

"So what's your current project?" Sharon asks.

"Come in, if you like, and I'll show you. This is more of an artistic venture, but it would tie in nicely with some olfo-receptor research. I like to combine this left-brain right-brain stuff."

We follow him into his house, which is awash with gadgets, meters and lengths of electrical wire. Unwashed dishes and piles of laundry abound. The whole of the upstairs clearly doubles as his impromptu lab, with shelves of files and books framing the extensive computerware on his desk. However, he picks up a cubic perspex case containing a small and perfect replica of his own unmistakeably bespectacled head. It is mottled green and brown, sculpted from a material I don't quite recognise.

"You made that?" Sharon asks.

"Yup."

"That's brilliant," I admire. "You really have a talent there."

"Thank you."

I peer closer at the miniature inscription at its base:

**Title**: Auto-portrait
**Artist**: G Douglas Ganavan
**Medium**: Bogeys

"It took nearly a year to collect the necessary material," he says.

"All of it yours?" I query.

"Oh, certainly, all mine. It's very pleasing to work with, though not too durable. You want me to show you how I fixed it?"

"Some other time, maybe," says Sharon. "We really have to go."

We take our leave and walk along the path to the hospital. She shakes her head and says, "That guy is seriously weird."

We find Edna and Lena sitting with a coffee each. "Hey, if it isn't our ontological doctor!" Edna greets. Sharon and Lena look puzzled, so Edna has to explain my wordy put-down of Marshall Snape. They seem amused.

Lena turns out to be a star. She is in her late thirties, black, nearly six foot tall, with a short crop of hair. She may look imposing but she laughs all the time, even when she says, "I don't take no shit from these people," which is her favourite turn of phrase.

Now we sit in the little lounge between the ward and emerg, waiting to see if the ambulance will deliver some horrible consignment of smoke inhalation or burns. Thankfully the siren has stopped, so we sit chatting with one eye each on the small hours television. This, though, is Jackfish Lake TV. While other channels cable out their unending dire fare of cops and robbers, chat shows and recycled comedy dross, the local station is a round-the-clock alternative. Sadly they haven't yet mastered the technology necessary to harness a moving picture and accompanying sound to the transmission, it is simply like watching the silent end of movie credits scroll slowly and unendingly up the screen. It is no more than Teletext which happens to move. The content turns out to be much the same as the radio, and what the hell else did I expect?

For any type of boat repairs phone Lyle Ingmarsson,
Marine Engineer 2275

Baptist Women's trip to Thompson Saturday $12
contact Shirley on 4319

"Fresh fruit? In Jackfish Lake?" I exclaim. "I never knew that."

"He doesn't always succeed in getting here," Sharon tells me. "And it's not that fresh, it's stopped off at every bar between here and Dauphin along the way."

After half an hour with no sign of any casualties we jump to the sound of the doors swinging open down the corridor. However, it is Brad, who ambles towards us and pours himself a coffee with the report, "Bartram's house is pretty much burnt to the ground. Whoever did it has disappeared, so can you guys let us know if anyone turns up in the next day or two with unexplained burns?"

I am wondering how to express my misgivings that this might actually be an unethical breach of patient confidentiality, but Edna puts it more succinctly than I could. "Piss off, Brad, and do your own dirty work," she says. "Hey—that's nothing personal now, finish your coffee first."


I haven't heard from Karla in the few days since our return. This is annoying because Lena has offered to work the weekend, to give me more time off and earn some extra cash herself. Karla gave me her phone number but I am reluctant to use it in case anyone else replies. Thursday night finds me on call and at eleven o'clock the telephone rings. I jump to answer it, hoping it might be her.

"Hello?"

"Hi, Cormack, it's Bertha."

"Oh. Hi."

"Well, sorry to disappoint you—"

"No, I didn't mean it like that. I didn't expect it to be work."

"I paged you. Didn't it go?"

"No."

"Must need charging up. Who were you expecting anyway?"

"Nobody special."

"Don't kid me. Word gets round, you know. Anyways can you come have a look at this guy over here?"

"What's the problem?"

"He don't feel too good."

"That's helpful, anything more specific?"

"No, but he don't look too good, neither."

The scales in emerg weigh up to 160kg, but even that is not enough to accommodate Yale. It seems he has been feeling rather peaky of late and, finally admitting this might have something to do with his weight, put himself on a Slimfast diet to get a little more trim. This has had disastrous results because, like most other members of his family, it turns out he is diabetic, and the cripplingly low calorie intake he has instituted means he has started digesting his own protein tissue to keep his blood glucose up. Now he flounders on a trolley, his massive tent of a T-shirt caked in dribble and sick. I call in Doug, who expresses great professional interest in this resultant biochemical fuck-up despite the lateness of the hour. "Type twos aren't supposed to get ketotic," he says. "It'll be fascinating to see how you correct this."

If only my faith in my ability matched his. I am not a diabetologist, but I know enough to appreciate that this is a potentially serious condition. Any further wobble of Yale's mineral balance, particularly his potassium, could send his already overloaded heart into terminal fibrillation. I explain everything to him, and advise we whisk him off to Winnipeg for expert care. He absolutely refuses, leaving me to skid frantically through my freebie rep textbook for help with walking this metabolic tightrope. He will need intravenous fluids, insulin, and potassium, and it is many a year since I have juggled with such a regime.

"Look, Yale," I reiterate. "You ought to be in Winnipeg, you know."

"I ain't goin a Winnipeg."

Again I try to explain the nature of his situation, his deranged physiology, the risks to his heart and brain of not treating it properly. "Is there anything about this you don't understand? Is there anything you want to ask me?"

He reflects a long moment or two and says, "Yuh."

"What's that, Yale? What do you want to know?"

"When can I go home?"

But I do it, I start the treatment just as my recipe says. I sit for an age writing up his treatment and investigations needed over the next twenty-four hours. Every time Doug checks out his mineral balance I ask him to do it again, and sure enough Yale's biochemical perfection is finally attained.

When I become more relaxed about his fate I ponder, "So do you reckon he has a brother called Harvard?"

"Not that I know to," Bertha answers. "What makes you think that?"


Saturday arrives, and my joy at having two whole days off is tempered by the fact that I do not know what to do. I could go to the lake to paint, I could go for a long walk, I could borrow Sharon's car for a drive. She has been rather cool towards me since I went to Winnipeg, though I am relieved that she persuaded Donald to accompany her on her Thompson trip. At least they brought back the consignment of gin and wine I requested, along with the stash of beer and assorted booze for everyone else, so we are all cheered up, just like the locals on a welfare weekend.

I know I could invite her for a compensatory day out, but I suspect she is jealous of my involvement with Karla, about which everyone within a thousand-mile radius must now know. Not that I should feel guilty, not at all, for I have never given Sharon the slightest hint that I have harboured any intentions—my thoughts are stopped by the phone.

"Philip?"

"Karla!"

"Hi! What are you doing today?"

"Nothing—I was just wondering what—"

"We'll pick you up in ten minutes, okay?"

"Yeah, great. Wonderful. Then what?"

"You'll see. We'll be outdoors, so bring a hat and some water and stuff."

We? I don't have too long to deliberate because within ten minutes she is indeed at my door. Alex is in the back of her car ("Hi, Alex, how's it going?" "Nyurh.") and she drives us off to meet Lorraine at the jetty, where, I discover, four kayaks are lined up on the gravelly beach.

"Whose are these?"

"Two are Lorraine's, I borrowed the other two. I thought it was time you saw something of Jackfish Lake apart from emerg and your tv. You ever done this before?"

"No, never."

"Here, put this on."

I don the life jacket and smile nervously, amusing Lorraine, who is loud, cheerful, and only modestly overweight. These boats look thin and flimsy, and it does not help that I have to wriggle into one with my legs fully extended onto the adjustable foot rest deep in the prow. So now I am left firmly trapped in it with the obvious worry of what to do if I capsize.

"Now what?"

"Paddle. It helps if you have one of these."

They pass the necessary implement to me, and push me off into the lake. I thrust the paddle cautiously into the water, to each side in turn. After a preliminary wobble I right myself by propelling forward. "Hey, it works!" I shout with joy for I am indeed moving across the surface of the lake. Years of batting and fielding have left my arms fairly strong, and I soon gain the confidence that this is a hugely enjoyable skill which I can master. In no time, it seems, I am out in the open lake, and the horizon which has been such a fixed part of my recent weeks is suddenly reversed. Turning my head proves to be rather unstabilising, though, and within a minute the others, Alex included, are swishing past. I wonder what I am doing wrong, and find that even one or two asymmetrical pulls of the paddle can skew me through many degrees. Karla waits for me to catch up.

"Take your time, we've got all day."

"Where are we going?"

"Muskik Island. It's not so far—just around the point there and towards the north side of the lake. We'll do it in about an hour—is that okay?"

"You bet! This is brilliant, Karla, just brilliant!"

The hospital and our cluster of dwellings are to our right, between the trees. Now though we u-turn away from them, downstream, around Fraser's Point. Its church stands on the headland, as white and poetic as the high clouds. The town blends invitingly into the trees, and even the Athabasca Bar—even United Provisions!—looks attractive from here. This different perspective, gained from only ten minutes gentle effort, is astonishing, and I wonder why everyone on reserve doesn't do this. Why don't they enjoy the serenity of their lake once in a while, and put a healthy distance between them and the source of their daily irritations? Then again, why don't they ever take a bike ride or a walk?

Slowly and steadily we skirt round the point, and a whole new expanse of lake opens up. The horizon never loses its thin circumference of trees. Now though, I can see the detail of islands scattered ahead, a handful among thousands in this vast territory. Lorraine is some way in front of us, Alex at her tail. Karla slows to my pace, though our meditative efforts and the beauty of the day leave us with little urge to talk. The only noise is the splash of water we disturb. I can't believe how exhilarating this simple exercise is. It is heightened by the closeness to the water, slunk unfeasibly low in it and separated from its infinity by a few millimetres of fibre glass. How impressive does that make bygone Cree in their kayaks of wood and hide?

After about an hour we indeed reach the first island. I am last to land, and the others help my craft ashore. When I extricate myself from it, everyone laughs.

"What's so funny?"

"You're supposed to keep the water outside the kayak," Lorraine says.

Only now do I notice that my shorts are soaking wet, my coarse attempts at paddling having created major turbulence. Lorraine chuckles and suggests I take them off to dry, but I decline and feel myself blush. This, incidentally, is something I still occasionally do. It was much worse when I was younger, of course, belatedly exposed to the presence of girls after the prolonged hormonal quarantine of Mountstephen School.

Lorraine produces a rucksack from behind her seat and we share the cookies and flask of coffee while the women chat with the ease and certainty that their firm feminine friendship brings. I worry that I should make conversation with Alex ("So how's school?" "Aahhdno." "Um…") but he wanders off to explore between the trees.

"Look! There it is!" Karla grabs my arm, points with her other hand to what is unmistakeably an eagle wheeling towards its nest. Its wing span is immense yet it combines elegance with utterly silent power. I gasp in amazement because this single sight of it is truly marvellous, it transcends description. I almost burst into tears.

After a while we paddle towards its island, but it is circumspect, it allows us to reach its shore and then it flees to the mainland. I can't take my eyes off it, I feel that its sighting, this kayak trip, has made my whole expedition worthwhile.

We move on to a third island and laze on its shore to eat lunch. I stretch out, Karla uses my belly as a pillow and closes her eyes. I put my arm across her waist and her hand reaches for mine. Lorraine is unabashed by this intimacy, Alex seems not to notice, let alone care. For an hour we do nothing but chat, absorb the sun, and let the eagle grace us with an occasional display.

"Mom, when are we going back?" Alex asks. "I'm staying at Howard's tonight."

"Oh, when we're ready," she murmurs.

"Well, I'm ready now."

"Come on, I'll take you," Lorraine offers. And then with a wink to us, "It's okay, I'll drop him off at Howard's, you can come back in your own time."

We politely protest, she kindly insists, and five minutes later we are waving them from view, alone on our island and unseen by anyone else in the world.

"Come on, let's swim," says Karla.

"I haven't brought my trunks."

"And boys from Shahbn mustn't swim without their trunks?"

We laugh at my absurdity, peel off our clothes, and run into the lake. Its water is as cool and clean as any on the planet. We fool around, we splash each other, our aquatic wrestling becomes erotic wrestling. We run back ashore, fall to the ground and make love.

Karla comes home with me and, wrapped together in bed, I say, "Wasn't that eagle amazing?"

"It sure was."

"Do you know, I think this has been the happiest day of my life."

"Don't bullshit me, Cormack."

"It's true—I can't remember the last time I had such a wonderful day."

"What about when you got married? When your daughters were born? When you became a doctor?"

"Yeah, sure, but they were over twenty years ago."

"Well, it's nice of you to say that, even if it is bullshit."

"There's only one little thing spoiling it."

"What's that?"

"I'm helluva itchy."

"Where?"

Now she mentions it, all over. My back is worst, so I roll away to turn on the bedside light and show her.

"No surprise you're itchy," she laughs. "You've got mosquito bites all over your ass."

Karla goes off next morning to pick up Alex then spend the day at home. I decide to do more painting, and take up my usual spot. The knowledge that I could go further afield is itself liberating, but I am secure enough here in the knowledge that Lena is on call, so I will not be disturbed. Memories of yesterday form a happy backdrop to my thoughts, and the relaxation aids my art. I am getting more adventurous, my intuition has free rein. Unexpected crops of colour appear on the paper, I am guided not so much my what I see or what I think I should see, but instead the concept of what I *might* see begins to enter my brain. My skill is still minimal, of course, but I have the firm intention of producing something other than a kitsch kiddy reproduction of water and boats and fluffy clouds. Only now, many weeks into my artistic venture, does it occur to me that I could actually complete this indoors, I no longer have to be at the scene to capture it, for the essence of it is now stored in the appropriate part of my brain. I wonder how much of it I really can retain, so I sit there for a minute on Karla's stool, facing across the lake with my eyes closed.

"Hi there, Philip."

"Oh, hi!" I was so focussed on my interior journey I didn't even hear Donald's footsteps coming up behind. In fact I am annoyed to be interrupted, for I feel I was entering a place I'd not been before, and I fear that I might never find the route again.

"Hope I'm not disturbing you."

"No, not at all." Donald is one of those rare people against whom it is not possible to harbour a harmful thought. "How are you?"

"I'm fine. I was thinking that as you're finally free of being on call for the day you might like to come out for a drive?"

"Yeah, good idea. Nice of you to ask."

"When you're ready, of course. Do carry on painting for a while."

"Can you give me half an hour or so to tidy this up?"

"Sure, I'll come round for you. See you soon."

What a kind and thoughtful man Donald is. I know from Sharon that he is only a few years older than me, fifty-four or -five, but his quietly avuncular manner belongs to a staid and conservative

131

breed. After smudging on a few last flashes of pastel I transport my work indoors feeling pleased with its progress. I wash then fix myself a sandwich, looking forward to my afternoon out. When the doorbell rings I assume he has come to pick me up.

"Oh—hi, Karla, I didn't expect to see you."

"Sorry to surprise you. Are you entertaining someone else?"

"No, of course not, I was just going out for a drive with Donald, that's all."

"Oh, okay. That's fine."

"Why, what's the matter, is there a problem?"

"Well, yeah, kind of. Can I see you when you get back?"

"Of course you can. But I don't have to go out, I can tell Donald something's turned up."

"No, no, please don't do that. It might look suspicious."

"What do you mean, suspicious? What's going on?"

"I'll tell you later. Ring me at home when you get back."

With that she is gone. From my doorstep I watch her head back to her car. Donald is outside chatting to Sharon, who nods curt greetings to Karla as she walks intently past.

"Just coming, Donald," I shout. I close the door and join them. "Hi, Sharon. Donald and I are just off for a drive."

Donald asks her, "Hey, why don't you come along? Bring that mad dog of yours."

"No, thanks all the same," she says. "I have things to do."

We drive off, my mind still bothered by what Karla's problem might be.

"I've found out where there's an eagle's nest," Donald says. "I could take you to see it if you like."

"I saw one yesterday, actually. Out on one of the islands."

"Oh—okay, we don't have to do that. I know, we'll go to the dump instead."

"The dump?"

"Yeah, it's up near the mine."

"But why?"

"The bears often go there for food."

Donald is keen on photographing wildlife and he is excited

to arrive there to find a bear and her three young cubs foraging the garbage. We drive surprisingly close, and wind the windows down to watch. When he clicks the shutter to capture them they give a distrustful look.

"Perfect!" he says. "Aren't they amazing?"

I suppose they are, but there is something incongruous and not a little demeaning about seeing these imposing animals as they scavenge the discarded crates and packaging, the festering fruit, the unwanted furniture and appliances, the drained bottles and jars of this semi-civilised outpost. I half expect to see them sitting in line on an old settee watching a telly they have rigged up while swigging hopefully at the empty Budweiser cans. Here and there fires smoulder, and the charred underlay of rubbish is as black as the bears themselves. Donald tells me how dangerous they are if provoked, and I can imagine it. But somehow this makes it all the more undignified for them to be scratching away at the putrid debris unwanted by the folk of Jackfish Lake.

"Okay, beavers next."

We drive to Fraser's Point then walk down a rough track between trees. It emerges at a small stream, where he says, "We'll just sit here and wait."

In front of us is an obvious dam. Where the stream narrows a rough construct of branches has been shored up to block the flow, and behind it the water has dilated into a sizeable lake. After ten minutes Donald nudges me and whispers, "Here they come," and I turn to see two beavers swimming towards us, each with half a small tree clamped in its teeth. In front of us they manoeuvre the branch into position, and I see there is considerable skill in their construction technique. Each is laid longitudinally, not transversely across the stream, the distal leafy section downstream so that the mass of vegetation wedges together under the pressure of water instead of flowing off to the lake. One animal seems to be engineer-in-chief, the others goes back for more supplies.

"Clever little devils, huh?"

I agree, and the senior beaver suddenly surfaces three feet before us, surprisingly muscular, its sleek-oiled coat repelling water away. Donald's camera clicks and it dives back under the surface to attend to its intricate industry once more.

On the way back I thank Donald for showing me another snippet of the nation's wildlife, and as he parks the car he asks, "Say, Philip, are you still up for that trip to the north in October or November?"

"Um, yeah, I don't see why not."

"Excellent! Do you want to come in for a coffee, maybe look at a few possible routes?"

"Okay," I say, then regret my acceptance as I remember Karla's troubled visit.

Inside he attends to the coffee while I spread maps on the floor. "I have better ones than those on my desk. None of the regular maps show the north."

"Why's that?"

"I suppose no one is too interested. It's only lakes and natives, after all."

I smile and we consider all the places we could go. The prospect of driving across the Rockies in autumn is thrilling, of course, but might I not be wanting to spend time with Karla instead?

Donald describes excursions he has made in the past, to places like Buffalo Narrows and Fort MacKay, then he unexpectedly says, "Philip, you know I told you about my son and my wife?"

"Yes."

"Well, how long would you say it should take someone to recover from a loss like that?"

"I don't know, Donald, people vary enormously."

"Sure, but Wendy and Peter have been gone three years now, do you think I should be over it by now?"

"I shouldn't think you ever get over a trauma like that, not completely."

"No, but people are supposed to move on and find other happiness in their life."

"Aren't you doing that? Are you still depressed?"

"I don't know, I wouldn't necessarily say depressed. But I have

134

this—this emptiness, this void, and I really don't know how to fill it."

I look at him with his neat white hair and youthful skin, and that, as far as I can see, is that. "I'm sure that's inevitable, Donald. But you've got your photography, you've got friends."

"Maybe you're right," he says. "Maybe it just needs more time. Hey, more coffee?"

The mention of friends brings Karla's predicament back to me. "No thanks, Donald, I've got a couple of phone calls to make."

"Oh, okay. I'll see you some other time." As I walk from his house he calls, "And Philip—"

"Yeah?"

"Thank you for coming. Thank you."


She answers straight away. "Stay there, I'll come round."

Ten minutes later she arrives, looking cool in a pale blue T-shirt, her hair tied back into a barely sustainable bunch, her sunglasses jutted up onto her head. I would like to kiss her, but she is clearly troubled by something.

"Philip, I want to ask you a favour. If you say no, if you don't want to get involved in this, that's fine, I won't mention it again."

"Tell me what it is."

"You know the police said about the fire at Bartram's place, to let them know if anyone turns up with burns?"

"Yeah."

"Well—well, someone I know might be involved. He's got burns which look infected and he's too scared to come to the hospital."

"But it's still confidential, Karla, I could see him in emerg and wouldn't tell the police."

"That might be the case in England, but not here. They'd just come and look through the register, in fact they've already done that. Edna caught Brad Casper taking notes last night when he brought in an MHA. And Ellie's his little spy."

"But that's not legal, surely?"

"Sure it isn't, but this is cops dealing with Cree."

"So what do you want me to do?"

"This guy has burns on his leg, and I don't know whether he needs antibiotics, or to go down for a skin graft, or what. Could you take an unofficial look at him and give me some advice?"

"I'm not an expert on burns, Karla. And if it's that bad, he'll just have to go to hospital and take the flak."

"I know."

I sigh. "Where is he?"

"I'll take you—but only if you're sure."

I sigh again. "Okay. Take me. I'm sure."


This time it's a house out beyond the airstrip, off reserve. A track curves off the pitted road and the dilapidated structure huddles in a shallow dip, totally unseen. Adjoining it is a shed which leans at about seventy-five degrees sympathy with the prevailing wind. A battered pick-up stands in the drive, and Karla parks next to it. Four wooden steps lead up to the front door.

Karla hammers on it and shouts, "Wilson, it's me."

Heavy bolts are heard being drawn back, though it would take little effort for an intruder to smash through the door. It is opened by a small man wearing a grubby orange shirt and a baseball cap. He is young, but his face is pocked and drawn, he looks unwell. My first thought is that he has been starved not only of food but of light. A spell in prison perhaps.

"Wilson, this is Philip. Philip—meet Wilson, my brother."

"Hi." He steps fractionally back to let us in, and I guess it would be inappropriate to shake hands. He clearly would not be a candidate for membership of St Lanyon's Country Club, but at least their relationship explains Karla's involvement in this unsavoury affair.

The shack is dirty and dark, with rough wooden shutters defending the place against light. In the kitchen I make out a scatter of rubbish, mugs and cans and cigarette ends accumulated for weeks on the floor. Every corner of air is stained by the faint but unmistakeable stench of scorched human flesh.

"You want me to see this burn?" I ask him.

"Not me," he says. "Through there."

We go into to the next room, which is equally squalid. Slumped in a chair, beer in hand, is the shadowy figure of Marshall Snape. He looks at me and grunts. After three months here I am learning to discern the subtleties of these various emitted noises and his does not register highly on the welcoming scale.

"Marshall, show Philip your leg," Karla commands. He stands with laboured reluctance to lower his trousers and let her unwrap the heavy dressing from his thigh.

"How did you do it?" I ask.

Karla anticipates his silence. "He needs to know, and it won't go anywhere else."

"Gasolene," he says. "Splashed on my pants, then a spark set it on fire."

His leg is indeed a mess. An area the size of a side plate has been seared of its skin. Yellow slough is forming on the cooked pink flesh and the unleashed smell is nauseously bad.

"I've been dressing it daily with Flamazine," Karla says.

"I ain't going to hospital," says Marshall. "Not here, not Winnipeg, not anywhere."

"Do you have a fever?" I ask.

"No, but it fucking hurts."

"Well, it's certainly infected. You need antibiotics, at least. Are you allergic to anything?"

"No. And can you get me any painkillers?"

I hesitate, and Karla says, "Say no if it's a problem, Philip."

"That's more difficult," I tell him, "but I'll see what I can do."

His nod is as close to a thank you as I can expect. Karla attends to his leg, and I see that she has already accumulated a fair supply of dressings, presumably illicitly, presumably from the ward.

"Thank you, Philip," she says on his behalf. "I'll bring the antibiotics tomorrow."

"Tonight would be better," I suggest.

"Okay, thanks."

We grunt our farewells, and I offer to see Marshall's leg again in a few days. Back in the car, Karla thanks me once more.

"You're welcome. That leg is pretty bad, you know."

She nods, clearly tense and concerned.

"So Marshall is a friend of your brother's?"

She nods again, pauses, then says, "Yeah, he's always been Wilson's best friend. He's also—" Her voice tapers into the air.

"Also what?"

"He's also Alex's Dad."

Karla can see that I am shocked by this revelation. "It was thirteen years ago, Philip. I was hardly eighteen at the time."

Maybe so, but the thought of her liaison, however long ago, with that lowlife is deeply repugnant. When I think back to my few girlfriends before Mary (Jacqui Harriot-Webb with her horses and that lovely racing-green MGB, the delightful Lucy from Sturminster Newton, Diana the speech therapist whom I met at the Rag Week Ball) it makes me see that Karla and I are social constellations apart. I feel cheapened, drawn into the morass of sexual life on this infected incestuous reserve. The airport car park is Sunday deserted, but she pulls into it and switches the engine off.

"Listen, Philip, I know what you're thinking—"

"No, you don't."

"I do, I've made you feel dirty. I'm sorry for that, but you have to understand that I was eighteen, and all I wanted was to escape from this place. You know by now what it's like here. Marshall always seemed like a bit of a hero, he wasn't afraid to speak out or do things about the injustice—"

"Things like arson, you mean?"

"I'm not defending what he did. I'm just saying that when I was young I found him attractive because he was a rebel. We weren't together for long, but I was careless and got pregnant."

"So do you have any other children anywhere?"

"No! Hey, what is this?"

"I only asked."

"Well, I'm only telling you go fuck yourself." With that she starts the car and screeches off down the road, giving the impression that she is deliberately seeking out every rut and bump. She turns into the hospital drive and skids to a halt behind trees, as near as anywhere possible round here for being unseen.

"I'll wait here," she says.

"For what?"

"You said you'd get Marshall his antibiotics. You wanna do that now?"

I am tempted to say bugger Marshall and his antibiotics, and I am slightly less tempted to knock on Brad's door and tell him who set fire to Bartram's house. The only thing which deters me is the discovery that nice guy Brad doesn't always play to the rules either. And I suppose I have given my word, so I get out of the car and cut through the trees to emerg.

Edna is on duty. "Hi, Philip, what are you doing here?"

"I was wondering if you could let me have some fluclox?"

"Sure thing. What for?"

"Oh, I've got a few mosquito bites turned septic."

"You want me to take a look at them?"

"No, thanks. Um, can you make it the 500s rather than 250s?" I venture, knowing that this immediately challenges my excuse for needing them.

"Got a bit carried away with the sunbathing, ay?" she grins.

I am not sure how much to read into that. "Um, they're pretty painful—do you have any Tylenol Extras to spare?"

"Sure, how many?"

"A couple of dozen?"

She gets my supplies from the drug cupboard, smiles in a knowing sort of way, so I thank her and try to make my departure look as nonchalant as possible. I wonder if I should adopt a limp.

I give them to Karla, who says, "Thank you. Anyway, it's an aboriginal tradition."

"What is?"

"When the man of the house dies or leaves, the rest of the tribe set fire to it. You might call it arson, but to us it's getting rid of the bad spirits which remain, and also it's a statement that we aren't attached to material things. Unlike some cultures."

With that she drives away from me, taut-faced at high speed, leaving me to assume that our relationship has gone up in flames as well.


Next day I get an email from Mary. She and NYK now want to get married, so it falls to me to instigate a divorce. If I wouldn't mind doing the honours, of course. I shout an obscenity in the general direction of NYK as the phrase "giving away the bride" takes on a new and sickening turn. But she says it can wait until I return, for she wants to be as reasonable and civil as possible over this. By the way, she has seen a solicitor, who assures her that a fifty-fifty split is called for, whoever has been technically wronged. After all, we were equal partners in marriage, and how could I ever recompense her commitment to housewifing and mothering for all those years? She has sacrificed full-time work for me and my daughters, not that she is complaining, although it is only natural for her to wonder sometimes about the career possibilities she spurned. She was always one of the top five per cent throughout university, whereas I, if I care to remember, always just scraped by.

I know I have a right to feel angry about this, especially when I think of all the extra years I will have to flog myself in order to secure a decent pension, now that she can leech half of it away. Didn't I read somewhere that doctors who retire at sixty-five can only expect to live until they're sixty-seven? But there is no point in becoming an embittered and sour old man, it would only drive me to alcoholism or a stroke, a Pyrrhic satisfaction I can well do without. Instead, the letter leaves me with a feeling of emptiness, and although I know that now is the time for me to move on, the question is—move on where?

At the Folkfest I stocked up on some CDs—Boys of the Lough, Mary Black, The Chieftains—and I spend the evening listening

141

to them while I write to some old friends. Most addresses in my book are from pre-email days, they are people with whom I have exchanged ink-on-paper letters over many a year, though the frequency of these has severely dwindled with time and the distraction of family and work.

But now I write to Gareth and then to Roderick Hart, who was my best friend at university. This became complicated, and severely eroded, because Mary disliked his dull wife. Then there is Tim Forrester, though I still feel guilty for neglecting him when he was so depressed (I was getting involved with Mary and doing house jobs at the time). And Jane Short, whom I lost touch with until our last reunion, though she was Mary's friend rather than mine. Oh, and Lesley Hardwick, though I think this address is old. But suddenly I want to tell all these estranged people what I am doing. I, Pacamac, am on an exciting adventure, the work is challenging but I am pleased to be helping some of the overlooked people in our so-called civilised world. I am also taking the opportunity to do some kayaking, absorb something of aboriginal culture, and plan to see more of this wonderful country. By the way, was I really such a plodder at medical school? By the way, my marriage has broken down.


At least I am getting to enjoy Lena's company. She is from a desperately poor South African background, but was one of a handful of such people to get a scholarship through university. She has battled against prejudice in the context of her colour and her gender, and it wouldn't surprise me if she were gay, not that I have any wish to get involved in that. When I ask if she ever thinks about going back to work with her own people she glares at me and I have to apologise, realising how patronising I sound.

"Doctors in South Africa get paid fuck all, Philip, why do you think they all come over here? And the rand is just about worthless, so I can make in a day here what it takes a month to earn back home. Anyway, my duty is to my family. I've bought a nice house for them all, and now I'm saving something so my nieces and nephews can get educated. After that, the rest is for me.

"You know, when I was a girl I only had one pair of clothes. When my mother washed them I just put them on again wet and made sure I played on the sunny side of the house. I was happy enough but I always promised myself I'd get out of that poverty, however hard I had to work. That's why these people really piss me off, you know—" she sweeps her hand out in the general expansive direction of the Cree, and shakes her head. "All the government handouts they get."

This shocks me, for I expected her to express some solidarity with them. "But they can't all train to be doctors, Lena. What else can they do out here?"

Instead of answering she asks, "Philip, when do you finish here?"

"End of October, why?"

"Because in November you can come to South Africa with me. I'll show you Cape Town and Table Mountain, and all the beaches and the wildlife and stuff, and I'll also take you to show you where I grew up. At least they have some spirit there, all they do here is whine."

I thank her for the offer, overlooking for a moment my agreement to a trip with Donald. But I like and admire her a lot, and she is certainly excellent at work. Because she has always had to strive twice as hard as everyone else to get anywhere she knows twice as much as the average doctor, or twenty times more than me. I can ask her about anything from scaphoid fractures to renal failure, and she tells me what I need to know. Yet just when I feel I am starting to gain a little understanding and sympathy for the plight of the aboriginal, she comes along with her radical views and confuses me. What, I wonder, would be the Lib Dem line on this? That, after all, is what I vote for at home. Radical reactionaries. Pragmatic principles. Cornish common sense.

And she is certainly honest. Today she has been asked to meet with the family of Billy, a diabetic in his sixties whom I have seen many times. He has been on dialysis three days a week, with the other four spent at home breathlessly shifting between his bed and his chair. His feet are ulcerated and he is half blind. He has a wretched life. Lena readmitted him to the ward yesterday and it is clear that the end is near, all his bodily systems have failed. Yet the family—every one of them, dozens of them—want to meet with the doctor to see if anything further can be done. I have been in this position before and know that twenty of them will be crammed into the little visitors' room, hanging on to Lena's every word in search of a glimmer of hope. Shouldn't he go down to Winnipeg? Can't he have a kidney transplant? Say what you like about these people, at least in times of illness, birth and death, the families rally intensely round. (This, as ever, reminds me to flinch with guilt. I really must phone Mum and Dad.) After half an hour with Lena they finally emerge, weeping and holding on to each other for support.

"So what did you say?" Edna asks quietly as they file back to their nearly departed uncle or brother or dad.

"I explained to them," Lena whispers back, "that you can't make chicken soup out of chicken shit."


Karla is on duty tonight, as am I. This is uncomfortable as I am not sure where our relationship stands now, if it stands at all. But we are too busy to chat, there are the usual "emergencies" to see, as well as Billy and his family on the ward. There is always a patient or a nursing assistant within earshot, so we just get on with what needs to be done. At three in the morning it quietens, and all I can think of is sleep. As usual I am thwarted, for before I can leave a young man hobbles into emerg.

"Hi, Morton," Karla greets. "How ya doin'?"

"Can I see a doctor?"

"What's the problem?" I intervene, understandably brusque given the time of night.

"I hurt my back."

"When?"

"Aahhdno."

"How did you do it?"

"Aahhdno."

"Have you ever had this before?"

"Aahhdno." Then, catching my exasperation, "Yeah, I guess I have."

"Don't you have any painkillers?"

"Aahhdno. My mom gives me some pills now and then."

I feel another rage of exasperation coming on, but it is soon clear that his Aahhdnos are genuine. There is nothing he would like more than to co-operate with my questioning, but the capacity is simply not there. He does not drink, but I learn from Karla that as a youth he got heavily into sniffing solvents—glue, lighter fuel, kerosene, anything that he and his friends could find to obliterate the tedium of their days. He is a good-looking man of thirty or so, a little plump but with kind eyes and surprisingly clear skin. However the higher functions of his brain have simply been dry-cleaned away.

I wonder what will happen—as it surely will—when heroin takes a hold on these reserves. I have already seen a couple of youths coming back from the city with injection sites infected in their arms, and a handful of people are already known to have hepatitis C. This is the perfect viral time bomb, ticking away in dark corners of the circulation, fuelled by alcohol and malnutrition, waiting to explode with a slow remorseless fall-out of fatigue, nausea, liver failure and death. Treatment is possible, but unreliable, unpleasant and expensive (too expensive for Indians?), so nowhere is there a sounder case for prevention being better than cure. The public health nurses have asked the band for funds for education and a needle exchange, but have been told that this would be seen to condone the problem. Drugs belong to the cities, they don't trouble us out here. They still haven't learnt the lessons from alcohol that denial and prohibition don't work. But everyone else in the world knows that heroin seeks out the young and disaffected, those from disrupted families, those with no future and no education, those kids who have no mental resources, no plans but to escape. Heroin and its suppliers have no conscience about this, even now they will be checking their radar for future lucrative markets. They will jump with excitement at their bleeping screens—Jackfish Lake, here we come!

Next morning I call in to Sharon's office. "I need a holiday. Now Lena's here I thought I'd take the chance to get away."

"Good idea. Where you planning to go?"

"I fancied the idea of Vancouver and the west."

"Good choice. Are you meeting up with your family?"

"I shouldn't think so. I'll probably go by myself."

"That's a shame," she says, emphasising the word long and hard. Sh-a-a-ame. I half expect her to tell me that she is due for some leave too.

"I don't mind, actually, in fact I quite like the idea of being able to go exactly where I please."

"When do you want to go?"

"Soon as I can get something fixed up. I thought I'd give some travel agents a ring."

She recommends a couple of names to me, and I thank her and leave. Suddenly I have a tremendous elation as I realise how small and stultifying this place is, how infinitely exciting the possibilities outside.

Karla is not on duty on Wednesday night, so on Thursday (I have the luxury of afternoons off now Lena is here) I decide to give her a ring. I do not like this uncertainty we are in, but if I have offended her I can at least apologise and remain on civil terms.

Her mother, I presume, answers, "Yallo?"

"Hi, is Karla there?"

"No."

"Oh. Can you give her a message?"

"Yes."

"Can you ask her to phone Philip? 6223?"

"Okay."

I am immediately annoyed with myself for committing myself to her return call. On a summer afternoon like this I really want to be out in a kayak or in front of my easel.

But within half an hour she turns up. "Hi. Mom said you'd called."

"Yeah—" I find myself uncertain where the weekend's spat has left us. "Karla, I'm sorry I upset you the other day. I shouldn't have said—"

"That's okay, it's no problem," she says, and walks towards me to kiss me full on the lips. "Would you mind taking a look at Marshall again, please?"

"What, now?"

"If that's all right. Then maybe we could get out on the lake."

So within five minutes we are bumping along the track to his refuge. It feels like a place the sun always misses, enclosed by sparse trees and approached only through this thin clearing to the north. I half expect it still to be covered in snow. This time Marshall is alone. He grunts a greeting and drops his track suit bottoms to reveal he is wearing nothing beneath. Given what I now know about Karla's past, it is a sight I don't particularly want to see, but she takes no notice as she rolls the bandage away from his leg.

"No better, no worse," she observes, and I agree. From her shoulder bag she produces another supply of Flamazine, gloves, plastic forceps and dressings. As she tends to her work I absorb what I can of the gloomy room. Although incapacitated and lying low, it is clear he has not troubled himself to tidy up. The debris seems much as it was a few days ago, though this time I notice, on the far corner of the floor, a gun.

"What do you reckon?" Karla asks.

"Just carry on, I suppose. If you don't want to go to hospital to get a skin graft, there's not much more we can do. Burns just take an age."

"Can you get me more painkillers?" he asks.

Although I was expecting this, I am not sure how to respond. Karla catches my hesitation and suggests, "Maybe you could write out a prescription in Wilson's name? Then I could get it tomorrow."

"Yeah, okay," I say, but then regret my assent. It is, after all, still fraud, sufficiently dishonest for the College to suspend my registration straight away. I imagine myself on the plane back home to England in disgrace, banned from working in this country ever again. Or worse, prosecuted, publicly shamed, sent to prison maybe—o happy fate—to share a cell with Marshall himself.

Back in the car I ask, "Did you take all those dressings from the ward?"

"Sure, but everyone does it. It's okay."

"It's not okay, Karla. Don't get yourself into trouble—please."

This time we paddle south, across the lake. No one else disturbs its surface, and I am aware of how visible we are to anyone on the reserve. People will be observing, "Looks like Karla MacRae out there. And that white doctor, ay?" "Hell, is she desperate or what?"

After about an hour we find a small inlet. As we sit on the grassy outcrop with the sun at our backs, I put my arm round her shoulder, and she rests her head into me.

"I'm not taking my clothes off, mind," I tell her.

"Why not? It's nearly the end of mosquito season."

But it is perfect just to sit here with her and chat. I tell Karla how staggering I find it that there is not one settlement for hundreds of miles on this land mass behind us, just as there is no sign of human intrusion, not a single artificial light, between Jackfish Lake and the North Pole. She shrugs, for it is not amazing to her, it is just the way it is.

"Do you think Donald is having it off with Sharon?" she asks instead.

"Donald and Sharon?!" I laugh.

"Sure. Why not?"

"But he's so much older than her."

"And you're not so much older than me?"

"What's that got to do with it? Anyway, she's so—"

148

"Yeah, you can say it, she's fat. But some men like that."

"Maybe, but I don't. And I get the impression she doesn't like you."

Karla laughs. "Well, she's jealous, isn't she?"

"Is she?"

"Sure she is. She talked of nothing for months and months about this doctor who was coming, how he had the cutest English accent, and his wife had just walked out on him. She had it in her head that you were the one for her."

"Poor Sharon. I—I've never led her on, you know."

"I know that."

But did I? How much telephonic flirting did I engage in during those months of marital loss? Is it a complete surprise that she allowed her imagination to roam so far? And, until I met her, didn't I do the same? I wonder why can't we rid ourselves of this silly emotional turmoil as we mature. Why did Mary have to upset an apple cart of domestic and financial stability to go flouncing off with NYK? Why can't we all just choose the easiest and most rational route through life, sparing our fellow humans the fall-out of disappointment and hurt?

"Yes," I conclude, "maybe Sharon and Donald should get together. They're both such nice people after all."

Karla emits something approaching a shriek, and I look round in alarm, expecting a crocodile or a snake. "What is it?"

"Shit, I just *hate* it when people say that."

Oh, God, now what have I done? "Say what?"

"That phrase, Such Nice People!"

"What's wrong with it?"

"That's what everyone says about white Canadians, oh, they're Such Nice People. Sure they are. And why do you think that should be?"

"I don't know. I guess they're generally content with their lot."

"Tscheee," she snorts amazement, contempt and pity my way. "I'll tell you why Canadians are all Such Nice Fucking People, shall I? It's because of their collective guilt at all the atrocities they've handed out to the aboriginals over the years. Theft of land, oppression, discrimination in any way you can think of, residential schools—did I tell you my mom was sent to a residential school?"

"No. But she's not so old?"

"Dead right, Philip, she's three years older than you. We aren't talking about something which happened two hundred years ago, we're talking about my mother, lots of my mother's friends, and lots of my friends' mothers. When she was six they came here and abducted her. They packed her off to the school at Blackwater Lake to "civilise" her, to make a good little Christian housewife out of her, but do you think they actually educated her? Do you think they cared about her or the effect that had on her parents? Do you think they fed her properly? Do you think they clothed her? Do you think they heated the school in winter? No to all of those. And by the way, do you think the teachers emotionally abused her? Do you think they physically abused her? Do you think they sexually abused her?"

Presumably, yes. I stare out at the sublime calm of the lake, substrate for these people for as long as anybody knows. I feel that it, too, has been bespoiled. How can I not feel guilty for Karla's family horrors? Guilt by association is still guilt.

"So yes to all of those," she confirms. "And you know what happens when she gets to fifteen? They decide this whole residential school business hasn't worked. She doesn't turn out to be a polite and docile girl who'll go work as a secretary or a maid for some rich prairie family and go to church on Sunday— no, she's a sullen, moody, uneducated failure. After all that time she hasn't actually learned anything about the glorious British Fucking Empire, so they might as well send her back to the reserve. And what do you think life's like for her on the reserve? She's been away for nine years, her mother's dead, her father's disappeared because he's given up hope of her ever coming back, she has no friends, she's lost touch with everything she knew, all the traditional ceremonies and beliefs don't mean a thing. She's confused, she doesn't know if she's white or if she's Cree. But the priests and teachers from Blackwater Lake and all those places like it, they go back to the city with their pensions and they say, 'We tried really hard with those Indians, you know, but you just can't get through to them, they don't want to know.' So people admire them for trying, and when they hear people like my mother—the few who were ever brave enough to complain they were raped—they say, 'How dare you make such allegations? That's just not believable, we are Such Nice People. We could *never* do a thing like that.'"

What can I say? What can I do? Even to touch her could be construed as abuse. Eventually I have the nerve to ask, "I suppose all that leaves you feeling confused too?"

She looks across to her reserve and her roots. She shrugs weakly, a yes more than a no. I could almost convince myself that there is a tear in the corner of her eye.

But after that she lightens. We walk a little way into the galaxy of trees, holding hands. When we return the sun is at its height so we cool off with another naked swim. This time Karla has had the foresight to bring a towel so we dry off then lie together squashed onto it. There is no need to make love. Suddenly I burst out laughing, overcome with the simple sensuality of it all.

"What's so funny?"

"Nothing. I'm just happy to be here."

"Good. I'm glad."

We laugh and lie there some more, hands linked. I know this can't be bettered, I know I should just relax and enjoy the moment, but I can't help myself. I seem to want even more. "Karla?"

"Hmm?"

"I've got two weeks holiday I want to take soon."

"So?"

"Well, I haven't been off reserve for weeks. I'm desperate to get away."

"You're desperate?!" she snaps. "You've been here less than three months and you're telling me *you're* desperate? What about all the people who can't afford the two hundred dollar air fare, the people who *never* get out of here? And this is actually one of the better reserves, you know, at least we have a road, we have electricity, at least we have water."

Hell, I've done it yet again. "I'm sorry, I'm really sorry. I didn't mean it like that. But I do need a holiday, so—will you come away with me?"

"When? Where to?"

"Whenever you can. Wherever you like. It doesn't matter, just come away with me somewhere."

"Yeah, okay," she says, as if she's just agreed to lend me a couple of bucks.

We head back, Karla leading the way. It is slightly upstream and in the middle of the lake I am suddenly drawn along by a narrow unseen channel, and I find myself battling against the current. The harder I paddle against it, the less headway I seem to make. I do not exactly panic, but suddenly I have an insight into the power of this sheer massive flow. It all looks still and benign but it occurs to me that this river system probably drains an area the size of Britain, and a vision appears of me, exhausted, washed away into the still chilly expanse of the Hudson Bay (**Tregaskis mourns lost kayak Doc**, the *West Briton* will run). I work even harder, my arms ache, I am still paddling on the spot. When I look up I see Karla gliding effortlessly back to me, her face consumed by mirth.

"Try paddling across it, not against it," she suggests.

Immediately I swing through ninety degrees and then can return to my initial intended course. "Oh—I get you. Thanks."

Already her skinny arms are pulling her ahead of me. "Don't you white folk know nothin'?" she asks.

Next day she catches me in emerg and asks me to write a prescription for Wilson. I do two separately, for fifty Tylenol Extra each, so as not to arouse Donald's suspicion. "That's so you don't cash them both today, leave the post-dated one till next week."

"Do I look that stupid?"

"Do I have to answer that now?"

"Ha ha," she says, but we know this is not a laughing matter. I still feel uneasy about this.

"Anyway, I've just been to see Sharon. I can take the middle two weeks in August off."

Lena is approaching us down the corridor. Karla folds the prescriptions into her pocket, winks and turns away.

"Oh, Karla," I call her back. "We're barbecuing tonight, would you like to come round?"

Her expression registers enthusiasm on a negative scale. "Am I invited?"

"I've just invited you."

"Maybe," she says. "I'll let you know."

We stand in utter awe of the latest display of natural beauty this country offers. "Amazing—no other word for it," I say, realising immediately that there are no words at all.

The barbecue is down to its embers, and we all stand jacketed under the cloudless night sky with our remnants of drinks to hand, our heads levered back to take in as much of this spectacle as we can. Sheets of phosphorescent green sweep back and forth, white lights shimmer in backdrop, they are never still. Sometimes there is a hint of purple, sometimes the rays are obscured as if something invisible has cast a shadow over the source of this vast bounty of light.

Sharon agrees. "It doesn't matter how many times you see them, they're awesome every time."

"Actually," Doug pronounces, "it's all caused by gaseous atoms in the Van Allen belt, or the magnetosphere, being ionised. Charged particles, mainly electrons in the outer part of the belt, drift towards the magnetic poles, then—"

"Doug?" Lena interrupts.

"What?"

"Shut the fuck up."

We chuckle back into silence and stand magnetised ourselves

153

by this cosmic extravaganza. After about twenty minutes it simply stops, leaving us humbled, privileged and elated to have witnessed the show.

Karla is the first to speak. "Actually, Doug, you're wrong."

"No, I'm not, I was reading it up last week."

"It has nothing to do with science at all. That's the spirits calling somebody back home."

"What, you mean—?"

"Yeah, I know it's wonderful and all, but the Cree don't like the lights. They mean somebody's going to die."

The chilly silence in which we stand pondering this is now shattered by my bleep. I laugh nervously as everyone looks my way.

Karla predicts, "That'll be Billy, his family are expecting him to go tonight."

I press the button to receive the message. "*Krrrshkrshkrrrshkrrr*," it says.

When I phone for a translation Bertha tells me it is in fact couple of drunks with minor stab wounds. I ask how Billy is and she says, "His resps are irregular, he won't last long."

Clearly I will have to go. I worry for a moment about leaving Karla, then I realise she has known all these people longer than I have, she hardly needs my protection. I say goodbye, squeeze her hand, and meet her smiling eyes through the darkness. I have the urge to tell her that none of her past matters to me any more. Who am I to judge her history? What significance is a bygone teenage fling compared to the imponderable awe of the Northern Lights?

Nine or ten of Billy's closest relatives huddle round his bed, bent forward on their hard chairs to focus on his every feeble breath. I preserve the silence, raising my hand to them as I round his bed. The last few pulses of his life issue from his heart, futile and feeble, failing to trouble his wrist. There is nothing for me to do, of course, except ensure he is not distressed. I have gone in there merely to show I have not abandoned them. I want to convey a simple mark of respect, and although I know that this action might be misconstrued as it passes across our cultural gulf, I mean it, so I do it just the same.

His eldest son follows me from the room. "How long do you think he'll last?"

"Not long. Probably not the night."

"You think he knows what's going on?"

"I really don't think so, Horace. Not now."

He nods and returns to the room to report back.


I recognise both of the drunks, and assume that the younger one, Jay Moose, is related in some way to Johnny. They were in the pub and began arguing, apparently about claims to one of the empty houses. Many families have now moved in to them and have erected satellite dishes outside to affirm their claim. TV dishes, it appears, are the totem poles of today, and Jay's was uprooted in a deeply sacrilegious act. He therefore jabbed a beer glass into his rival's face to confirm his accusation. In return he sports a stab wound just to the left of his navel. It is clean and discreet, almost aesthetic, and no more than an inch in length. It is horizontal in the crease of his skin and it barely bleeds. He appears untroubled as he rambles drunkenly away to anyone who might listen. No one does.

Calvin Beardy's laceration, on the other hand, is hardly minor. It zig-zags across his left cheek like a crazy meridian, with one peninsula of skin in particular dangling perilously loose. Fortunately his eye is spared as is the inside of the mouth. I decide to tackle him first and warn him it will take about an hour. He grimaces as I inject the local, and after that he lies perfectly silent and still. For that I am grateful, it is difficult enough without him bawling and thrashing about. But my suturing skills are improving, and it is satisfying to see this bloody mess restored into a neat if irregular scar. Bertha helps clean him up, and as we sit him forward the room is suddenly filled with a mournful wail. It has the same quality as the siren and for a moment I think Calvin is the source of this baleful noise.

155

"That's Billy gone," Bertha says.

One would imagine from the reaction that his death was entirely unexpected, a tragedy from the blue. The women howl and they embrace each other with grief. I steal past and confirm that Billy's heart is still, his eyes already glazed with the milky film of death. The family turn to me as I pronounce what they already know, and the crying is intensified. Horace steps forward to shake my hand. "We all want to thank you for what you done."

With the concentrated emotion of this I almost forget about Jay's knife wound, but it takes only a few minutes to clean it and insert three stitches. Bertha summons his taxi and we are thankful that Calvin has already been collected in a separate car.

Surprisingly there is no one else to see so I head home. Outside the house I stand awhile. The barbecue remnants have cooled to dust, and overhead fronds of cloud interplay with stars. There is no hint of the magical aurora, and I imagine the cosmic gods up there, pleased to have done their job. I would like to find Karla waiting for me so I can confirm to her that another soul has indeed been recalled. I would like her to tell me about more of her people's arcane customs and beliefs. I would love to submerge myself in the welcoming warmth of her body but instead my bed is empty and bare.

At three o'clock my phone rings. "Hi, Cormack."

Grunt.

"Your man with the stab wound's back."

"What—Calvin?"

"No, the other one, the kid."

"What's the matter?"

"Aahhdno. Says he don't feel too good."

It is probably his hangover setting in, but I suppose I had better see him. He looks a bit sweaty and his pulse rate has gone up. His wound looks clean and when I prod his abdomen he does not object too much. I enquire more closely about the offending weapon and he describes a long slim knife. Now I am beginning to worry in case there are any internal injuries and it occurs to

156

me that an x-ray might be helpful to see if there is any gas in his abdominal cavity as a result of a perforated bowel. Ellie arrives, and when we stand him up to get the appropriate film he looks decidedly ill.

"Pulse 140, bp 80/45," Bertha reports.

I don't know what is going on, but I don't like it very much. And because I don't know what's going on, I don't have much of an idea what to do.

"You wanna start an i-v?" Bertha prompts.

"Yeah, good idea." But this proves difficult as the veins in his arm are collapsing in sympathy with their owner. As I am prodding around trying to institute a drip he complains of pains in his chest. Bertha wheels in the ECG machine and its tracing looks ominously abnormal. I belatedly listen to his chest and something is clearly amiss—his heart sounds are muffled, almost inaudible. My brain belatedly tells me I have missed something very serious indeed.

A voice interrupts my rapidly mounting terror, "How you doing, Philip?"

"Lena! What are you doing here?"

"Bertha said there was a bit of a problem."

Any indignation at being undermined by Bertha's call for help is overwhelmed by relief. I explain what has happened and Lena diagnoses the situation straight away. "Cardiac tamponade. The knife's come up through his diaphragm and nicked his pericardium." She demonstrates its path with an upward thrust of her fist. "Get the Medevac a.s.a.p, Bertha. We may need to open his chest."

Open his chest? Christ! Lena may be used to doing stuff like that in Cape Town but my surgical skills these days begin with ingrowing toenails and end with sebaceous cysts. Lena gets Ellie to do a chest x-ray and it confirms the outline of the heart is bloated by the bleeding into the sac which contains it, splinting its movements as it tries to pump blood round Jay's vital organs.

Lena slows down the intravenous fluids I am pouring in. "Best not overload him. When's the Medevac in?"

157

"Within twenty minutes," Bertha reports. "They were on the way back from Thompson so I told them to get straight here."

After an agony of waiting the ambulance crew arrive to take him to the plane. "One of us better go with him," Lena says.

"Be my guest," I offer, and she laughs.

I tell her to phone from Winnipeg with news of his fate. There is no point in going to bed, for I know I will not sleep. Instead I slump in a chair in the coffee room, no company though for Bertha while my head swims with anxiety, despair of my utter incompetence, the certainty that Jay will die, the curse of the Northern Lights.

At six o'clock the phone rings, and I leap to answer it. "Hi," Lena says.

"Lena! What's happened?"

"He arrested as soon as we got into emerg here."

"Oh, shit!"

"But the cardiac guys were waiting for us, so they did a thoracotomy on the spot and cleared out his pericardium."

"So he's okay?"

"Yeah. On ICU for a day or two, but he should be fine now."

"Lena, you're an absolute star."

She laughs. "You mean that?"

"You bet I do."

"Okay, in that case I'm staying here to do some serious shopping. I'll see you in a couple of days."

For several days I am enveloped in a despondent fog. I fear every snuffly kid is incubating pneumonia or meningitis, and am aware of the nurses examining my every decision. After weeks of bumbling along and getting away with it I have been found out. But for Lena's timely appearance that night Jay would have died.

"Don't take it so badly," she tells me. "These things happen. The boy's all right."

"No thanks to me."

"Philip, we all miss things, we all make mistakes."

We are standing at the nurses' station on the ward. Karla is sitting there to write up her daily reports and Ellie is standing by to do a chest x-ray. Rose emerges from the stock room behind us and says, "You know, we've got through a hell of a lot of dressings this last two weeks. I don't understand where they've all disappeared."

I daren't catch Karla's eye but I look to see if Ellie responds. We all know whose little black book might collect such suspicious information.

All this is making me jaded and edgy. I desperately need a break, but I have postponed my holiday to fit in with Karla getting time off. It seems unbearable to wait that long, I want to go away with her now.

Meanwhile I have to get through another working day, and

there is nothing more unrewarding here than the diabetic clinic. Half of them don't turn up, and those that do seem to feel it is a little ritual to be endured to keep doctor happy. It is part of the strange process of western medicine in which ever more drugs (aspirin, atorvastatin, ramipril, atenolol, amlodipine, metformin, glipizide, rosiglitazone…) are dispensed at enormous cost, with no perceived benefit, to prolong a disease process which will kill their recipients just the same.

But they don't like to offend, just as they don't like to ask how many millions of dollars the directors of UP or Pepsi or Glaxo SKB are making from their demise, or how much "research" is driven by these pharmaceutical monsters. If they are aware of any bigger picture than their mouldering feet they don't tell me. I am still not sure whether this is due to a benign innate compliance or to a learned fear of the white man and his establishments. They don't say and I don't ask.

"How are you doing, Myrtle?"

"Fine."

"Have you been checking your glucose?"

"Yuh."

"So how are the readings?"

"Fine."

"Did you bring your diary?"

"No, I forgot."

"So what have the readings been?"

"Aahhdno. Between seven and nine."

This is what they all say. Word has got round that the doctor won't believe a result less than seven, and anything in double figures will result in a lecture about the horrible complications they're going to get anyway and a prescription for yet another drug. Better to play safe and claim between seven and nine.

Then there is the nonsense of testing their feet. The rationale behind this is that identifying subtle loss of sensation in good time will trigger an improvement in diabetic control and prevent further nerve damage with its resultant numbness, trauma and infected ulcers which never heal. Early interventions like this

160

should prevent the misery of osteomyelitis or an amputated toe or foot or leg.

That's the theory. This is the practice:

"Myrtle, I want you to lie down on the couch."

"On the what?"

"The couch—sorry! I mean the table, the bed."

It takes an age for her to remove her shoes and clamber her bulk across the room and lie herself down. She grips the sides of the couch and holds her head tautly up as if complete submission to the horizontal might kill her. Her anxiety fuels my anxiety that indeed it might.

"Okay. Now close your eyes and tell me whenever you feel anything touch your feet." I prod them in various prescribed places with the Zimmensteil-Grøen 10G monofilament, or whatever its technical name is (a bit of fishing line embedded in plastic, $35 each from PharmaCorp). She does not respond. "Didn't you feel anything?"

"Yuh."

"But I want you tell me each time I do it."

"Okay."

I test her again and she does not answer. "Did you not feel that?"

"Yuh, I felt that."

Dear God. I repeat the instructions and jab her foot lightly, once.

"Yuh," she says.

Alleluia. I touch another point.

"Yuh."

Then I stand back, holding my little implement behind me.

"Yuh…" she says. "Yuh…yuh…yuh…"

And it occurs to me that this is not simply a case of an old woman being stupid. We have sucked her into a game she does not want to play, a sulky child forced to endure Monopoly on Christmas Day. Clinical trials on the implications of good glycaemic control are as meaningless to her as smoke signals would be to me. Talks on empowerment are all very well at

Tregaskis Patients' Group meetings—but here? How confused we have made them. Maybe the snow gods and the Northern Lights carry more influence than my keenness to prescribe more drugs. Their attitude is not so much denial as simply being resigned to their fate. Perhaps these reservations should be called Indian resignations.

So it is a long and unfulfilling afternoon. The last patient is Janet Bell, a stout woman in her fifties who irritates me from the second she struts into the room.

"Never mind my diabetes, can you refer me to my dermatologist?"

"Why?"

She pulls down the neck of her jumper to reveal a crop of tiny warts.

I inspect them and tell her, "They're perfectly harmless. But if you want them removed I could do that for you here."

"I'd rather see my dermatologist."

"But there's no need, it's very straightforward to remove them with some liquid nitrogen."

"My dermatologist said if I ever have any skin problem I was worried about, I was to be sent back to him straight away."

I sigh with the recognition of this common scenario. She wants a trip to Winnipeg, and if she has been referred for a five-minute clinic appointment there, the magic travel warrant will ensure a free return flight. Although I can understand this cultivation of illness as a means of escape, both physically and emotionally, I also know that millions of dollars a year of public money are squandered on such journeys, and I feel I have some small responsibility to protect the public purse. I repeat my offer to relieve her of the offending lesions.

"So you're not gonna refer me?"

"No, madam, I am not."

She stands, and heads to the door with an indignant bustle. "Well, you just wait till my husband hears about this." I say nothing as I have the feeling she is going to enlighten me anyway. "My husband happens to be the Chief."

"Could you explain what difference that makes?" I ask, but she flounces out, leaving me to guess her muttered reply.


As soon as I get back to the house I am cheered by Karla's arrival. "Come on, we're taking you out."

"We?"

"Me and Alex."

"Out?"

"Out fishing."

"Fishing? I don't think so!"

I explain to her, as I have to every dumbfounded male I've met since I've been here, that I can't stand fishing. I hate the protracted tedium of standing in one place or sitting in a bobbing boat for hours on end, and I hate even more the prospect of grabbing, unhooking and killing them, then slicing their cold sloppy guts into a stinking bucket. Eating them is fine, but I prefer to leave the distasteful preparatory stuff to someone else. I don't like bowel surgery, gardening, car mechanics or fishing. I prefer not to dirty my hands.

"But Alex wanted to take you. And I was hoping you would." When she has that disappointed look in her brown eyes I want to soothe it away instantly. But this time I can't achieve it by holding her close in my protective arms, instead I have to go fucking fishing.

"Why?"

She drops onto the edge of the settee, so I sit next to her. "I'm worried about him, Philip. He spends a lot of time visiting Marshall lately. I've never minded that, I've let them see each other whenever they like, though you can imagine Marshall hasn't exactly been a rock all these years. But he's at a very impressionable age now, and at home it's normally just me and Mom and Evelyn. Marshall and Wilson are the only adult males he really knows and—well, sometimes I think he should have a more positive example to follow. It's not very good for him to be cooped up in that shit hole with those two, especially when you consider the circumstances."

"And he's all in favour of this bonding excursion with me?" He may be Karla's son, but in my company he's always been as staunchly mute as any other kid on the reserve.

"Of course he isn't. He only agreed because I told him you were dead keen to learn how to catch some pickerel."

"Thanks." For the first time it really dawns on me that our relationship has implications for Alex. And I realise that Karla might have entertained the possibility of me being more than someone who is passing through. This thrills and scares me equally, for I had assumed—because I thought she had assumed—that my return home would close this short chapter of our lives. "Karla?"

"Where do you think all this will end?"

"All what?"

"Me and you, of course."

"Why worry about that, why not just enjoy one day at a time? Why not come and try some fishing? You might even like it." With that she gets up and leaves, and I have to run to catch her as she dashes laughing to the car.

I say hello to Alex and he offers his gruntings in return. We head south to Jewel Falls, which Karla assures me is just the prettiest spot around here. It turns out little different to anywhere else I have seen, the "falls" are simply a collection of rocks at a narrow point of the river, causing a little turbulence in the slow flow. Karla gives me one of the two rods, propels me to stand on the bank, and instructs Alex to instruct me what to do. I have a queasy fear that I will be expected to impale maggots or worms onto the hook, a further anxiety that I will lash the barb through my finger or my lip. Fortunately we have some inanimate glittery objects as bait. For ten minutes nothing happens, then, amazingly, my line jolts, so I gingerly turn the reel. "Quick!" Alex yells. "It'll get away!"

But for the first time in my life I have caught a fish, a pickerel at that. To Alex's amusement I recoil at its muscular flapping, but he rescues me from my squeamishness by grabbing it, freeing it from its hook, and securing it into a net he has rigged in the water to keep our catch alive. For a moment or less I can understand the attraction of all this, but of course this early success is a fluke. No matter how many times Alex shows me I cannot consistently get the simple co-ordination of releasing the catch on the line as I cast out. He flicks out his hook on a serious calculus curve to an intended spot well beyond midstream. My efforts plop feebly into the river a few feet in front of me, or worse, fail embarrassingly even to reach the water as I brake the line in mid air. When I eventually feel another pull on the rod I am too tentative to haul it in, and the fish squirms clear. Alex is not impressed. He catches five pickerel and a couple of jackfish, which he wants to reject back into the river. Karla tries to persuade him that, cooked properly, they make a decent meal ("Okay, they're a bit stringy, but you get used to them."). I stand there bored and useless, reflecting on the aptness of the jackfish being such an inferior catch.

Finally Karla frees me from my misery by calling me back to sit with her, and rewards my feeble attempts at blokemanship with a beer from her bag. We sit together, happy to say little, and Alex impresses me, makes me a little jealous, by engrossing himself for two solid hours in this rudimentary sporting pursuit.

The light fades and we head back, Alex proud of his catch. I expect Karla to drop me off at the hospital, but she says, "Come back and say hello to Mom."

"Are you sure?"

"Of course I'm sure, I wouldn't ask if I weren't. Don't you want to meet her?"

"Yes, I do—I just didn't mean it like that."

Their wooden house is a jumbled mish-mash of artefacts, the chaotic abode of people who have an aversion to throwing things out. There are, as far as I can see in the gloom, at least three sheds in the garden in varying states of disrepair. "Full of Dad's old stuff," Karla tells me. "Wilson keeps promising to sort it out, but I guess I'll end up doing it myself."

The living room is bare-floored and dominated by an old glass-fronted cabinet which contains an assortment of plates, jugs and dishes which first appears as English as any country cottage I have seen at home. Further inspection, though, reveals a collection of kitsch crockery, souvenirs from Moose Jaw, Flin Flon, and Thunder Bay. The curtains are patchy and thin. The walls are packed with family photos—the children in instalments of growing, Karla's graduation, her father proud and smiling in his boat. But I get the impression that he was the one who kept the house in order. Since his death I sense that upkeep of the place is now too much for them—Ruth being invalid, Wilson indolent, Evelyn incapable, and Karla indifferent to the clutter which surrounds them all. But these are the first people I have seen in their homes since I have been here, and I feel strangely privileged at this.

"Hi," says Karla's mum.

"Hi—"

"Ruth, you can call her Ruth," Karla tells me.

"Hi, Ruth."

Although I know she is of similar age to me, her hair is swept into a simple grey pony tail and she is already stooped with an early curving spine. She walks with a heavy arthritic limp but her face is young—a rare achievement here—and she seems pleased enough to see me. Despite her years of hardship she has, like Karla, questioning and potentially mischievous eyes. She offers the statutory coffee which has been idling in its jug all day, and catches my hesitation.

"You can have a beer if you prefer—Evelyn, go get him one of Wilson's beers."

Evelyn, lurking in the doorway, giggles at the audacity of this.

"Go on, Evey, Philip's a guest," Karla says. "And get one for me."

So we sit round the table and Ruth asks, "You staying for something to eat?"

"Oh, no thanks, I—"

"What do you mean, no thanks?" Karla demands. "Where else you going to eat?"

"Well, nowhere. I—I suppose I was being polite."

"Polite!" sneers Karla. "What's with this polite? It's an English thing, Mom—if your house is on fire and you're trapped on the top floor, the firefighters come and shout, 'Hey, we'll save your life if you jump into this blanket,' you have to reply, 'No, no, I don't want to put you to any trouble. You just carry on, old chap.' "

We laugh, and Evelyn smiles admiringly at her sister's wit. Presumably her mental limitations have freed her from the obligation to acquire the general grumpiness of the reserve. She draws her chair close to mine, clearly relishing the visit of this foreign guest. Alex comes in and mumbles to his mom.

"He wants to know if you'd like to help him prepare the fish," Karla tells me.

"No, thanks—and this time I'm not being polite."

"Oh, go on, show an interest—let him show you how it's done."

So, outside in the darkening yard, he wordlessly demonstrates a surprisingly elaborate ritual of slicing away scales, guts, gills, head and bones, with a slick whittling precision I cannot help but admire. He knows his fish anatomy and he is meticulous in his task. Finally he presents five pickerel, now white and dissected and looking invitingly edible, to Ruth. She washes them again and fries them into a simple crumbed coating, and their smell sizzles with anticipation across the room. The meal is presented simply, with potatoes but nothing green, and we gather round the table to enjoy it.

"Hey, this is really great," I say. "Thank you very much."

"Thank you for catching them," says Ruth. Karla and I laugh as Alex's look darts accusingly up.

"I really didn't contribute very much," I admit.

"Well, who cares? It's good to have you as a guest of the MacRae family," says Ruth.

I thank them again, then decide I should stop this spiral of thanking before risking another lecture on being polite. "So—" I say instead, "MacRae—does that mean you have some Scottish blood?"

Karla slams her fork onto the table and stares at me. I don't know what *faux pas* is in Cree, but I have clearly made a large one.

"Philip—do I look fucking Scottish?"

Evelyn giggles at her sister's choice of words, Alex stares and Ruth tuts, I feel, in sympathy with me. At least Wilson isn't here.

"No, I suppose not."

"Correct. That's because I'm not Scottish, I'm Cree."

"I know that, but—well, all the surnames here—MacPherson, Fraser—"

"Shit, Philip, how long have you been here?"

Ruth intervenes, calmly, to explain. "A hundred years ago the government sent agents up here to open schools, to try to educate us dumb Indians. They couldn't get their tongues round our names like Muminawatum and Karsakuwigamak, so they gave us nice easy names instead. You can guess where the agents came from."

I can indeed. "So why don't people change back to their traditional names?"

"A few have, I guess, but generally we don't get attached to the significance of names like you do. It doesn't matter too much what you're called, it's who you are and what you do that counts. But on the other hand some people carry their enforced names like a stigma, or a war wound—and some of them were really cruel, you know. If you look at the names across these reserves—Patchinose, Brightnose, Cutlip, Whiskey, Tobacco…there's even a family of Donkeys in London House, and that was all just the agents, you know—"

"Taking the piss," says Karla.

"Sure. So people keep those names to remind themselves of that abuse. Why should they change them? Why should they be ashamed? They didn't do anything wrong."

I suppose not. Ruth goes on to tell me, in an even voice, what life was like in Blackwater Lake, her residential school. She shows me a photo of it, snipped years later from a magazine, a great Victorian four-storey block imposing and incongruous on the flat landscape. The English school abroad. It is stark and Dickensian, and I try to imagine the daily horror of the hundreds of children herded into it in the name of patriotism and progress and God. I know from Karla that it is not something she likes to dwell on, but—like it or not as we sit round this plain table—our nations' history is staring us in the face. She answers the questions I am too polite to ask.

Which was worst—the beatings, the cold, or the lack of food? The lack of food.

Whose best friend ran away? Ruth's.

Whose body was found two weeks later frozen into a ditch? Ruth's best friend.

What was Ruth's punishment for speaking Cree? Being made to stand in the snow with no shoes.

So who got frostbite? Ruth.

What was the title of the man who sexually abused her? Reverend.

When did the Canadian government admit that residential schools were a failure? 1948.

So when was the last one finally closed? 1986.

Who publicly congratulated the Anglican Church in 1969 for its role in educating Indian children, particularly in residential schools? Jean Chrétien, our recently retired Prime Minister.

"But I knew I'd get back home one day. That was the only thing that kept me going, and of course when it finally happened it was a terrible disappointment. My mom had been really ill with a bad chest, and she'd died a few months before I got back. My dad had just disappeared—they said he was drowned in the lake, but I never found out for sure. So I lived with my aunt for a while, but it must have been real hard for them, she had six children of her own. It was bad enough trying to feed and clothe them without some other kid she hadn't seen for ten years suddenly turning up. And on top of that, the traditional ways had all gone, people seemed to have lost heart. I remember one year going to the powwow at London House. I was really looking forward to it because I thought it would help rediscover the part of my culture I'd lost, but it ended up as a massive party, everyone just got drunk.

"Anyways," she suddenly concludes, "why aren't your family here?"

Alex goes to occupy himself in the sheds outside, storing the fishing gear neat for the next trip. The rest of us sit in the dim light of the room, Evelyn attentive to my every word as I tell them about my daughters, my work and Cornish life. She is particularly thrilled to hear that I have a sister called Eve. "That's like my name!" she says more than once. Ruth shows courtesy and interest, and asks me about the weather, my home, what people wear, what the shops are like, and—most intriguing to her—the sea.

"I reckon we should all come and see it before we die," she says.

"Yes, you should," I say. "And you ought to see Scotland because, whatever you say about the names and the agents and all that, it's really wonderful. And there is an odd sort of similarity with here. I know here is dead flat and the Highlands are mountainous, but the population is very scattered in the Highlands, and the way of life doesn't really change. People build their houses here in the same way as Scottish crofts, they drink too much for their own good, and they leave their scrap cars outside their homes to rot for years."

"Yeah, I'd like to see Scotland," Karla says.

"Me too!" Evelyn exclaims. "I'll come!"

But Karla immediately deflates her excitement. "Hey, come on, it's a nice idea but I can't even afford to take you guys to Winnipeg, let alone Scotland."

And it is only with that remark that I fully realise how hard life is for Karla. She has a good job by the standards of the reserve, but she has to support these three other people, and no doubt Wilson pesters her for funds as well. Yet in this small dim room I feel the true kinship of a family, and I know this is a bond which has been lost to me for many a year, if not my entire life. When the old-fashioned clock gongs midnight, Karla offers to drive me home. I stand up, don jacket and shoes, and thank them for their hospitality. Ruth shakes my hand, Evelyn hugs me, and I really don't want to go.

A Sunday afternoon off, and I am at a loose end because Karla is at work. I am rescued by the doorbell and find that its ringer is Doug.

"Hi, Philip, I was wondering if you'd like to come for a walk."

A walk? With Doug? But walking seems such an unDouglike activity. "Yeah, good idea. Where to?"

"Anywhere, absolutely anywhere. I'll follow you."

"Okay—along the shore then?"

"No, no, we should drive somewhere first, somewhere we've not been before."

It is easier, I have discovered, to try not to analyse Doug's train of thought. "Whatever you say. Anyone else coming?"

"No. There was no reply from Donald, and Sharon said she was busy. I think I might have interrupted something—she seemed a bit flustered somehow. You don't think she and Donald are, you know—?"

"I've no idea, but you're the second person to ask me that."

Doug chats on as he drives away. A police car turns into the hospital as we leave, and I feel relieved not to be on call. I am halfway through my stint here, and I allow myself a little waft of satisfaction at my achievement. The work is still demanding, but, the scrape with Jay aside, I have coped. I am feeling more relaxed and able to appreciate time off with these good people like Donald and Doug. We pass the charred shell of Bartram's house, past the turn-off to the dump, and head towards the mine. Just before we reach it Doug stops the car and points to an overgrown track on our left.

"You ever been up there?"

"No."

"Me neither. Lead the way."

The path leads to a small clearing but there is no discernible route on from here. However Doug urges me to forge ahead through the mat of trees. Recalling my first day's experience I start to feel uneasy. "Doug, are you trying to get us lost?"

"Sure."

"Can I ask why?"

"Sure you can. Go ahead."

"Okay, why are you trying to get us lost?"

He flourishes from his pocket something resembling a small mobile phone. It proves to be a satellite tracking gadget which has recorded our every twist and turn. Excitedly he demonstrates, ten yards forward, then sixty degrees to the left, a squared figure of eight, an abrupt diversion to the right. Our every move is mirrored in its fiendish gizmo trace. After half an hour we decide to return, and Doug's confidence in his technology clearly exceeds mine. All I know is that we should keep the sun roughly behind us as we head back, and I envisage night falling about us while Doug peers frantically at his toy as it malfunctions us to death. "Maybe I should have checked the batteries," he would reflect.

O me of little faith! As my anxiety rises in this unlandmarked place, a small clearing appears. This leads easily back to the car, and Doug's satisfaction is complete.

"So the Cree and the Inuit don't have the monopoly on these magical powers," he says as we head back towards the town. "This thing is so accurate I could drive back without looking at the road."

"Not a good idea, Doug."

"No, really—" He waves his toy in front of me to prove his point. "Look—there's a left hand curve coming up—"

Suddenly the world capsizes. "Aarrgh!" we shout unimaginatively above the tumult of noise as we career into the roadside ditch. The car clouts my head, rock scrapes horribly against the side of the vehicle and we crunch to a halt. A welter of steam fizzes from the bonnet, the engine dies, and I am aware of a thundering great lump dripping something warm and sticky and wet from the vicinity of my right ear.

We sit there for a moment, still strapped in to the upended car. After the enormity of the crash the silence seems profound. "Are you okay?" Doug asks.

"I seem to have bashed my head. What about you?"

"On an analogue scale of global okayness from zero to ten, I estimate my present score as 3.139 recurring."

"Doug?"

"Yeah?"

"If—just suppose—you had a major head injury to the point where your brain processes were seriously scrambled—"

"Yeah?"

"Well, how would anyone know the difference?"

At the thought of this we both explode into laughter—the result, I guess, of shock, fright, relief and stupidity all compounded into one explosion, and we feed off each other's hilarity like schoolkids for several minutes. Then, as we finally subside into the sobriety our situation deserves, Brad's head appears before us at an angle of 120 degrees. How does he do that? Where is the ground? Which of us is upside down? Doug and I relapse into hysterics again.

"Jesus Christ!" says Brad. "What are you guys *on*?"

An ambulance is summoned (oh, the humiliation!) and by the time we reach the hospital my head hurts. It seems to have sprouted a head of its own but the bleeding has pretty much stopped. Karla is horrified to see me, though it is soon clear that I'm not too bad. She cleans me up, summons Lena to insert a couple of stitches, gives me some Tylenol Extra, and sends me on my way.

I take two painkillers, lie on my bed, and before I can worry too much about the risk of having an intra-cranial bleed, I am deeply asleep. As if reacting to my earlier frivolity, I have an unpleasant dream in which I am passenger in a speeding car, its unidentified driver hurling me round bends and through junctions with escalating recklessness. I am on a journey somewhere, but don't know why it's so urgent, where it will end. I am telling the driver to slow down, slow down—then there is an ominous banging noise, pain in my head.

Euh? The local anaesthetic is wearing off and my head pulsates with pain. But someone is knocking at the door, and as the afternoon's events crowd back into my muddled mind, I assume Karla has come to visit. Instead I find Sharon on the doorstep, looking distressed. Behind her is a policeman, one I have not seen before.

"Hi, Sharon, come in."

"Hi. This is—"

"Gus Riddoch, RCMP," he greets. He flashes his ID and follows her into the house.

"Hi, take a seat. You want a statement about this accident?"

"Accident?" asks Sharon, surprised.

"Well, yeah." I point to my bump. "It was nothing really, Doug just skidded into a ditch."

"Oh, I didn't know about that. Are you all right?"

"Just a couple of stitches and a bit shaken up. Isn't that why you're here?"

She sits on the edge of the settee, sighs, pauses, fidgets her fingers over her face. Officer Riddoch intervenes. "Doctor Cormack, can you give any explanation as to why significant quantities of narcotic drugs appear to have gone missing from your hospital pharmacy in recent weeks?"

# 1.12

I assure Officer Riddoch that I have never taken controlled drugs from the hospital for any reason, and have no idea who might be responsible for such a thing.

"Have you ever had any suspicions that any of your colleagues might be abusing meperidine?"

"Meperidine?" I have to search for the translation for a moment, that's pethidine. "No, absolutely not."

"And what about you?" he asks Sharon.

She appears genuinely bemused. "No, I really have no idea."

Surely to God, Karla can't have been so stupid as to acquire some for Marshall? But I remember how blasé she was about taking dressings from the ward, and imagine how manipulative he might be. He kept pestering for Tylenol Extras, and his leg must have been giving him severe pain.

I think I am being calm about this but Sharon asks, "Philip? Are you all right?"

"What?"

"Are you okay? You're a bit pale and sweaty."

I am aware of Riddoch scrutinising me in a policey sort of way, and feel sure he suspects something at once. "Am I? Must be this crack on the head. I think I need an early night."

"You'll be okay for work tomorrow?"

"Oh, yes, sure. Unless I wake up dead."

My nervous joke falls deservedly flat, and I instantly feel foolish and tinged with guilt. Riddoch gets up. "I'm sorry about your mishap, Doc, I hope you're better soon." Then, to Sharon, "Okay, who's next?"

"You've seen Lena, Doug was out—on to the nurses, I guess."

I wish them goodnight and imagine Riddoch jotting into his mental notebook: English Doc…seems a bit edgy…merits another visit, I think.

As soon as they have gone I rush to the phone to warn Karla. She is on duty for a further hour and I presume she will be the first person they see. I pick up the receiver then hesitate—my phone calls could be easily monitored, and me alerting Karla within milliseconds of Riddoch's departure would look incriminating. And what if the calls are tapped, would they be doing that? I don't know, for I have never in my life been in trouble with the police. No, that's not strictly true, I got stopped for speeding once on the A303 at Ilminster (or maybe it was Ilchester, I always get them mixed up) but fortunately the old stethoscope on the passenger seat wheeze worked a treat and the bobby let me off in exchange for a few words of advice about his tennis elbow. I had a TR6 at the time, a rather flash white one—

Cormack, get a grip! Perhaps it is the head injury, but my mental state is one or two notches short of panic. I am a law-abiding citizen, I have no place getting involved in arson, perjury, or theft of narcotics. This is all new to me, and I feel a vague suspicion that if I transgressed the law here, or was suspected thereof, the police would not be so gallant as my man on the A303. I feel I must warn Karla, but even now, while I have dithered, Riddoch is probably showing her his ID and noting that she, too, looks a bit on edge. Perhaps I could phone her on some other pretext, though I have no idea what. Before I know it, I am ringing emerg but it is engaged.

What I need is a drink. My decent wine and gin from Sharon's last Thompson trip didn't last long, but I remember the dregs of a barbecue a couple of weeks ago, Sharon left some cherry brandy (cherry brandy!!) in my cupboard. It tastes awful but it will do. While I savour its syrupy chemical punch the phone rings and I rush to pick it up.

"Karla?"

"Hello, Philip? Is that you?"

"Yes." There is something very odd about the voice because, it takes a second to realise, it is English. It is male and unfamiliar, and after three months in Jackfish Lake it sounds ridiculously plummy, as if it might belong to a 1950s' BBC newscaster or the toff in a Carry On film. It takes another few seconds of slow cerebration to realise that—oh, God!—that's how I must have sounded to the locals on my arrival here. "Who is that?"

"It's David here. David Kenning."

"Who?"

"David Kenning. You know—I, er, I'm living with Mary now."

Mary? I almost ask. Mary who? "Oh, right—it's NYK. Yes?"

He pauses a moment, understandably confused. I decide not to explain. "Yes—she asked me to phone you. She's in hospital, she's really not very well."

"What's the problem?"

"She broke her ankle while we were on holiday in Tuscany—just tripped down a couple of steps, you know—then when we got home she had a thrombosis and a pulmonary embolus. She was in intensive care for a couple of days, but she is improving, she's back on the ward."

"So what do you want me to do?"

"Hm? Well—nothing, but we thought you ought to know that she's been seriously ill. Obviously she'll be off work for a while, and the girls have been very concerned. She just asked me to let you know."

"That's all right, then," I tell him. "You've told me. But you're the main man now, so you can deal with it, can't you? I don't give a toss."

I feel I could go on—at some length—but I don't really want any involvement with David Fucking Kenning. Why didn't Beth or Stella let me know instead? I slam the phone down and pour myself another drink because this anxiety is still stifling my mind.

If Karla doesn't ring soon I'll wait until she's back home. I don't *really* think she'd be silly enough to steal pethidine, but—but Marshall Snape unnerves me, he could put her under lots of pressure. I take a further slug of cherry brandy, then chase that with one or two more. Then I realise how much my head throbs, so I take a couple more Tylenol Extras and lie down on the bed. The only thing which consoles me—in fact it makes me laugh aloud—is the knowledge that NYK sounds like a complete and utter twat.

The phone rings once more. My head hurts. For a moment the two experiences are inseparable, they merge into a grating clatter I desperately want to end.

"Heurrh?"

"Philip? It's Sharon. How are you?"

"Heurrh. Not good. Headache."

"I'm sorry to disturb you, but we have a bit of a problem over here. Could you come to my office when you're ready?"

"Heurrh." I manage to focus on the clock. Nine-fifteen. I must have had two or three hours of really dense sleep, and now I feel that only parts of my brain have been wrenched from it. My initial thought is please oh please don't tell me that Lena is planning to leave. "What's up?"

"I'd rather not say on the phone. It's about the problem we saw you about last night."

"Okay." I put the phone down and wonder why I am groggy and uneasy like this. It all takes several minutes to come back. The accident…Mary in hospital…the missing drugs…the visit from the police—whoa, **last night**?! Did Sharon say **last night**? My hand reflexly feels my head, and the bump is still there with the stitches scabbed stickily into my scalp. Have I been unconscious? Do I need a scan? Then I stagger to the kitchen and see the packet of painkillers and the empty bottle of cherry brandy. Jesus, how could I have been so stupid? I open the curtains and the morning sun is indeed directly across the lake. Then another panic—Karla! Why didn't she contact me last night? I rush to the phone and Ruth answers. No, she ain't here, she had to go out, she seemed a bit distressed. And no, she don't know where she's gone.

As I get dressed I have the urge to drive off in Sharon's car to Marshall's little hovel. But—even if I find Karla there, then what? It would only add to our incrimination. Instead I try to clean myself up, though this does nothing to help my head. It seems to take an awfully long time to do everyday things like dress and wash and affix shoes to the correct feet, but eventually I stumble into Sharon's office to find her visibly anxious, Riddoch stone-faced at her side. Presumably he wants to see if I am any less shifty than yesterday, and he wouldn't need the benefit of an advanced detectiving course to put that down as a no.

"Hi, Sharon. Good morning, officer."

He nods curtly, she says, "Philip, we have a problem in that we have no access to the pharmacy today."

"Why?"

"Because the police are investigating it."

"How can we run a hospital without a pharmacy?" I ask.

Riddoch intervenes by handing me a prescription in the name of Jay Moose for five meperidine injections. It appears to have been issued by me. "Is that your signature, doctor?"

I inspect it closely and hope my hand conceals its urge to shake. "Well, yes—hang on, no I don't believe it is. I think someone must have forged it."

"What about this?" He hands me a further prescription, this time in the late Billy Schenk's name, then one for Marion Ross.

"No. I didn't write them."

"How can you be so sure?"

This is, I have to concede, a fair question, for the mark of Dr P A Cormack has deteriorated into little more than a rushed flourish, what with so many demands on it over the years to authenticate repeat prescriptions, pathology forms and sick certificates, letters to expedite appointments and request anything from urgent rehousing to the provision of elastic tights or stairlifts or plastic mattresses or lumbar corsets or NHS wigs or protein drinks or the plea to excuse Verity from PE this week because her tummy aches are really really bad. Those fractions of a second saved add up to several zillion over twenty-five years. "I—well, I know for a fact that I haven't written a prescription for five meperidine injections since I've been here. Not for those people or anyone else."

"Are you sure about that?"

"Yes."

"But that could still be your signature? You might have signed a blank prescription?"

"Um—no, I don't think so."

"But you're not absolutely certain?"

"Um—no. I think they're very good forgeries."

"Do you have any idea who might have written these?"

"No."

"Thank you for your assistance, Dr Cormack, that will be all for now."

I leave the room, unsettled by the way he said that. Was it heavy with respect or irony? Does he suspect something I don't know?

Around the nurses' station everyone is discussing the crisis.

"Where the fuck are we supposed to get drugs from when our cupboard's empty?"

"Aahhdno. But Sharon says pharmacy's a no-go area until the police have finished going through the books."

"Hi, Philip. What's going on?"

"I've no idea."

"Hey, I hear you had a little adventure with Doug. How's your head?"

"Not good. Listen, does anyone know where Karla is?"

Nobody does. She's off until Thursday now, and much as I would like to drive off to find her, I can't. I am on call.

"Lena's gone to bed, she was up most of the night," Edna informs me. "She said to let you know there's a fifteen-year-old primip in labour."

"What! What the hell is she doing here? Why isn't she in Winnipeg?"

"Only found out she was pregnant two hours ago. Thought she had a build-up of gas."

Shit, this is all I need. I really don't want to be in this place any more. I am an ageing, unadventurous, semi-alcoholic, semi-divorced failing doctor. From now on—let's forget this nonsense idea of a challenging sabbatical—all I want is the Quiet Life. With a capital Q and capital L.

The morning is fairly routine but for the squeals of the labouring schoolkid, who has unfortunately progressed too far to risk transfer to the city. My anxiety settings are on red once more, though it is a consolation to know that in the event of my obstetric skills falling short I could always call upon Lena to help. By lunchtime (Cree breakfast time) my headache is wearing off and I head back to the house to eat.

Ten minutes later there is someone at my door.

"Karla!"

"Philip—how are you?"

"I was about to ask you that, I've been really worried—"

She flings herself into my arms and I think for a moment she is going to cry. "I'm sorry I didn't call you to see how you were last night, especially with the police and all, but I had a problem—"

"Is this all to do with Marshall?"

"Yeah, he came round to the house and gave me a real hard time."

"But why? You've been helping him."

"I know, but he was mad—well, it's all about you."

"Me? Why?"

"Because he's jealous, that's why. He still has feelings for me, and—well, it's a big issue for him that you're white. He was drunk and I was worried that he might try to find you, so I just had to keep him talking and drinking until he more or less passed out."

"Christ! So where is he now?"

"I don't know. He seems to have disappeared."

Oh hell. Adding the threat of grievous bodily harm to my list of worries is all I need. I have a fleeting picture of myself in receipt of a flashing knife wound, up under the ribs and nicking the heart, the ignominy of being Medevacced out, surgeons and police in wait. "Karla, I hate to ask you this, but—about the police—oh, shit!" I shout as the phone interrupts.

"Hi, Philip, it's Edna. You gonna come and pull this baby out?"

"What, now?"

"Well, I could ask her to hold on to it until you finish eating, but it looks pretty imminent to me."

"Oh, shit!" I confirm.

"You're welcome," she says. "See you soon."

"Sorry, Karla, I have to go and deliver this baby."

"You trying to avoid me or something? That excuse is wearing a little thin."

In the labour room the family support has amassed, flabby women in their thirties with their obligatory hair (invariably long, black and straight, but customised by an ornate frontal tuft or severely cropped fringe to distinguish them from their peers) and effete black jackets proclaiming the family name, MOOSE, or in one instance, MOO F. They seem very excited by this unheralded addition to their ranks, though I rather suspect they must have guessed. ("Hey, Lindy, why you taken to wearin them baggy clothes all the time? You tryin a hide somethin?" A grunt of denial in reply.) To be fair, little Miss Moose is making a damn good job of propelling the baby's head from between her legs, and I scrub into gown and gloves, praying to whatever gods govern such occasions that my services are not required. Sure enough I have to perform only the minimum show of basic midwifery as a modest-sized girl slithers out in a chorus of blood and liquor, screams and squeals.

"Oh, she's lovely!" the unexpectant mother sobs.

"What you gonna call her?" Edna asks.

"Cinderella," she replies.

After that a steady trickle of dross prevents me from contacting Karla. By now everyone knows about the police and the missing

182

drugs, and although rumours abound, nobody has any firm clues. Ellie points out that this problem has only come to light since Lena arrived, but I say that nobody really knows how long it's been going on.

"Since you arrived then," Edna suggests.

Bertha arrives, off duty, to see what is happening.

"Usual kind of day—raided by the cops, no pharmacy, and another concealed teenage pregnancy," Edna tells her.

"So I heard. How's the baby?" Bertha wants to know.

"Fine. Nice little girl," I tell her. "Though Cinderella Moose sounds more like a hair gel than a baby to me."

My quip falls on silence, and Bertha glares. "That happens to be my niece," she says.

Oh double shit. Well done, that man. "I'm sorry, Bertha—"

Then the phone rings and Edna answers, "Sure, he's standing right here, I'll send him along." She replaces the phone and says, "This Riddoch guy wants to see you in Sharon's office. So it is you after all!"

I go straight there. Sharon is seated at her desk in a state best described as silent hysterics. She tries to stifle blubs and shrieks into her hands, which still fail to disguise the fact that her face is bloated and blotched. Riddoch stands behind her, a hand tentative on her shoulder, and for a moment I think she is under arrest. He indicates me to sit.

"What's the matter?"

"You want me to tell him?" Riddoch asks her.

She manages, between spasms of heaving weeps, to nod her head.

Riddoch faces me but looks to the floor. "The body of a man believed to be Donald Medev, your pharmacist, has been found in his car near Jewel Falls. He appears to have taken his own life. We also believe he has been unlawfully acquiring narcotics, and abusing them, from numerous hospitals in the country over the last three years."

"Oh, my God!" I get up to comfort Sharon, kneel to embrace her shaking bulk. She turns to cling to me, burying her head in my neck. "Sharon, I'm so sorry."

I wonder if there was indeed anything going on between them, and I have the odd feeling that she is wanting me to ask. But no, of course this is not the time. She cries and I feel a hot and sickening pain myself. I remember rejecting him the other day when he was so in need of a friend, and all the other slights and rebuffs in the past. If only I had had more time for him, not let myself be distracted by Karla or by work. I think of the invitation to accompany him on his November tour of the north, and now, despairingly too late, I can picture us motoring the snowy roads of Alberta, resting at barely chartered settlements, staying at out of season motels, stopping to photograph the formation of silent birds or to absorb the low sun as it picks out white skylines with a clarity which would have lifted our hearts.

If only we had got there—if only I had agreed to go—I feel he would still be alive.

Karla's grip tightens into my hand as the drunk meanders past. I know what she is thinking—if he spots her with me he will approach her with a rambling invective about being a traitor to their race. But she does not flinch away, she keeps an alert eye on him, braced like a cat. What would I do if he stumbles into aggression with us? Punch him on the nose? Run away? Try to soothe him with some mellow Shahbn diplomacy ("Look here, old chap, let's not make a scene...")? I really do not know.

Certainly we would not expect any assistance from members of the surrounding public. If this man's intention is to stun them into shuffling embarrassment, he succeeds. Every last one of them is wishing him to evaporate into space so their leisurely Sunday can be resumed without such a blatant reminder of this virus which plagues their country. Their thought waves unite around us—Christ, you try giving them special treatment, all that welfare, you try keeping them out of harm's way, you really think the only solution is...

He has a plastic carrier bag in one hand, a can of beer in the other. He wears a Budweiser cap. "S'right, I'm jus another drunken fuckin native, tryin a find somewhere a sit down in my own fuckin country. Yeah, I'll jus sit down here if s'alright with you—" Then, as the horrified middle-aged couple—him lemon polo-shirted, his wife with the peak of a sun visor elasticated round her permed head, and pleated shorts hoicked over a bulging swimming costume—scrabble up their belongings and head away, he calls after them, "Hey, s'okay, I'm clean, y'know, I may be an Indian but I know how to wash my ass."

But instead of sitting he lurches on. People look round slyly, and, as their eyes fall on Karla and wonder whether to incriminate her for this spectacle ("But she's pretty, she's with a white guy…"), we can see the fleeting expressions of fear. Where are the Goddam police when you need them most?

Yet in many ways we have found Vancouver to be a wonderful city, as cosmopolitan and relaxed as any you could wish to find. This is Pacific Canada, so Chinese and Japanese abound, and there seems to be no separateness about them. They are all constituents of the country's great mixture—Orientals, Europeans, students, tourists, the elderly, the gay. All these nations are represented here, but only one, the First one, stands alienated from the rest.

The drunk moves on, people tut and try once more to relax. But even the simple act of lying on a summer city beach seems too organised and restrained. Felled tree trunks are laid out on the sand, parallel to the gently sploshing curve of the sea's edge and precisely spaced, so families and couples can recline against them and—more important!—stake out their claim of sand. Even in this most liberal part of the country, it seems, an innate tarpiness breaks through.

So far we have had four days here, exploring the sights of Stanley Park, Gas Town, the shops, the bars and the art galleries. We have eaten out on Japanese and Mexican, we have supped *cappuccino* and *cafe latte* on leisurely terraces, we have bought clothes and books and gifts. Tomorrow we are hiring a car for a tour of Vancouver Island. But for tonight we sprawl ourselves and our belongings across this luxury hotel room. Decadent, I know, but we are drinking sparkling wine in the luxury of our hot scented bath.

"Philip, can I ask you a question?"

"Sure."

"Will you answer honestly?"

"Yes."

"Do you promise?"

"I promise."

"Okay. Are you trying to impress me with all this?"

I lie back to consider, not wishing to lighten the gravity with an unconsidered yes or no. Even so, she laughs.

"What's so funny?"

"You have big blob of suds on your head." She reaches forward to flick them away and I cannot resist a reflex fondle of her breasts. She kisses me and leans back. "Answer the question," she says.

"Do you mean, 'Am I lavishing you with material treats in the hope it makes you think what a great guy I am?'?"

"Pretty much, yeah."

"Then no."

"That's good to know," she says. Then, with her eyes suddenly sharpened at me, and an undertone of calm menace in her voice, "Because if I ever thought you were trying to buy my affection, that would be the worst insult you could hit me with. Not only would I never speak to you again, I would hate you for it as long as I lived. Do you understand that?"

"Yes, I do." And I hope my answers are right. I hope I have answered truthfully, one hundred per cent, from the bottom of my soul.

We mooch on the bed, go through the actions of packing, though completing this task will take no more than ten minutes tomorrow. I flit through the tv channels, ever hopeful of an update on the Fourth Test. Instead there is tennis, athletics, hockey, basketball and Australian football. For a moment this intrigues me, as an accident would, for I swear it is the most gruesome and messy game ever invented by man. They play on a pitch the size of Sheffield and launch into a random mêlée of kicking, hurling, scrumming and sub-lethal tackles.

"Look at that!" I exclaim, appalled. "It's awful, no aesthetics to it at all. And those vests they wear! What a thoroughly ugly game!"

187

Karla considers it. "Looks kind of exciting to me. And wow! Look at the muscles on that big blond guy!"

I change programme quickly, and she dives onto me in a quest for the remote control. She likes these physical jousts, I am discovering, and tells me that when she was young she used to wrestle with Wilson all the time. This faintly disturbs me, makes me jealous, for I cannot picture Wilson as anything but a sulky, shabby, and slightly undernourished young man. Certainly the thought of any contact with Eve used to repel me and break me into boyhood sweats. Even the touching of my girlfriends got filed into certain permissible situations (cramped in-car snogs with Jacqui, bathed in a horsey smell; holding hands when walking out; the overpowering intimacy of sex, the retreat afterwards to apologise for having encroached) and—only *now* does it occur to me that these habits were maintained with Mary, both in and out of the marital bed. A stiff and stuffy husband for all those years. Here I am, fifty-one next month, finally discovering the fun and erotic undertones of a damn good romp.

Karla sits bare-legged on my chest, trying to pin my wrists to the bed. She is unexpectedly strong, her hair is ruffled wild, eyes dark with determination. I could, with my greater weight, thrust her off, but she catches me by surprise, tweaks a tickling finger under my ribs.

"Stop!" I shriek with tortured laughter. "Aarrgh! Stop! You win!"

She flashes her prize at the television, and although she cannot retrieve the Aussie hunk, ninety-three other channels panorama by—cop programmes, chat shows, news, Yankee sport, more cops, more shooting, punchy rappers, and films elongating a threadbare plot but inevitably featuring a handsome unassuming hero with a glossy wife and an unspeakably precocious kid with a voice like a duck on helium. One third of what we catch in this random sample are commercials, claims for achieving a happier life and spiritual fulfilment by way of better washing powder, bigger DIY stores, sexier aftershave, more absorbent diapers, slushier music, sleeker cars. After ten or fifteen minutes she turns it off and asks, "So did you notice anything about all of that?"

"Still no cricket."

"Anything else?"

"Yes, it was all crap."

"Anything else?"

"Aahhdno, you tell me."

"How many people have we seen on that selection of Canadian prime time tv?"

"Loads. Three hundred perhaps? Five hundred?"

"Okay. And how many of them were aboriginal?"

"None that I remember."

"Correct. None."

I sigh. One minute we are enjoying a robust parasexual knockabout, and the next she reverts to her serious single subject sociological comment. "I know, but—"

"But nothing, Philip. Okay, it's just a random few minutes of shit, but that's how it is on every channel, every night. They make a big fuss because a black guy finally gets to appear on Friends, but there's no way in the next thousand years you'll ever see an aboriginal. I'm sorry to burden you with that observation, I'm sorry if it disturbs your pleasant day, but it's something we have to live with. Its in our consciousness—my consciousness—all the time, and you'll have to accept that if you want any sort of relationship with me. According to our own media, we don't exist except as the bad guy in the westerns or the drunk on the local news. We just don't exist, we've been airbrushed out so you white folk don't feel uncomfortable. It's televisual genocide, is what it is."


The next day is bright, warm and sunny. We collect our hire car and set off for the ferry, whose meandering passage through the flotilla of islands is breathtaking. Karla says its the most beautiful place she's ever seen. We lounge on deck, our fingers interlinked or mine caressing her sunned neck or hers creeping naughtily into my back pocket, all the time exhilarated and absorbed by the view.

189

Victoria is predictably British, but we do not stay, for we want to head west to the Pacific to see where the continent ends. After a lifetime of land, Karla is besotted with the sea. Meanwhile I am enthralled by the possibilities of the map, and am surprised to see that the reserves around here are not confined to remote unwanted territories, but nestle between the island's green and civilised towns. Pauquachin. Tsartlip. Esquimalt. Tsawout. At least their inhabitants don't suffer the blight of isolation, at least they can get a half-hour bus to the city, they can lie on a beach in the sun.

"What tribes are they?" I ask Karla.

"Aahhdno. Apache or Cherokee probably. Maybe Spokane."

I am a little surprised at her indifference. I had assumed she carried a mental atlas of other aboriginals' whereabouts, their history and geography wedded into the culture of her own.

"Do you want to visit any of these places?" I ask.

She looks at me astounded and wounded at the same time. "Sure. I'll just go and knock on a few doors and say, 'Hi there, everybody, I'm Karla, I'm a Cree!' And while I'm doing that you could try the houses down this street here and see if there are any English people around. You might even find somebody from good old Shahbn."

"Okay, I'm sorry, it was a stupid remark." I slump back against the bench we have found to rest on, Pacamac the social dunce.

But Karla looks to me and smiles. "Thank you, Philip," she says.

"For what?"

"For offering." She kisses my cheek and squeezes me to her as hard as she has ever done before.


And so the two weeks go. We drive across the island, stopping often to pay homage to red magnificent trees. Their grandeur humbles me, but also makes me fearful for them. I know that British Columbia is being shorn of them, huge mountainsides to the north are being hacked bare, logging towns thrive on their reduction to paper and pulp. We stand for a few brief moments in this great arboreal oasis, knowing even this is threatened for the sake of some short-term gain—magazines, coffee tables and kitchen units which the world must have today.

Then, on the coast, we recline on reclusive beaches, their sand clean, their sea clear. On the last day we take a boat trip to spot whales, and we see them, we watch them arching their great sleek bulks from the sea. They parade before us and leave us in awe. Underpinning this great privilege, though, there is again a small nucleus of pain. How fragile they are for all their mass, how tenuous their hold on man's sea. What will their future bring?

But despite this awareness of the frailty of all things—no, *because* of this realisation—I am suddenly overwhelmed by the importance of now. What matters is me, here, on this bumpy boat with Karla. Now.

On deck we relax into the warm wind, heading back to Tofino. She sits against the rail of this dumpy little tub, eyes closed as the wind skims through her hair. Her face seems utterly relaxed, although it scrunches into a slight frown when someone stands up to cast her into momentary shade. At that precise moment I decide I am in love.

Why then? The twitch of her nose? Her indignation at someone stealing her sun? Realising the transience of our lives? All of that, for sure, but also I feel I am discovering a new Karla here. Freed from the daily hardships of reserve life, she is vibrant, gorgeous and relaxed. Yes, she bears her hardship well, but what does a future in Jackfish Lake have to offer her? I, on the other hand, have money and comforts, and I want to share them with her and I want to show her the outside world. Which is not buying her affection, I feel sure.

# 1.14

Despite my love for Karla (I have declared it, too, on the last evening of our holiday, sitting on one of the regimented sun-and-surf-bleached logs to watch the English Bay sunset. I thought it romantic, but it may just have been predictable and corny. "You're very sweet," she said.), returning to Jackfish Lake is hard. Everyone asks if we had a good time, for yes, our relationship is public now. I can almost imagine it being transmitted on the waves of Radio JFL, "Charlene Weiss has a satellite dish for sale, phone 8115…Karla MacRae and that English doctor are back from their holidays on the six o'clock flight…Robert MacDonald, go home to your mom…"

On Monday morning I call into Sharon's office. She looks tired and subdued, and seems to have put on weight. "Hi, Philip, welcome back. How was your trip?"

"Good, thanks. How are you?"

"Um, not bad." Our eyes meet and she amends this to, "No, actually I feel like shit."

"I'm really sorry…"

"It's not your fault, Philip. It's—well, Doug and I went to Donald's funeral, and you know there were only six people there. The two of us, a brother from Toronto, and three neighbours from back in Brandon. It just makes me feel awful that he was so lonely and so troubled, and none of us recognised that. And I should have kept a check on the pharmacy supplies, I should have picked up how much meperidine he was ordering. If I'd done that, maybe we could have got him some help."

I sit at the chair by her desk, incriminated myself. "You can't blame yourself, Sharon, you trusted him, we all did. And you were a good friend to him."

"He suddenly started to come and talk to me, tell me about his wife and son..." Now she bursts into tears again, great gushings and howlings of them, and, suffused with secondary guilt, I take on my comforter role once more.


After the culture and civilisation of Vancouver and the natural beauty which surrounds it, the reserve seems dirtier and more depressing than ever. Walking over to the hospital to assess the evening's minor ailments and injuries, I pass their owners loitering as ever outside the door. Every one of them is smoking, and despite the rubbish bin provided, the ground around them is strewn with fag ends, chip and chocolate wrappers, and pincered Pepsi cans.

"For Christ's sake!" I snap. "I thought you people were supposed to have a respect for the land."

I am met, of course, by the usual inscrutable stares. For a second I worry that Marshall Snape might be among them with a stealthy knife about his person, but as far as I can see he is not. It briefly troubles me that I am so irritable, fresh back from my holiday. I am supposed to be in love.

But Edna is on duty, and this cheers me up. "Philip, welcome back!"

"Thank you."

"So did you have lots of sex?"

"Edna!"

"Well, that's what everyone wants to know. Never mind all this 'Did you have a nice time? How were the art galleries?' crap."

"Actually, the art galleries were very good. There was a joint exhibition of Emily Carr, Frida Kahlo and Georgia O'Keefe. Some of her flower paintings are just amazing."

The names clearly mean nothing to her, and there is no reason why they should. I didn't intend to sound superior or name-

193

droppy, and anyway how much have I learned about leading figures in aboriginal culture or art since I've been in Jackfish Lake? It is hardly surprising that cerebral and aesthetic functions do not blossom here, for it is as much as one can do to keep warm, exchange some daily contact with one's neighbour, go to church, listen to the radio, play bingo, and try not to worry about being struck down by diabetes or a stroke.

"Maslow's hierarchy of needs," I recall from some distant residue of memory.

"Hey, now, don't you get ontological with me!" Edna objects. "And you didn't answer my question."

I evade it again and she goes on to present me with a run-down of news I have missed:

"We had a baby with meningitis—shit, that was a sick kid, but Lena was on the ball, filled it with penicillin, Medevacced it straight out...

"Oh, and Lena had a fight with the chief's wife. She wanted a free ride out for some clinic appointment, but Lena stood her ground...

"And the band want to buy up all the empty houses. They figure they're worthless anyway, so they can put in an offer of next to nothing to the mine...

"Remember Calvin Beardy, the guy whose face you stitched up? The one who stabbed Johnny Moose's nephew? Well, he's locked up, but Johnny damn nearly killed his son—fractured his skull, another Medevac, gee, Lena was busy last weekend. Johnny's disappeared, of course, in Winnipeg, I guess...

"We've got a pharmacist coming tomorrow, it's been desperate without one. The Pharmacists Society or whatever they are said we'd have to close the hospital, but we managed with Rose and that stupid dispenser who works there—all illegal, of course...

"Sharon's taking this business with Donald real bad. You know, it's terrible to say this, but I wasn't completely surprised. I know it was awful, what happened to his wife and boy, but sometimes I'd go down to pharmacy and he'd be there, not quite with it, you know. He's not the first to come up here with a load of baggage, though. Did you ever hear about the Newfie pathologist we had? He was some kind of pervert, tried to suffocate a student nurse while they were at it, got himself arrested in the end..."

Suddenly I yearn for Cornwall, for the safe and stuffy comfort of my study, the camaraderie of the Dog and Pheasant, the perfectly rolled green of the cricket pitch on a Sunday afternoon, the homely streets of Truro, its bookshops, the coastal path at St Anthony's Head. Even the prospect of work there doesn't seem so bad.


In the evening, at the first slackening of work, I phone Karla and say, "I want to see you."

"When?"

"Now. As soon as I can. Any time. All of the time."

I imagine her face creasing into her laugh. "I was just going out with Alex to see Lorraine."

"Oh, all right."

"Come on, Philip, I haven't seen him for two weeks. And you're on call."

"Yes, I know, but—"

"But what?"

"But I wanted to see you, that's all."

She laughs again. "I'll come round tomorrow evening, about six."

Before I can say anything more, let alone how much I love her, she is gone. So now I start wondering if she takes this seriously. She has had her luxury holiday, so is that it? I hope not, but why shouldn't she take advantage of me? Why shouldn't she milk this rich white man for all she can get and score a few points for the Cree? She has never misled me, promised me her future or anything like that. So why can't I enjoy each day, make the most of this venture—the challenging work, the different culture, a relationship with a woman twenty years younger than me—and stop torturing myself with the future?

Suddenly it occurs to me that this sabbatical isn't just about experiencing and working in a different environment for a few passing months, it's about me, and how I am to cope with the next instalment of my life. If I am dissatisfied (and for some impalpable reason I am) is that the fault of Jackfish Lake? Isn't the point of this exercise to discover something about *me*? I should be learning something here, but I can't quite see where the lesson lies. But I do know that learning must involve repairing and making amends, and some emotional reflex lures me to my desk, the address book in its drawer, then the phone.

"Hello?"

Damn. A deep male grunt, disturbed from sleep. Perhaps I'll cut my losses and ask if Irvine's there.

"Oh, hi," I say, as cheerily as I can. "Is that you, Giles?"

"Yeah," without recognition in his tone.

"Hi, it's me, Philip. Is Eve there?"

There is an unduly long pause, his squat hairy hand presumably occluding their whispered irritation.

"Hi, Eve, it's me. How are you?"

"Well, I was asleep. It's after one o'clock."

Drat, I suppose it is. In my impulse to connect with her I seem to have miscalculated the time difference. "Sorry. Did I wake you up?"

"Of course you bloody woke us up. What's wrong?"

"Nothing's wrong, I just wanted a chat."

"A chat! At this time of night! For the first time in twenty years you phone just for a chat—"

"I'm sorry, I'll call back tomorrow if you like. Hey, it's not really twenty years—"

I expect her to carry on berating me, but instead her tone suddenly softens and she says, "Hang on, I'll talk to you downstairs." I imagine her husband grumping questions at her as she rises from the bed.

"Go on, then, chat," she resumes.

"Oh, okay—um—"

"I presume you had something reasonably important to say."

"Not really. Well, yes—listen, Eve, I was thinking. When we were young, was I really horrible to you?"

"Yes. Can I go back to bed now?"

"What, all of the time?"

"Most of it."

"Oh, shit. I'm really sorry. Do you hate me for it?"

"Um," she considers. "No, not really. Not now. I guess that's just the way you were. I suppose now I feel sorry that you were so insecure."

"But you did? You hated me then?"

"Yes. Does that come as a surprise?"

"Oh, hell. I wonder why I was so awful."

"Is this why you're phoning me up, for some sort of absolution?" I picture her sitting in her top-notch fitted kitchen, ungainly and plain without her make-up, her dressing gown clamped over her thighs. She is a bigger version of our mother, taller and imposing, certainly more assured. Materially, at least, she has carved out some success in her life. She set up her own employment agency, which now specialises in nannies recruited from overseas for wealthy London families. Thanks to her, young women can exchange the hardship of Latvia or the Philippines for a round-the-clock stewardship of some little Elspeth in Epsom or Hugo in Hampstead. But she takes the responsibility that goes with the income, she makes sure the girls are not exploited, she has a conscience too. Her husband is a forensic accountant, which I think means he investigates fraud, so they have a very large income, a luxury house in Surrey and two muscular hyper-confident boys who succeed wherever they turn (both of them Oxbridge material and future England rugby captains, according to the last mass-produced Christmas bulletin). All of this sits oddly with the sister I remember, big and lumbering, with timid watchful eyes tucked into her round face. She was always more clever than me, naturally so; I had to store rote facts in my brain whereas she could assess situations and understand their implications with a restrained nod of her head. She knows more than she lets on, that girl, that's what everyone said.

Because of their physical resemblance, it was assumed she would behave like Mum, so vapid and innocuous, forever in the

197

thrall and under the thumb of Dad. Even finishing a sentence proved too decisive for our mother. "Put those toys away or. Your father will be home from. We'll send you to bed without." But no, Eve proved to have more mettle, which makes her tolerance of my boyhood malice all the more strange.

And perhaps now, forty years on, thousands of miles and a quarter of a day apart, I have suddenly answered my own question. I knew all along that she was mentally superior, she had the resources to get back at me if only she had dared. I thought I had to bully her to keep me out of fourth place in our family hierarchy, whereas she knew all along that my every sly punch, trip or kick confirmed my unworthiness for anything but bottom of the pile.

"No, I just need to know."

"Why? Why now, I mean."

"Because—because I'm working out here in Nowhereville, and I seem to be getting into a new relationship. I suppose it's all making me a bit introspective."

She doesn't ask about Mary or who this liaison is with, and why indeed should she? When was the last time I phoned to enquire about her and her family, my brother-in-law and nephews, the only ones I have? "I think you were always angry because Dad never had any time for you, he sent you away to school," she says. "Not that he had any more for me, if that's any consolation. I just don't think he was suited to fatherhood, he was always so pre-occupied by his work and one thing or another. But boys need their dads, I suppose."

Is that it, is it as simple as that? Dad ignores boy, so boy spites girl, who would kick cat if she had one, but doesn't, so makes success of her life instead. Eve goes on to recollect some instances of my bullying: burning her favourite dolls; pinching her budding nipples; scissoring chunks of hair from the back of her sleeping head. "Do you know what was the worst thing you did?" she asks.

"No."

"Telling me I was adopted."

"Oh, shit, I'd forgotten about that one. That was just meant as a joke."

"Some joke, Philip, I was devastated. It was weeks before I told Mum about that."

"Oh, dear, I'm sorry."

"And on the subject of your parents—when did you last speak to them?"

"About a month ago. I sent them a postcard from Vancouver last week."

"That was nice of you. When did you last see them?"

"Christmas, I think. Why?"

"Only that they're your parents too. I go to see them every two or three weeks. They're both nearly eighty now, and Dad's memory is going. And you know Mum's always been totally reliant on him, so I'm just telling you that they're not going to be able to cope in that big house for too much longer."

"No, I suppose not."

She gives me examples of his misbehaviour—locking them both out of the house, forgetting where he's parked the car, becoming more abusive to Mum—and for a second I am irritated because Eve seems to assume I don't know what a confused elderly person is like. "So you'll have to get a bit more involved when you get home, I can't do everything, you know. Anyway, it's half past one and I'm going back to bed. You can call me back at a more reasonable time if you like. I don't even know where you are, only that you're in Canada somewhere. You haven't let me know."

"No, I suppose I haven't—"

With that she says goodnight and the line goes dead. My impulse to grasp out for some familial support and warmth has left me deflated. I notice that the temperature here is falling, evenings are accelerating in towards winter. Night clouds are congregating outside to blacken the lake, and, as I stand and stare at them, I reflect on the fact that my half-century report doesn't amount to very much:

**As a son**—Indifferent and ungrateful. A selfish boy!

**As a brother**—Shows no interest whatsoever, unless wants something in return.

**As a father**—Full of good intentions but neglectful, has contributed little for many years.

**As a doctor**—Knowledge and attitude fall well short of the standard required.

**As a cricketer**—Enthusiastic but—it needs to be said—lacks natural talent.

**As a husband**—Failed.

**General comment**—Sadly, it now seems unlikely that Philip will fulfil the modest potential he once had. Little cause for optimism for what lies ahead.

The interim report on Jackfish Lake Indian Hospital isn't too promising either. I finish at the end of October, and Lena will follow a month after that. Sharon is trying with perpetual lack of success to find replacements for us, but will be leaving herself for Phoenix Farm in the hope of shedding some weight and some gloom. Brad, meanwhile, is elated by the news that he is being posted to Thompson, so Ellie will go with him of course. There have been no applicants for the posts of manager, radiographer or doctor, but at least we have a temporary pharmacist, a small, shy Chinaman named Li who has declined all out-of-hours offers of coffee, meals and drinks. It looks like the social gatherings here for the winter will comprise him and the ever reclusive Doug.

"So how will the hospital cope when we all leave?" I ask Karla. She has come round to see me with a view to a drive somewhere off reserve ("Anywhere to get away from this place for a while," she pleads.) but unfortunately Jewel Falls is now off limits because of its association with poor Donald. It's on the only road out of here so we have no option but to head along it but stop some place else. I notice that she seems a little down, her usual sparkle is subdued, and she seems to have been wearing the same scruffy shorts, baseball cap and increasingly smeared Bryan Adams T-shirt every day since our return.

"We'll get by, we've done it before," she replies. "That's just the way it is, we make do with a second-class health service. They haven't had a doctor at London House for two years. There wasn't one when I was there as a student."

"So what happens when someone comes in with chest pain?"

"The nurses do what they can. They can't Medevac everyone out, so they just do their best. Sometimes they get it wrong."

"But people could die, surely?"

"Sure they could, and they do. But they're only natives, ay?"

At times like this, when I get reminded first-hand of the First Nations' plight, my mood plummets, my conscience stirs grumpily from its sleep, and the course of denial seems the best and most comfortable one to steer. I understand why white Canadians avoid any contact with these people and pretend they don't exist. Hell, all they do is drink and get diabetes, you think they'd take some responsibility for themselves...

"Karla?"

"Hmm?"

"Do you think all this, this racial business, is surmountable? You know, with regard to us?"

"Philip?"

"Hmm?"

"What the fuck are you trying to say?"

"Sorry. I suppose I mean do you think you could ever have a serious relationship with a white man?"

"Aren't I having one? Aren't you serious? Aren't you white?"

"Yes, of course, but I mean long-term. Would there always be a barrier?"

"Are you saying I make you feel guilty about our past?"

"Well, yes."

"But why? You're not personally responsible for people dying in London House, are you? Or what happened to my mom?"

"Well, no."

"So don't feel guilty about it."

This, I feel, hasn't answered my question. We sit together in the car, now hampered by an inconclusive silence. The question

201

fills the vehicle, it feels like the most important one I have ever asked. "What I'm saying is, would you come to England and live with me?"

"I don't know. Do you want me to?"

I want to say yes, why else would I have asked her, but the conditioning of a cautious lifetime wins through. "I don't know."

"Thank God that's decided then," she observes, and we hold onto each other and laugh.

The phone seems to ring for ever. They can't possibly be out, something must be wrong.

Eventually, "Hello?"

"Hello, Mum, it's me. Philip."

"Oh, hello, dear. Hang on, I'll go and get your dad."

"No, wait a minute. How are you?"

"All right, I suppose."

"So how's Dad?"

"Ohh," she sighs. I imagine that wan and pudgy face, always looking as if to burst into tears. "Not very good. His memory's going, I think. He's starting to wander at. Gets up. Four in the morning, confused. And irritable! Oh, he's terrible since. I don't know. Loses things. Keys. All the time, keys. Still driving. 'Where's my bloody keys?' Eve says to hide them so he can't, but he. Oh, I don't know what to do with him. Whether he's safe. Whether to report him. He'd go mad."

I think I get the drift. "Well, can you get any help? Have you seen Dr Carson about him?"

"Doctor? What could he do? Aren't any tablets. Don't suppose."

"It might help if he's getting restless at night."

"Wouldn't take them. Wouldn't see anyone. Doesn't see there's a. Thinks everything's fine."

I know she is right. How many times have I been at the doctor end of this scenario, seeing the husband slowly dementing, refusing all help until there's a crisis, the wife becomes ill, has a fall, or simply cracks up herself under the caring strain? The daughters (or sons) live at the other end of the country (or world) and assuage their long-distance guilt by demanding that something be done. So nurses and social services visit, do assessments, complete care plans, organise days in unhomely homes where the telly is all there is. The husband can't see the bally need for being there, he hates it, he deeply resents not knowing where anything is kept, being told when to eat, that he can't have a gin or go out for a walk. This makes him more argumentative, more unmanageable, so then the psychiatrist is called. The wife can't cope, the home can't cope, but there's a hospital bed half a county away. There aren't any buses, the wife can't visit so feels guilty and mopes, the husband feels neglected and progresses from cantankerous to frankly mad. More sedatives are given, his frail frame fails, he falls, pneumonia steals in. And so he dies, and, after fifty-five years of marriage, her grief proves terminal too. They are buried together in the churchyard where they married, two hundred miles from any living relative, and thus the problem is solved.

"Philip? Philip? Is that you?"

"Oh, hello, Dad. How are you?"

"Not too bad, you know. Trying to tidy up the garden but it's all getting a bit much. Think we'll have to get someone in to give a hand."

"I thought you had someone?"

"No, always done it myself. But there's leaves everywhere, all over the bloody grass. What are you up to, anyway?"

"I'm still in Canada, for another month."

"Canada, eh? Haven't seen anything of Geoffrey, I suppose?"

Shit, Dad, Geoffrey's dead. "No, I haven't."

"And how's whatshername, Mary? Is she enjoying herself over there?"

He wasn't this bad the last time I spoke to him, a month or maybe two ago. He must have had a mini-stroke or some such, the smaller tributaries which supply his brain steadily silting up, his memory cells starving quietly in their dark. It doesn't surprise me, for—no matter what neurologists and evidence-based papers say—I swear there is a personality type predisposed to Alzheimer's Disease. My father fits this bill exactly, he was always precise, controlling, rigid and argumentative. Even now, as he speaks, he will be wearing a collar and tie. His gardening jacket is the one with leather patched elbows, his shirt is checked, trousers cord, shoes brogue brown, his pullover diamond-hatched, v-necked and bought from Pritchard's Country Outfitters in town. I even know which socks he has on, a bottle-green pair, their little woollen tentacles warming but faintly itching his feet. Later, he will change into a finer, darker suit (though they are all thinning shinily from unremitting use) and he will choose from his old oak wardrobe one of the identical white shirts his wife still irons for him with obsessive obsequious care.

September the twenty-sixth, and I open my door to a thin powdering of snow. Snow! The cricket season has barely finished, but here we are getting a formal warning that wintry hostilities will soon be resumed. This is nothing, of course, it won't last, but the polar wind slices through clothes and bodies like a cheese wire through Brie. They say here that if the snow has settled before Hallowe'en it makes for a long winter, and only now with this first herald patch of white do I really appreciate the hardship and the everyday endurance which getting through seasons entails.

In the last two weeks my contact with the world beyond Jackfish Lake has consisted of one brief phone call with each of my daughters. Beth told me she was fine, still at her summer waitressing, waiting for term to start. This, I know, tells little of what her life is really like—worries, threats, friends, hopes, how she might expose herself to injudicious drinking or drugs or sex or debt. And I don't want to know these details, she is adult and circumspect now. She is a fine young woman, despite or because of me.

Stella's conversation, though, was more direct. She was really annoyed that I'd been so rude to NYK about Mary. Didn't I know that Mary had been seriously ill? And Mary was cross enough to be ill, on Intensive Care with her plastered leg, even more cross to learn of my attitude on the phone. Stella suggested I call Mary to apologise, and for a second or two I thought I might. But then I pictured her small dark face pinched into dissatisfaction and it seemed that this had been its natural state for several years. Why had I put up with it for so long? Okay, maybe because I hadn't noticed it, but why should I expose myself now to even more crossness, was it my problem if Mary was ill? Apart from that, I couldn't quite remember what I was supposed to have said.

So much, then, for reparation. So much for good intentions, like phoning Eve back or keeping contact with Mum and Dad. Most of my free time is spent with Karla and I am finding that (she was right) we don't have to *do* anything, we don't have to *go* anywhere, simply being together is enough. Sometimes we have lakeside strolls, some evenings we just sit in my kitchen, sometimes she watches my attempts to paint. If we are free at weekends, we kayak across the lake, though the snow makes me sad that such expeditions must now be at an end. Tonight she finishes work at seven and collects me on her way home. We may go to see Lorraine later, but for now we eat the meal Ruth has made— cheap meat converted into an edible pie, then bannock cakes and coffee—and we chat.

Evelyn still treats my every word with adoration, laughs heartily at every mild joke, and tells me I am her best friend. Alex still says little, but I feel his silence is now within acceptable limits, it can probably be classified as Creely normal, tolerant rather than aggrieved.

"Did I ever show you these?" Ruth asks. She hobbles to the bulky sideboard and I expect her to extract more photos. I have already seen the highlights of the family collection: the usual babies and gap-toothed kids; Joe fishing in his boat; the year they held the powwow at Jackfish Lake; Wilson (Wilson!) receiving his relay medal at the Junior Aboriginal Games.

But suddenly she jumps, insofar as her gnarled joints permit, in the direction of the radio. "Hey, it's eight o'clock!"

"Damn, I forgot to get a ticket!" Karla says.

Radio JFL bingo at least accounts for one of the quietest hours of the day in emerg. When the broadcast ends at nine o'clock all but a handful of the local populace will be disappointed, and they will simultaneously remember their everyday malaise and the bodily niggles which have pestered them for the last few weeks. "No luck today, Horace. Never mind, I think I'll get on down to emerg, see if I can get someone take a look at this knee."

We catch the tail end of the message board, "Elsie Monias is looking for a ride to Thompson on Saturday, phone her on 6664 if you can oblige…Ed Rivers is selling off fishing tackle in his workshop all Saturday…phone 7801 if you've found Des Carter's jacket…Robert MacDonald, go home to your mom…"

"It's *always* Robert MacDonald!" Karla says. "I think Sherry chucks him out every morning, then sits down for bingo and thinks, 'Hey, I don't believe I've seen Robert all day, must give the radio a call.'"

"Shush, it's starting," Ruth interrupts.

What follows is incomprehensible. The three women pore over Ruth's tickets, but instead of some pedestrian parlour game where numbers are called out and leisurely ticked off, there is a whole sub-set of different rules, different cards, and different sequences of lines, diagonals and corners to complete in pursuit of the prizes. They don't win, of course, but at least there is some vicarious consolation in learning who phones in to the radio station to claim victory. "Hey, that's Bertha's sister!" Karla exclaims. "Five hundred bucks!"

But the real money is in the provincial lottery, they explain. I recall it from the adverts, the WinniLooneyPot or somesuch ("A looney is a Canadian dollar, you see, that's the name of the bird on the note," Ruth explains. "He does know that, Mom, he's been here nearly six months."), with its subsidiary scratch cards and games with absurd names like ManiMoneyPot or MiniWinniLooneyLottoWotaLot, which they try to explain to me— "Stop, I can't keep up with it," I laugh, head in hands. Evelyn laughs at my laughter, then Ruth at hers.

"You may think it's funny," Karla admonishes, "but it's serious business around here. I mean, you know about 9/11, don't you, Philip?"

"What, you mean the Twin Towers?"

"Hell no, not that. If you ask people round here what happened that day, they'll say, 'Yup, that was the day Deborah Moose won eighty thousand bucks on the bingo.'"

"She never?" I know the woman as a large and regular attender at midnight emerg, either escorting one of her stroppy teenagers or complaining herself of bellyache or vomiting likely due to dietary or beery excess. She does not strike me as a member of the Jackfish Lake *nouveau riche.* "Eighty thousand! So what happened to it all?"

"Went to Winnipeg and spent it in a year. Drinking and gambling, I guess."

"Stupid woman!" says Ruth.

"Well, yes and no," Karla says. "Who would have done anything different around here? What do people expect, they're ground into a life of poverty year after year, no prospect of a decent job, they resort to drink, then when they win a fortune they're expected to be sensible about it. It's not as if there's anyone out there to give them rational advice on what to do with it, is there? It just depresses me so much because when white people hear of that happening they sneer and say, 'There you go, give these natives some money and they just waste it on drink, they can't manage their own lives.' Then I'm angry at Deborah Moose because she's let every damn one of us down."

"I don't think that," I say. "I can understand how it happens."

Karla looks at me, squeezes my thigh, and smiles. She rests her head on my shoulder and says, "Yes, but not everyone is as understanding as you."

I congratulate myself on this, taking it to be true. Perhaps I really have learnt something about these people who seemed so surly and unwelcoming when I arrived. However a quiet voice behind us asks, "And since when have you been such an expert, Cormack?" We turn to find Wilson MacRae slouching and wiry against the frame of the door. "What the fuck you *doing* here, anyway?"

# 1.15

Indeed, after six months the patients seem to have mellowed towards me, not by virtue of me being particularly good at my job, but simply because I have stayed with them. This marks considerable endurance compared to what they have known. Some of them have got to say hello, a few ask how I am or where I'm from, some even spend time on a chat. Last week Bernard the Chief, visiting a friend on the ward, came over to speak to me. I was expecting him to accost me for denying his wife her free trip to the city that day, but instead he shook my hand and thanked me for my contribution to the community. And now?

"What's this? They say you're leaving us?"

"Yes, back to my practice in England."

"Hell, same old story. You just get used to somebody and then they're off. Who's taking your place?"

"Well, Lena —Dr Khonje—will be here for a little while yet—"

"And then she'll be gone and there'll be no one, I guess. Always the way up here, people never stop. The nurses do their best, but when you've got diabetes and a heart condition..."

It would be an exaggeration to say I am now fond of the Cree, but, as Karla has pointed out, who am I to patronise them with my fondness anyway?

Tonight is our farewell party—Sharon is leaving too—and we are gathered in her house. Stodgy snacks and supplies of drink have been consumed (she's not exactly in training for Phoenix Farm), and everyone is making complimentary remarks. I feel uncommonly emotional, not because I am taken in by their flattery, but primarily because I have achieved what I set out to do. I came here, almost by mistake, and against weighty professional and social odds I have survived.

Of course we are all feeling Donald's absence, and in a way I feel that this is also his party. We are rejoicing in the honour of having known him and at the same time coming to terms with our helplessness—that was the course chosen for him in this life, and if we at least diluted his grief with some moments of friendship, so be it. We could have done more for him but we are human, and given his gracious nature, we think he would have forgiven us that. None of this is spoken, but for the first time in my life I feel I am in touch with the communal thoughts and feelings of friends. There is some transcendent quality in the air, I feel sure.

Doug stands and clears his throat, "Okay, Philip, I guess it's appropriate for me to thank you for being a great friend and a fine doctor in your time here." More coughing here, a noise like a croupy moose, "But although that's clearly not the case, we thought it mean not to make a presentation anyway." Everyone laughs and he produces a card and a wrapped gift. "No, seriously, it's been great to work with you, and we wish you all the best. I hope you'll look back on your stay here with affection, especially the time spent in my car."

I finger my scalp and say, "Thank you. I'll think of you, Doug, every time I touch my commemorative scar. Now this isn't one of your works of snot art, is it?" I read the card and peel paper from a dinner plate, painstakingly made and expertly glazed with a view of a famous local landmark. "That's just wonderful," I admire. "The United Provisions store, Jackfish Lake."

"Every time you eat from it you will be reminded of that great institution and its cornucopia of goods," says Doug. I thank him again. We laugh. We shake hands. We hug.

Then Sharon gives me a Jackfish Lake T-shirt, Brad and Ellie have bought me a Jackfish Lake waterproof, Edna donates a

Jackfish Lake baseball cap. I put them all on, pose for photos, and thank everyone for their friendship and generosity. I say, truthfully, that it has been a privilege to live and work here, to be accepted here, I feel humble and grateful and will always remember them and, oh yes, come and visit me in England and make acquaintance with our two great traditions, cricket and rain. No, make that three, I forgot the warm beer. Then it is Sharon's turn, we thank her and she thanks us, we wish all the mutual future bests, and she unwraps what turns out to be a rather beautiful glass statue of a flying goose. She is moved. She cries. We drink and chat late into the night, and I feel near to tears myself for when was the last time I basked in such camaraderie as this? Even if I never see them again, they will remain in my heart as friends. Living in this relative hardship concentrates the bonds between us, and I make a point of hugging everyone present, saying I will miss them very much.

My presents will have to be packed away with the ones from last night. Ruth insisted on a farewell meal, pickerel of course, and gave me a pair of moccasins she had made herself. Evelyn gave chocolates, which we shared, and Alex sheepishly offered a book, *A Beginner's Guide To Fishing*. I thanked him and promised to put it to use when I got back home. There was nothing from Wilson, of course, but I thought it best not joke about that.

As she drove me home Karla said, "Thank you, Philip."

"Thank you for what?"

"For being so nice to Mom."

"Was I?"

"Of course. All the white men she's known in the past have either been abusers in some way, or cops trying to track down her son. You're the first decent one she's met, and I think it's helped her a lot."

I found myself too choked to reply. If that was true my trip would have been worthwhile, but what sort of comment on white or male supremacy is that?

---

So I reverse my journey, flying—for the last time?—away from Jackfish Lake. The flight was delayed by low cloud, and I was surprised at how anxious this made me feel. Farewells said, I just wanted to *go*. But it finally took off in time for this connection to Montreal. Below is a Great Lake, Superior I think, and to the right is the vast sprawl of the United States. But from up here there are no boundaries. Land is land, varied in its nature for sure, but its ownership seems arbitrary and unfair. I read in the newspaper (for yes, I am back in civilisation now) that a new breed of Russian billionaire is topping the planet's rich list on the strength of, I guess, land not dissimilar to this. Because of what can be plundered from under it, an elite band of speculators reigns, but how can that gold or oil or uranium be *theirs*? Will that wealth be spread between the common people of those lands, the Alaskans or the Khazaks or the Cree? No, of course not, it will—

"Ow!"

Karla, sitting beside me, has tweaked the inside of my thigh. "Welcome back! You were way deep in thought."

"Yeah, a once-in-a-lifetime experience and you interrupt it." She smiles, we nibble a surreptitious little kiss, and I try to explain to her where my thinking was heading.

"So maybe the Cree and Inuit were right, maybe we can teach you guys something after all."

"Too right. Nearly every war in the history of the world must have been over some dispute about territory."

"Philip," she says, "we'll make an Injun of you yet."

I still have ten days before I start work again at home. Karla has managed to get a week off, and after a lot of persuasion she has agreed to let me pay for a further trip. The point is, we still don't know if this is it, the end of us, or whether she is willing to take a leap to be with me in the great Cornish unknown.


Montreal is cosmopolitan, but less spectacular and more workaday than Vancouver. We like it a lot. Then we take a coach to Quebec, which is more French than France, its picturesque charm attracting tourists from all over the world. The Japanese amuse us, little regiments of them commandeering pavements, pointing pocket cameras as they go. They stick reflexly together as if still confined in their imaginary bus.

"At least we can get a decent French meal," I observe as we compare restaurant menus in the old town. "And a bottle of good wine."

So I practise my French on the waiter, then as we eat I tell Karla that one of the best things about living in Cornwall is its proximity to France. You can get a ferry from Plymouth to Roscoff, I say, and it's like being on a giant floating hotel. And as soon as you drive through Brittany, with its fields of artichokes and thoughtfully roofed farmhouses and quiet villages snoozing through midday and its beautiful coastline with its rocks glistening pink in the sun—oh, as soon as you set foot in France all stress disappears, it is impossible not to relax. Then there are the towns, the calm exquisite towns like Morlaix, Vannes and Vendôme, where lunch lasts hours and the evening shops gently reawaken to assure everybody that this is the most civilised way possible to organise a daily life. For yes, I could live in France, I could retire there. In fact, Karla, as soon as I possibly can, in the new year maybe, I think I'll go over for a few days and look at properties. Suddenly I am driven by a vision, as near to perfection as I can get, of living with Karla in France, a small town close to the sea—Guérande or Crozon, perhaps—me working part-time with my passable French, maybe coming back to Canada for periodic locums—

"But you have a house," Karla interrupts. "You mean you'd buy another one, a second one?"

"Sure. I think I could manage that. It all depends on the divorce settlement, of course, but I could maybe buy a small place in Brittany to visit for holidays, let it out when I wasn't there, or, yes, I might sell up in Cornwall and just move."

"I thought you liked Cornwall."

"Well, I do. But I like France as well, it would be a wonderful place to live."

"But you think it's okay to have two houses?"

"Yes, it's quite a common thing to do—"

"That doesn't make it right."

"No, but it's acceptable in Europe now for people to move to different countries. It's good that different races mix and integrate, you must agree with that?"

"Sure, but not if you buy up all the French people's homes. You told me that young families where you live can't afford to buy homes because rich people from London or wherever have a second home there."

"Yes, but it's rather different in France. There's a surplus of houses, in fact the rural areas are under-populated and in decline."

"Bullshit. It's the same principle, the same as those Russian guys making fortunes out of the oil which should belong to the people. I take back what I said about you being an aboriginal at heart, you're just another capitalist, another hypocrite."

"Come on, Karla—" I begin, but she just looks at me and shrugs. We sit here in *La Belle Cuisine*, this *chic* restaurant, eating *moules marinières* and drinking *Sancerre,* and she does not look out of place. Her hair is cut simply, short and straight, her brown eyes and strong cheeks could almost pass her as French. She wears her usual denim jacket (which is at least not emblazoned MACRAE) but has made the concession of buying new jeans.

"Come on, what?"

I fear for a moment we are heading towards a classic scene-in-a-restaurant showdown, and imagine her blazing out as heads turn and hushed comments are made about what else to expect when bringing a native to a place like this. "Look, I'm sorry, I can see that you're right. But you know, people still want to do what's best for themselves and their families. If they work hard, they want to see some sort of reward. I know it's ultimately the same principle as people acquiring oilfields, but it's on a much smaller scale."

I see her question coming but she asks it all the same, "So does that make it right?"

"No, but—but France is full of empty farmhouses. So what if

I was to buy one for myself? Why does it make you so angry? What's this really all about?"

She considers over a mouthful of lamb, another one of wine, then asks, "Philip, can we go some place else?"

"What, now?! We're halfway through—"

"I don't mean right now, I don't mean this meal. It's the city I don't like, can we leave tomorrow?"

"Of course, where do you want to go?"

"Wherever you choose. Do you mind?"

I was actually looking forward to a couple of days exploring the steep twee streets, perhaps enjoying a river trip, getting a tour inside *Le Château Frontenac*. But I say, "No, I don't mind, as long as you tell me why."

"I'm sorry, but it's the same old story. I guess you'll be really glad to get away from me spouting on about our history."

"But what's the problem with Quebec?"

"It's just that it's always been so fiercely French. All those years they've dominated Canadian politics, arguing whether they want independence, as if they're the only two groups of people in the country who matter, the English and the French. As if the people who were here before them don't exist at all."

There is nothing I can say in French or English defence. "How about we hire a car and go off into the country?"

"That would be lovely. I'm sorry I didn't think this through before we arrived, but I didn't think it would affect me so badly. What about the hotel? Haven't you booked it for another two nights?"

"Don't worry, I can cancel it. We'll go wherever you like."

"Thank you, you're very kind to me," she smiles. I bask in appreciation before she adds, "Still a fucking hypocrite, but very kind."


One evening later, counting down the handful left together before we part, we stroll the harbour of a village on the vast St Lawrence. It broadens away to our left, miles wide, and I can now understand, forty years on, why our geography teacher Limpy Whittenstone banged on about it for so long. I tell Karla this, how the scale and significance of this mighty waterway meant nothing to the well bred teenage oiks of a Shahbn school. We were all pre-occupied by our own conflict, for testosterone loitered on every corner of our circulation like the sixth-form bullies we could never quite escape. But official school policy denied the existence of girls or sex, so how were we to cope with this hormonal maelstrom? Was it okay to explore each others' erections? Was it okay to wank? And what were we to do when Limpy invited us after class to his study for extra tuition and inevitably sat too close, resting his hand with such casual intent on the inside of our thigh?

"So did you do it with other boys?" asks Karla.

"No, it really never appealed to me. And I don't think I gave out any encouraging messages, I never got propositioned like some of the other kids."

"Always the ladies' man, ay?"

"I don't know about that. I suppose we're all different, all societies have their own ways. Posh public schools in England breed matron fixations and homosexuals, boredom and poverty in Jackfish Lake leads to teenage pregnancies and drink. Who's to moralise about what's right?"

"Correct," she commends me, as a teacher might. I think of our conversation last night, how we're all hypocrites when it suits us, distinguished only by the question of degree. All of us?

I tell her, "Karla, I think you're the most honest person I've ever met."

Had we been here a month ago the trees would have been ravishing red, the stuff of postcards and decorative coffee-table books. Even now the decaying leaves are issuing ironically rich and beautiful hues. The sky, in its last hour of blueness, is razor clear. We sit, privileged to witness it all, on a small bench beside the St Lawrence waterway, Tadoussac, Quebec. The place is important because we are together, and this might not happen again. So I want to fix it all in my memory, every last detail of it, of us, the exact where and when. She is wearing her thicker coat, corded, grey, hood pulled up against the chill. As I glance left all I can see of her face is the tip of her nose. Her gloved hand holds mine. Our knees nudge against each other and our feet alternate. Hers. Mine. Hers. Mine.

"I went to see one of the elders last week," she says.

"Why?"

"To ask her where to find some good buffalo milk, why the fuck do you think?"

"Sorry. So what did she say?"

"Nothing I didn't in my heart know already, which I guess means it's right."

"And?"

"Well, she said my first priority was Alex, because children always come first. Then I have a duty to do what is right—spiritually, emotionally and practically—for myself. After that I have to remember my duty to my people, the Cree."

"So what would be best for Alex?"

"Academically he isn't all that great. To go to university he'd have to perform better than most white kids, and I know that isn't going to happen. Where he is he'll get a basic education, no more. Then if he stays in Jackfish Lake he's unlikely to get a job. If he moves to Winnipeg he might get work in a MacDonald's or cleaning streets. Or, if three hundred years of prejudice magically disappear, he might get a decent job. He may well turn to drink or drugs, I realise that, and he may end up with assorted children all over the province, like his father did. He may end up in jail. What do you think will happen to him if we come to live with you?"

"Well, he'll get into the local secondary school, which is in the village. It's small but very good. There aren't many kids from ethnic minorities, but I don't think he'll come up against any discrimination. He might have some novelty value, but most Cornish people are very hospitable at heart. He'd have a better chance of going on to college or university, I'm sure. After that,

I can't say what his job prospects would be, but they'd be better than in Jackfish Lake. In all honesty, Karla, he'd have far more opportunity and face less prejudice if you came to live with me."

"Okay, so what about the problem that he wants to stay where he is? He wants to stay a Cree."

"I know it's natural at that age not to want to move halfway across the world, but he'd still be a Cree. And you can't let him blackmail you, Karla, you do have a life of your own."

"I know that, but I don't want to drag him kicking and screaming to England, he'd just make our lives hell. I know I could leave him behind with Mom, but I don't want to do that, and I won't."

"So what have you decided?"

"I've decided that in three months time you'll probably have forgotten me anyway, or at least you'll see that it was all a completely stupid idea. I think that after the winter you'll have met someone else, but if not, if you *really* want me to come and live with you, you can ask me and I'll talk it over again with Alex then. But I think this is just a holiday romance."

"No, I'm convinced this is for real, I do love you," I protest.

"I know that's what you think," she says.

Her doubt saddens me because sometimes I think that she knows me more truthfully than I know myself.

## 2.1

The traditional Easter weather system drizzles in from the west. The clouds are too ponderous to elevate themselves above ground, they simply slouch on saturated fields and blanket the county in palpable particles of wet. Somewhere out there the trees are thrusting lushly, crocuses and daffodils flourish, but all I can see from my car window is an endless lassitude of grey. That and the square white backside of a caravan with its obligatory self-proclaiming slogan mockingly in my face. AVONDALE—HOME FROM HOME.

"Oh, move, you stupid fuckwit!" I shout.

I am on the lane which winds between Trebrack and Polmartin, and because every rainbound visitor to the county unerringly decides that they must go for a drive somewhere after a leisurely breakfast the usual rural gridlock has ensued. A Range Rover towing the caravan in front of me has met a Ford Granada hauling an even larger one on this narrow bend. Neither driver appears to have the ability to reverse, so instead they edge hopefully forward, ever forward, into an intractable wedge. By now a queue has formed behind them in both directions, horns blast in exasperation, so opting out is not possible. Granada has halted on the inner curve of the bend, leans an elbow on the window sill and looks back worriedly at his home on wheels as Range Rover tries to circumnavigate.

"No, you're nearly there, keep going," Granada insists.

So Range Rover inches on. Just as it seems salvation is at hand,

218

and millimetres of daylight appear between the offending vehicles, Range Rover emits an agonised curse as the near side of his precious vehicle cracks into a concealed hedgerow stone.

"Yes!" I cheer, punching the air. "Result!"

Not that my evolution into an irredeemable old curmudgeon is yet complete, but I am in a desperate hurry. It is Thursday morning, and I am taking the afternoon off. I really don't want to be working at all, but my partners George and Julia moaned predictably about taking leave on the eve of this public holiday. For of course it is exceptionally busy, it is just too much for the local populace to bear that the doctors' surgery might be closed for four whole days. So I have seen a roomful of kids with coughs and colds, brought along by their mothers "just in case" they get worse.

"We didn't want him to be ill over the holiday," they plead, as if I have the power to divert the incubation period of their various viruses into a timescale which miraculously by-passes the days we set aside to commemorate the crucifixion and resurrection of our Lord.

Then I have five visits, infuriatingly scattered across the corners of our practice. After the Avalon Nursing Home in Tregaskis and an old duck with a chest infection in Trebrack, I now have to get to Polmartin, Wheal Ansty and then Carricktown. It is already ten to one, I should by now be counting down the last minutes of my duty and heading for the open road. Thirty seconds later there is another delay because all local farmers like to give their tractors a holiday weekend chug out with the express intention of slowing down and pissing off the emmits. I applaud this activity in principle, but not when the resultant queue includes me.

Just before two o'clock, I get to my final call, and at least it sounds from the receptionist's message as if Caroline Lane has a straightforward vertigo attack which shouldn't detain me too long. Her husband Barnaby opens the door.

"Ah, Philip. Jolly good of you to come." Actually it isn't, I don't have a lot of choice, and I am not exactly visiting in a generous frame of mind. "Before you see her, could I just have a word?"

He has no idea how fucking irritating this is. I just want to see the woman, sort out the problem and leave. By now I should be cutting past the clouds of Dartmoor, leaving the slow spray of Tesco lorries and clapped-out camper vans in my wake. Like my father, Barnaby Lane is a retired architect, though he still takes on selected commissions. But his house is a quirky eyesore, a sixties aberration of concrete rectangles, oversized windows and wooden-railed balconies mish-mashed together so that it is impossible to tell where one storey ends and the next begins. Split level houses were his trademark, so there are a few steps here, a few over there, up a bit to the kitchen, down (as it fashionably was in his heyday) to the bedroom where his wife ails. He should never really have got planning permission to build on this green rounded spur of land with Ansty Stream down there on three sides, but of course he is a member of the Tregaskis mafia, the clique of Masons and Round Tablers and rural Rotarians who meet and play golf and take good care of each others' business needs. Because they also raise considerable sums of money for local charities any tweaking of legal niceties can safely be overlooked. Barnaby considers himself stylish, too. He still has a florid head of curls, which flops silver onto his collar. I half expect to see him with a cigarette holder and a cape.

"Can I get you a coffee?"

"No, thanks, I'm a bit pushed for time."

"Right ho." Underneath that debonair mask he is clearly an anxious man. "You know I wouldn't dream of calling you out (But you just have, I resist the urge to point out.), but she's dizzy and throwing up, and—well, the fact is I've been really worried about her for some time. I don't know if she's depressed, or what—"

I know I should gather some more background information, but I cut him short and make towards her room.

"Here's Philip, darling, would you like me to stay?" He takes the hint of my back turning towards him. "Right, I'll leave you to tell him what's going on."

220

She does indeed look rough. Her normally bouffant hair (she clings to the sixties too) straggles in semi-lacquered clumps across her head, and it occurs to me that her hair resembles the house—balconies everywhere, of questionable practical and decorative value. Without make-up she appears vulnerable and old. At first she only admits to a stomach bug but when I ask, as now I must, if anything else is troubling her, she floods her face with tears.

"I don't know where to start," she sobs. My gloom deepens as I glance at her overly ornate bedside clock.

Yet I consider myself a friend of the Lanes, I am a part of that same circle who meet at dinner parties, in the pub, at Gareth and Lyn's regular soirées, and at the summer barbecues on St Anselm's beach. Their youngest son once dated Beth. We have a bond—not intimate but certainly amicable and respectful—because we are worthy citizens in this worthy community of ours.

Normally I would set aside whatever time was needed to sit with Caroline, who turns out to be depressed and insecure and anxious, seemingly because her mother is terminally ill. I may be incompetent (May be? I am!) but at least I too have always tried to adhere to this code of looking after one's own. This is digressing, but soon after I arrived here it was Barnaby who asked me if I wanted to consider joining their lodge. I must have seemed like ideal Mason material, but my refusal surprised him, they had probably never been turned down before. It was not that I declined out of any fine principles I held, but the truth is that Mary strongly disapproved, and she felt I was already giving far too much of my time to cricket and to work. So I made my excuses to Barnaby and his fellows, who did not seem to hold this against me. At heart I was still regarded as one of them, and that was what I felt myself to be. In the past I would have sympathised with Caroline's difficulties and given her as much of my time as she needed. I would have explored all her invisible concerns about mortality and mothering and whatever else, and she would have been grateful in return and told everyone how wonderful I was. But now I tell her, maybe a little too curtly, this is all far too complicated for now, and she must make an appointment to see me after the weekend. She accepts this with a wan and apologetic smile, but I can tell that Barnaby is none too chuffed.

Much has changed in a year, not least at work. Twelve months ago George and Julia could see I was stressed, they sympathised with me on marital grounds, and they thought that happiness and efficiency would be restored when I returned revitalised from my sabbatical. So, it must be said, did I. But yesterday I turned up at our routine practice meeting expecting to discuss the usual tripe about the new contract, staffing, and the scandal of our accountants' latest fees, to be confronted by the two of them and our practice manager Noreen in an unmistakeably terse mood.

After dealing with the routine stuff in record time I thought I might be able to set about the mass of paperwork and emails which had been in arrears since the morning of my return, but George coughed portentously (he can do that) and fiddled his pencil into slow hypnotic cartwheels as he peered at me over his *pince-nez* specs. He is older and greyer than me but his plush round face wears well. His smile is ready and affable, but it is not always possible to tell what lurks behind. He simply asked, "Philip, how do you think things have been going since you've been back?"

The truth is that my sojourn in Jackfish Lake has been throwing up some sharp perspectives about work since my return. Out there I was able to practise *real* medicine, I delivered babies, reduced fractures, treated heart attacks and pneumonia, I dealt with seriously sick children unaided, I rediscovered all those skills I thought my training was for. Now it seems my time is divided between feckless whingers who do all they can to avoid taking responsibility for themselves and the pampered over-privileged who expect me to correct every little deficiency in their lives. (A prime example this morning: Caroline has been pestering me about a manky finger nail [yes, that's right, a fingernail] and on establishing there wasn't a fungal infection in it, I told her there was nothing I could do. "But there must be, Philip," she bemoaned.

*But there must be... .* That's the level of expectation I find myself up against, and it doesn't half piss me off.)

"Um, all right," I mumble, though. "Why?"

"Why? Because the receptionists are fed up with your perpetual short temper, several patients have complained about your off-handedness, and Julia and I both feel you're not really very interested in the practice any more."

Um, clearly not all right then. Before I could reply, Julia—ever keen to assert herself and for once in agreement with George—waded in. "The fact is, we really thought you might have come back from your Canada trip in a positive frame of mind, but that's clearly not the case. When Ben was doing your locum the staff were happy and everything was running smoothly, but now it's all back to what it was before. We know you've had the trauma with Mary, we've tried to make allowances for that, but that's all done and dusted now. We don't want to be thinking in terms of dissolving the practice, or anything as drastic as that, but we do—both of us—feel as if we're tidying up after you for much of the time. Things will have to change."

So—even more not all right than I had imagined, but no one had said anything to warn me. There had been no avuncular chats from George or tactful close-the-door-behind-you sessions in Noreen's office to say there was a problem. I tried to defend myself and stated my commitment to the practice, my intention to be nice to all the staff, whatever, and it ended with George menacingly proposing a further meeting to review the situation in one month's time.

But afterwards I felt shocked and betrayed, for I had never in my career been put in such a position as this. Then a great anger came over me. Certainly I had my limitations, as I had discovered, but at least I had gone away to challenge myself and widen my horizons while they sat on their complacent backsides before their well-to-do and unctuously thankful patients. "Bastards!" I hissed into the confidence of my room.

Suddenly I realised what must have precipitated this crisis. A few days before I had seen Eleanor de Vere, whose husband

Daniel has established himself as a notable photographer on the strength of a series of giant and deliberately blurred seascapes. "Not so much depicting the sea as the essence of sea," as the critic in the *Independent* wrote, his clipping now fading with several summers of sunlight in the gallery window. This helped excavate him a niche with visitors from London, and now the simple application of an inflated price tag appears to convince a certain breed of people that his work must indeed have great merit. (£1,250 for a photo of some waves? Yes, the emperor is finely clad today.) What Eleanor does with her time—apart from a couple of mid-morning hours sitting decoratively in the gallery sipping jasmine tea and scanning the Sunday supplements—has always remained unclear.

"Philip, what *am* I to do about my cholesterol?" she had demanded. I checked her result and looked at her in her trim woollen suit, not picked up on a Sunday morning in Par market, to be sure. "I mean, it's gone up to 6.2. I eat loads of olives, I adore them, I eat fish twice a week, hardly any meat, I've started using Benecol instead of butter. What else can I do? Do I need to go on tablets? Tell me about these statin things—are there any side-effects, how do they work?"

"Do you smoke?"

"Only socially, four or five at the most. Okay, say ten on a bad day."

"Well, you should stop smoking."

"Oh, I knew you were going to say that. I want to know what I should I be eating, Philip. What about avocadoes? What about prawns, are they okay?"

I sighed, established that her weight and blood pressure were fine, and told her, "It's really not a problem, all your other risk factors for heart disease are low, apart from the smoking. You can eat whatever you like, you can eat butter instead of that chemical slop for a start."

"You're telling me I can eat butter?!" Her face squirmed into horrified disbelief.

"Yes, butter is actually a natural product, you know, unlike those tubs of manufactured shit the supermarkets brainwash you into buying. They're all just a massive marketing con, like bottled water, and Coca-Cola. Of course you can eat some bloody butter, just don't worry about it."

"But I am worried, that's why I'm here. Can I see a nutritionist or a dietician or someone?"

"No, we can't refer everyone with a borderline cholesterol to a dietician, they'd end up having to see half the county." I think I may have laughed at the implausibility of this.

"Can I see one privately? I'm quite prepared to pay."

"No, they don't take private referrals! They're a specialised service, they're not interested in the well-off worried well. And anyway, if you can afford to pay, you've probably got nothing to worry about. If you were forced to eat crap food and live in poverty on some native American reserve, then I'd be concerned, but you're a normal-sized middle-class English woman on a healthy diet. If you're so worried about your health why don't you stop smoking?"

"Oh, Philip, it's only half a dozen a day."

"Well, that's your choice," I concluded. "You're a responsible adult. But eat what the hell you like, and stop being so bloody neurotic about your cholesterol."

Eleanor and Daniel are good friends of Julia, of course. Word would have got back to her about my rudeness, my disregard for one so dedicated to her own health. It's ironic, I reflect, that back in Jackfish Lake lives were at put at risk by my mediocre skills, but people put up with that as a fact of everyday medical life. Here, one tactless remark to the hyper-precious wife of an overblown third-rate artist means all hell breaks loose.

"Bastards!" I shout again, rather louder this time.


So yesterday I finally got back home to soothe my injustice with a gin. Until Mary fucked off with NYK my life was stable and pleasant, apart from the stresses of work. It was all very well for the unmarried Julia to sit there and say my marital breakdown was all in the past, but who was she to say how long my recovery should take, what I should feel, how I should behave?

Take the divorce. I came back in November to an officious letter from Mary's solicitor, proposing we sell Dene House, our family home for all those years, and split the proceeds fifty-fifty. As simple and ruthless and final as that. I could have challenged it, pointing out whose earnings finally paid off the mortgage last year and which party's adultery terminated the marriage, but no, I agreed, because I did not want to taint any of our lives with vindictive, lengthy and expensive wrangling, I wanted to play fair. I wanted to be reasonable and decent even though Mary was refusing to speak to me because of that perceived telephone slight when she was in hospital. I phoned her to tell her it was nothing, but the reply I got was, "I have nothing more to say to you about that, Philip. You've got my solicitor's address."

So we sold Dene House for £395,000, which sounds a lot. Indeed, half of that added to the considerable proceeds of NYK's little pad could, and did, buy them a very desirable four-bedroomed property just outside Truro, complete with outhouses, several acres of land, and a tranquil poolful of carp. It sounds wonderful, a perfect venue for their Amnesty Fucking International meetings, I'm sure. My half has gone towards a three-bedroom cottage—9 Chapel Lane—in the middle of Tregaskis. It needs a fair bit of work, for there are damp stains of mould on the west-facing wall, the electrics are outdated, skirting boards and outside doors need to be replaced. The windows are small, the ceilings low, the garden cramped, and—after finally paying off our last penny of debt on Dene House last year—I have had to take out a mortgage for thirty grand. I could have moved into Truro but prices were even higher there, and I cannot bear to commit myself to work for any more years than I absolutely must.

At least Stella has mellowed back towards me. She has visited now and then and no longer seems fussed about what I said or didn't say to Mary. That isn't her business, and she wants to stay on good terms with her dad. For now she is living with the opposition, but in October will be off to university. Cornwall is too small for her ("It's so *boring*. There's nothing to *do*."). She has outgrown us and will soon be moving on to a life of her own.

And, ironically—or is this the natural circle of events?—I am replacing my girls with my parents. I don't know whether this is admirable or sad, but I have spent one or two weekends up there easing my guilty despair at their demise by doing odd son-like jobs around the house. Not that I'm capable of anything too adventurous (Pacamac the handyman? I think not.) but Dad's fading muscles leave him increasingly unsteady on the ground, let alone on step ladders, while Mum remains generically hopeless. A gardener is fine, but I resent the idea of some two-bit tradesman cashing in on their incapacity for trivial tasks. So I spent last weekend re-fixing unsafe curtain rails, washing the top shelf kitchen plates of their years of greasy dust, renewing light bulbs, shopping, weeding the drive, and clearing the attic and various cupboards of clothes which will not be worn again, ornaments and dishes beyond further admiration or use, and stacks of architects' magazines which will never be read.

"Dad, have you thought of moving to a smaller house?" I asked.

"Makes no difference to me, but it would break your mother's heart if we left. It's the family home, and she's still very attached to that."

So, "Mum, have you ever thought of moving to a smaller house?" I asked.

"Moving? Smaller? Make life easier, but your father wouldn't. Don't think he'll ever."

Sitting between them at dinner, I sought an open consensus of their views.

"I wouldn't mind, but I think it would be too much of a wrench for."

"I'd move tomorrow, dear, I've always said so. I just think it would be too much of an upheaval for you."

"Okay, you both say you're prepared to move to a smaller house. So let's give it some serious consideration."

"Oh, I don't think so, your father's familiar with. Might get confused if."

"What do you mean, confused? I'm perfectly happy to go and live somewhere else, but I don't think you'd be able to manage it, to be frank."

"Why don't I get some details from the estate agents?" I suggest. "Then at least you can see what the possibilities are."

"No, there's no point, you know what she's like. She'll agree to it when you're here, but as soon as you're gone, everything will change."

"It's no use saying I'm the one who. You've always been so set in your. I'll do whatever. I just don't think you."

After several such exchanges the impetus of my good intentions faltered, and I let the matter drop.

And now I sit in my car, immobilised by the Annual Festival of Roadworks, a traditional Bank Holiday gala of illuminated delays which enables thousands of motorists to stop and watch men in hard helmets and fluorescent tabards lean on their shovels and smoke as they watch them back. I am thinking of nominating these at Moorlands Junction as my favourites for Roadworks of the Year.

I am already two hours late, but the anger has drained out of me. There just doesn't seem to be any point in it any more. It has been replaced by an eerily calm introspection, an acceptance of whatever my future will bring. So what if George and Julia contrive to get rid of me? Two divorces in one year? So? As I drum my fingers onto the static steering wheel I get a sudden insight into something, a glimpse into a potential beyond. If I really have been so irritable, something must be wrong with me, not the rest of the world. Now—here, this minute—is the time to put it aside and take with gratitude what's ahead, and not be despondent if my plans fail.

Or maybe it's more mundane than that, maybe the big lesson of my life-changing sabbatical was that I should simply spend more time with my ailing mum and dad.

My resolution to remain calm for the rest of my life lasts four hours. It is seven o'clock and I am locked, lost, in the labyrinthine concrete techno-mess of Heathrow. I had the sign for short-stay parking for Terminal 3 clearly in my sights but I was displaced by a convoy of coaches into the wrong lane and now I have been sucked into a vortex of 450 degree turns, merging slip roads, underground passes and directions to unwanted places like Cargo Terminal and Customs House. I scream a futile anguished scream, an undignified admission of panic, but it is not unleashed out of concern for myself. Somewhere in this chaos of the world's maddest airport Karla and Alex are standing bewildered and scared, wondering what the hell is going on.

I tried to phone the airline to say I would be late, but of course got only an amputated voice telling me to press 1 for reservations, 2 for cancellations, and so on. All I wanted was a person, a palpably sentient and sympathetic being to whom I could say, "Look, I've been horribly delayed, and two very special people will be at their wits' end wondering where I am. Could you let them know?" And he or she would reply, "But of course, sir. What are their names and where are they coming from? I'll broadcast them a reassuring message at once." No such fucking luck.

Eventually I park the car and follow directions to Arrivals. I keep checking my mobile and wonder why she hasn't rung me. Maybe there aren't any public phone boxes, maybe they've all been vandalised, she can't work out how to use them, she has no money, I gave her the wrong number, she hasn't turned up...I fear I may simply never find her because the Arrivals lounge (lounge??) is a seething crowd of desperate and disparate exhausted-looking people. They have come from every continent to find that England greets them with this—a grubby concentration of overpriced crap food outlets with unswept floors staffed by disinterested young girls who have been emotionally immunised against the drama around them. Beer-necked England-shirted youths slob across several seats. Fat middle-aged men in sportswear return from Florida with their cheap sunburn already rubbing raw. Plump Asian women look anxiously about, their trolleys piled high with belongings, their satellites of children fearful of being sucked forever away. Blank faced couriers lean on rails, bearing hand scrawled notices seeking EDOUARD LEFEBRE or FAMILY HONG. Big-coated businessmen stride off, plugged assertively into their mobile phones. With apprehension curdling my stomach I wonder what Karla will be making of all this. More to the point, I wish I knew where in this God-forsaken place she was.

There is no information kiosk or meeting point, no friendly reception staff. Everyone rushes about, crammed tight and tense into this tiny arena. Before I fall into complete despair that I have fouled up her arrival into this new life ("If he can't get here to meet us, then we're going straight back home."), it dawns on me to check one of the computerised screens. It tells me that flight KLM 671H from Amsterdam will now arrive at 2130. It has been delayed four hours.

By then they will be exhausted and none of us will be fit for the drive home. At the Tourist Information desk a helpful young woman books us into a nearby hotel, so I take the car there to check in, shower and de-panic, and return to Heathrow on the bus. I have a very necessary beer followed by another one, then line up with the dozens of others who wait. Passengers from all over the world are processed through Customs and appear from the door, popping out like random bemused lottery balls. Finally, suddenly, unreally, Karla appears.

She simply says, "Hi," and walks into my arms. I squeeze her to me and feel tears of relief (fatigue, excitement, apprehension?) form in the corner of my eye as Alex looks on. He is silent and bewildered, with the darting eyes of the universal lost child.

A hotel room again. We both know that relationships moulded only within such confines are likely to be unfounded and false. In January I used my remaining few days of leave to go back to Winnipeg, fearing our bond might have faded with the separation of time. Although I offered to return to Jackfish Lake, Karla felt it better to meet alone to discuss where our future lay. We would have no privacy at her house especially with Wilson there lying low for the winter, she said, as if he ever did anything else. And anyway planes were so unreliable at that time of year, I could fly up there and be stranded for a month. The city was viciously cold, minus thirty when I arrived, but it remained remarkably unparalysed as buses and cars and their workers burrowed along the snow-banked streets. So back to the Prince Albert it was, greeted by staff as an old friend and received by Karla with uncertainty until I convinced her that this crazy venture could work.

Now, though, she does not look so sure. She has had her hair trimmed, which emphasises the youthfulness of her face. She is not masculine or sexless, but she bears the broad-boned purity of race which is intrinsically attractive whether borne by a boy or a girl. In the cosmos of London she would pass unnoticed as someone whose blood line was Inca or Asian or Moor.

We eat in the hotel bar, Alex in quiet awe of the brash sophisticated newness of it all: leather seats and dim lights; endless sparkling optics of alcohol freely on display; waistcoated waiters bearing gigantic steaks; mobile phones with attention-seeking tones; slim young girls with heaving cleavages, jewelled navels and low slung jeans exposing tattooed sacrums and tacky Top Shop thongs. And, above all, the sheer density of people—families, couples, stag parties, sunseekers, businessmen—the same population as Jackfish Lake crammed into the concentrated chaos of one hotel.

The menu horrifies Karla: "Shit, Philip, £3.50 for a glass of wine! How many loonies is that?"

"About eight."

"Eight!? Are you kidding? And what's this continental breakfast deal?"

"Well, it's a selection of croissants—you know, pastries and things like that —"

She raises her voice with horror, "Holy cow, that's forty dollars for some fancy bits of bread! Mom could live for a week on that!"

People at the next table turn to look at her. I smile an apology which is weakened by the fact that she does indeed have a point.

Alex chooses chicken from the menu and when it arrives he eats with a ravished gusto. Even though it is standard battery-bred restaurant fare I suspect it is the plumpest most wholesome poultry he has ever had. Karla, however, picks at her meal: "I'm sorry, but I'm exhausted," she says. "I can't bear to waste it, but—"

"I'll have it," Alex claims, with the relish of someone who is seriously underfed.

I have booked a family room, fearing that a night of solitude in this unknown new world might be too much for Alex to bear. Only now he is here do I *really* appreciate what this upheaval means to him. Until now I have considered my happiness and Karla's, and I fear I have underestimated how much agonising she has done on his behalf. While he is in the bathroom (no doubt the plushest he has seen—we hear taps gushing experimentally from hot to cold, full blast to off, him gasping behind the door) she thanks me for my choice.

Karla emerges from her turn in the bathroom in plain white pyjamas, looking ravishing despite her fatigue. Alex gets into his bed, we into ours, and in the darkness I hold her tightly and whisper that I love her, though I suspect she is already asleep.

———————

At breakfast next morning Alex asks, "Can we go into London today?"

This causes me a minor degree of dumbfoundment, for I believe it is the longest sentence I have heard him assemble. It almost ranks alongside Beth's first such landmark, "Where's cat gone?" uttered somewhat in advance of the age of two. My pleasure at this breakthrough is tempered by the fact that I really do not want to spend Good Friday traipsing round the usual city sights with millions of tourists before our four- or five-hour drive back to Cornwall. My expression must reflect this.

"We can go another time, Alex. Don't you want to go and see your new home?"

"I'll see that anyway. Why not go to London now we're here?"

I explain again that we have a long journey, the traffic will be bad, we can come some other time, maybe on the train. I don't want to set a precedent by giving in to him on day one, though on the other hand I have no wish to alienate him or reinforce any feeling that he has no choice about anything in this new country where he is being forced to live. But he sticks to his guns. He has done some research at school and told his friends about Buckingham Palace, Madame Tussaud's, the London Eye. I turn to Karla for guidance but she simply shrugs, handing the decision back to me.

"It would be better to come another day," I decide. "I think we should get on home."

The speed and density of motorway traffic appals them, but after a while Karla relaxes back into her seat. She is more refreshed today, and as we spin past affable Wiltshire fields she tells me news of Jackfish Lake.

There is at least a doctor, a gruff and arrogant South African everybody hates. "Everyone's hoping you'll come back," she says, and while I am genuinely touched by this flattery, I feel that I could live my remaining days quite happily without working there again. No replacement has been found for Sharon, so Rose is filling in with her usual grumpy efficiency. Bertha, now found to be diabetic, has been depressed and unwell. Li the pharmacist is still there, and Doug remains quite mad. She tells me that his latest interest is robots, "I think that's because he was once one himself."

At home, Ruth's arthritis is giving her a hard time, and Evelyn took badly to her beloved sister and nephew's departure. ("Mom, Evelyn will be okay, won't she?" Alex chips in. "Sure she will," she replies, conviction missing from her voice.) Wilson comes and goes as usual, but is lost and bad-tempered too.

"What happened to Marshall?" I ask, mainly out of professional interest in the evolution of his burns.

"That's a sore point at the moment. As far as I know he's still in prison."

"In prison!" I exclaim. "Did he get done for Bartram's house fire?"

Karla grimaces her eyes towards the back seat. I almost swerve the car in anticipation of a sharp dig in the ribs, and am sheepishly aware of Alex's attention on the alert.

"No," Karla says calmly. "He's been—let's just say he was found in possession of some stuff which didn't exactly belong to him."

I make a high priority mental note to find out what other topics should be discussed only away from Alex's ears. Is he really innocent to Marshall's criminal activities? Is arson really considered acceptable in reserves like Jackfish Lake? I try to imagine the reaction around Tregaskis (George! The de Veres! Mary!!!) when news filters back from Alex's new and inquisitive friends that his father is serving time in Winnipeg nick.

So this is it, your new home. Our new home. The words and the concept sit awkwardly, as if it really can be constructed as mathematically as that. This is a house, we are its occupants, *ergo* this is our home. I think back to my own childhood and the place my parents still live, and I understand their reluctance to leave. I can chide them for playing their blame-laying games, but of course the fabric of Montfort House is now interchangeable with theirs. However rational uprooting them into a warden-patrolled assembly unit may be, it will still presage the death of them, it will be the first removal of a vital link in the chain of memory and attachment and kin.

Will this modest cottage ever gain the same significance? I know it won't, for Alex—who is the taciturn crux of this union—is already bonded elsewhere. His home is the north, sno-moing the winter road to Weskip Lake, fishing, learning to speak Cree, training for next year's Junior Aboriginal Games. I watch him as he stands in the small high-walled garden. After the endless expanse of Canada I try to hem him into this?

They have been unpacking while I make full English belated breakfast. (Local bacon! Fresh mushrooms! Yellow eggs! Beans without molasses! Sugar-free bread! At least Alex's nutritional shortcomings will soon be corrected, and I envisage him gaining several rapid inches and a couple of muscular stone. Maybe the time-honoured technique of food bribery will compensate for any romantic attachments to home.) Within an hour it all seems to be done, for they have remarkably few belongings. Alex in particular has minimal requirements for his new life—odd mementoes from his friends like his dozen or so baseball caps and the bright carved model of a traditional boat which takes pride of place in his room, and a couple of sets of clothes whose scruffy dullness seems even more pronounced outside their natural habitat. Today's outfit is a simple T-shirt and jeans devoid of commercial logos. Admirable as this innocence is, I imagine the astonished and condescending response of his peers at finding that their new colleague bears not so much as a Nike swoosh. He has no books, no mobile phone, no walkman, no CDs. Anyway—now we are encamped in our new house/home, what are we to do?

What else? "Come on, then, let's go!"

"Go where?"

"To the sea!"

We get in the car and I take them to see their new neighbourhood. The roads, they note, are all replete with tarmac, even off reserve. Alex asks why the houses are joined together like that and why the cars are so small. It takes two minutes to tour Tregaskis, and I point out the places of interest—pub, church, surgery, cricket pitch, and oh, look!—there's the pub again. I decide to avoid The Greenery, our own little rustic ghetto where local reprobates and rent-dodgers are housed, and soon we are in the tight high-banked lanes whose signposts entice us to Chygolden, Parc Gweal and St Anselm's Bay.

"Weird names," Karla says, and I explain the Celtic influence, how the west of Scotland, Ireland, Cornwall, Brittany ("They named a place for Britney?" Alex asks.) and Galicia are linked by this romantic and mysterious race, their sea-faring and saints memorised in a thousand villages, their legends as arcane and durable as those of the Cree. I tell them about King Arthur, Excalibur, the reputed lost land of Lyonnesse. They were a remarkable people, spiritual and wise.

"So why didn't they build straight roads?" asks Alex.

But who—Cornish or Celt or Cree—can fail to be moved by

the sea? I take the back lane to Gant Cove and suddenly the land falls away before us and we are dizzily atop the cliff with the green ocean sparkling and cresting and crashing below. We get out of the car and Karla stands squeezing my arm, flinching into the clear incisive wind.

"It's the most beautiful place on earth," she declares.

"You said that on Vancouver Island."

She wields a mock fist at my pedantic streak, I grab her wrist and sneak a kiss behind Alex's back. He is totally absorbed, and my excitement is augmented by encompassing this, his first view of the sea. Imagine it! How we take it for granted here, it defies belief to be deprived of it until such an age. I compare it to spending the first thirteen years of one's life under permanent clouds, only for them to dramatically clear for a whole new element, breathtakingly blue and infinite, to be revealed. Karla smiles and nods, and for a moment I believe I can read her thoughts—that whatever becomes of us, however misguided this relationship is, at least we have given Alex this.

We get back into the car, wind down the steep valley, and emerge again to walk on the shingly beach. The day is chilly and grey, spray hisses off the surface onto our faces, and we take off our shoes to splash through the incoming tide. We can submerge ourselves in it another day, a warmer one, but for now it is enough to make contact and walk through it with hands held. Karla is in the middle, and she laughs as I indulge in the British tradition of rolling up my trousers in the vain hope of keeping them dry. We walk the full length of the cove and hope that the ocean's brutal beautiful power will strengthen us on our way.

"So, Alex, what do you think of the sea?" I ask.

"Aahhdno," he replies.

This sight-seeing, this prolongation of holiday falsity, is all very well but sooner or later it must end and anyday routine take its place. Our biggest concern has been schooling for Alex. On the face of it, that is not a problem for there is a comprehensive school right here in the village. We are repeatedly told it is barely big

237

enough to be viable, for Tregaskis itself has an ageing population. But this gives the school a good reputation, everyone thinks of it as small and friendly, and it does passably well in the hallowed examination league. It serves a large area and pupils are bussed in from the surrounding rural miles, though, as in the practice, these are drawn from two distinct groups. The two or three school buses, decrepit old charabancs picked up at bygone auctions by Jack Cobb, our very own yokel entrepreneur, meander the local lanes twice daily in term times and bear their amateurish crest COBBS' LUXURY TRAVEL on peeling green windscreen stickers and over the fading bodywork name of the previous owner, PARADISE TOURS OF DUDLEY. I have intimate knowledge of these vehicles, for the cricket club has always hired them for away fixtures. Cricketers pissed *en masse* are only slightly less bawdy than football or rugby players, and I have lost many slow hours to journeys back from places like Gwilliam and St Minn. The worn brown upholstery and smell of dank sick is now shared with local youths who disgorge sloppily with shirts mutinously flapping as they try to puff off the reek of their last fag before entering school. These are the kids from the "Cornish units", the slabbed grey council edifices built to house bottom of the range farm workers two or three generations ago. They are scattered in settlements of six or eight, far from pub or shop, and I know from work that deprivation often lurks there too. The extent of this is obscured from tourists and from the privileged others who may live less than a mile away. But small-scale farming is imperilled, secure work is scarce, and men who would in better days be humble labourers of the land have either moved to the towns or stay on to cobble up black-market cars or justify their enforced idleness on grounds of bad chests or backs. They turn up every three months for their certificates, hoping I won't question them too much, resenting the wait for their next cigarette. I comply with this though I could—and should—ask what *really* ails them. But they are reticent by nature, and anyway I know that at the heart of them is a despair. They see their growing children, academically below par, on the verge of a workless world and all too vulnerable to the distracting pull of alco-pops, all-day snooker, violent videos, humdrum crime, drugs, pulp TV and unwitting parenthood. We both know there is nothing we can do about this so we agree instead on a prescription for painkillers, a certificate of deceit.

The second and now much larger group is delivered to the school in Range Rovers and other four-wheel drives, which are legitimate here because this is Cornwall, where the roads are prone to horrible hazards like mud. These are families liberated from London by the ease of commuting or the advent of e-work, and, more important, the considerable wealth they have amassed by happening to acquire a home-county house several years ago. Now they can sell up and buy "quality of life" instead. This is understandable, this is fine, except that they pitch up here with nothing but the expectation that we in this honest place must meet their demands for schooling, public transport, doctors, hospitals, roads, restaurants, culture, weather, and—most critical— favourable house prices. Our own indigenous people learned long ago not to expect anything in return.

Anyway, the county's true elite go to public school in Truro and we all know what outstanding citizens such institutions produce. But for the majority of parents in the county, school fees are too prohibitive, so many of those whose offspring rough it with the riff-raff in Tregaskis make out that they do so in an act of wise generosity. "It's so good for them to mix with kids of different backgrounds," they say. "It gives them a much more rounded education." On the face of it these pupils are indistinguishable from their less privileged peers. They scruff their uniform to the technical limit—girls' skirts rise up goose-pimpled legs, green sweaters are torn and stained, shoes elaborately unlaced, and bodily adornments get more indiscreet by the day until teachers quell the uprising and it starts all over again in some other sneakily disobedient form. But overheard clips of conversation show which polarity they occupy;

"Becky's having a sleepover tomorrow, her mum says we can stay in the studio…"

"They want me to go to Badminton with them, but it's *so* fucking tedious…"

"My sister got an iPod for her birthday, jammy cow…"

A year or two ago my automatic opinion would have been to send any boy of mine off to public school (Why didn't the girls go? Because Mary objected, she was always more of a socialist than me, and she liked to have them around the home.), but now I'm not so sure. Has Karla changed my thinking on this? Would any such school now remind me of Blackwater Lake? Anyway, thanks to Mary, the moral considerations are now academic. Any reserves I might have raided for fees have been sunk into her and NYK's luxurious new home.

So Alex goes off to school, looking as forlorn as only one's own child can. His uniform is conspicuous, new-boy neat. We have offered to accompany him on the short walk through the village, but he knows that to appear on his first day with Mummy or semi-Daddy in tow will attract only scorn from his peers. Yesterday when teachers got their pupil-free day to ease themselves in (Why don't we ban patients from the surgery for three or four days a year to give ourselves some breathing space, by the way? Bloody teachers!), we took him for a look round the school. He got his timetable and his bearings and they were terribly nice to him, as you would expect. But today?

Karla watches him from the front door, biting hard into her lower lip, and I try to hug some confidence into her. "Don't worry, he'll be all right."

"You don't *know* that, Philip, you just don't know," she says as she turns her back to me. "I was hoping he might have met someone his own age in the last few days, it would have made it a little easier."

Possibly so, but we have spent the last week or two doing necessary shopping—mainly to replace his dowdy clothes—and seeing the usual Cornish sights like Truro and St Ives. And anyway I do not know any thirteen-year-olds socially, nor the parents of such. All our friends over the years have been a similar vintage to us, so their offspring are either now living independently or on the verge of doing so, and certainly not inclined to take some mute youngster from the woollybacks of Canada under their wing.

They are still "our" friends, not mine, you notice, because we were always couples and families together. In the months since Mary moved away I have felt aloof and uncertain with Steve and Kim, even with Gareth and Lyn, as if we are all not quite sure how we are bonded now. Even the subject of Karla's arrival has seemed delicate. For instance, when we met up at Christmas:

"What's this, I hear you're jetting off back to Canada," Lyn said. "You must really like it over there."

"Mm, yes. Well, I'm actually going to visit a young lady I met there. We got quite attached, you know."

"Good for you, Philip. I mean, life goes on, and all that."

"Sure. I, um, the fact is she might be coming over here if all goes well."

"How marvellous! You never said anything about that, you dark horse. You must bring her round to meet us. Gareth—Philip's whizzing off to see his lady friend in the new year, he hopes to bring her over here soon."

"Oh, excellent!"

"So what's her name?"

"Karla."

"And when might she come over here?"

"Oh, not for a while yet. Easter, perhaps."

"You must be so excited. Are we here at Easter, darling? Or is that when we were planning to visit James?"

"I think it might be. Did we tell you he's still in Japan? Having a marvellous time over there, teaching English. We thought we'd better go and visit while we've got the chance."

"I don't blame you."

"It's a place I've always wanted to go. And do you know, Philip, they play cricket?"

"Really?"

"Yes, they're really keen. I've already emailed Nagasaki Cricket

Club—can you believe there is such a thing?—that's where James is staying, and they've said I *must* pay them a visit..."

Similarly when I dropped into coffee conversation with George and Julia last week that I was off to Heathrow to collect the woman who was coming to live with me, the response was an eyebrow raised in diffident condescension, as if this was a Filipino housekeeper I was hiring for a few weeks to make my dinner and iron my shirts, or a mail-order Russian bride.

Oh God. The thought of George triggers an oppressive panic. Karla still stands on the doorstep watching the corner Alex has just turned. I put a hand on her shoulder and this time she turns to face me. "I'm sorry," I tell her, "but I have to go to work."

A morning of flat-out exasperation it is too. Every working day is now ruled by the computer. Our brave new contract dictates that everyone who steps through the door must be regarded as a reservoir of data which must be updated, processed and logged into annual reports. Good morning, Mr Wilkins, I need to weigh you, measure your height and waist, and check your blood pressure. How much do you drink? Do you smoke? Well, don't. You need to get your cholesterol checked so on your way out make an appointment for that, and oh yes see the nurse in the asthma clinic. What's that, your wife's just died, you're depressed?

Then it's the usual daily trayful of DSS reports, DVLA reports, drug company bumph, prescribing cost statements, minutes of Primary Care Trust board meetings, invitations to irrelevant lectures and interminable case conferences, and demands for defence union subscriptions, increased again of course. With each day the backlog grows, and with it the feeling of despair. Somewhere in those kilograms of crap lurks the odd important document, somebody's mortgage fallen through because I haven't sent off the insurance report, urgent medication needed yesterday, referral letters still waiting to be signed.

And I know where the problem lies. Since my sabbatical I have discovered why some doctors—like the urbane George and the assertive intelligent Julia—cope with the escalating workload which affects us all, while those such as myself are left in a state of flailing inefficiency. They can discriminate between what they must do and what they can discard or entrust to somebody else. For although I was keen and conscientious when I started here I was also, and forever will be, Doctor Plod. Mary was right. For a long time I could compensate for my average intellect by approaching work in a methodical manner. What needed to be done got done eventually and systematically, but now I have reached plod overload, I have de-compensated, my brain cannot cope with these volumes of input any more.

So what is the solution? I really do not know, but at least I can tell Karla all this when I get home. At one o'clock, mindful of her all-day isolation, I call into the house for a snatch of lunch. She has local papers and nursing journals spread on the kitchen table as she looks for suitable posts.

"Look, Philip, there's a job on the renal unit in Plymouth. I can apply for that." I am not entirely sure that occasional supervision of the two-bit clockwork dialysis machine at Jackfish Lake equips her to work in a regional centre of excellence. "What's the matter?" she asks as she catches my expression.

"Plymouth's quite a long way, you know."

"But I looked on the map, it's no distance."

"It's no great Canadian distance, but it would take about an hour and a half each way, it's a really slow road. That's three hours a day travelling."

"I could take the train."

"Even slower, even less reliable."

Her shoulders slump. "Thanks for the encouragement."

"I'm just being realistic. You can still apply, but you need to know these things. Come on, let's have some lunch."

Lunch! I look forward to flavourful slices of smoked salmon on freshly baked rolls, complemented by the zip of lime juice and black pepper and some tangy crescents of red onion. One of the joys of the last two weeks has been introducing Karla to quality food, simply prepared by my own modestly skilled hand, for in the months of single living and anticipation of her arrival I have been expanding my culinary repertoire. And I have already introduced her to the joy of country pubs, with their stout tables, hushed lights, and the civilised burr of conversation a backdrop to our meal. Lunch? How many times in my life has the clatter of the phone or the shrill electronic warble of a bleep pierced my plans for food or relaxation or personal contact? However many it's been, add one.

"Where *are* you?" Noreen demands. "We're all waiting, and George is getting rather vexed."

"Waiting? For what?"

"For you. It's our monthly QOF meeting, remember?"

"Quaff meeting?" I echo with confusion. Are we all going down the pub?

"Quality Outcome Framework, Philip, the new contract update. We've got a hundred and one things to get through."

I am tempted to say fuck George and fuck the new contract. Who's bothered if we lose an iota or two of computerised points in this crazy system? George is, for one, because there's money in it. If care can't be quantified it no longer exists. Its provision will now become a medical *Wisden*; blood pressures and body mass indices tabulated like runs and wickets into bar charts and growth rates, publicly set against arbitrary targets of performance and cost, measured against neighbours and compared with previous years. General practice has been reduced to computer searches and Read codes, and although this systematic approach might once have suited my temperament, I no longer have the heart. Every doctor in the county will look to our various performance tables and find P A Cormack, P A Cormack, P A Cormack at the bottom of every one.

My gloom is deepened by the knowledge that I am on probation. For now I have to maintain my role of the proper doctor, play the game and observe the rules. "I'll be there in five minutes," I say. I apologise to Karla and kiss her, but she turns her attention away from me and into her afternoon alone.

It is clear from our meeting that while I have been away everyone else has graduated into this new realm of medicine. That I have been left behind is apparent in the basic questions I still need to ask and George's response to them, teacher peering over his glasses at the dim kid at the back.

There is also the likelihood of a further complaint. Lauren Wallis comes in during the afternoon to discuss her "migraines", but it is clear that they are in fact boring old no-street-cred tension headaches. She has just moved here from Surrey, so I don't know her well. Her husband still works there in film production or something like that—but he travels, so they too have moved down here for the cheaper housing, fresher air and better schools. I try to tell her that migraines are episodic and by definition (From *hemi-krania*, I explain, passing on the benefit of my Shahbn Greek.) affect only half of the head. But she knows best, she is in tune with her body, she has cut out caffeine and wheat. All this is discussed with the backdrop of her six-year-old son Anton, fidgeting and interrupting, pulling books from my shelves and turning on the taps.

"Can you turn that off, please, Anton?" I ask.

"Oh, it's no use telling him. He's autistic, he doesn't understand."

I give him a sharp look of disapproval, and he seems to fucking understand to me. He sits next to his mother for a minute, waits for her train of self-indulgent symptoms to resume, then begins to open my drawers.

"Don't do that, please, you might trap your fingers," I say.

"I told you it's not as easy as that," she snaps. "He's not been right since his MMR, it makes no difference what you say to him."

I know—I just *know* within thirty seconds of seeing him—that it does, for he looks at me again and obeys. But she has now spent years on an elaborate construction of his role as autistic, his free and chaotic will damaged by toxic vaccines and conspiring doctors. Now he is beyond control and she is helpless, a slave to him and to "migraines", a slave to God knows what else. I wonder what the husband-father is like, sympathise with his choice to be absent, and in a rare moment of insight I understand that Anton actually *wants* to be controlled. He wants nothing more than maternal love expressed in terms of confinement and protection. He does not want the responsibility of his own immature whim-led explorations any more. I understand that, however long it takes, it is my duty to explain this to her, and oddly I do not mind. This, after all, is one of the few occasions where I can rise above the computerised risk management business that general practice has become and make profound contact with somebody and actually help them in a time of need. If adults choose to become illness junkies, that is their right, but when they seek to project their prejudices onto their children it starts to smack of abuse and I am obliged to intervene.

"Look," I begin calmly, "whether he's autistic or not, he still needs—"

"How dare you!" she interrupts, standing up. "How dare you lecture me on what he needs! Are you an expert on autism? Are you? Are you? Have you had any training at all? Come on, Anton, we're going home." And she wrenches his surprised jerky form behind her as she pauses only to slam the door.


When I get back home at six-thirty I immediately pour us a drink (Karla is getting to like gin and tonic—there are many good things about England, you see) and tell her about our meeting, my encounter with the unfortunate Anton, and the rest of my shitty day. And I have to tell her that even if she and her colleagues in Jackfish Lake misguidedly saw me as a good doctor, that is certainly not the view of my partners and a fair few patients here. Yes, I had hoped to return from Canada invigorated and positive, but I seem to be demoralised and confused. For nearly an hour I tell her of the friction in the practice, how work and fatigue eroded my marriage, my determination that it won't happen again. Now I feel I am at a crossroads, I must adapt, maybe go part time. She sits at the table, all that foreign historical wisdom quietly concentrated into her slim frame, incongruous in this little Cornish house. My only certainty is that I am glad to have her here, and I squeeze her hand and tell her so. She smiles unconvincingly, breaks free from my hand to stand up.

"Karla? What's the matter?"

"Nothing. I'm sorry you're having these problems, and I guess it's good that you've told me."

"But?"

"But I thought you might have asked how Alex was at his first day of school."

# 2.4

Gareth and Lyn look like brother and sister. He is shorter than me but sturdily built, suggesting passable fitness for his age, a man who plays a good game of squash. She has rounded a little with time but her face is sharp and the overriding impression is of trim alertness. They share the same shading—freckle-coloured hair which has matured into a sandy grey, his now mildly sparse, and skin which has been tastefully exposed to the sun. Mary used to say that people who look alike make happy marriages, a piece of family philosophy handed down unfounded, but in our four individual instances true.

They are just back from visiting James and are holding another open house. Karla is nervous, knowing she will be scrutinised by these dozen or so friends of the doctor, all so politely nosey about this foreign young dolly he has acquired. I keep a supportive hand to her waist and introduce her to our hosts. Lyn welcomes her with an effusive kiss to each cheek. This is hardly a standard Jackfish Lake greeting, but Karla reacts admirably with a winning smile and a "Thank you for inviting me. That's very kind." Lyn goes to greet more arrivals, so we chat to Barnaby and Caroline. She has evidently recovered from her fit of the vapours (She never did make that appointment to discuss them, not with me at least. She might have gone to see that nice understanding Julia instead.), and I am relieved that there is no sign of Mary and NYK. More hellos are said, more drinks are poured, Karla fields predictable questions as she endures a polite society initiation of people seeking boundaries and foundations before they can move onto warmth. How are you settling down? What do you think of Cornwall? How's your boy? Where are you from? Have you found work? For an hour or so she responds with a corresponding English restraint but I know she is still not relaxed. Her normal posture is of strong composure, so her fidgeting is noticeable. She knocks back two generous glasses of red wine rather quickly and her cheeks take on the hint of a flush.

Then Lyn returns with her customary quickfire talk, "Karla, darling, how are you coping with all these weird and wonderful people? It's lovely to see you at last. How are you liking it over here?"

"Fine, I think we'll really enjoy it, thanks."

"And where's your darling boy? Is he settling in?"

"He's at home watching TV. He feels he has to catch up with all the strange programmes his friends watch, then he'll have something to talk about. What are they called, Philip?"

"EastEnders? Hollyoaks? Not the kind of thing I follow myself." Indeed, no. I have caught him watching such banal offerings and tried to get him to switch to something more edifying on more than one occasion. He has silently refused.

"Something like that. I guess school is still a little strange, but I think he'll be okay."

"I'm sure he will. People are so friendly here, aren't they, Gareth? I'm sorry not to have invited you round earlier, but we only got back from Japan last week. It's an amazing country, you really must go, you'd adore the place (she addresses this to Karla for some reason). And the people or so courteous. James was really worried when he got there, everyone was really formal at first, and he had to wear a suit for work—I mean, James in a suit, imagine!—and they have all these odd customs, of course. For instance, did you know (touching her hand onto Karla's forearm in that confiding way) it's extremely rude to lock your door. There's absolutely no crime, and they take it to mean you don't trust people if you leave your house locked. I suppose it used to be like that round here, didn't it, not so long ago? Do you get much street crime in Canada, Karla?"

"Yeah, we've had quite a few houses burned down on the reserve this last year. Plus the usual stabbings."

"Oh, goodness!" Lyn stops, momentarily capsized from her flow but righting herself with impressive speed. "Anyway, at the end of the first week the headmaster invited James to his house after school, and he thought it would be really stuffy, you know. Of course, it was straight into the karaoke and they all got *absolutely* pissed. Can you imagine it? James—karaoke!"

She goes on at some length about their trip, what a wonderful country it is, how lovely the gardens are, and yes they really do have those little capsule hotels but women aren't allowed to stay in them, how unfair is that? Gareth comes by to top up glasses once more. He is an excellent host, continually circulating to see to his guests' needs even at the cost of excluding himself from the backdrop of laughter and steadily loosening conversation. On this occasion, though, he stops to confirm how marvellous their visit was.

"So how long were you there?" Karla asks.

"Four weeks. No, in fact it was nearly five."

"That must have been quite an experience. You must have a real good job to afford a trip like that. What do you do?"

Gareth looks unsure, as am I, whether this is asked in innocence or mischief. "I was in property development for some years, though it's all very low key now."

"Shit, so you don't really work at all?"

"Well, not as such. I do have certain—"

"Gee, I'm sorry if it's none of my business, but I have a lot of trouble getting my head around that one. I've never met anyone who could take a five-week vacation before. When people on our reserve don't work it's because they have no choice."

Gareth smiles awkwardly and looks to me for some sort of lead. I fail to supply it, but fortunately Steve and Kim arrive. Kim is always revered as being more broadminded than the rest of us, the one who does yoga, who is learning to do reiki massage, who knows about things like chakras and auras and herbs. You would think she should have waist-length hennaed hair and swirling kaftans, but she is small and blonde and simply dressed. She looks younger than her years, and her slightly pudgy face would be featureless but for her striking bright blue eyes.

"So! This must be Karla—how lovely!" She kisses her theatrically on both cheeks. Karla responds stiffly but smiles. "What do you think of Cornwall?"

"It's just beautiful. After being so far from the sea, it's amazing to be able to see it so often."

"You're from the middle of Canada then?"

"Yes, Manitoba. As far inland as you can get."

"And which tribe do you belong to, Karla?"

"I'm Cree."

"Cree! Wow, and you actually live on a reserve?"

"Yes."

"How amazing!"

"It's not so amazing when it's minus thirty in January and you can't afford fuel because your man spends what little money you have on drink. Not that Philip does that, of course."

"Not quite," I amend. "Not yet."

Our laughter is perhaps a little over-egged, and Kim continues, "No, I'm sure, but every country has its pockets of deprivation, doesn't it? At least you've still got your native traditions and all that ancient wisdom, which is more than we have here."

"If we have, it's no thanks to the English, but the truth is that most people today have lost touch with all that. They might go to the occasional powwow, but it doesn't really affect the way they live. Ancient customs don't feed us or keep us warm."

"That's *really* sad." Kim looks genuinely offended by this, as if years of her own accumulated wisdom have been thrown away. "I was reading a book recently about the native Americans, and it was amazing that they knew so much about religion and mythology and health—everything really. Apparently the Hopi Indians burn candles in their ears to remove wax. Isn't that amazing? Do your people do that?"

"No, they don't," says Karla. "But I read in a book once that if the English don't have a shit at seven o'clock every morning, they need to have an enema. Do your people do that?"

I have the impulse to burst into mortified laughter but Kim's hurt stare deters me. Lyn looks around for an excuse to escape, and Gareth says, "Karla, dear, your glass is empty again. Can I get you another drink?"

In bed later I say to Karla, "Nothing like going straight in at the deep end, then."

"Are you trying to say I was rude?"

"Well, you might have been a bit, um, direct with Gareth and Kim."

"Good."

"Oh, come on, Karla, he's a very nice person, and he happens to be my best friend."

"I'm sure he's a real nice guy and all that, but he's also damn lucky that he can go wherever he likes in the world without having to work. I don't see any harm in pointing that out to him."

"No, but—"

"But what? But I mustn't upset him because he's your friend?"

"No, that's not what I meant—"

"You told me I was the most honest person you'd ever met. Now you're saying you want me to change that?"

"No, of course not."

"Good. Because if you just want me to come over here to look pretty and say nice things to your friends without making them uncomfortable, then we should forget this whole business now because I just can't do it. This is the way I am."

I feel I should tell her that it's possible to be honest without being blunt and confrontational like that, but she turns to face me and I can see even through the fading light that her eyes are focused and uncompromising. "Yes, okay," I say instead. "Goodnight."

She is still trying to get a job and has sent off applications for the few local posts which arise. The c.v. she encloses, prepared in her own biroed hand, does not look guaranteed to impress:

*Karla Ruth MACRAE*          *Date of Birth—2/22/1974*
Education—Jackfish Lake High School, MB, Canada
Qualifed—University Of Manitoba School of Nursing 1999
This was based mainly at Thompson Hospital and covered all Aspects of Nursing Care
Posts held—Registred Nurse, Jackfish Lake Indian Hospital.
gaining experience in Trauma, Diabetic Care, and Supervision of small Renal Dialysis Unit (1999-2004). Also lots of Pediatrics.
Referees—Mrs Rose Guthrie, Clinic Manager, Jackfish Lake
Hospital, Manitoba ROB 4WW Canada
Miss Jane Monias, Nurse Tutor. Thompson Hospital, Thompson MB.

"Doesn't it seem funny describing Rose as clinic manager?" she chuckles. "I wonder if she's still as pissed off with it all."

I offer a distracted grunt and feel her gaze darting into the back of my neck. "What's wrong with it?" she demands.

"Nothing—"

"But what? What's the problem?"

"Karla, relax, there's no problem. But there'll be lots of applicants for this job, so you just have to present yourself in the best possible way, so they'll want to interview you. Put in as much detail as you can about your courses and certificates, and all your experience, and do it on the computer. It'll look much more professional. I'll help you do it if you like." Immediately she rips her application into myriad shreds. "Karla!"

"Well, you said it wasn't good enough, you said that I had to do it again. So that's what I'm doing."

"But there's no need to take it to heart like that." She is sitting at the kitchen table, elbows propped, chin slumped into hands. I edge onto the chair beside her and put my arm round her shoulder. "Come on, Karla, what's up?"

"I don't think this is going to work," she says quietly.

"What?"

"This. Everything. You. Me. Alex. Here."

"Hey, come on, give it time, you've only been here a month. You'll find work, it just takes longer than you think. You mustn't give up yet. You know, after my first three days in Jackfish Lake, I was all set to come straight back home. It was all so strange, I thought I'd never handle the work."

"But it was different for you, you only had yourself to think of."

"Sure, but—are you saying this is all down to Alex?"

"Not entirely, but he's really unhappy, Philip."

"But he says school is going okay."

"He's told you that, and I've told you that, because I thought he just needed time to settle in. But he comes home every day and cries."

"Why? Is anyone giving him trouble?"

"No. But he's lonely, he's made no friends. He doesn't have anything in common with the local kids."

"Karla, it really is early days yet, I'm sure he'll be okay, kids are very adaptable."

She looks at me with her soft brown eyes and I know they have something more to say. "Philip, it's not only that."

"So what is it?"

"I'm sorry to say this, but he doesn't like you. I know you can't help it, I know you've tried, but he still sees you as the person who's taken him away from his home and everything he knows."

"Well, I can understand that, I suppose—"

"He just can't connect with you, Philip. I'm sorry, I'm not blaming you, but—I know Marshall and Wilson have been good for nothing for much of their lives, but they've both looked after Alex in their way. They've taken him fishing, camping, skating, on sno-mo trips, to powwows, shown him lots of practical stuff. It's different here, he doesn't have anything in common with you, he finds you very remote."

I sigh. She gives me that look again and I know that more is to come. "And the truth is, so do I."

Remote? But, I try to tell her, I have never felt more comfortable with anyone, I have opened up to her with all the candour I have. "Karla?"

"What?"

"Do you love me, or did you just want to escape? It's okay to tell me the truth—all I want is to know."

She shifts her position onto my lap, arm round my shoulder but looking away. Eventually she replies. "I really don't know any more. I thought I loved you, and I honestly wouldn't have come otherwise. I'm not as cynical as that. But can you love someone in isolation, Philip? If you take me away from my culture and my family and my friends, I'm not really me any more, I'm not complete. Love you or not I feel like half a person here, I feel lost and disconnected. And Alex feels even worse.

"You know, lots of women on the reserve like Edna and Bertha always swore that they would never marry anyone but a Cree. They might say they would do anything to get away from that place, but they don't mean it. I know life is hard and I know we've lost a lot of our traditional values over the years, but if we marry out of our tribe it will dilute it even further, and within a generation the Cree identity will be completely lost. You might say that shouldn't matter to the two of us, but it kind of takes a hold of you, you know? You can't separate the people from their environment. So I think I probably love you as an individual person, but I guess I'm no longer sure if that's enough. I'm sorry if I've misled you, or if you think I've taken advantage of you, but I'm trying to be honest."

"But aren't you overplaying this cultural thing?" I ask. "I'm not saying anything against the Cree, but people integrate these days, they have to. You only have to go to London or Birmingham to see that different races inter-marry. That's how countries become

255

cosmopolitan and tolerant of each other, it all has to start on an individual basis. It's normal now, surely it's a good thing?"

"Maybe it's good if you come into somewhere strange with your extended family, or if there's a community already there to help you. But otherwise it's so difficult—how many Cree are there in Cornwall, or even in England? And anyway, there's another thing that bothers me."

"What's that?"

"It's that people here have so much."

"But wasn't that one reason for coming? There are more opportunities for Alex, and for you."

"I know, I know. I don't want to sound ungrateful, but seeing all this—everyone's comfortable homes, their five or six holidays a year, people like Gareth and Lyn living luxurious lives without having to work—I'm sorry if I embarrassed you the other night but it makes me sad and it makes me angry. It makes me think of what Mom went through, and how people like Marshall and Wilson will never get a job because society discriminates against them just on account of their race. And being here makes part of me feel like a traitor, like I'm selling out. What do you say to that?"

Why ask me? That we love each other, that it would make more material sense to make our lives together here than on her isolated and deprived reserve, is my simplistic and emotionally constipated way of looking at it. "It's just the way the world is, Karla, it's unfair and it always will be, there's nothing wrong with looking after your own needs. So are you telling me you want to go back home?"

She looks at me and manages to smile. "No, I'm not giving up yet, it wouldn't be fair on Alex or on you." She gazes out of the window at the twee and utterly comfortable skyline of our Cornish village. The cottages across the road, walls smug with ivy, conceal tasteful extensions which contain Rayburns and extensive wine racks and Ikea units hosting elegant cutlery, crafted serviette rings, Creuset kitchenware, candlestick holders for every day of the week, fruit and spices from all over the world. Holiday

256

homes, a third of the village now, await Volvoed owners on their next weekend break, and are delegated to agencies who employ the local women to clean them once a week. Suddenly I think the Cree may have a point—maybe the people from The Greenery should take them over or raze them to the ground. But of course I know they won't. This is Cornwall, this is England, this is a civilisation where poverty is contained, where its subjects are made soporific and pliant by *Coronation Street* and *Big Brother*, dreams of the lottery, the tits in The Sun, cheap flights to Spain, football and beer, DVDs and drugs. For the first time in my life it is revealed to me that all this unseemly stuff is indeed sanctioned by the Government, because it is a distraction from any revolutionary thoughts, it keeps people in their place. I have an urge to rush up to The Greenery, to hammer on all their doors and shout, "Come on, wake up, it's okay to revolt against all this! You've been oppressed and deceived—do it, do it!" But I will do no such thing, of course, for I too know my place.

Our cheeks touch. Side by side, they glance together in our pensive state. All these greater factors—in particular her burden of history and duty and punishment and tradition—orbit around us, their diverse gravities tug us in subtle and unknowable ways. No, it is clearly not just a question of me and Karla, and what is "best" for us. For a minute or two we are silent, thrown together from our far quarters to be clamped together on this hard chair in this small room in this pleasant village. Her eyes house sadness as she says, "I'll give it until the summer, I guess."

So already I have a deadline. After just four weeks I fear our partnership is already serving its notice. Unless she establishes herself as a woman of the county and Alex successfully steers himself through the dwindling school term, my romance will end. It will be remembered fuzzily as the doctor's aberration, a pretty memento from his time abroad—oh, yes, and didn't she have a sulky son? But I don't want it to fail on my part for any lack of will. At very least I will not be remote.

In bed I kiss and hold her tight. "I don't want to lose you," I say. I want to—I absolutely have to—reveal my true self, and the thought of this, the unbridled passion of Pacamac, makes me stifle a laugh.

"What is it?" she smiles, and I try my best to explain, so now our laughter is open and shared. Like never before I want to make love to her, I think I might have caught a glimpse of new and selfless depths. My hands explore her body but for once she defends it, her muscles are on guard.

"What's the matter?"

"Sssh," she says. "These walls are so thin, I don't want Alex to hear. He's not been sleeping well at night."

I sigh loudly and turn away into a rejected schoolboy huff. After a few minutes she turns in parallel with me and lays a hand gently on my hip. She tells me, "Anyway, Edna says there's another reason she would never want a baby with a white guy, no matter how dishy he was."

"What's that, then?"

"Because she could never have a kid without a treaty number. It would cost her a fortune, that's why."

I roll back to hold her and decide that the ability to laugh together is more important than sex.


A few days later she gets a letter in the post. There are usually one or two a week from Ruth, sometimes one from Lorraine, but this is different, this is official. "Look, Philip! Look!" Excitement and optimism lift her face.

She has been offered an interview at one of the smaller community hospitals, one of those low-tech care of the elderly units where patients receive basic nursing care within visiting distance of relatives when they are recovering from their hip replacements or strokes, or are simply "off their legs". It is easily within her capabilities, and I see that the letter is from Helena Crisp, a nursing officer whom I know in a friend-of-a-friend sort of way.

"Hey, that's excellent, I could give her a ring if you like."

"What do you mean, give her a ring?"

"Well, I know her—"

"Philip, how dare you! How dare you! I don't want your fucking government hand-out shit, thank you, I want to get this job on my own merit."

"I know, that, I know. I only—"

Only what? I know what she means, of course, but I am trying to help. And everyone does it, don't they? I try to tell her that this is how the system works, for all the official policies of not discriminating against anyone on the strength of their race or gender or age or total lack of ability, we all know that first impressions and the word-of-mouth recommendation of a trusted colleague count for ten times more than diplomas or degrees. Down here in Cornwall, you see, it's rather a tight community where the personal touch thankfully still has influence. These politically correct directives are all very well in London, but down here they don't really apply, for *this* is the real world, this is where—

"Karla?"

The minute-long elation of her offer is demolished as she slams out of the door.

Then I have to go to work, and I spend the whole morning distracted by leaving her in this state. Nor is she home when I phone mid-morning, and my anxiety levels rise. Is this it? Has she decided to head back home? I intend to try again but the frantic despair of the day prevents me, and it occurs to me that this is what really gets me down. I now want to abdicate from this throne to which subjects flock to be absolved of their pathology or their responsibility. I'm in agonies of pain all of the time. I can't seem to lose weight. I think my son's on drugs. I feel so tired. I'm depressed. How can my own life ever be fulfilling when I am inundated by this constant misery, and am made to feel it is my duty to relieve it? A quarter of a century working for the NHS has conditioned me to believe that the population's fatigue, obesity, unemployment, addictions, anxiety and general unhappiness are mine to resolve, and I must drown myself in pools of guilt if I don't flog myself for every waking hour of the week in this pursuit.

I call in at one-thirty and she is about to leave the house. "Where are you going?"

"I have to go to the school."

"Why?"

"Because Alex's teacher wants to speak to me. Can you come with me?"

"What, now? I have to be back at work. Is it so urgent?"

"Maybe not, but as there's a problem and I have nothing else to do all day, I thought I might as well go now. Are you coming or not?"

I really should say no, but I think of all those home versus work conflicts over the years, and the marital carnage that resulted. My dilemma comes out as a sigh.

"You don't *have* to, he's not your son."

"I know that, but—yes, I'll come with you. Let's go."

The school is like schools everywhere, a flat-roofed blocky maze of concrete and glass, unimaginative and seemingly unplanned. Miss Chater has a free period, and we are directed to her room. She seems ludicrously young, and I wonder how she can maintain authority over these dozens of adolescents in her charge. I think she must teach maths because her hair is so geometrically cut, black and straight and precisely angled to frame her circular face. We say hello and shake hands.

"It's really good to have Alex here, you know. I've really taken a liking to him."

"But?" Karla questions at once.

If this directness unsettles Miss Chater, she does not let it show. "But yes, there are a couple of concerns, which is why I asked if you'd like to come. I know it must be really difficult for him, coming from a different culture and all that, and being fairly quiet by nature. But he's socialising more, it's taking time, and he's starting to make friends."

"But?" repeats Karla.

"I don't now how forthcoming he is at home—"

"He isn't," I say.

"He tells *me* things," Karla says.

"—but I thought it wise to inform you that some boys from The Greenery estate have taken him under their wing. It might be harmless, and I know Alex has to sort these things out for himself, but past experience says that they might not be a good influence to someone who is new to the school."

I nod, having a good idea who she means. The Gibbs family, presumably, with their house constantly bathed in cigarette smoke and daytime telly, the big lumbering boys lounging louche outside and somehow attracting girls who are scarcely mature but simper and smoke with their new-found breasts thrusting out of tiny T-shirts which proclaim **up for it** and **i want u**. I imagine Alex, vulnerable and still barely into puberty, being a curiosity to them, an immigrant to convert to their way of life of furtive fags, swearing, drinking cider, shoplifting excursions in the village Spar, truancy and a general contempt for the values of school.

"What do you mean?" asks Karla.

"Well," says Miss Chater, "I'm sure Dr Cormack will confirm that there are a minority of pupils here who don't place education high on their priorities, and who take a certain delight in being disruptive."

"But at least they're taking an interest in Alex, they're speaking to him."

"Certainly, but they may well have ulterior motives. I don't think it would be very good for him—"

"How do you know what's good for him?" Karla demands. "Do you have any idea at all what hardships he's had, what it's like being brought up on a reserve?

"No, of course not—"

"Well, don't lecture me on—"

"Karla!" I interrupt. "Calm down, Miss Chater's trying to help."

"I'm sure she is, but she doesn't necessarily know what's best for Alex. He does talk to me, you know, and he says that at least those kids from the rough houses try to make friends with him, at least he feels okay with them. All the others, you know the rich ones who think they're so smart, they just ignore him, they treat him like shit."

Miss Chater, to her credit, keeps calm. "I'm not trying to tell you who he should and shouldn't mix with, I just thought I should let you have the information so you know what's happening. Anyway, there's another problem, which is more important."

"What?"

"You know he's one of the youngest in the class, don't you? Most of the others are now fourteen? Well, Alex's literacy skills are rather delayed."

"By how much?" I ask.

"His reading age is just under ten."

"Hey! What are you saying?" Karla snaps. "Are you saying he's stupid or something? Are you saying his schooling back home was substandard, because if so—"

"I'm not accusing him or you or his previous school of anything, I just wanted to talk to you so we could decide what's best for him," Miss Chater says quietly.

"Okay, so what do you think that might be?"

"Drop him back a year. I think that would help him socially and academically. There are a few weeks left this school year so if we do it now he can get to know the pupils in the year below and the teachers."

I catch Karla's glare and say, "That sounds like a good idea, you know, it might help him to adapt." It seems right now that he is making a better fist of it than his mother, and I smile Miss Chater an apology on Karla's behalf. She reciprocates and I see that, despite her youth, she is mature and conventional and sweet. She is from a nice middle-class background and she has never experienced hardship of any kind. I find myself hoping she never will. Her engagement ring is, like her, pretty and precise, neither cheap nor showy, and for one fierce moment I am jealous of her intended spouse. He is undoubtedly conventional too, I expect he works with computers or in a bank, but he can have everyday innocent conversations with her without the fear of provoking a backlash of cultural protest. Furthermore he has permission to rip off her sensible clothes, ruffle her orderly hair, trigger her ecstasy in bed. He can do all that and then they can lie together, united and cocooned in their world, safe, perfectly safe.

Then comes a further anxiety. This evening Beth phones to say she will be back in Cornwall at the weekend, so clearly we will all have to meet up. After all, Karla keeps bombarding me with questions about them (When did you say Beth was home from London? Don't you want them to meet me or something?) so it is already building up towards one of those taut meet-the-family occasions. At first I wonder about a neutral venue, taking them all out to lunch in Truro or a country pub, but this will only add formality. So I invite my daughters round on Sunday afternoon.

It is everything I anticipate it to be. We have prepared three o'clock tea, with bannock cakes as per Ruth's recipe, and Karla is clearly impressed by my girls. Beth has gained confidence from her years away, and she tells us of her university course although Karla admits to not knowing who Samuel Beckett is, or seeing how preparing a 10,000 word dissertation on him can prepare anyone for the hardships of life ahead. Stella is more cagey, and they politely exchange extracts of each other's lives between offers of more tea and compliments on the cake. Alex drifts uneasily between us and homework and TV, but details of his origin are too intimate for today. Karla seems to have accepted for once that a little restraint may have a place. Even so, I fear that my daughters' thoughts are dominated by outrage at her age, seeing that their staid and dependable dad has gone the way of middle-aged loners everywhere and taken on a young bit of stuff.

It is clear that the distance between them is unbridgeable. Matters would be eased if the one common touchstone between them—me—were warm and spontaneous and outgoing, but I am morbidly self-conscious (I may even blush) and my embarrassment stifles us all.

# 2.5

It is a long time since I have approached Montfort House with anything like affection. In recent years the drive past the tall once-red brick walls which retain the sizeable garden, and my walk along the increasingly bedraggled path has been accompanied by an anticipatory gloom. The interior seems darker with every visit, my parents who were both so imposing in their way are now shrinking to occupy an ever smaller proportion of their rambling abode. Dad is seventy-nine today and I cannot connect the moment of this to anything but doom and decline. And today I recognise something else which underpins my apprehension at coming back here, a mixture of resentment and loss which stems from the knowledge that my lifelong connection with this house may not endure much longer. This is not a new feeling, it has rankled idly for some years, and I now suspect that it stems from the fact that I was sent away, a mere eight miles but nonetheless away, from what should have been an ideal boyhood home. The spare bedrooms, the enormous attic, the garden with trees to climb and build dens in, the sheds, the lush lawn perfect for cricket, the neighbouring friends, the—

"Oh, bugger," I utter my dismay.

"What?" asks Karla. "What's the matter?"

I point out the lumbering boys now in sight, a two-man scrum tumbling on the grass in pursuit of a rugby ball. "Henry and Mark, I didn't know they were here. I didn't see Giles's car."

"But Philip, aren't they your nephews? Aren't you glad to see them?"

"Well, yes, I suppose so, but they're a bit boisterous, always niggling each other and scrapping."

"So do they have criminal records? Do they take drugs? Do they sniff gas?"

They don't, of course. We get out of the car to meet them. Henry is fifteen, Mark a year less, but they are both threateningly mature with a combination of their father's swarthy musculature and their mother's height. We introduce ourselves and they assess Alex as he stands shyly, looking half their size and age.

"Ever played rugby?" Henry asks him.

"No."

"Come on then, we'll teach you."

Without a glance of permission from us, he is off to learn his new art, so I lead Karla into the house. It takes a moment to adjust to the exclusion of light, but she peers around the cavernous hallway with its sombre oaky doors and stairway angling up to uninviting heights. It occurs to me that this space on which the gloom of the house converges is probably bigger than the room in which Karla, Alex, Ruth and Evelyn have all lived for so many years. But, despite the vast acreage at their disposal, my parents seem to spend most of their waking time in the kitchen, though this too is now a clutter of darkness and—a humiliating admission of my mother's failure to cope—dirt. The pulley dangles from the ceiling with bygone clothes to dry, and every surface is occupied by a musty chaos of jars, books, newspapers, cutlery and crockery, bread and its crumbs, elderly fruit, cereal packets, pens, batteries and Mum's little wicker pots which overflow with their own quota of detritus—combs, elastic bands, purses, nail clippers, spectacles, skin creams and all the other myriad accumulations which they have put "to one side" for improbable future use. Mum is fussing at the Rayburn while Dad sits on his usual high-backed chair with the *Telegraph* spread on the table before him. It's barely six weeks since I've been here but I swear that my mother has shrunk. Her size always used to mitigate against her lack of mettle, but now that physical presence has gone.

"Hi, Mum, hi, Dad!"

"Philip!"

"Hello, son, never heard you come in."

"This is Karla. I told you she was coming with me."

"Hi," she smiles. "It's real good to meet you."

"Hello, dear." Mum wipes her hands on her apron, Dad stands, and in turn they shake hands with her, formal and polite. There is not a chance in a million that they will offer her a hug, and I wonder if Karla might see in this introductory instant why the son they produced is also cool and aloof, some might say remote.

"How d'you do, m'dear," says Dad. "So where've you come from, eh?"

"Manitoba. Right in the middle of Canada."

I know what Dad is going to say, and indeed he follows the limited script which his brain now retains, "Canada, eh? Haven't come across our Geoffrey by any chance? Can't remember which part he lives in now."

Mum and Karla look to me as if I'm some sort of expert here. Do I correct him gently but invoke embarrassment in front of his new guest? Or should I say nothing and reinforce this delusion that his brother is still alive? The fact is, it makes no difference. He will be impervious to whatever I say, any new fact or feeling will not be stored.

"Dad, Geoffrey's dead."

"What?! When? We only had a card from him last week."

"I don't think so, Dad, it's been quite a time now. It must have slipped your mind."

"May! You never told me Geoffrey was dead!"

"I did, dear, but it was a very long time—"

"My own brother! She hides things from me all the time, you see what she's like? My own brother's dead, and I'm the last to know!"

Suddenly he is agitated, I fear he will burst into tears. He moves from behind the table to reveal remnants of meals on his jumper and a streaky sheen on his trousers where urine has overflowed, unnoticed, away. From mid-air in my own memory I pluck out a vision of him—me aged eight or ten in his study, light flooding through the bay window, him silver-haired and dapper at his drawing board even then, set-square and meticulous pens and pencils to hand, piles of plans stacked white and heavy on the table, and each one packed precise with data—distance and floor space, the height of walls and depth of drains, the angle of doors and plot of electrics, annotated comment neat and precise and perpendicular on every page. Even the paper itself seemed impressive, demanding respect with its restrained pearly gloss and its size. This was him as he was meant to be, in his element, not a husband or father but an architect every minute of his lucid life. Now this—if he can't draw plans, he may as well abandon himself to decay.

"Dad, nobody's hiding things from you, but your memory's not what it was. It can't be helped, it's just one of those unfortunate things."

"Unfortunate?" he shouts. "I'll say it's bally unfortunate. Somebody tells you your brother's dead, then makes out—"

"Oh, Ronald!" Mum wails. She makes a feebly protective move towards him, arms outstretched as if to a rushing child. It is clear from her voice and posture that what scant reserve she ever had has now gone.

"Stop pestering me, woman!" He flails an arm towards her, a foot or two away but enough to make her recoil and it is only Karla's foresight that steadies her.

At this moment of chaos, Eve and Giles arrive laden—the latter clearly reluctantly—with supermarket bags. "Oh, you're here then. We arrived this morning to find that there was no food in the house."

"Hi. Dad's just got himself a little bit upset."

"Yes, well now you see what it's like." I brace myself for a beration, but Eve spots Karla and smiles. "You must be Karla," and she greets her with a wholehearted hug. "I'm sorry you've suddenly been landed with all this, but—well, this is how things are right now."

"Please don't apologise. I understand."

Dad settles quickly with the distraction of his daughter, Mum sits down in another fluster but just short of tears, Giles offers a cursory greeting then goes off to spend some quality time with his mobile. "We've a hell of a lot on at work," he explains, in a pre-emptive objection to being here. But it's Saturday, I feel like saying. I thought you were a fucking accountant.

Eve packs away the shopping and makes us all a coffee, over which she extracts a preliminary biography from Karla. Then she asks her, "Come on then, are you ready?"

"Ready for what?"

"I'm taking you into Sherborne for lunch and some retail therapy. I need a break from him (her eyes point to the door Giles has passed through once more) and those boys, so I thought we could have a girls' day out."

I am about to point out that Karla might have an ethical problem with retail therapy, especially the type available in Shahbn, but she is already smiling with enthusiasm. "Sounds great," she says, "I'd like that."

"And I'm sure Philip needs to catch up with what's happening here with Mum and Dad," says Eve. She links arms with Karla and leads her to the car.

The rest of the weekend stumbles uneasily by. We have a celebratory dinner, though Dad is not sure why. Giles remains peeved and persistently directs his irritation at Mark via his wife, "Why can that boy never sit through a meal time like a reasonable adult?" "What is wrong with him that he can't survive a single hour without those stupid computer games?" I don't believe he once speaks directly to Karla, for she is not nor ever will be one of his type. But at least Henry and his brother include Alex in their furtive electronic musings and after the meal they walk to the traditional old village store and video rental outlet to hire *Trainspotting*, which Alex has never heard of, let alone seen. He watches it intently, but later admits that he has not understood a word.

We retire about eleven, and Karla puts on the dress she has bought, a pink floral cotton creation from Laura Ashley or Monsoon or somewhere like that.

"It's not really me, but Eve just insisted," she apologises. "I wonder if I could take it back without offending her."

"Karla, you look absolutely gorgeous," I tell her, and I make love to her while she still wears it, frantic and impulsive, sprawled anyhow across the bed now occupying what was once my boyhood room.



We get back home on Sunday evening to receive good news twice. Karla opens a letter from Helena Crisp, "Look! Look!" she shows me her invitation to an interview on Thursday of this week. One of the nearby community hospitals has a vacancy in their Minor Injury Unit, and Helena thinks her experience would be better suited to that than the elder care post for which she applied. "That would be ideal—after Jackfish Lake I could handle anything like that." I am sure that she could, for the sprains and dog bites and summer sunburns would keep her happily occupied.

"That's great!" I congratulate her, and I hope as hard as I can that the expectation lighting up her eyes doesn't plummet into disappointment.

Then there is an ansafone message from Gareth, "Listen, Philip, Jon Tullo tells me there's a new crop of kids this year who want to resurrect the junior cricket team. He's roped me in to give them a coaching session on Wednesday at six, so I'm roping you in to help. And you'd better bring that lad of yours along too."

Suddenly I have a conviction that everything will be all right. Karla will find rewarding work which will bind her to our community, and I will further my fathering of Alex by guiding him through the niceties of cricket. I really can't understand why I hadn't thought to do this before.

# 2.6

Is there anything more idyllic? What could attract someone to the delights of English rural life if not an evening of cricket? The sun is shining, a warm light breeze refreshes us, and fourteen boys have gathered for a session on the village pitch. To be honest, not many of them are interested in the finer points of technique, they just want a couple of hours of gently competitive activity. The slow strategy of the three- or five-day game is not for them, for they are bred on action replays, glossed-up soft-focus highlights of highlights which do away with the bother of preparation and perspiration to concentrate all on the gratification of the winning goal or try or six, and the excruciating slow-mo celebrations thereof. They have all seen the tawdry and sacrilegious innovation which is 20Twenty or Twenty20 or 2wenti2wenti or whatever its stupid subliterate textified name is, but unless Gareth and I give in to them and offer some enjoyment they will not come back.

So the two of us will field for both sides (Tregaskis village v Rest of the World) in a twenty-over game, and those boys who want to stay on for some specialised tuition after the allotted overs can do so. Of course I have given Alex some abbreviated lessons in the last few evenings, though the first time I brought him here to lob a routine throw towards him he underestimated the density of the ball and it crashed through his cupped hands and into his breast bone, knocking him to the ground. Undeterred he got up, to learn how to grip the bat, where to stand, and how to bowl. But his arms are still spindly and it is clear he will not have the strength to hurl the ball back to the wicket from much of a range.

His team fields first, and I put him in the slips. Before long it is clear that he has one attribute which most of his colleagues lack, because he concentrates on every ball. He maintains this from one over to the next while the other boys' attention dawdles on to some movement in the pavilion, an exchanged smirk or remark, or the lurid internal workings of the male teenage brain. Sometimes he dashes off, naively out of position, in enthusiastic pursuit of a shot, but this is to be understood. And halfway through the innings the opposing opener, known to be the best batsman on the pitch and seemingly capable of winning the game on his own, snicks a thick edge low to Alex's right. Before we know it, Alex is already diving, anticipating, gathering the ball securely in his outstretched hand. What a hero! What a catch!

As last man in he doesn't get much chance to bat, because they are clearly going to lose. But he makes contact with one or two routine balls. The first time it surprises him, he looks out in anticipation of a boundary, whereas the reality is a mistimed shot which backspins to a halt within a few feet. Then he repeats his manoeuvre, gains a little more momentum this time, and is still standing stunned when his colleague yells, "Run!" I applaud heartily—Alex is off the mark.

Six or seven of the boys stay on for an hour or so, as Gareth and I attend to basic matters of technique. Lyn, Kim and Karla have been watching, and afterwards we go for a drink and meal in the pub. I am grateful, incidentally, that Kim has come to look on Karla's introductory outburst towards her with an amused forgiveness, though Gareth finds it difficult to conceal his wariness when she is around. But now we are all complimenting Alex on how well he played. "Hey, you made that catch real good!" Karla says. "Why don't they give you some gloves?"

Gareth tells her, "What you might not have noticed is his footwork. Most kids when they're batting just stand rooted to the spot until the very last millisecond, when it's too late. But I was watching how he automatically adjusted his position from almost before the ball left the bowler's arm. He probably wasn't aware of it himself, it was subconscious, but that's the mark of a true batsman. I think he could be quite a decent cricketer."

Alex looks up from his meal. He doesn't notice us smiling at his moustache of tomato soup, a reminder that he has not yet left the habits of childhood behind. "So when's the next game?" he asks. "When can I play again?"

If only this contentment extended to the realm of work. Every week creates more demands than the one before. Patients either display a confounding level of ignorance about their own health care, or (the majority here) flap neurotically about every media-driven scare they encounter. There seems to be no solidly sensible middle ground. This week some high-profile but totally unqualified friend of Cherie Blair has pontificated in the *Mail on Sunday* about the horrific side-effects of childhood vaccinations, so now earnest mummies are caught in the throes of their latest dilemma. "It's so hard to know who to believe, isn't it?" they flock to me to agonise. Actually, madam, it isn't. You can either rely on scores upon scores of proven studies by reputable scientists from all over the world, or you can take the word of some bimboid "lifestyle guru" besotted with the easy and irresponsible influence which vacuous celebrity brings. Other life-threatening concerns this week have included:

Tamsin's allergist says can she get hair analysis on the NHS?

Can you put some elastic stockings on my prescription as we're flying to our gîte near Carcassonne for the summer and I don't want to get a thrombosis?

Is it all right for my wife to eat grilled goat's cheese when she's pregnant?

Answers: a) No. b) Certainly not. c) It depends whether you're grilling the cheese or the goat.

If the patients don't finish me off, the computer certainly will. No consultation can begin before the obstacle course of hazard warnings is negotiated. Every time I obliterate one another flashes up to take its place. **This patient has not been offered smoking cessation advice. This diabetic has not had peripheral pulses recorded. This patient is overdue a cervical smear. This doctor's mental faculties have really gone to ratshit.** This slows every surgery and I am aware that more time is spent inspecting the screen than the patient. It also a constant reminder that my contribution to the George Retirement Fund is unacceptable. We are due to meet again next week to assess my performance and productivity, but all I can see is that the health gains to the population seem to be gallingly small for the effort and money invested in all this. My computer tells me that Ernie Pellow, who hasn't eaten a vegetable for most of his ninety-one years unless it's encased in his daily pasty, is due for a cholesterol check. For fuck's sake, computer, why? He gave up smoking when he had his mini-stroke at eighty-eight, isn't that enough? His son takes him to the pub for a Sunday lunchtime Guinness and, if the weather is good, to his favourite quayside bench at Leazey to survey the fishing boats which appear pretty much unchanged from the days he worked them himself. But of course I must not deny him access to health care on the basis of age alone. The National Service Framework (That's another thing! What does that mean? I thought National Service was abolished in 1956. Framework to me suggests scaffolding. Who invents these ridiculous titles? People with recalcitrant mental health problems here are now referred to something called the Assertive Outreach Team. How does that give any clue as to who they are and what they do? ["I think I ought to refer you to the Assertive Outreach Team, Darren." "Yer fuckin wot?"] Why not be honest and call it the When All Else Fails Team? And, guess what, they are not based in an office but something called a Resource Centre. A couple of weeks ago I went to a study day and on registering was given a folder of relevant reading matter. "Here's your resource pack," I was told. "Madam," I wanted to reply, "please do not insult me with your pretentious euphemisms. This is not a resource pack, it's a bleeding folder!") warns me that age discrimination is not always explicit. I do know that, just as I know that in the very unlikely event of me living to ninety-one, I do not wish to take handfuls of pharmaceuticals every day just to keep my biochemical markers within the government's limits. I can't get through a single surgery without wondering what's the point of it all. Every minor discontent and abnormality must be corrected as the population's threshold for imperfection drops.

Are our lives here on this green and clement peninsula of our prosperous nation really so bad? I know they aren't because Karla continues to phone her mother two or three times a week. Again there is no doctor in Jackfish Lake. The pompous South African only lasted four weeks, so now the nurses try to muddle through. They dish out Amoxil to chesty kids, organise Medevacs for chest pains, and backslab the angulated ankles of drunks. They can do this as well as I did, but meanwhile the asthmatics, depressives, epileptics, hypertensives and diabetics receive no care, and many more of these go undetected as a population's hearts and legs and kidneys and brains are bathed in a substrate of UP-sponsored fatty salty sticky blood.

Now we learn that Evelyn is diabetic too. She became lethargic and thirsty, Ruth took her to emerg, and a blood test confirmed the worst. Karla tells me the news and our eyes meet. Hers are filmed with tears for we both know what Evelyn's future holds. It will be a slow and painful decline without any prospect of escape.

The good news (well, everything is relative) is that Marshall has been released from jail. Nobody, however, seems to know where he is.

# 2.7

It is a beautiful evening. The dappled sea barely moves, it is as if the whole ocean is asleep. Alex and a couple of other children harvest driftwood from all corners of the beach, which is deserted but for the dozen of us who have gathered. I am glad that Karla is here to experience this, one of the delights of Cornwall. Steve, as ever, is barbecue monitor, but he is happy to have Alex assist. They chat easily (What about? I am jealous to know.) and indeed Alex calls out, "Mom, Steve says he'll take me out fishing on Sunday. Is that okay?"

"Sure, honey," she replies. "And thank you, Steve."

He waves a piece of wood in acknowledgement, then attends to the task in hand. He is a busy person, Steve, always constructing or tinkering or keeping assiduously fit. For long periods he will say nothing, then he will embark on a lengthy description or anecdote, only to suddenly stop. It is as if he has not quite mastered the concept of conversation being a two-way process, but for all that his demeanour is spontaneous and sociable, his actions are generous, and he is generally well liked. He is also darkly lean and handsome. All the women clearly think he's gorgeous, and as we men find him too nice to trouble with our jealousy, no one makes a fuss.

More people arrive. This Friday at Six gathering at St Anselm's Bay has been going on for years. Sometimes half a dozen people attend, often—for birthdays or when friends of friends arrive for a weekend away—there can be thirty or more. Children are welcome too. They amuse themselves easily in this setting, especially when parents mellow with wine, and it is good to see Alex and the others collecting wood or investigating pools marooned in the rocks as the tide ebbs quietly away. The shore is still a source of novelty and wonder to him, and now he calls out with joy at the discovery of an everyday small crab.

We are chatting to Barnaby and Caroline, who asks Karla, "So do you have barbecues in Canada?"

"No, we've never heard of such a thing."

"Really?" Caroline replies. "They're quite popular here, aren't they? People have all these automated garden sets now, gas or whatever, but traditionally it's just cooking outdoors on wood and…" she falters as she catches our expressions. "She's pulling my leg, isn't she, Philip?"

"I'm sorry, that's real bad of me," Karla admits. "Actually the last barbecue I went to was in February, out in the middle of the lake."

"A barbecue in the middle of the lake?"

"Sure. When it's frozen solid we just drive out onto it and light fires."

"She's pulling my leg, isn't she, Philip?" Caroline repeats.

"No, I don't think so. Not this time."

Caroline laughs again, touching an affected hand onto Karla's arm. "I'm sorry, but we're so dreadfully ignorant here about other people's cultures, aren't we?"

"Maybe, but it's the same back home. Folk in Jackfish Lake don't exactly have a wide view on the world. They have enough problems of their own."

Caroline nods with exaggerated vigour, like a TV news reporter under instruction to be seen to be keen. "Yes, I'm sure, but we really should be better informed, don't you think? We're so wrapped up in our own comfortable lives, we're completely oblivious to the fact that other cultures have their own wisdom too, aren't we? I mean, I read something amazing the other day. Did you know that the Hopi Indians burn candles in their ears to melt wax?"

I close my eyes and brace myself for the impact. For a second I think I might have been spared it, for Karla's voice is quiet and calm. "Do you know what, if I was a Hopi Indian on some squalid reserve living off a shit diet courtesy of some meagre handout from the world's richest government, who pride themselves on being so God-fearing and civilised, but happened to have built their whole colossal wealth on land unlawfully taken from people like the Hopi in the first place, if I was such a person I'd be very, very pissed off if the only thing white people knew about my culture was some trivial and utterly irrelevant crap about ear wax, and then went on to make some patronising remark about the ancient knowledge that we've carelessly lost."

"I'm sorry, Philip, I just can't help it. Tomorrow I'll book me and Alex a ticket back to Winnipeg, then you won't have to worry about losing any more of your friends."

We are in bed, lights off, hands held, lying on our backs and staring into parallel dark. Maybe this is symbolic, the way it must be, never to intersect. "No, Karla, I want you to stay."

"But I get so angry all the time. I'll never fit in here, you must be able to see that."

"Did you see that newspaper article the other day about the English woman who went off to Africa and married some tribal king? They had nothing in common, not even the same language, but they recognised something between each other which transcended all their differences. She even had his children."

"Are you saying you want to start making babies with me?"

"Well, no." I hadn't really envisaged that, though I am momentarily taken by the vision of a hybrid son and heir. "I'm too old now, but it would be interesting to see the outcome— half Shahbn, half Cree. We could call him Piers de Montfort Tobacco Cormack, or Jocelyn Moose MacRae..."

"Or if it's a girl, Cinderella Jackfish Pacamac."

"Hm, maybe we'll put the baby idea on hold."

We laugh, silence settles, then she asks, "Do you think we have that something?"

"Euh? Of course. Don't you?"

"I really don't know any more, Philip. I really don't know."

This response disappoints me dreadfully, but I sleep sporadically and am aware of her getting up in the early hours to go downstairs. At ten in the morning we are both still dressing gowned and slow, mulling over kitchen table coffee and newspapers when the doorbell goes. Caroline comes in and presents Karla with a large bouquet of flowers. "I'm sorry I offended you, I apologise. These are on behalf of all of us, really, just to say we really like having you here."

For a moment I think Karla might burst into tears, but she gives a composed smile, exchanges a hug, and says, "Thank you. You're very kind."


Thursday arrives, and at least Alex is happy. He has agreed to be put into the lower year, and he finds the work more manageable. His literacy is still poor, but he has an enquiring mind and an aptitude for maths. His new classmates seem to accept him, even if it is again the clique from The Greenery who attract him into their circle. In the morning I leave for work and am slightly perturbed to see the Gibbs twins loitering slobbily outside.

However I am more preoccupied by my own day, which will centre on the meeting with Julia and George. In the last month I have kept my head down and done my best, I cannot think of anything which might give them cause for concern but I still feel myself in the position of a football manager given a vote of "confidence" by his board.

So it proves. I have done nothing to merit criticism, and nothing worth special praise. George asks if I have anything to say, and I don't. He suggests a further meeting in three months, by which time—the crux of the matter, I suspect—my financial contribution from the cumulated bytes of attained blood pressure targets and proffered advice on tobacco, alcohol and exercise will have been assessed. I wonder if the latter objective can be technically and cost-effectively achieved by phoning Radio Cornwall with the story that a virulent new superbug is transmitted in pasties and clotted cream, or maybe sponsoring a plane to fly over the practice area trailing a banner which instructs STOP SMOKING, CUT DOWN THE BOOZE AND GET OFF YOUR FAT ARSES NOW AND THEN.

"Something amusing you, Philip?" asks George.

"No, no, just a bit of lettuce between my teeth."

However, I haven't forgotten that the most important event of the day is Karla's interview. I rush home after work and in the first second of entering the house see that the outcome is not good. She is sitting at the kitchen table with a bottle of red wine already halfway drunk.

"Karla?" I pull up a chair beside her, sit and grasp her hand.

She does not look at me, but gives a false smile and shrugs.

"Tell me what happened."

She tops up her wine, I pour one for myself, and she says, "I got interviewed by two women in suits. They were both real pleasant, and asked me about what I did back home. They seemed to be impressed, but in the end they said they couldn't employ me because I didn't have a work permit. I said I'd apply for one, but they told me that takes five or six months. And anyway I can't apply for a work permit until I've got the offer of a specific job, and they want someone now."

"But that's terrible!" I sympathise. "That's a real Catch 22."

"A what?"

"Oh, never mind. But why did they interview you if they knew they couldn't give you a job?"

"That's what I asked them. Shit, Philip, I got really angry—I don't think they'd *ever* want to employ me now."

I can imagine the scene. "So what did they say?"

"They figured I'd be around for a while, so they said they'd offer me a job to start in December, so I can apply for a work permit now on the strength of that."

"Well, that's something, isn't it?"

"No!" she shouts. "I want something *now*! I don't think I can do this housewife stuff for six months, Philip, I think I'd rather go home."

So what are we to do? Just as it seems that our biggest worry—Alex's schooling—is being resolved, we find that Karla is being prevented from getting a job, and I am in danger of losing mine. But I hug her to me and say—lamely, I know—"Don't worry, everything will be all right."

"How will it?" she asks. "How?"

How? Because of cricket, of course. I declined the offer of accompanying Alex on his fishing trip with Steve (He came back with several mackerel and said, "Sea fishing's brilliant!"), but we catch one-day games on television and I try to raise his interest in the daily scorecards. He doesn't understand the points system of run rates and bonus points, and is scornful of the number of drawn games ("They play four whole days and nobody wins?"). I concede that he has a point. More important, we have a couple more evening sessions with the juniors, and Gareth reports that he has fixed up a game for the following week—a real game on a real pitch, here!—against the boys of St Minn. None of the team can be more excited than me, for some of them are already losing interest or staking out excuses to miss the game. It will be a struggle to find an eleven so it seems certain that Alex, if only by default, will play.

"Did I tell you about my first game for the seconds at Mountstephen?" I ask. "I used to open the batting because I could stay at the crease for ages. I never scored so many runs, but I could wear the bowling down so that the better batsmen could take advantage and start playing their shots. Anyway, we were away at some school in Taunton, and I was horrified when we got there because the pitch was tarmacced—they'd dug up the grass and put down a tarmac strip between the wickets. We'd never seen such a thing, and of course the first ball I faced reared up at about a hundred miles an hour and thwacked me on the shoulder. I broke my collar bone and couldn't play again that year."

"Thanks for telling him that," says Karla.

"You're welcome," I reply.

At least the anticipation of this game buoys me through the days of work. "There's more to this life than general fucking practice!" I announce to nobody. I am sitting in my car and trying to summon enthusiasm to enter the Avalon Nursing Home, where several elderly people await my attention. It does not help that I suddenly have a vision of my father's imminent and unwilling admission to an establishment such as this. I have not fulfilled my intention to pay further visits, as Eve's regular phone calls remind me. Mum's had another fall, she's going to fracture her hip one day. They won't have a carer come in, do you think you can have a word? Dad got lost this morning, we had to phone the police. You said you were going to visit, Philip. Yes, yes, I am. But when?

And if it's not them on the phone, it's Ruth. Evelyn is on tablets but they give her the runs. Edna is her "doctor" but isn't too sure what to do, could I phone her up? Also her eyesight's gone funny and there's no longer an optometrist there. Ruth feels depressed, which makes Karla guiltily think she should go back. We are both failing our families and I think it is this conflict which—for the first time in our small history—is making us cranky and sad.

I am escorted round the Avalon by a young oriental nurse I have never seen before. Oriental? In Tregaskis? She is courteous and efficient ("Dr Cormack, we are very worried about the circulation of Mrs Jeffrey's foot. Would you be so good as to look at it please?") and on the way out I catch Jane Tullo, who is the manager, or matron, or nurse in charge, or whatever her title is now.

"Hi, Jane, she's new, isn't she?"

"Yes, and really good too. We could do with some more like that, we're desperate for staff."

"Where's she from?"

"The Philippines, only arrived last month."

"But—doesn't she have all the hassle of getting a work permit? I thought all that took months."

"No idea, I found her in a recruitment agency, so I let them deal with all that."

"So do you still have vacancies?"

"Sure, do you want a job?"

"Not me, but my—a friend of mine from Canada is a qualified nurse—"

"Tell her to give me a ring."

I rush home to tell Karla this. "Of course, it's only the routine care of the elderly stuff…"

"I know what it involves, Philip, and I don't care. I just want to work, I'm so bored!"

She phones Jane Tullo and comes back to tell me, "I've got an interview."

"When?"

"Now."


Wednesday evening is perfect. Eleven teenage boys are kitted out in pristine whites and baseball caps, some of which bear **Greetings from Jackfish Lake**. They are seated around the dressing room benches while Gareth gives them last-minute tips as I nod fervently on. "Keep to basics, don't try anything clever, don't worry about the heroics. Just concentrate on your stance, your footwork, straight bat, anticipate the line of the ball. If you're not receiving, remember to follow up, and, most important, *call* if you see a run. If you do that well, you'll probably nick enough singles to win…"

There are spectators too. Many are parents, of course, some of them from St Minn. But there is also a fair collection of other villagers—old men glad of a sociable distraction, cricket club diehards, inattentive friends of the team, and people like Steve and Kim who throw their support behind any community activity, however eccentric, however mundane. They sit next to Karla and me on the pavilion benches, and behind us white cloths conceal sandwiches on trestle tables and the urns of tea and bottles of ale which await. I look around with satisfaction at the interest our little contest has attracted, and only hope that Alex will not look sorely out of place. Someone standing near the pavilion catches my eye and gives a restrained wave. Oh, my God, it's Mary and NYK—what the hell are they doing here? I motion a civil hand in return and flinch quickly back.

"What's the matter?" asks Karla.

"Mary's here."

I am relieved that she does not spin reflexly round to inspect her. Instead she shrugs and asks, "That's okay, isn't it?" I suppose it is, but it is not her presence which unsettles me so much as the realisation—even from a distance—that she looks so radiantly well.

The game starts at five, St Minn bat first and reach 71 for 6. Alex takes two simple catches, but drops a difficult one which falls a foot or two in front of him. But this is an attainable target, Gareth congratulates them for bowling and fielding so well. "Don't be too impatient," he tells the openers. "If you get a good length ball, just block it, there'll be plenty of opportunities to score."

If only they would heed his words. Within three overs, as many wickets have gone. Both openers have lashed out at straightforwardly accurate balls, both have been clean bowled. But our two best players keep calm, notch efficient singles where they can and our impetus slowly mounts. Victory is within our sights. Then things change again, we lose four quick wickets and Alex comes in, sixteen short of a win. If he is nervous, it does not show. The first ball is wide, he makes to swing out at it but thankfully desists. The next two are on line for middle stump, but he blocks them, bat plumb straight.

"Good defence, Alex!" Gareth calls.

Then, luckily, he is off the mark, a thick edge which squirms past slips to scramble a single. The fielder panics, and throws hopelessly wide of the mark. "Yes!" yells Roddy Tullo, urging a second run. "No!" replies Alex, "You can't!" But Roddy is halfway down the wicket, Alex firm in his crease, and this time the ball is fielded cleanly to run poor Roddy out. I feel responsible for this, for I have told Alex never to run from an overthrow, and in this instance it would have been perfectly safe. Roddy is upset, but here comes our secret weapon, a big lad called Danny Spinks. He has power but no discipline, certainly no great technique. If Alex can hold firm while Danny connects with some loose bowling we may yet win. For two, then three overs, he does. Twelve runs needed with four overs and two wickets left.

Even the non-cricketers can see we are in for a tense climax. Alex somehow knows he can leave it to his partner to score. He defends admirably, then gets a lucky single to hand over the strike. Danny swipes madly at the following delivery, failing to connect. Despite Gareth's tuition, he is clearly not one for caution, for he clouts the next ball recklessly high into the air. Our eyes follow its trajectory, trying at the same time to assess the fielder scampering to get under it and the progress of the batsmen in notching a run or even two while the ball traverses the sky.

Then something wrong happens, something bizarre and disconcerting, clearly out of place. It is an explosion of sorts, and it distorts not only sound waves but time. Seconds slow, and in them I can look round and absorb everything—the looks of shock and bemusement, the spillage of beer and tea, the clattering in my ears of the loudest registerable noise. I catch the briefest imprint of Mary's face, frozen in alarm towards me. Somehow my mind deciphers the cause of these shock waves detonating through space. It is unmistakeably wood against wood, it is the broad face of willow—a ferociously wielded bat—hammered flat onto the table just two feet behind us. Crockery shatters, cutlery clatters, glass crashes to the floor, women scream, and out on the pitch all attention springs away from Danny's airborne shot to, it would seem, me. Then there is a momentary aftermath, a rebound of hyper-silence. In it I turn around and gasp to see that the man stood brandishing the bat is also looking squarely into my eyes.

"Hey, what the fuck's this, Cornwall Cree Nation?" he demands quietly, and it takes me an unreal second to recognise the figure of Marshall Snape.

Karla reacts more quickly than me. She steps up to confront him and demand, "Marshall! What the fuck do you think you're *doing*?"

"I've come to visit Alex," he says calmly. "Where is he?"

"He's out there playing cricket. He's having a good time, so leave him alone."

Marshall looks up and makes out the figure of his son, English schoolboy personified. He is standing in his whites at the crease, blinking in this direction, the cause of the commotion as yet unknown to him. "So what's with this cricket shit? Who ever heard of a Cree playing cricket?"

He makes towards the pitch and I stand to restrain him with a hand on his arm. "No, leave him."

Marshall spins round, and although he is three or four inches shorter and several stone lighter than me, he looks up into my eyes with measured threat. "Don't you tell me when I can or can't see my boy. And don't you touch me like that."

I take my hand way and say, "Look, he's enjoying his game and it's nearly finished. Then you can see him, all right?"

"No, not all right, Cormack! I'm gonna see him now." He marches down the few pavilion steps and crosses the boundary rope, bat still in his hand. Indignant voices are now raised in protest at the sight of this dishevelled, scruff-haired, and (tut tut!) black-clad figure striding onto the pitch, "Look here!" "I say!" "For God's sake...?" but nobody dares intervene. "Hey, Alex!" he shouts.

Then Karla runs after him, "Marshall, leave him! How dare you ruin their game!" He turns to her and they exchange heated words. Clearly I have to take some responsibility, so I join them on the grass, just about at long leg, excruciatingly conscious of the scandalised spectators looking on. This, then, is what I have brought to the gentility of our village.

By now Jon Tullo, who is umpiring, also arrives on the scene. "What the hell's going on, Philip?"

"I'm sorry, I'll sort it out. Come on, Marshall, you can see Alex as soon as they've done. The game's nearly over."

"You stay out of this," he snaps. "You're the cause of this whole fucking problem anyway."

Now Karla pulls him to face her, but drops her voice low. "This isn't helping anyone, least of all Alex. Let him finish his game and then you can see him. Otherwise I call the cops and you're on the next plane home."

Marshall glares at her and then, without a word, heads back to the pavilion. We follow sheepishly and he sits inside on a dressing-room bench to light a cigarette. I suppose it's best not to tell him that smoking isn't allowed in this graceful but highly flammable little wooden edifice, donated to the community by the Dene family in 1929. Karla stands over him but says to me, "You go watch the rest of the game, I'll stay here."

I fumble back to my seat, mortified by the surreptitious stares. As I sit I squirm a sly glance back at the pavilion, fearful that Marshall will re-emerge. My gaze meets Mary's, and she gives a barely perceptible shake of the head before turning scornfully away.

How can I concentrate on the match, and anyway, what does it matter now? The fielder under the skier was presumably distracted by our commotion, for Danny remains at the crease. But within two overs it is finished as Danny swings at thin air to be bowled, then Alex snicks a catch behind. The fielders celebrate and sportingly usher the batsmen back towards us, but as I stand to applaud I see from the corner of my eye that a further problem has occurred.

I don't know who summoned them, but two policemen are entering the pavilion. This, I curse, must be the fastest ever response time to an incident in Tregaskis. When Noreen phoned them last year because some kids were trying to break into a car parked outside the surgery, the response she got was, "Hang on, I'll have to pass this one through to Camborne, I think your lads are having their crib." I try to squeeze past the kids and parents converging on the dressing rooms, and by the time I get there Marshall is already being questioned.

"It's okay, officer, there's no problem," I interrupt. "I'll pay for any damage caused."

The nearer constable turns and prepares to dismiss me. Fortunately his colleague recognises me and says, "Hello there, Doc, been having a spot of bother?"

"No, it's nothing really."

"We got a phone call to say there was a disturbance of some sort, someone thrashing about with a cricket bat." They stare accusingly at Marshall. "Do you have any identification?"

"Sure." Marshall extracts a shabby batch of papers from his jacket pocket, selects his passport from this and hands it over.

"Do you have an address in Cornwall?"

"I'm staying with him."

The police look to me for confirmation. "Yes, that's right. 9 Chapel Lane, Tregaskis."

The officer I don't know records the details in his notebook and calls into base on his phone, "Hello, love, do you have anything on Lincoln Delaney, 4.12.67, Canadian national born Winnipeg?"

Karla and I sneak a glance. I've no idea who Lincoln Delaney is or was, but it would serve Marshall right if he's wanted by Interpol, the FBI, the RCMP, Devon and Cornwall Constabulary and MI5. Suddenly Alex emerges from the crowd which has filled the room and runs silently into the arms of his dad. "Hi, son, you're looking good," Marshall greets him and they sit enclosed in a hug until the police decide to move the suspect into their car pending further statements and the results of their record check.

"How can he be in trouble when he's only just got here?" Alex asks Karla.

"You know Marshall, that's always been one of his talents."

"What's he doing here anyway?"

"I think he just wanted to see you," she replies. "And if the cops ask you, he's called Lincoln Delaney today."

"Duh?" asks Alex.

"Exactly," Karla shrugs back. "Duh?"

"Excuse me," an indignant father interrupts her, "but the boys are waiting to get changed if you don't mind."

Then Jon Tullo's voice pipes through the air, "My God, who's been smoking in here?" and for some reason it irritates me deeply. Far be it from me to leap to the defence of fag-lovers' rights, but does it really matter, I want to demand of him, in the greater context of global injustice and suffering—do we really care?

I edge Karla outside. The low sun shines, catching only the top of the church spire. The rest of the village languishes in cool shadow, occasional wisps of smoke rise in pale silhouettes. It all seems so insignificant, one trifling settlement caught in a vast intersection of space and time. Yet to all these people—Lacoste-sweatered fathers ushering their Sheridans and Willoughbys back to their BMWs and convertible Saabs—it is a supremely pleasant universe blessed by their very presence in it, where all that matters is the favourable value of their property and the assured provision of BUPA health checks and Waitrose produce from all over the world.

"I'm really sorry," she says, squeezing my arm. "I feel responsible—"

"No, it's okay. It doesn't really matter any more." Because it doesn't. I don't care what the repercussions are, I don't care what anyone says.

More people edge away with a restrained nod towards me. Alex joins us and his team mates take their leave of him with considerably more warmth. "Nice one, Alex, see you tomorrow!" "Orright, Alex? Same time next week?"

I expect the police to arrest "Lincoln Delaney" as an illegal immigrant, but they finally confirm they have no record of him, and that nobody present seems to want to press charges. I assure them I will pay for the assorted breakages of crockery and glasses, and they let him out of the car with a warning glare. This leaves the four of us to stand, Marshall's arm on Alex's shoulder, Karla's arm still linked to mine.

Gareth and Jon are already getting stuck into the clearing up with plenty of volunteers, so I decide to leave them to it. More youthful cricketers and their protective parents ebb away home with disparaging looks. Some amble round the corner to the pub, where they will greet each other with animated warmth, having something tasty and unexpected, rather more than the cricket to discuss. I imagine the drama being retold in the households of Tregaskis and St Minn and thereafter spreading in exponential fashion through the county. God, it might even get a mention on *Spotlight Southwest*. Truly it could, for only last week they ran a story on two bakers from Tavistock doing a sponsored slim.

In the meantime, what are we to do? I can hardly book Marshall in to the executive suite of St Lanyon Country Club, so I guess he'll just have to stay with us.

# 2.9

"Hey, this is good," Marshall approves his meal. "What you call this?"

"Sea bass."

"Where you catch it?"

"In the sea, funnily enough. Though we bought this from Tesco."

"You bought it? All this fucking sea, and you buy fish?"

"Steve's taking me fishing again on Saturday," Alex tells him. "Do you want to come?"

"Hang on, Steve might not want to invite him," I point out.

"Hey!" Marshall objects. "Who asked you? Fishermen make for good buddies, there's a kind of brotherhood, but I guess you don't know nothing about that."

"Okay, okay, we'll ask Steve," I say, and immediately envisage a twenty-year friendship biting the dust.

"Good. Any more of this?"

"No more fish but there's veg," Karla says. "By the way, when did you last eat?"

"Aahhdno. Yesterday, I guess. That shit on the plane."

It surprises me from the way he bolts it down that it was as recent as that. I am beginning to wonder if he stowed away in some unlit sub zero cargo hold for the flight, for he appears more unkempt than ever, he has no money, only a single shoulder bag which contains a spare T-shirt, a couple of pairs of boxers, a **London House** cap for Alex, and a small supply of cigarettes. I wonder how he might have found funds for the fare.

"So why didn't you tell us you were coming?" I want to know.

"Because I wanted to make sure my boy was being looked after. I wanted just to turn up and see what things were really like."

"Of course he's okay, aren't you, Alex?" Karla says and Alex nods. "You think I'd stay here with him if he wasn't?"

"Yeah, I can see he's eating okay and got nice clothes and all that stuff. But what I mean is are you turning him into some polite little English kid? Seems to me that you are. He should be playing hockey not fucking cricket."

Karla's voice escalates. "Now wait a minute! Don't start lecturing me on how to raise my boy. You haven't done a lot to help in the last thirteen years, and if he was to follow your example, he'd spend half his life in jail!"

Now Marshall is shouting too, "Shit, who's been brainwashing you? It's easy to keep out of jail when you've got work, a nice house, plenty of money—"

"I know that, so maybe that's why I brought him here!"

"Yeah, maybe that's true! I know you, you saw this rich white guy and decided that was your chance—"

"That's not true!"

"Oh, calm down!" I plead, hands outstretched. "You're not achieving anything by arguing in front of Alex like this. I think we all need a good night's sleep." Fortunately I prevent myself from adding, "and a nice cup of tea."

"You have any more beer?" asks Marshall.

I point to the cupboard. "Sure, help yourself."

"That's all your warm English shit," he objects. "You don't have nothin' in the fridge?"


When I wake next morning I experience several milliseconds of relative euphoria before the recall of yesterday's events set in. "Oh, God," I groan, and it is not only the embarrassing little fracas at the cricket which swirls round my brain, but the feeling of constraint which Marshall's presence has brought to our family house. In bed last night, Karla and I felt obliged to whisper as Marshall rummaged noisily downstairs, fending off his jet lag with early hours television and beer.

I eat a picky breakfast and as soon as I arrive in the surgery the worst is confirmed. "George wants a meeting at lunchtime," Noreen tells me, and I don't feel the need to ask why. I fear that every patient is scrutinising me with the knowledge of yesterday's sordid little spectacle newly gossiped into their minds.

So at one o'clock precisely (George insists on starting on time) we sit round the common room table, upright, silent and stern. His preamble comes as no surprise. "The fact is, Philip, after expressing our recent concerns about your performance, we were (the condescending little look over the specs here) a little perturbed to hear about the rather unseemly incident last evening. It really shows the practice in a very unfavourable light, you know. Of course, we've only a second-hand account of what happened, there may be mitigating circumstances we know nothing about..."

He pauses to give me a chance to explain, but I refuse to give him the honour of access to my personal affairs.

Julia duly gets her four penn'orth in, "I know we've said before how terribly reluctant we'd be to dissolve the partnership, especially in view of the number of years we've—"

"It's all right, you can stop pussyfooting around. I know you can't bear to think of the precious image of the practice being tarnished, George, but you don't have to worry about that now, because I resign. I've had enough of it, more than enough." I swear I see a fleeting smile of satisfaction play across his face, which I have the urge to punch. But maybe one altercation is enough. "I think the practice agreement stipulates three months' notice, but I'll leave earlier if you happen to find a replacement in that time."

He takes off his glasses to inspect the lenses and polish them on his tie, and says, "Funnily enough, Ben came round for lunch yesterday. He really enjoyed his time here doing your locum, and he still hasn't taken on anything permanent. I'm sure he'd be seriously interested, and he could probably start quite soon."

Bastard. They have obviously had detailed discussions about this, and presumably Julia has been in on them too. At least I have the Pyrrhic satisfaction of resigning before I am sacked. Without any further word I get up and leave the room. It is tempting to walk out forever, right now, but I suppose I have some commitment to the patients booked in for the afternoon slog. Only when I sit down does the enormity of what I have done slam into me. Without any forethought I have blurted out my resignation with nothing in the way of alternative plans. For a moment I wonder if I can go back to George and unresign, but no, the deed is done. I confirm my intention in writing, sign my hurried scrawl, and seal this into an envelope in George's tray in the office. Then, back behind the closed door of my room, I recline deep into my chair, stretch my feet up onto the desk, and link my hands behind my head, buoyed by a feeling of deep and totally inexplicable calm.

At six-thirty I get home and find Karla and Marshall at the kitchen table, well on their way through a bottle of red wine—a *Domaine Guy de Sauvanes*, as it happens, one I have been laying down for a special occasion. Perhaps today, in its perverse way, *is* special, but I still resent it being frittered on Marshall's indiscriminate palate.

Karla pours one for me and smiles, "Hi, how was your day?"

"It was certainly interesting. I resigned."

"You did what!? You mean you don't have a job?"

"No, I suppose not."

Marshall holds up a hand into what is known in common parlance, I do believe, as a high five. "Yeah, man!" he shouts. "Join the club!"

Next day I arrive at work heavy with the expectation of what lies ahead. At the end of morning surgery I am asked to see Ernie Pellow's ankle, which is ulcerated, but not too seriously, it is nothing too bad.

"Thank you, doctor," says his daughter-in-law on receipt of my brief attention. "Here, what's all this about you leaving?"

And so the day continues, with sideways looks from patients and their imagined waiting-room discussions tormenting my head. Julia and George give the impression they would rather bathe naked in a tub of horse manure than exchange pleasantries with me. Working three months notice here will clearly be intolerable, but I suspect that George has already been scheming with Ben to see how soon he can start. So I am left to reflect on another breakdown, one more partnership that started with good intentions and warmth. How many more will fail?

On returning home I dutifully ask Karla how Alex's day has been.

"Oh, he's fine, in fact he seems to have become a minor celebrity on the strength of Wednesday night's performance."

"That's something, I suppose, I was worried they'd give him a hard time. Anyway, where's Marshall?"

Karla shrugs. "He went for a walk, said he wanted to be outside."

I shudder at the thought of him at large in Tregaskis—calling on the vicar, bumping into George, loitering outside de Vere's gallery and swearing volubly at the prices of the photographs on display...well, maybe that last scenario wouldn't be so bad. "Look, Karla, I'll still find work, you know. There's plenty of locums available, I'd be able to pick and choose. I might have to travel around a bit, but—" I catch her expression, mouth angled down, the usual spirit of her eyes not there. "What is it? What's the matter?"

"I got a phone call from your friend Mrs Tullo at the Avalon."

"Oh, yes?"

"You know she said she'd contact that recruitment agency, that they'd get in touch with me within the week?"

"Yes."

"She phoned—or her secretary phoned—to say the job's gone. They don't want me any more."

"Oh, Karla!" I hug her with my sympathy, try to find

encouraging words. But the timing of this rejection cannot be co-incidence. All I can do is share her despair. This was meant to be a new life for her, a salvation. How can things get any worse? "That's not fair, that's—"

"I know, I know, it's discrimination and prejudice and fear. I know it well enough now, I know the smell of it, I know the excuses, I know the way people refuse to look you in the eye, get someone else to deliver the dirty news. I just thought that over here it might not be so bad."

How ineffably stupid I feel. Despite all those months of grappling with the bureaucracy of my own sabbatical, I did not give one thought to investigating such requirements for Karla. Why not? I know already. It was an obstacle I chose to ignore in case it ever stopped her coming here. Denial fails again.

The phone rings. I answer the voice of Jim Asprey, landlord of the pub. "Hello, Doc, sorry to trouble you, but we're having a spot of bother here. We've got a young fellow causing a bit of a disturbance, says he's staying with you."

# 3.1

<hr>

"Come on, Dad, drink your tea."

"I've told you, I'm not drinking anything."

"Why not?"

"Because she's poisoned it." His finger menaces Mum, who quivers and snivels in distress.

"I haven't, I haven't," she bleats. "I haven't, Philip, really."

"I do know that, Mother. Just ignore him, you're making him worse." For she reinforces his behaviour by giving credence to these allegations. Her response means more attention is paid to them and hence to him. They are regressing into childhood, two sibs squabbling, Eve and me.

"But he thinks I'm trying to, and I'm not."

"I know, but you can't reason with him when he's like this, he's totally impervious to it."

"But why does he think? I'm not!"

"Yes, Mother, I know!" I don't intend to raise my voice, but it's two in the morning, and we are all—except Dad—exhausted. His tea, of course, *is* doctored. Haloperidol liquid is supposed to sedate him, though I know that its effect will be slight. But we are desperate and we cling to the hope that anything might soothe him, even if we are neglecting to get his informed consent about taking the medication. At this fraught moment we are not too fussed about infringing his stated human rights, we just want some bloody sleep.

This is now a regular thing. He drowses through the day and

defies all attempts to rouse him into fruitful activity ("Come on, Dad, let's go for a walk." "Walk? Where to? What for? Don't want a bally walk."). A sign of his decline is that he no longer bothers getting dressed, he has taken to spending most of the time wearing his bottle-green sleeveless pullover on top of his pyjamas. I try to recall from thirty-year old physiology lectures which bit of the brain governs the awareness of time. Is it the pineal body? Whatever it is, his has now atrophied away, and its supply of primordial chemicals which tunes his body to the fundamentals of night and day, light and dark, has been exhausted. In these terms my father is now less evolved than a plant.

Yet something about his mental decline does not ring quite true. I have seen hundreds of people with Alzheimers over the years, I am familiar with their pattern of listless disorientation, their indifference to time and place, the leeching of insight from their eyes. Dad is different, his recall more inconsistent, impossible to predict. At times he is as sharp as he ever was, picking up nuances of tone and attitude in my voice. "Don't patronise me, Philip," he scolded just now when I tried to convince him that a full night's sleep might be for his own good. "I've never been a good sleeper, so I'm not going to start to conform to your timetable now." He is still articulate, eloquent even, and although some swathes of memory indeed seem to have been erased away, others unexpectedly remain. "That damn Foster man and his bloody gherkin thing!" he recalls from the news. "That's not architecture. That's not a gherkin, it's a phallus."

So I am not quite sure how much manipulation goes on. We all suspect—Eve, I, and the impartial Karla—that he is lusting for attention, regressing into a childhood bathed in his mother-wife's attention. It always has been thus, of course, so why should he (or she) change a lifelong habit now? I only wish my mother would show a little resolve. I tell her, "You mustn't let him bully you, it just encourages him all the more."

"I don't! I'm not! I just!"

Essentially she is scared, because she has always relied on him to make every minutest decision of their history. She never had to find a job, and her son was farmed off to boarding school. What was left for her to do but care for her daughter and witter after her husband's every demand? Being bullied and belittled was worth it because it was preferable to nothing at all, and it is still her allotted role, it's another strange symbiosis in the wonders of marital life. And when one symbiont dies, the other will surely die too.

But—the thought suddenly rattles my tired brain that at least my parents' relationship has surpassed the intensity of anything I have achieved myself. My marriage to Mary was little more than a co-existence. Sure, we were companions, but she became a component of my days along with work, the girls and cricket, and of course she must have longed for much more. Now we have split up I am surviving and she is thriving. What must I learn from that?

"Where are you going?" Mum asks.

"Upstairs. Back in a minute."

I steal into our room and, as I expect, the noise has kept Karla awake. She is sitting up in bed reading through the letter and collection of news cuttings her mother has sent. "Hey, Ken's dead," she says.

"Ken?"

"You know, the drunk. They found him at the side of the road, think he'd been hit by a car. That's awful, I kind of liked Ken."

"Did you?"

"Yeah, did you know his story? His wife died in a house fire, they'd only been married about a year. He was a real handsome guy in his day, but he never recovered from that. He just started drinking and—"

"Karla?"

She looks up and I hold her as hard as I can. Ruth's arthritic note and the account of Ken's demise scrunch against her breast. "Thank you for that," she says when I finally relax my hold. "What was that for? Are you okay down there? Is there anything you want me to do?"

"No, there's nothing I want you to do but stay with me."

"I can do that," she smiles.

Back downstairs Dad wants to go for a walk.

"No, Ronald, you can't!" my mother bleats as she tugs his sleeve back from the door.

He whips his arm away. "What do you mean, I can't? Why not, woman? It's a free country, let go of me!"

"But it's two in the morning!"

"So what? What difference does that make?"

"It's two in the. You can't!"

"Come on, Dad!" I intervene, but this only makes him worse.

"Why can't I go for a walk whenever I like?" he persists, as we stand in the hallway, arguing in circles, repeating our words. It's dark. It's cold. You'll get lost. You'll fall. You should be in bed. You mustn't. You can't. All of these answers inflame him, make him ever more determined to go. I put an arm round his shoulder and he shrugs me off. Mum grabs for his hand again, he swats at her like a pesky insect. Our voices rise in unison as all pretence of logic and rapport and decorum is lost. In the midst of this unseemly scuffle we are distracted by the sound of a key in the front door. It opens into us and Dad demands, "Who the bloody hell's this?"

"Hey, what's going on?" asks Marshall. "You shouldn't treat your elders like that."

"And who the devil are you?"

"I'm Marshall Snape, sir. I met you earlier today."

"Well, you need a bloody hair cut."

"I reckon you're right. Do you know where I can get one?"

"Billy Kingham in Market Street. Only charges three and six."

"Oh, Ronald, Billy Kingham's long gone," Mum cries, but responds to my wave to shush.

"Anyway, where are you from?" asks Dad.

"Jackfish Lake Cree Nation, Manitoba, Canada."

Dad's face lights up. "Canada, eh? Haven't come across my brother Geoffrey, I suppose?"

Mum heaves her predicted sigh of exasperation, and yet again I have to motion her to shut up.

"No, I don't believe so. What does he look like?"

"Smaller than me, a bit thin on top nowadays. You'd know him because he walks with a limp. Osteomyelitis when he was a youngster, bloody lucky to survive. He was confined to bed for six months, that was all they could do back then."

"Why don't you sit down and tell me about him?" Marshall suggests. "Do you have a whisky anywhere?"

"Certainly. Old Bushmill's any good to you? Philip, do the honours, would you?"

Dad calms quickly and we lead him back to the kitchen table. I pour two drinks, think about one for myself, but Marshall suggests, "Hey, you two are looking pretty damn tired. Why don't you go off to bed while I talk to him for a while?"

Mum looks uncertain, as I probably do myself. But if Marshall can occupy him for an hour, then I tell her we should take advantage and try to get some rest.

"Now tell me about your brother," Marshall is saying. "What happened to his leg?"

When I wake it is after nine o'clock. Apparently Dad talked solidly for three hours then took meekly to his bed, where he remains. Marshall is also asleep, his timing still set to the rhythm of Jackfish Lake.


We have been here now for nearly four weeks. It seemed to be the obvious answer, for my three months notice was mutually waived. Ben had indeed been primed by George, he was keen to start at once, and I was desperate to get out. We could have stayed in Tregaskis, but there seemed little prospect of Karla getting work, and I knew my reputation locally would have been darkened by rumours following my abrupt resignation. Here in Penscott Abbas we are nearer to a larger population, I can easily find locum work, we are close to civilisation (Bristol an hour away—concerts, the theatre, opera, county cricket) and the main line train. It also helps my parents, not to mention Eve and Giles. My overdraft of guilt can be paid off, steadily and virtuously, in my own time.

In addition the house in Tregaskis is for sale. When it sells I will be solvent again, and in due course Ben will buy out my share of the practice, so there will be money to spare for holidays, I can take them when I choose and work part-time. It all makes such good sense.

But the real reason for the move is deeper. After Marshall's unseemly intrusion into our lives I discovered that my network of friends did not run very deep, so I suppose I should thank him perversely for that. In the days after the incident the veneer of camaraderie with all those people was cracked. Quite simply— if unconsciously—I put them all to the test, and I waited to see who would contact us to offer friendship and support. And although Alex's friends from The Greenery frequently came to the door, nobody called to see Karla and me, nor did anyone phone. There was no contact from Gareth to arrange further cricket, nothing from the Lanes, nothing from Steve and Kim. After twenty years hard labour in the practice, no one rang from work to enquire of my health or my plans. Beth and Stella both phoned, and I love and thank them for that. But now I know—I just know— that life there strolls on without me. Ben will be picking up diagnoses I have missed, investigations I have failed to perform, the legacies of my substandard practice will be revealed to him day by day. George and Julia will be smug in their good fortune, congratulating themselves that they tolerated me for so long. Friday at Six will be in full summer swing, they will all be congregating weekly with their white wine chilled into their insulated picnic bags, huddling around the barbie in their sleeveless fleeces to discuss where they'll be spending the winter ("Barnaby's brother-in-law has just done up this super little barn near Gerona. He says we can stay there for as long as we like." "Anywhere near the Costa Brava's getting *so* expensive, though, isn't it? We're seriously considering Croatia, you can still buy for next to nothing there.") and again I *know* that newly insinuated

301

and perfectly integrated into the heart of these gatherings will be the arm-linked figures of Mary and NYK. I am already a member of their past, of relevance to them now only out of snooping interest of how much I am asking for my house.

At least Karla has found work, through the agency Jane Tullo used. A wealthy family in Anstock, six miles away, has a severely handicapped son. His brain damage relates to some rare but catastrophic syndrome but they have continued to care for him at home. Now his mother wants to resume her career but has despaired that the usual crop of school leavers or well-intentioned but untrained carers might not cope with the boy's alarming choking attacks or fits. Karla deals unflappably with this, the parents are grateful and pay her well. She takes Toby out in his bulky electric chair, which slots into their modified people carrier, and whizzes off to do their shopping or take him to the park. Already she has won their confidence, and—finally freed from their enslavement to him—they are asking her to work the occasional evening so they can dare to go out once in a while.

There is plenty of locum work for me. It is liberating to walk into a surgery for the day, see the patients, and then go home without the burden of budgets, staff, meetings, PCT missives, NICE guidelines, paperwork, business decisions and the dreaded QOF targets to worry about. The manager of the practice I was in today asked if I missed the continuity of running my own practice. I answered with a thoughtful, "No, I can't say that I do," but what I truly meant was an instant and joyous, "**Do I, fuck??!!**"

This is all very fine, but it leaves us with the bizarre domestic situation of Marshall Snape looking after Mum and Dad.

By a weirdly ironic little tweak of fortune I have found a week's locum work in Shahbn, and the doctors happen to be the medical officers for good old Mountstephen School. They hold a regular weekly session there to do routine checks on asthmatics and see the accumulated sprains and sore throats and rashes which Matron knows will cure themselves but ("You know how parents worry...") had still better be checked out. Of course this is a private arrangement, and the practice is paid handsomely to ensure that the precious little scholars get nothing but the best. The money involved means that I, a mere stand-in, am denied the pleasure of this, despite my stated sentimental interest. However, at five o'clock on Friday a call is requested to a boy with abdominal pain. None of the other partners are keen to infringe on weekend time, so I volunteer to go.

So, yes, I drive up the approach road, rugby field on my left, Hartley's Copse over to the right, as the imposing stone frontage and its foursquare windows rebuff the afternoon sun. Round the back I go, between science block and gym, and through the double door where the grand hall still basks, its walls harbouring echoes of the shrill voices of assembly for all those years. But the tennis courts are now a car park, the corner of the field behind the pavilion has been replaced by a utilitarian glass block, the staff room has acquired an extension—it has all expanded gracelessly within its confines, yet it looks demeaningly small. It is suddenly revealed to me that behind that grand two-dimensional facade an awful lot of shabbiness is crammed. As I park the car to enter the sick bay I think of my thousands of hours of schooling, seven years behind a desk—stolidly conscientious and less readily distracted than my peers—exposed to a million facts. But how many of them were useful? How many have I retained? One per cent of French perhaps, but algebra? Geometry? Physics? What was Boyle's Law again? Christ, why didn't they just let me play cricket? Why did I let Jack Jarvis put me off? Some extra coaching might have let me carve out a sort of career, nothing spectacular I know, but maybe a few years at minor county level. The money wouldn't have been much, but I would have been happy, I really would.

Beyond those doors to my left I once lived and ate and slept, joked and read, chattered and laughed, wanked and shat. This is the place where I experienced the tortured hormonal shifts of puberty, converted sexual frustration into bullying, was one of the pack forever chasing Chubby Briscoe into the toilets and dunking him in the bog. I think of all the dark nights up in that dorm telling crass jokes, picturing girls' bodies, farting, sniggering, acting lewd and brash while at the same time deeply frightened of the adulthood ahead. How would I know what to do? What grown-ups could I copy? The teachers—the homosexual geographer or the war-wounded musician? My distant dad?

Sister Robinson is a cheerful buxom woman, thirty-five to forty, and the object no doubt of a dormful of carnal desires. I wonder if it thrills her that her imagined unleashed breasts bless so many deposits of adolescent sperm. She shows me to the boy in the sick bay, who has nothing seriously wrong. I examine and reassure him, then give in to the urge to say that I was once a pupil here, and that he is bloody lucky because Matron in my day was dumpy and old, smelling of Savlon and fags. The alert boy, lying chipper and clean in his brisk bed, reprieved of serious illness, laughs at this with brightness in his eyes. I know that whatever he does in life will be done well. He will excel in business, in academia or as a lawyer, bright and smart and witty, everything I am not. And a great sadness engulfs me. Does anyone here now recall Pacamac? Of course they don't. A bulky, well-meaning but average boy, least memorable of the lot.


The visit has unsettled me. It is not yet five-thirty, an early finish for me, yet somehow I have no urge to rush home. So I detour back to Penscott Abbas in a random saw-tooth path—right there, left here—to pass through places which, despite being a handful of miles from my childhood home, I hardly know. On impulse I stop in Frentley Parva, a village which still focuses cosily on its green and its pond like a slumbering family round a Christmas fire. Its only potential activity is an antique shop, its door ajar and quietly lit to attract customers of a suitable kind. None of the residents of these twee sandstone homes, every last one of them manicured to discreet perfection, know who I am. I get the impression that each window secretes an observer, just stepped back across the frontier where the occlusion of darkness begins. A restrained sign on a lamp post alerts me to Neighbourhood Watch, and I have the urge to amend it to Fearsomely Paranoid Telegraph-Toting Smug-Arsed Neighbourhood Snoop. I laugh aloud at my anarchic impulse and the woman in the dim depths of the antique shop looks up.

When I get home I find myself immersed in what, in any language and any culture, is clearly an argument. Karla is as angry as I have ever seen her. She is standing with her hands on her head in tormented abstraction, her hair ruffled, face afire. Marshall, the recipient of her wrath, lolls onto the back two legs of his chair, his dirty-booted feet on the kitchen table, provocatively calm. Between them stands Alex, his eyes dilated with anxiety and evident guilt for being the unwitting epicentre of this storm.

"Marshall, don't rock back on your chair like that, please. It's an antique."

"Jeez, Karla, how do you put up with this shit? We're having an important discussion here."

"I can see that, but it's still no reason to break Mum and Dad's best furniture," I answer for her. "And anyway it's not very hygienic to be spreading dog mess or whatever onto the dining table."

This time Karla turns my way, not speaking, but clearly telling me to shut up.

"Important discussion or not, I don't want Salmonella, thank you," I defend myself. "Anyway, what's the big problem?"

"Alex, tell Philip where you've been today," Karla commands.

"Out."

"Out where?"

"Out fishing."

"Who with?"

"Marshall and Ronald."

"And tell Philip where you were yesterday."

"Out."

"Out where?"

"Out fishing."

"Who with?"

Sigh. "Marshall and Ronald."

For one silly fleeting second I feel oddly pleased. Alex is occupied, settling into his new home, integrating himself—and thereby Karla—into his surrogate home. "But," I realise, "shouldn't he be at school?"

"Oh, well done," she congratulates me. "You're really on the ball today."

"But—is there a problem with school, Alex?"

He hesitates and will have to skew a glance for guidance. But which way, to which parent? Tellingly, he looks left.

"Go ahead, tell him," Marshall encourages.

"I hate school. I don't want to go no more."

Karla says, "But you've only just started, it will take a little time. You didn't like Tregaskis at first but you were fine in—"

"But I don't want do it all again!" he shouts. "I did it once to please you, and it was really hard. Then as soon as I got to like it and make some friends you made me move again! The kids in this place are assholes and the teachers are assholes. End of story."

Marshall motions a quiet nod of support then says, "You don't understand that the Cree learn by watching and by doing, not by looking at books and sitting in some classroom all day listening to all the shit you get here."

"Look, Alex," I say, careful to ignore Marshall's contribution. "I know it's been difficult for you, I really appreciate that, but you shouldn't just give up on school. I have lots of days when I don't want to go to work, but sometimes you really have to stick at things if you want any reward."

"What reward? I'm just not interested in your history or German, or your fucking religious education shit. I want to learn *my* history, I want to go fishing and kayaking, I want to be a Cree. I don't want to live in this country no more, I want to go home and see my friends and Granma and Evelyn and Wilson again. I've done my best here because I thought it was what Mom wanted, but now it's my turn to speak."

For a moment I am impressed by the fact that Alex is becoming quite articulate. Then—maybe it's the mention of Wilson which triggers me—after maintaining a brief impartial calm, it's my turn to shout. "Well, I hope you're satisfied, Marshall. You've dumped this boy on Karla for years on end, and now she's brought him here to build a new life you just come over and unsettle him. I think you're jealous that you never had opportunities like this yourself."

"Well, it's easy for you to be an expert, isn't it?" he asks coolly. "You come over and bless us with your presence for a few months then fuck off back to your nice big house when you've had enough. Anyway, it wasn't me that couldn't hold a job down this time, was it? And it wasn't me that insisted on taking him out of school these last two days."

"No? So who was it?"

"Ronald."

"Oh, come on, you expect me to believe that?"

"Go ask him you like. He said it would be good to have a guys' trip out. Said it was good after all these years to find a boy he could take fishing. Ain't that right, Alex?"

"Yeah, that's what he said."

Fishing? Dad? I don't believe it. Okay, he took me to West Bay for a day when I was eight or so, and I remember the hours of feeling cold and bored. What kid would develop an enthusiasm on the strength of that? It wouldn't surprise me if Marshall has coerced his son into lying, and I know that I cannot get a reliable account of events from my father. "So where did you go? How did you get there?"

"Some place on the coast, Something Regis. We went in Ronald's car."

"But Dad's not fit to drive!"

"Who says he drove? I drove."

"You don't have a licence, or insurance, or—"

"Okay, so Alex drove. Who cares? You need to loosen up, Cormack, that might be part of the problem round here."

Me, loosen up? But I am looser than I have ever been. Who

307

could ever have imagined the Pacamac of old venturing into the social injustice of the North Americas, let alone bringing back an indigenous woman and her son? Isn't that adventurous? Isn't that liberated? Why, only half an hour ago I was on the verge of defacing a Neighbourhood Watch sign on Frentley Parva village green.

"What about you, what do you want to do about it?" I ask Karla. But the anger of a few minutes ago has drained from her. She looks up at me with those brown eyes and in them I believe I can see her future and her past. Sorrow, vigour, oppression and love are all there, but above all these is entrapment. Whatever she does, wherever she goes there will be conflict, the inescapable wrestle of free will and history, loyalty and ambition, duty and desire. And there is nothing noble about this battle, it is as sordid as any gut-splattered minefield in Sudan or Baghdad. She is a casualty too, four times over—a second-generation legacy of what whites do to not-whites, Christians do to heathens, men do to women, rich do to the poor. We cannot escape the unequal foundation of our relationship, which is based on correcting what—however indirectly or distantly—I have done to her.

"I want what's best for Alex," she says.

"Which is?"

She looks away and does not speak. I know there is no need.


The school year is ending soon anyway. Marshall has said that he will stay for two more weeks of his son's company and then head back home. I have a fear that he is bluffing and will stay in this house forever, but he produces a crumpled airline ticket from the bottom of his bag. He says he misses his friends and the unconfined outdoors (which makes it ironic that he should choose to spend so much time in jail) and a myriad other things which are beyond my conventional comprehension.

Karla has immersed herself in the care of the handicapped Toby. I am fully occupied with my locums, in fact I am turning down work. Meanwhile the summer is uneasily hot and the normally plush fields of Dorset are already brown with drought. As I drive to Shahbn or Sherrborrne or wherever my day's work is, it worries me to sense how our weather is changing. In particular—I don't need more guilt than I already have, but it visits me just the same— I know whose climate will suffer more than most. Arctic ice will perish, and with it Inuit life. Fish and seals, bears and birds will die. Beneath reserves like Jackfish Lake the permafrost will melt. Homes and roads, bridges and airstrips will crumble. Throughout the north of the continent, buildings like the Athabasca Bar and United Provisions will become unsafe. Insurance claims will be trumped by small print get-out clauses, the government will plead poverty, the people will get no help. And whose technology, whose central heating and armies of kitchen gadgets and tumble driers, whose Range Rovers, whose holidays on tax-free fuel and accumulated air miles will have infected them with this destruction? The white man's. Ours. Mine.

The heat has made Dad particularly fractious. He lies in bed, fidgets, flings off the clothes, and gets up with Mum scampering behind him and stoking his fever even more. What are you doing, Ronald? Come back to bed. You won't go out, will you, you mustn't, you'll get lost. Let me make you a. Or a tablet, I'll get you one from the. Oh, where's Philip, I wonder if he's in—**Shut up, woman, bloody well leave me alone!**

We have admitted tacit defeat and slotted in to his timing. He brazenly goes to bed in the afternoon while Mum dozes in a chair. She wakes pale and stiff-jointed, instantly fraught and unrefreshed. Oh, where is he? Has he gone to? I told him not to, he'll never sleep tonight. She has sentenced herself to death by fretting, and I fear she will peg out before him.

So as usual I drive home with trepidation. Alex is unhappy, Karla is quietly tormented, and Dad's nocturnal ramblings, whether demented or calculated, are straining everyone in the house. Marshall is entirely unpredictable, sometimes swanning off in Dad's Jag (with his happy permission) with Alex in the front seat and fishy paraphernalia slopping out on the leathered back, or setting off on random all-day walks. It would appear that we are quietly colluding with Alex's truancy in these last few days of term, ostensibly to spend time with his father, but it still admits to defeat.

Further horror greets me today. Marshall and Alex are sitting cross-legged on the lawn, encircled by a sprawling inexplicable mesh of rope and twine. At first sight it looks as if they are repairing fishing nets, but the material is too thick and coarse.

"Hey, what's going on?!" I demand when I then see the six-foot wooden stakes and the two sizeable holes hacked out of the middle of Dad's once pristine lawn.

"Cool it, man, I'm doing you a favour," Marshall replies.

"A favour? How the hell is destroying my father's pride and joy doing anyone a favour?"

"You'll find out soon enough. Why don't you get us both a beer?"

"Oh, certainly! And perhaps you'd like a selection from the wide and entirely free buffet we have on offer here. Can I get you some olives, perhaps? Some anchovies? Smoked salmon? Accompanied by a fine dry sherry?"

He looks up with bemused innocence on his face. "Why are you so pissed off all the time, Cormack? I really don't know what your problem is."

"Actually, it's you!" I want to shout, but I desist. Because, of course, he's not.

I head indoors, where Karla is scouring the kitchen for food. She is standing on a chair and it is clear that the contents of the upper reaches of these big dark cupboards are musty and outdated. Cubic glass jars contain unidentifiable pulses or beans, their age and safety unknown. Behind them she finds eight large tins of fish soup, brought back on Dad's insistence from their last French holiday seven years ago.

"Oh, I'd forgotten about them," Mum says as she hovers round Karla's feet.

"They're way out of date," Karla tells her. "I'll make an omelette instead."

"I could do a shepherd's pie," Mum offers.

"No, there are mushrooms here, I'll do an omelette."

"Or I could make a nice casserole."

"No, it's okay."

"Or there are some pies in the freezer if you."

"No!" Karla shouts. "Omelettes are fine!"

I intervene, "Karla, let's go out for a walk."

"But I'm going to make dinner."

"No, come on. That can wait."

It is hot and hazy, English summer at its slightly doleful height. Dorset's mild hills embrace us and we head along the lane out of the village to the footpath which will take us down to Audley's Copse. We haven't done much of this lately—walking, talking, holding hands—and it is evident in this rare interlude alone that she is subdued. This is not the Karla of old.

"I'm sorry if I shouted at your mother."

"Don't worry, I know how trying she can be. It's not that I'm bothered about, I just find it awfully difficult with Marshall around all the time. I know he has a right to see Alex, but he is rather intrusive. And do you keep giving him money?"

"Shit, don't tell me this is just about money! He doesn't have any of his own, does he? Anyway, Ronald's been giving him some as well."

"Has he? How much?"

"How should I know? You'll have to ask him."

I might have known he would be leeching off someone, but that's not why we're here. "No, it's not just about the money. Look, Karla—"

Look, what? I don't know what to say or what to ask, I only know that something is amiss, and no, it's not all down to Marshall. Suddenly I realise that I must reclaim her, I do not want another relationship to drift impassively into routine and courtesy, ever more distant by the day. We are standing just inside the woods, shade and light scrambled madly by the flickering leaves. I pull her to me and kiss her, I want nothing more than to fall upon the leaf-bed ground and make love to her, naked and exposed. This urge transcends sex, I know. It would just be the

311

most extreme form of impulse, recklessness and passion I can imagine, it would show her that my desire for her exceeds all else. But she tenses against me and looks away.

"What's the matter?"

"I'm worried about Mom and Evelyn. I'm missing them, I guess."

"Are you saying you want to go back home?"

She nods, then summons herself to look at me. "I don't know—maybe if it was just me, I'd stay, but Alex isn't happy here, he wants to go back. I'm sorry, but I just keep thinking of what the elder told me, that my first responsibility is to him."

A deluge of despair engulfs me, though it doesn't quite extinguish a flicker of anger. "This is nothing to do with Marshall being here, is it?" I have an irrational, but nonetheless agonising vision of them resuming their liaison and living in bliss back in Jackfish Lake. Maybe the real purpose of his visit was to reclaim her, maybe—

"Do me a favour here!" she shouts, but on this occasion she catches my hangdog eyes and lets her anger subside. She hugs my arm and says, "No, it's nothing to do with him. It's been wonderful over here, and I'll always be grateful to you, but—I don't know, I don't think this can ever be our home."

"Okay, so I'll come back to Canada with you. Anywhere you want to go, back to Jackfish Lake, wherever."

She looks at me with those historic brown eyes, kisses me gently on the lips, and asks, "Would you do that, Philip? Would you really?"

"Of course. Why not?"

"I don't know. I just assumed you wouldn't want to leave England now you're back."

"I want to be where you are, Karla, end of story," I say, though I recall my amused comment when Sharon told me of Lena's imminent return to Jackfish Lake. "She's been here before? And she wants to come back?"

"What's the matter?" Karla asks, catching my stifled smile.

I tell her, then add, "I wonder what Sharon's doing now."

I don't really want to go home, into public—least of all when Marshall is a member of it—with the burden of this sentence hanging over me. We walk back in arm-linked silence and at the door she seems to read my mind. "Don't worry, Marshall's going home next week, I won't say anything to him."

We eat a quiet dinner then slump blankly before the telly, my mind filled only with sorrow at the end of this venture. But tomorrow I will tell Karla again that I *do* love her, I *will* go back to Canada with her if she will permit me. It is nearly eleven o'clock and she sits at the table to write to Ruth. I imagine her delight at receiving this latest missive, "Evelyn! She's coming home! I knew it wouldn't last!"

Mum slumps in dozing respite in her chair, and suddenly I startle up, for something is missing. The house is peaceful and unblemished by Dad's ranting. Where the hell has he gone? The fact that his shoes are still neat in the hall rack means nothing, he could still have slipped out dressing-gowned and slippered for a meander round the village. The possibilities are sickeningly endless, as they used to be when we waited for Beth and Stella to return late from teenage nights out. I appreciate that everyone around here knows him, but he could still have been accosted by rowdy drunks, stepped in front of a car, or fallen unseen behind a neighbour's hedge. I walk to the end of the drive, and two boy racers zoom by. They fuel my anxiety, though I know it is illogical. But perhaps I should start my search for him by checking the house.

"Dad?"

A half moon illuminates the garden. The dry scent of lilac is detected and the high shadowy walls fend off any sounds of traffic. In the partial darkness I can make out the parallel heaps of Marshall and Alex stretched out on the lawn. Beyond them an unfamiliar structure bridges the air, and as I approach it I find it harbours the faint snores of someone securely asleep. Dad is suspended in a hammock, a single token blanket sufficient in this warmth. I creep closer and there can be no mistaking the fact that

313

his face has been cleansed of all its cantankerous anguish. I had never expected to see him—not this side of death—so convincingly serene.

He sleeps there for the next three nights too, and there is no doubt that his daily behaviour has improved. We are sitting round the old oak kitchen table eating Sunday brunch—yes, all six of us! What kind of nuclear family is this?

"Marshall," I say (for credit where it's due, as all good Shahbn scholars attest), "Dad's been much better since you fixed up that hammock for him. Thanks very much."

"You're welcome. I don't think it's all down to the hammock, though."

"Isn't it?"

"No, I think the calamus has helped too."

"The what?"

"Calamus, it's the root of a medicinal plant. You never heard of it?"

"No. Where did you get that from?"

"I asked one of the healers back home to send it over. As soon as I saw Ronald I guessed it would help."

"So how long has he been having that?"

"About two weeks, I guess."

"But hang on!" I object. "Don't you think you should have asked? Some of these so-called natural remedies are really toxic, you know."

"Come on, we've been using calamus for hundreds of years, it's safer than all that shit you give out."

"That's not the point. I appreciate your concern, I really do, but I'm not sure that you have the right to start giving him all these herbs and things without asking."

Before Marshall can defend himself, Dad intervenes, "But he asked me."

"I should think he did, but even so—"

"Even so, piffle. Just because you're a doctor doesn't mean you know everything. And I certainly don't need to ask your

314

permission to take whatever sort of medication I like. I'm of perfectly sound mind, as Dr Carson has confirmed."

"Dr Carson confirmed? When did you see him?"

"Day before yesterday, Marshall took me."

"Marshall took you?"

"Good God, man, stop talking like a parrot. Yes, Marshall took me because there was nobody else here. Everyone insists I'm not fit to drive, your mother can't, so Marshall gives me a run out in the Jag now and then, which is more than anyone else does."

"But is he insured?"

"Of course he's bally insured, I phoned them up the other week."

I desist from asking whether it's Marshall Snape or Lincoln Delaney who's covered to drive Dad's car, for I am more troubled by his rapid promotion through the ranks of Dad's closest associates. I have a vision of going back to Canada with Karla and Alex at the end of the summer, leaving Marshall employed as Dad's factotum here. Perhaps we could then send Ruth and Evelyn over to Penscott Abbas as well? The permutations are endless, I suppose, maybe there is scope for a reality TV show here. Delinquent ex-Partner Swap. Changing Demented Dads.

"What's funny?" Karla demands.

"Nothing. Sorry. Something stuck in my teeth."

"Anyways," Marshall informs me, "you good Christian people should know about calamus root because it's in the Bible. Don't you know Solomon's Song?"


On Monday I have only a half day's work booked, so I get home at lunchtime feeling sad that Karla is not there to share the afternoon with me. It seems that on the few occasions neither of us is working, our attention is centred on Dad's erratic demands and Mum's whining. Then there is the worry that Marshall is taking centre stage, that Alex is spending far more time with him than with his mother. But at least his return is now booked for five day's time.

315

"Oh, Philip, oh, Philip," Mum bleats as soon as I enter the house, scurrying to meet me. She really does wring her hands, washing anxiety into every pore so she is constantly bathed in the stuff. Maybe I should ask Marshall to sort her out too with some potent traditional herbs.

"What is it?"

"Oh, Philip, I'm so worried."

"What is it this time?"

"They've gone. Your father and Alex and."

"That's okay, they often go out, they've probably gone fishing."

"No, not this time. They've gone to London."

"London! How?"

"I don't know. They set off in the car just after you."

"They can't have driven all the way, Mum, they probably left the car at the station." Even so, the prospects are appallingly endless. "But there's no point in worrying yourself to death. We can't do anything, we'll just have to wait for them to come back."

"I know that, but what if?"

But what if, indeed. That has been the guiding philosophy of my mother's life. In any situation, think of the ten worst things that could happen, and worry about them. When they don't, try not to waste time feeling relieved but move on to the next scenario and the next ten potential pitfalls. I don't think of myself as an anxious person, I feel she has immunised me against that, but spending all this time with her and Dad is throwing up all sorts of questions about how they imprinted their influence on me. It occurs to me now that my stolidity, my lack of adventure (my aversion to adventure!) is an antidote to her anxiety. The only way to avoid life's millions of disasters is to put one foot steadfastly in front of the other, slow and methodical, never looking too far ahead. A full-blown obsessive disorder is but one over-compensatory step away. So maybe my sabbatical in a challenging place and my foolhardy relationship with Karla has all been a belated rebellion, a severing of subconscious apron strings which tethered me to my neurotic mum.

And if that is true, what now? Having used Karla to fulfil my mission, can I now dispose of her? I honestly don't think I am callous enough to do that, but on the other hand do I really love her? In my way, yes, but whether my way is sufficient remains to be seen. I quietly curse this mess of parental legacies. Whether learnt or inherited their consequences are still the same. And—there is no escaping this destination now—my thoughts must turn to my own parenting, deficient as it has been. I have the impulse to phone the girls to see if they might refute this, but I know what their answers would be.

Have I been a good father? *Not especially. We never saw you much.*

Are you angry at me? *No, that was just the way it was.*

Is there anything else you want to say to me? *No thanks, I'm just going out.*

"Mum?"

"Hmm?"

"Why did you send me away to boarding school?"

"Well, it was what your father wanted, he thought it was for the best."

"Yes, but why? I could have gone as a day boy, I could have lived at home, like Eve did."

"I know."

"So why did I have to board?"

"You know what Ronald's always been like, him and his ideas."

She stands at the kitchen window, still big in physical stature but nonetheless frail and lost. Although her years here must soon end, it is as if she has never had any impact on this sober house and the garden which she surveys. "Didn't he think you were capable of bringing us up?"

She considers this in silence then offers a faint shake of the head. "No, dear, I don't believe he."

I go to stand behind her and lay my hands light on her shoulders. I wonder how her psyche has coped with this insult for so many years, wonder again why it has taken half my adult life to find it out.

———

317

At six o'clock Karla returns, looking tired and wan. "Where's Alex?"

"It looks like they've all gone to London for the day."

"London? Marshall and Alex and Ronald let loose in London? Are they all crazy? Whose idea was that? Why did you let them do that, for God's sake, why—?"

"Hey, calm down. They went just after we left this morning. I'm sure they'll be all right." Of course I am not sure of this at all, but I don't want Karla's anger directed onto me. "Come and sit down, I'll get you a drink."

I go to the kitchen to open the white wine I have thoughtfully set aside in the fridge. She thanks me for it, apologises for her crossness, which is entirely down to fatigue. As if to prove this she curls across the settee and into sleep, her cool bare feet resting on my lap. I stroke them lightly and sit there trapped, vowing that I will never in my life do anything to cause her unhappiness or harm.

They stagger into the house at ten-thirty, Alex laughing with excitement, Dad flushed and unsteady, Marshall as pissed as a laboratory rat.

"I hope you haven't driven Dad's car in that state!" I shout.

"Where the *hell* do you think you've been?" Karla demands.

"Ronald, I really don't think you," Mum wails.

"Jeez, it's good to be made welcome when you get home, ay, Ron?" Marshall asks.

"But I've been frantic with worry," Mum cries.

Ronald sits in his chair and scans the newspaper headlines. "For God's sake, woman, you're always frantic with worry. Why don't you take a day off?"

It is clearly my duty to maintain a degree of calm. "It's okay, they're back and they're safe. There's no harm done—but I really do think, Marshall, it was a bit irresponsible of you. Dad does get confused, you know—"

"Nonsense, I know London like the back of my hand."

"Yes, but you have got yourself lost on more than one occasion."

"No, I haven't. Every time I want to go for a walk by myself, someone comes rushing after me to tell me I'll get lost."

"But, Ronald, you."

"We got the train to Paddington, we bought a day ticket for the tube and followed the maps, and I took the A-Z. We did an open-top bus tour of the sights, and Alex had a marvellous time. The car's still at the station, we got a taxi back because Marshall's had a beer or two. We wanted to go to London, so what's wrong with that?"

"Why didn't you wait until I had a day off?" I ask. "Karla and I could have taken you."

Alex pounces on my words. "You said that the first day I got here, but you've never taken me yet. You haven't taken me anywhere."

"I don't think that's entirely true—" I begin, but Alex is already slamming his way up to his room.

"Shit, we've all had a great day out, and now you've upset him," Marshall says.

"Me? Me? Don't start blaming everything on me!" I tell him, and our exchange escalates; one old woman blubs as the other four people shout and accuse, unleash prejudices and long-held grudges, hurl undifferentiated aggression onto those they are supposed to love, all respect and dignity lost.

An anonymous café on a dual carriageway in southern England: Roadside Slop or The Sulky Waitress or whatever it is called. The paper place mats map out the identical fare available to travellers at identical establishments from Airdrie to Exeter. I imagine that in all of these there are family units deliberating on what to have with their chips as the rumble of trucks on tarmac mingles with local radio, whose update of accidents and traffic jams provides the only clue as to which part of the country they are in. Then I wonder if there can be a more pathetic specimen in the whole western world than the driver (invariably male) who phones in with traffic updates and glories in the guise of his adopted name. "Cowboy Bob tells us the A31 east of Ringwood is prone to delays because of roadworks…thanks to Roadrunner for alerting us to an accident on the southbound carriageway of the M27 between junctions 8 and 9…and Radar Rex has just phoned to say a lorry has shed its load on the B3081…"

"Radar Rex!" I exclaim. "Jesus Christ!"

"What's the matter with that?" Karla asks.

"These sad people who have nothing to do but give themselves silly names."

"What's wrong with that? Sounds very public-spirited to me."

"Yes, maybe so—but Radar Rex, I ask you!"

"If that's the biggest thing in your life you have to complain about, then you're a very lucky person."

"I didn't say it was the biggest thing. I just said that—" But she's right, it isn't worth pursuing.

"Hey, this looks good!" Alex interrupts as his burger and fries arrive.

I don't intend to cast disapproval in his direction, but presumably I do, because Karla tells me, "Oh, leave him be!"

So Alex looks at me, no doubt wondering why he has offended me, and I protest to Karla, "I never said a word!"

"You don't have to."

I sigh heavily. Then I expect her to say, "Don't sigh like that," but she doesn't, so I in turn desist from raising the stakes. "Stop playing with that," she says instead.

"What?"

"That."

Unawares, I have been fiddling with one of the annoyingly individualised little packets of pepper. These are all prepared in the name of hygiene and security, I suppose, yet more trees culled to make paper sachets housing exactly 3.625 grammes of pepper so as to safeguard us against the risk of a potential poisoner infiltrating the nation's cruets. The Condiment Killer Strikes Again, I imagine.

"For God's sake, what's so funny?"

"Nothing. Sorry."

She looks at me with that mixture of scorn and puzzlement, and I have the fleeting idea that if I can take her into my confidence and explain my endearingly eccentric internal humour pathways, our intimacy will be restored. But now is not the time, and I fear that there will never be such a time between us again. We are on our way back from London, having taken Marshall to catch his flight home. Already it seems surreal, as if we have had a visitor from another galaxy. Personally I was relieved to see the back of him, for I still clutch onto a faint hope that his departure will leave Karla and I to define ourselves in our family role. I even bought him a present, a decent rucksack, to commemorate his time in our home.

"Here, Marshall, this is for you, I wanted to thank you for the time you spent with Dad."

"You didn't have to do that, you don't owe me nothing."

"Maybe, but please take it anyway."

"Thank you," he said.

So we waved him off at the airport, his new Quiksilver bag holding little more than he had when he arrived. He hugged Karla and Alex, accepted my shake of the hand, then slouched off to the departure lounge without a backwards look, his Jackfish Lake cap and same old day-in-day-out jacket conspicuously dowdy even in the diversity of Heathrow.

And in these last three hours Alex has taken his leaving badly. At first he cried hard, then he spent the journey looking wistful through the car window, with Karla turning repeatedly to ask if he was all right. The arrival of his meal perks him briefly, but I can see the gloom returning, gradually weighing him down.

When we get home, Karla heads straight for bed. She kisses me quickly on the cheek and I note how her tiredness impersonates age. Small lines underpin her eyes, the vital and elastic tissue around her mouth is dormant, this is how she will look in five years time. This saddens me no end, for I know this process will career out of control in the hardship of Jackfish Lake.

"Of course!" I suddenly shout.

"What is it?" asks Mum, startled. "What have you?"

Without replying I race to the computer, summon the list of my favourite websites, and—yes!—still preserved from more than a year ago is the locum agency which led to my fateful spell in Jackfish Lake. Excited all over again, I survey the opportunities in store:

> **Arborg.** Immediately available long-term locum...no good, they need Obstetrics.
>
> **Neepawa.** GP/Anesthesiologist needed...well, that's no use.
>
> **Jackfish Lake.** The great outdoors! 300km N of Thompson. Short or long term locum available. $240,000

pa basic plus on call. Accommodation supplied. Occasional intra-partum care only. For further details contact...

**Indian Head**. Busy practice seeks short- or long-term help...the word "busy" seems to put me off.

**Buffalo Narrows**. Highly profitable single man practice...single man? I'm not getting lumbered by myself again.

**Wynsdale**. Friendly practice needs f/t or p/t help. Prepared to be flexible and to wait for the right person...

"Yes!" I shout softly. "Oh yes, oh yes, oh yes!"

For this, I feel certain, is the answer to my prayers. There is no way of knowing if this is the practice Uncle Geoffrey was in, but it doesn't matter. I have a tie to the town, I have been there, I know what it's like. I can picture us now in one of its neat and roomy houses, Alex and his friends free to exploit the basement, to play pool there, watch videos, or stroll to the swimming pool nearby. He will flourish at school. Karla will easily find worthwhile work. This is exactly what we are looking for—a civilised and tolerant place, a home for all of us regardless of tribe or creed.

I tap out a letter of application, attach my c.v. and despatch it into the ether. There is a slight hesitancy when it comes to the matter of referees, but I feel that George will be gentleman enough to help me out. Then, while the impetus of excitement is still there, I wing my next email across the sea:

Dear Sharon,

Sorry not to have contacted you for so long. I really hope you are well. How was Phoenix Farm?? As you probably know, Karla and Alex have been over here with me for some months now, though we have left Cornwall and are living with my Mum and Dad. Settling down here has been understandably difficult for them, especially Alex (though Marshall Snape had a cracking time, I think

I will omit). Thus I am applying for a job in Wynsdale, Sask, where my Uncle Geoffrey once practised and I studied!!! I am wondering if you would be so good as to give me a reference if they contact you? It would be great to get back to Canada and be able to visit you again.


Love,   Philip

"Come on, Alex, I'll take you to the cricket."

His face wrinkles with disinterest.

"Somerset against Surrey at Taunton. We can be there in an hour, it should be really good."

"Don't want to."

"Or we could get out for a while and give you some batting practice. We ought to see if there's a club round here to get you playing again before the season ends."

"I don't really like cricket any more."

This statement, I fear, ends any chance I have of bonding with the boy. In Marshall's time here he was happy, animated, almost communicative, but now he has relapsed into being a small bewildered refugee, alone in a foreign world. It is Saturday morning, Karla is working until five, so I feel obliged to involve myself with him for some, at least, of the coming hours. School has finished and he has found no holiday friends. "We could go to Bristol. Wouldn't you like to see the suspension bridge, or the zoo?"

He concentrates on the television, whose juvenile presenters giggle with estuary English silliness before introducing some skimpy-bloused female singer. "Aahhdno."

"Dad? Fancy a trip to the cricket?" I ask in an all-or-nothing bid. If he is keen, that will put more pressure on Alex, who would hardly relish being left alone all day with his surrogate gran.

"No, thanks, I'm going to start my *inukshuk*."

"Your what?"

"My *inukshuk*. It's an Inuit thing, it's a stone cairn built in the shape of a human, thought you'd know about them. They marked paths or places where they buried food, but they also had spiritual connotations as well."

"How do you know all this?"

"Marshall told me. Look." He produces one of his old sketch books, but instead of architectural drafts in his own hand he shows me page after page of deftly sketched stone humanoids, arms and heads and trunks counterpoised and chunkily elegant on their backdrop of white.

"But Marshall's not Inuit, he's Cree!" I object. "He drew these?"

"Yes."

Lucky he sobered up to get that tendon repaired, I reflect. His simple pencil lines are clean and bold, conveying the basics of shadow and weight. It surprises me that he has such talent, and for a moment I feel jealous for his certainly exceeds mine. My own artistic venture has long since ground to a halt, and I determine to resume it as soon as I can. But compared to Marshall's instinctive skill, I am a simple technician, another Painter Plod.

"And you're going to build one?" I ask.

"Yes, there's a huge pile of stones behind the shed from when I knocked down that wall. Alex—coming to help?"

"Sure," the boy replies, following my father eagerly through the door.


I haven't yet told Karla about the job in Wynsdale. They may well contact me to say the post has been filled or that I am unsuitable, in which case there is no point in building up her hopes. But I have been checking my email two or three times a day, and now—look!—there is a message from an unfamiliar address:

Hi Philip

It was just lovely to hear from you! I was beginning to think you'd forgotten all about me! I'm glad you and

Karla are well and I hope that everything works out for you, over there or back here. <u>Of course</u> I'll give you a reference! Wynsdale isn't so far from here (Canadian not far, that is)—well within visiting distance.

I've had an eventful time—I got down to 160 pounds at Phoenix and now I'm 149—I've reached my target of 150!!! And I'm at the gym every day! Found a job as clinic manager near Osborne village, where I'm renting a house. I'm so happy—there are photos attached of me and Paul, who I'm living with. We're getting married in October— please come!! I'll let you know the date nearer the time, probably the 3rd.

Lots of love, Sharon

I open the attachment and there indeed are her photos. Not that I would have known it to be her, a smiling girl in a pale blue suit and shoulder-length, honey-coloured hair, happy and desirable. She is not exactly slim, for her face still retains a mature roundness, but the adipose collar which made her look masculine has gone. Yes, she is an attractive woman now. She links arms with a man who is tall and crew cut, older than her, and, I can tell, unimaginative and honest. It is clear he is perfect for her. He will be loving and loyal, and I envy the simplicity of her ambition. I click them back into their e-vacuum, consumed by the realisation that I hate Paul very much.


"Mom! Come and look at this!" Alex shouts as she comes in from work. He grabs her hand and drags her through to the garden. "Look!" Their *inukshuk* stands on the far corner of the lawn, sturdy and reassuring, three foot tall.
"Hey, that's wonderful! Who made that?"
"Me and Ronald."
Dad nods in modest acknowledgement and ruffles Alex's hair.

"Not the sort of architecture I'm used to, but interesting all the same."

"It's brilliant, isn't it, Philip?"

We smile at their unlikely alliance, and I have to concede that it is. I realise that Dad is more animated than he has been for months. I keep to the back of my mind the thought that it may be anything to do with the daily dose of calamus he insists on continuing to take. (Maybe I could look into this and put my name on the medical research map by confirming this herbal cure for Alzheimer's Disease. But no, I don't suppose I will.) He still has lapses of memory but it is as if he has decided not to give himself over to the role of being terminally demented just yet. He is calmer and he has stopped playing his cantankerous games. He no longer derides Mum or takes advantage of her, he lets arguments lapse instead of haranguing them to death. She in turn seems happier and I even get glimpses of the affection they must once have had to sustain them through so many years. Even his dress code has relaxed. In London he bought his first ever pair of jeans, and now he stands in the garden wearing them, along with a baseball cap bearing a red maple leaf.

"How about we build one in the front garden tomorrow?" he asks Alex.

"Sure thing!" the boy replies.


My reply arrives on Monday. Mrs Rae Marquise, clinic manager, says that the doctors are very interested in my application and will be taking up references. One of them will contact me for a telephone interview later in the week, when would be a good time? If they can fast track my bureaucratic hurdles, would I be interested in doing a locum for a month or two later in the year? Then, after a period of mutual assessment, we might consider a permanent post. There is more information about the job—the salary is good, I can opt out of Obstetric care because one of the other practices in town tends to do it all...it sounds ideal. This time my judgement of this is more measured, for I know what the town is like. The patient group will be more sober and less knife-happy than those in Jackfish Lake, and true emergencies can be packed off to Regina, less than an hour's ambulance trip away.

I remember Uncle Geoffrey's homely little office (the term amused and confused me as "surgery" did them) in the main street. I forget the names of the receptionists but patients would drop by with an excuse for a chat and to keep in touch with local events. It's Gilbert and Sullivan night on Friday. Don't forget the flower show. There's a trip to the classic car exhibition at the airfield this weekend. I recall that I went there myself, lost a day in admiration of those swirling curves of bodywork, brilliant chrome, the extravagant *chic* of those Chryslers and Chevvies and Caddies. Going back to Wynsdale would be the perfect and obvious and most symmetrical solution. It is friendly and industrious and respectful, all those things which Jackfish Lake is not.

I print out the letter. "Karla—look!"

She is in the kitchen, compiling a list of requirements from the shop. "What's that?"

"Well, read it, find out!"

She does so, but her expression is perplexed. "Where's this from?"

"Wynsdale."

"Where?"

"Wynsdale, Saskatchewan. Where I did my student elective with Uncle Geoffrey."

"And now you've applied for a job there?"

"Well, yes. This is the response."

"You never said anything to me."

"No, because I thought it would probably come to nothing."

"Sure, but you could still have told me you were thinking of something as important as this."

"Okay, okay, I'm sorry!"

"You don't sound sorry."

"Oh, Karla! Look, I'm excited because this might be the answer for us. I can see how difficult it is for Alex over here, so a place like this in Canada would be ideal. You could visit Ruth and Evelyn, they could visit us, they could even live with us if they liked. Alex would have no problem integrating, the schools are good..." My voice tapers off, squashed by her stony response.

"Philip, are you kidding? Are you stupid? Don't you know how conservative, how prejudiced these small prairie towns are? I mean, redneck or what? They treat aboriginals like shit."

"Nobody would treat you badly, you'd be nursing there, you'd be with me—"

"Exactly!" she shouts. "They'd make an exception if I was married to a nice white doctor, they'd drop their prejudice then! They'd still shit all over any other Cree or Méti, but I could just turn a blind eye to that, couldn't I, I'd be—"

"But Wynsdale isn't like that! I lived there for two months, remember."

"Yeah, and how many aboriginals did you come across?"

"I don't know, not many, I admit."

"Sure, not many at all, probably none. You weren't aware of any because they were ostracised and ignored, they just don't integrate into places like that. Even Winnipeg would be better."

I am trying hard not to feel completely crushed. "Okay, if you don't like the idea of Wynsdale, I'll get a job in Winnipeg."

Her look at me is quizzical, as if she were seeing me for the first time. "But you thought Cornwall would work, and it didn't. You thought here would work, and it isn't—"

"What do you mean, it isn't? If it weren't for Marshall inviting himself and causing so much disruption, we might all have got on fine—"

She interrupts my interruption, her voice carrying on where it left off, decisive but calm. "You say you know what Wynsdale is like, but you still think it's a place where we all could live. I don't think you know me or Alex at all, you just like the idea of rescuing us and giving us a better life. There's no way we could ever be happy or be absorbed into a place like that. I'm sorry, but my mind's made up, it would be best if we just go back home. I'll book our tickets tomorrow."

"Karla, if you want to go back to Jackfish Lake, I'll come with you!"

Now she raises her voice, "You just don't get it! You don't get what I'm saying, this isn't going to work wherever we decide to live."

"But it can!"

"I don't think so," she says, but more reflectively now. "Our place is back home, Philip, it's as simple as that. However difficult it might be for me, I have to go home."

"What do you mean, difficult?"

Even though she is rejecting me, her brown eyes express confusion and warmth and, I do believe, love. "To a lot of people—especially the men—going off with a white man has labelled me as a traitor and a whore. It's the worst thing a woman can do."

"So don't go back!"

"It's not as simple as that. I can't run away from what I've done, I made that decision and I don't have any other home. The sooner I go back and face it, the better."

"But people over there have no right to moralise like that! You know what they're like—all that drinking, screwing around—"

"I know all that," she says quietly. "I'm really sorry, Philip, but the prairies wouldn't work. Alex and I are going back to Jackfish Lake."

Even in evening drizzle the village of Penscott Abbas seems remarkably alluring and safe. Rain refracts the few amber street lights into a warm protective glow. The several thatched roofs disdainfully deflect the water which drifts down through the air. Other eaves tumble luxuriously almost to the ground, and beneath them their occupants lounge on sofas with single malts, check their share prices in the *Financial Times*, and maybe contemplate a weekend shoot.

A mellifluous hum issues from the pub. I decide to enter it, to indulge myself with a pint and some sad contemplation. Why am I not content with all this? What could be more idyllic? This is rural England at its finest and I could live the rest of my days here in Montfort House, maybe sell it for something smaller when my parents finally expire. I would find work with ease, and no doubt a new partner would appear to me. She would be presentable and intelligent, of independent means, divorced or widowed, and a tad conservative, yes. She would think herself fortunate to conjoin me in this utterly pleasant life. All these things would evolve, I have no uncertainty about that. But do I want them? Would they be enough?

I imagine myself in session with Jayne, our counsellor in Tregaskis, or some counterpart elsewhere. I have always admired her ability to amend lives with no tools but her own detached perception and provision of time. No fobbing off with Prozac prescriptions for her! No passing the referral to someone else because a five-minute answer isn't there. How I could use her gently probing skills for myself. Perhaps she could tease out what ails me and point me in the gentle direction of a solution for my life.

I sit in a quiet corner to see if a beer or two will clear my thinking on this, but on this occasion it fails. Instead I look about me and see the self-congratulation it has induced. A group of well-turned-out men stand at the bar in their plain but expensive shirts, assured in their sartorial understatement while their perfect enunciation brays with confidence. One of them is a GP, I feel sure—I've never seen him before but his accumulated mannerisms and his v-necked pullover with its emblem on the chest and a dozen other things I can't define make my diagnosis secure. They are laughing, loudly lauding themselves, shored securely into a group. It's their version of Friday at Six. I could and should be *one of them*, and I still can't work out whether my silent resentment in their direction is because belonging to their ilk is, in the deep obscurity of my heart, the first or the very last thing I want.

When I get back home everyone is in bed but Dad. He sits at the kitchen table which is covered by a shower of small flat stones he has gathered from the garden, and an army of miniature *inukshuks* he has made.

"Simple cantilever, you see," he demonstrates with a rectangular head squashing two outstretched arms into perfect balance. "Take off the head and everything collapses." And it does, in a clatter of stone and soil. "Whatsisname was telling me that there are different types—some have small holes which you can look through and they align you with the next resting place. Then some of them mark fords or food stores, but I think most of them just represent the human form. When you're travelling across the Arctic for days without seeing anyone it's a comfort to know you're not completely alone. It's very important not to feel alone."

"Dad?"

"Hmm?"

"Why did you send me away to boarding school?"

"Thought it was for the best," he says, without shifting concentration from his humanoids to me.

"I know that. But I could have gone as a day boy. Why didn't you want me to do that?"

"If you're now telling me you wanted to stay at home, I have to point out to you that you're about forty years too late."

"I just want to know why. Didn't you think Mum would manage us?"

Now he looks up to consider. "Nothing to do with that. Just wanted you to have the benefit of the whole public school caboodle. To be honest I don't think I was ever cut out to be a parent, I expect you've realised that yourself. I suppose I might have quite liked the idea of having the end product, but I was never very interested in all the effort that goes into it. All that baby stuff, all that bonding you're supposed to do." His face creases into distaste.

"You seem to be bonding all right with Alex," I point out, having to admit here a sliver of jealousy towards a thirteen-year-old boy.

"Well, I'm older and wiser, now, aren't I? I might be going a bit senile, but there are still certain things you can learn. Anyway,

I could see that your mother missed you, so that's why Eve didn't board. If she'd gone away too, I don't know what your mother would have done. Apart from that—"

He pauses, occupied again by his little stone men.

"What?"

"Thought you needed all the help you could get, to be frank, you were never very bright."

## 4.1

Dad lies in the single bed of a side ward in the small cottage hospital. Mother looks lost on the low chair as she holds his insensate hand. She is not actually crying at the moment, though she has done so for much of the last two weeks since he was felled by his stroke. Eve is at his other side, his right, but at least she spends some time in his service by comforting his head into the stacked pillows or dabbing a salve of moisture to his mouth. It seems likely that this day, the ninth of November, will be his last. He cannot eat or drink, his breathing has slowed to a stop-start afterthought, and he does not have the strength to cough away the infection which has gathered in his chest. We know from the scan he had a fortnight ago that there is a haemorrhage at the base of his brain. It cannot be removed, it will not dissolve, it will ferry him conclusively to his grave.

But these days of waiting are hard. We speak to him as if he is still with us, but try to accept that he has already gone. What grieves me most is being deprived of truly knowing him. I will never discover what emotions his dedication to work concealed. This, it pains me, is a terrible deficiency in a relationship so fundamental to our lives. It would be good to report that a momentous conciliatory bond was formed in his last days, but that will clearly not be the case.

The thought of this makes me look at my watch. "See you later," I say as I quietly leave.

---

Penscott Junction is a mile or two from the town. The railway gives us a convenient option for travelling off round the country, but because it is on some circuitous route to the south coast and not the main line to London, commuters are deterred. Hanging baskets decorate the platforms and their floral displays are watered every day. The carved wooden valances around the hundred-year-old brickwork are freshly painted and bright in the sun. Visitors unerringly remark on what a clean and pleasant station this is.

The 11.33 arrives on time and from it step Beth and Stella. Beth is smiling and colourful in her chunky woollen jacket and matching hat. Stella, more fashionable and less practical, shivers as her light jacket and exposed midriff are exposed to the chilly air. We say hello and I hug them as hard as I ever have in my life.

"How's Grandad?"

"Gradually failing, I don't think he'll last much longer."

"What about Grandma, how's she bearing up?"

"As badly as she ever does."

"Poor Grandma, are we going to see them?"

"Later. Would you like a walk first, some coffee and something to eat?"

"That would be great."

I know that by dallying in town I could miss my father's last minutes on this earth, but I reckon he will be oblivious to that. There is nothing more I can do for him, and what matters more than anything in these coming minutes and hours and days is spending time with my daughters. The Dorset Coffee House is predictably twee but we enter it. We sit down, order drinks and teacakes and croissants, and Beth removes her hat. She is an attractive woman now, thanks to inheriting her mother's features rather than mine. Her face and eyes are sharp but her colouring is lighter and warmer than Mary's, her thick hair rich and brown.

"So?" I prompt.

"So what?"

"So what's been happening in your life?"

And for the next hour or so she tells me all the chatty little details about her new flatmate, her lazy landlord, the tutor who fancies her, her trip last week to her best friend Rosie's home. Stella came to London to stay a couple of weeks ago, and they had a wonderful time ("It was great, wasn't it, Stel?" "Yeah, wicked."). It's a good idea of hers to take a gap year, she wishes she'd done the same. Even if you don't go anywhere spectacular, you can still stop and think about what you really want to do.

They chat easily and happily, they touch and smile. Stella is younger and quieter, but they are equals, it is clear that there is no undertow of jealousy beneath their love. I look back at all my nasty boyhood rancour towards Eve and it occurs to me that if there is one great blessing in my life it is the fact that my daughters are fine young women and they remain close friends.

"I spoke to Mum yesterday, she seems really happy now—oh, sorry, I didn't mean it like that."

"It's okay, I think I'm over that now."

"And what about Karla? Are you going to visit her again?"

"No, I don't think so."

"Good."

"Why, didn't you like her?"

"Yes, I liked her well enough, but I'm sure it wouldn't have worked."

"Wouldn't it?"

"No, you just wanted to rescue her, didn't you?"

"God, was it that obvious?"

Beth laughs and says, "Yes." Stella agrees.

"So do you think she took advantage of me?"

"I don't think I know her well enough to answer that. Though I suppose it was understandable if she did."

For a moment I want to protest—no, there was more to it than that, much more! There really was a rare bond, something which transcended the differences and distances between us. Whether it was true love doesn't matter, it was as intense and adventurous as anything in my life. It was much more than a relationship of mutual convenience, Beth, it was...but whatever, now it has gone.

We amble through town and I buy them each a pair of winter boots. They protest, but they are still students, and these are gifts I can easily afford. "Thank you, Dad, it's just what I need." They kiss me on the cheek and I wish the recipe for all happiness was as straightforward as that.

When we get back to the hospital Mum's wails are audible at the end of the corridor. Eve is ushering her from his door, and we collect together in the cramped visitors' room. It is clear from Eve's expression that even at this time of loss her concern is wearing thin.

"He's gone now, Mum, try and calm down."

"I just don't know what I'm going to *do*," Mum says, crying even louder at this prospect. "I just don't know *what* I'll do."

I suppose this is not the time to point out to Mum that her husband treated her abysmally for much of his life. Yes, he could be charming and kind, but devoted? Respectful? Was she completely blind to his imperfections? Did she have some romantic newly-wed vision of him preserved in her brain? Did his nature change or evolve after they were wed? Was his bullying part of the deal, was it something the depths of her psyche needed in order to survive? We'll never know the answers, though one thing is already clear. Whatever it was my father provided—arrogance, a grudging dependency, a perversely expressed affection—it was indispensable. Without it she is lost. I know already that she will be one of those people whose grief reaction is prolonged and exclusive to anything else. Her reliance on him has been so complete she will barely be able to exist.

"Oh, I miss him so much," she will weep next week, next month and next year, and any year remaining to her after that.

I will reply, "Yes, mother, but he's long gone now," and my anger at her blubbing helplessness will cause me endless guilt.

Eve looks at me, and I know what she is saying: I have a full-time job, a husband and two boys to look after; you, on the other hand, are independent, you are already living free of charge in

338

Mum and Dad's house; I have done more than my share of looking after them in recent years; now it's your turn, so don't you dare fuck off back to Canada or on any other hare-brained scheme like that.

# 4.2

I think I probably met Edward Cooper many years ago. As a solicitor he was an occasional acquaintance of Dad's, but now we are sitting in his office I feel a mild hostility towards the man. Everything about him is heavy—his manner, his build, his silver hair and his daunting head, his glasses, his country tweedy jacket and (I admit to guessing this as I can't see them) his brown brogue shoes, probably purchased from Pritchard's Country Outfitters. His practice has expanded to take on several partners and the premises are an improvised ramble of three old houses, two adjacent and one three doors away, in the main street of this antique county town. Shahbn not Sherrborrne for sure. But behind these fine sandstone exteriors, every possible expense has been spared. The waiting room is bare and plastic-chaired, and while his office boasts the expected walnut desk and a voluminous chair for him, we are huddled in a sparse undecorated expanse. There are no pictures on the walls, only a single illegible framed certificate, presumably authorising him to do what he does. **Edward Haynes Cooper**, I imagine it, **licensed to hold the general public over a metaphorical barrel and blind them with lego-babble at their own phenomenal expense**.

"Sorry, Dr Cormack," he says. "You find something amusing?"

I try to convert my snigger into a stifled weep and Eve glares at me as if I am a mischievous child. "No, on the contrary. Please carry on."

In fact I now recollect Dad complaining about him a few months

340

ago, when his memory was certainly sharp. "That bastard solicitor," he fumed. "Only wanted him to witness my signature on something, cost me a hundred and seventy quid." It distresses me to think how much he is making out of the legal process of Dad's will, but we have no choice but to gather here attentive in his thrall. Eve squeezes Mum's hand. They both sit—Mum huddled forward, her daughter erect—in their black coats, publicly grieving still. I wear my dark suit but suddenly feel resentful of this, not out of any disrespect for Dad, but because it feels like I am honouring this country solicitor who is only doing his routine job.

Furthermore I am thinking of Karla. When I phoned her to tell her of Dad's demise she was, sincerely I think, upset. She and her family are fine. Alex is back with his friends, Ruth still has her arthritis and Evelyn her diabetes, but they are both much happier for Karla's return. It grieves me to think of her ageing into spinsterhood in the service of these needy relatives. It is selfish, I know, but I still wish I could relieve her of that burden and have her vitality—and yes, her sexual energy—for myself. It was in my mind to suggest I could return to Jackfish Lake, but it was clearly not the right time. But with each week since her return I have felt my impetus fail. I have had my adventure, I can convince myself that I did an exciting and vaguely philanthropic deed (even if it was unintentional, even if it was handsomely paid) but for the rest of my life I think I will prefer to play safe. It is not our lot, as a family, to change the world.

Know us by our children, and you could say we have all had reasonable success. Eve has her profitable career and two hearty boys who are well equipped for materialistic life. I will never be short of work or money, and I have two lovely daughters. I have seen for myself that hardships exist, and I know that Karla is once again submerged in them, but I attempted a salvage operation, and I can only do so much.

Cooper rambles on, savouring the sound of his sonorous voice. Dad has appointed me executor of the will, and he explains the implications of this. I don't know how onerous or honoured this

341

duty is, but I am relieved that Cooper wasn't chosen for the task, for the commission would have been a further massive expense. Despite the gravity of the occasion, the legalese has a hypnotic effect, and I can now understand how patients can sit through a critical consultation and retain next to nothing of what they have been told. I suddenly take heed, though, at, "I have here a letter dated 24th of June this year, from Dr Henry Carson of Penscott Abbas, confirming that he deems the late Mr Ronald Benjamin Cormack to possess sufficient mental faculties to amend his will."

What? I look at Eve and this is clearly news to her too.

"On the same day Mr Cormack attended my office to deliver the following short letter; 'Enjoying the privilege of reflection which old age bestows, I am pleased to see that my two children have sufficient means to supply all their reasonable needs, and indeed, the wherewithal to take financial care of their mother, whose requirements are not great. The events of recent weeks have confirmed to me that I have contributed little to the greater human need. In view of this I hereby confirm my intention to leave all my material wealth and property and goods to my friend Mr Marshall Snape."

"**What?!**" yells Eve, as Mother gasps with feeble astonishment beside her.

Cooper continues, "The only condition is that Mrs Cormack shall be allowed to live free of charge in Montfort House for as along as she wishes or until her death. All other assets apart from Montfort House and its contents shall be bequeathed immediately to Mr Snape. It would appear that bank, building society, shares and various other funds amount to about £242,000."

For a moment I don't believe it either, it must be some wholly unsustainable scam on Marshall's part. But Cooper's sombre solicitor stare confirms that it is true.

Suddenly I have a vision of Marshall Snape drinking cold Budweisers while he lounges on the verandah of the biggest house that Jackfish Lake has ever seen. He will have had it built at Fraser's Point and it will command a flawless view of the lake and the small private jetty which will moor his two or three boats.

It will put Bartram's chalet to shame, it will have a sauna and a bar, a fleet of sno-mos and a couple of brand new Chevvy pick-ups outside. He will be a celebrity and will not care one jot that his new-found friends are attracted only by his wealth and the prodigious parties he gives. For he will face a real prospect of a future without prison, as will his son. They will be free to spend as many days as they choose out fishing on the lake.

I am aware of Mum and Eve turning to me in horror, but I can't control it, I really can't. My stomach is convulsing with riots of laughter and tears are scorching my face.